DARKNESS, I

Also by Tanith Lee

DARK DANCE
PERSONAL DARKNESS

TANITH LEE

DARKNESS, I

THIRD IN THE
BLOOD OPERA SEQUENCE

St. Martin's Press ✖ New York

DARKNESS, I. Copyright © 1994 by Tanith Lee.
All rights reserved. Printed in the United States of
America. No part of this book may be used or
reproduced in any manner whatsoever without written
permission except in the case of brief quotations
embodied in critical articles or reviews.
For information, address St. Martin's Press,
175 Fifth Avenue, New York, N.Y. 10010.

Library of Congress Cataloging-in-Publication Data

Lee, Tanith.
Darkness, I : third in the blood opera
sequence / by Tanith Lee.
p.   cm.
ISBN 0-312-13956-X
I. Title.
PR6062.E4163D37   1996
823'.914—dc20   95-41848   CIP

First published in Great Britain
by Little, Brown and Company

First U.S. Edition: January 1996
10 9 8 7 6 5 4 3 2 1

To Jacques Post and Maarten Asscher
With thanks for the first gifts of Holland.

O, my heart, confess not against me as a witness!

Magical inscription on a Scarabaeus

Chapter One

THE CHILD ON THE TOMB:
A little mound of stone, and above it this slim, breastless figure. She was draped in a classical way. Yet her blind blank face reminded him – he did not know why – of the effigies of Easter Island, which he had seen in pictures. There was no name, or date.

The grave stood just outside the boundary of the air-strip, behind the barbed wire. And beyond the flat unearthly plain rolled all the way to the distant hills, raked by a chill dry wind.

Sometimes a pilot might leave a flower at the stone child's feet. One or two of them called her Santa Blanca. The missions from this place were not overt, probably often outside the law . . . even so, he did not understand why they felt they must placate the child. He had never left her a flower.

Miguel Chodil walked.

The sun was glaring in a sky of dilute stratos.

The white shape of the twin-engined plane looked too solid, as if she could not fly. But then, that was her trick. Last night, there had been a red moon over the city. The ancient peoples would have said that foretold a death. But whose? In a whole night, after all, someone was bound to die.

They had already loaded her up. Chodil boarded, and cast a quick inspecting eye along her belly.

1

It was always similar.

Boxes that probably held books, containers of oil and kerosene, various tinned stores, such as any base might require. But there, glowing in their crate, golden oranges, and dark pink peaches, the yellow candles of bananas. And in the straw, greenish Peruvian brandy.

Chodil checked the lashings, and, satisfied, went forward into the cockpit.

Out on the runway a guard had come up, and was standing staring at the aircraft, his Kalashnikov across his shoulder. Chodil waited. The guard moved away suddenly, as if he had seen evidence of some threat.

Chodil tried the plane over.

She made her usual sounds. She felt alert and springy. Perhaps too eager. '*Calma* . . .' he said.

As he took her down the runway, her accustomed rocking motion was familiar as the rhythm of a horse. He knew better than she when she would try to swerve, and kept her steady.

He drew her up into a shallow accelerating climb, and she levelled perfectly, settling on the wide blue sky in a drone of power.

Fifty minutes and he would need to take her down again to her first refuelling, and later there would come the second stop, where the Russians would offer him vodka and he would pretend to drink – it broke their hearts when you did not play with them. Two unmapped isles, the second whiter than the first, its coast littered with the bones of blue whales, creatures, it seemed to him, too big to love.

As he flew south, Miguel laid out his final destination from memory. He had, after all, made this journey twenty times.

The blue crystal sky would dip eventually through into a blue crystal sea. And there the cumulus had dropped upon the water in white ice, floating cliffs and domes and castles. And the terrible white land rose behind, to its points of mountains.

Death was only that. That whiteness. The lost creatures that roamed its fringes, the inner stopped clock of its cold white heart.

Chodil grimaced. He sang to the plane, and told her of the woman he had had in the city. He liked to make the plane a little jealous.

Three hours to go.

Chapter Two

WHEN THE SNOW BEGAN TO fall, she was at the back of the procession, lagging behind, unsure. She had a feeling, despite the grandeur, that it was all some hoax. Something stupid, which seemed to irritate, but not alarm her.

She knew what she was seeing. They were Ancient Egyptians. The women in tight-lapped gowns of half-transparent white linen, some with bare round breasts, and the men in kilts of linen or leather. They wore too, redolent of every epic, the characteristic collars, with garnets and blue glass paste on ribs of gold. Black wigs. Eye make-up like the lines around the eyes of lynxes. You could not mistake them.

Here and there a fan of ostrich feathers waved. Others were wheeling supermarket trolleys piled with golden vessels and cones of scented wax.

They toiled upward, up towards the great pyramid.

It seemed to her the pyramid was constructed of old books, some of which were even dilapidated paperbacks.

Women wailed. It was a funeral. Who was dead?

In the dream, she thought, *Oh, it's Ruth.*

And when she thought this, the dusk sky opened and the snow began to fall.

The Egyptians stopped. They seemed appropriately to freeze. Rachaela found herself, perhaps unwillingly,

4

walking forward now through the static lines of men and women. She came up to where a priest was. He had a leopard-skin over his shoulder, and on his head was the pointed mask of a black jackal with tall ears.

Adamus . . .

Of course, he had returned from death himself, to oversee the obsequies.

The mummy-case was leaning above a shaft in the side of the pyramid. It was golden, richer even than the case of the famous boy king, Tutankhamun. The form of a girl was painted on it, and she had two long black plaits. Yes, it was Ruth all right.

They lowered the sarcophagus into the depths.

I should feel something. Should I?

Then the case had vanished, and she stood there, feeling nothing, not even the cold of the falling snow.

They were all gone, and it was night now. The snow ended.

Above the pyramid a single star blazed like a diamond.

And Ruth's ka slid up out of the tomb.

Rachaela knew about the ka – like her dead daughter, Rachaela had read Haggard's novel, *Morning Star*. And what was a ka? Astral body more than ghost. The double that was freed at the negation of the flesh.

Ruth's ka was very glamorous. It wore a black dress with silver embroidery at the throat, and its black hair hung long and lustrous down its spine. The face of Ruth's ka was beautifully made up, the lips pale red, the eyes like smoulder.

'Hallo, Ruth,' Rachaela said.

'Hallo, Mummy.'

And then the ka came towards Rachaela, and Ruth held out her right hand.

On the tips of her fingers rested a still, soft flame.

Rachaela meant to back away, but she could not. Ruth, starter of fires —

Ruth was in front of her, near enough Rachaela could

smell the perfume her ka had put on – Lancôme? – and hear the rustle of her dress.

Ruth extended the star of flame upon her hand.

And Rachaela discovered that she had opened her mouth, wide, in a rictus, as once in her childhood she had had to do at the dentist's —

And then there she was in his chair, the old black kind that you felt should have had straps to tie you down.

'Now,' he said, the faceless memory, leaning forward, 'I think you've done a bit of damage here. Too many sweets, I shouldn't wonder. This will be a little bit uncomfortable, I expect, but you'll be a brave girl, won't you?'

And then Rachaela knew that Ruth had put the flame into her mouth, even before the dentist loomed over her again with his buzzing stinging wasp of a drill, to give her the only filling of her life.

And he said, 'Now just swallow that little flame, please, and then rinse round.'

Rachaela swallowed the flame.

She woke up with her head pressed into the pillow. Rachaela was alone . . . She turned, slowly, stiffly, unknotting her muscles, and Althene lay beside her, silently asleep.

Who are you? Rachaela thought.

Even unconscious, her face wiped of cosmetics, her hair stranded by the movements of somnolence, Althene was utterly herself, complete.

Well, since you're foolish enough to be here beside me, I could wake you up, tell you my troubles.

I dreamed of my dead and murdered murderess-demon of a daughter.

Taking care, rather awkwardly Rachaela angled herself out of bed, and curled the sheet back over Althene.

It was warm and close, a hot late-summer night. From the open window, scents of trees, plums, a hint of the river.

Rachaela went out of the bedroom noiselessly and into the bathroom. Washed by white moonlight through the opaque pane, she saw her shade in the mirror. A Klimt woman, young and high-breasted, with a pushing pregnant belly.

Almost eight months.

No, she had to be rational. She was not very big. Like that last time, when she had fooled half London that she had only grown overweight.

Last time, with Ruth.

But Ruth had been born, and Ruth had grown up. Ruth had become a woman at eleven, and presently she had become also terrible, a killer . . . and then, conversely, beautiful, and loved. Until she broke the rules of her lover. Until she killed again. Ruth, lady with the knife, bringer of fire. And when he disowned her, her Malach – white-haired warrior-priest – there in that second house of stained-glass windows, how she had screamed.

They had thought she ran away with Camillo. And yet, Camillo was her enemy, the ordinary unkind kind. He would never have helped Ruth. And Ruth, any way, had been beyond help by then.

What night had it been, when the telephone rang – Tuesday, Thursday? And Rachaela, half sleeping, heard Althene speaking very low. And then, Althene in the doorway, like a phantom. A messenger from the dead.

'What is it?'

'It's nothing. Go back to sleep.'

'I want to know.'

'Well, you're awake now. I shall have to tell you.'

And Althene sighed. She came forward and Rachaela sat up. Althene said, 'I don't know how you will feel. Eric called us.'

Rachaela said, 'It's Ruth.'

'Yes. But also not.'

'She's dead,' said Rachaela.

'Apparently.'

It seemed a busy bicycling couple had found her, in a wood. Someone had stabbed Ruth through the left breast into the heart. By the time her body was come upon, her beauty had dispersed for ever. Food for worms.

Rachaela said, 'She was dead when he left her. She died that moment. Will they tell him too, Malach?'

'I expect he will be told,' said Althene.

Rachaela lay down again. She looked up at the ceiling in the dark, and Althene went away. *What do I feel?*

But then, and now, two weeks after Eric had phoned them (no doubt Michael had dialled), Rachaela could only remember how Ruth had screamed when Malach cast her off.

Had she screamed like that, too, when the knife went into her?

And had Camillo done that?

'Damn,' said Rachaela softly, to the moonlit bathroom. 'Fuck this.' *Out. Get out of my mind.*

But this was why she had dreamed of the demon. Of Ruth. Because of the phone call. And because of the new, the other life, of which somehow she had not rid herself.

Althene had said, 'I can find you a doctor. If you don't want the pregnancy to go on. And you don't.' But Rachaela had not wanted that interruption, not yet. An abortion – illness, trauma. However well she was treated, however little fuss was made. She wanted to be with Althene, and to pretend that nothing was in her womb.

So, the cold, blustery, wet spring, walks by the river, dinners in strange little restaurants, sex in the blue bedroom of the flat. Nothing to fear now. And the companionable cosy hours, painting, Althene reading, or the games with clothes and make-up, that there had been before. Hot buttered toast and tea. A mother who was also a lover who was also a husband. Time piled up in an hour-glass. If only it could be made to stand still.

Although, in a way it had. Rachaela had only to look at

herself again. Her firm moon-white body, twenty-six years of age, a woman well over forty —

Scarabae time.

Althene did not say, *'My* child. A Scarabae child. You *must.'*

So it was easy, to let things slide. As if the child was not real. Now it was too late.

The doctor eventually provided was polite, gentle, and encouraging. She did not query Althene's presence. They were Ms Day and Ms Simon. But luscious Althene, although she could not be blamed, was secretely and fundamentally the cause. The father of Rachaela's burden.

I don't want it. Why didn't I let go?

She looked: The belly. Who was there?

One of the cats, black-faced Jacob, came into the bathroom. Only cats were permitted to disturb the night.

Rachaela lifted him, and he balanced a second, clawless, purring, on the handy ledge of her fecund stomach. Then he climbed up on to her shoulder and sang in her hair.

She could have learned the gender of the baby. But she had resisted that.

She did not want it, did not want the responsibility of killing it, wished it did not exist, pretended it did not exist.

Just like the time before.

'I think someone is watching the flat.'

'Who?' Althene crossed the conservatory and came out beside her on the south-facing balcony.

From below, they would appear to be two young women. One slenderly pregnant.

'Someone was under the garden wall. It's happened before. The other night I heard a noise—'

'One of the cats,' said Althene.

'Juliet was out. But yesterday I saw a man going by, and he stood out there, by the river, looking up.'

Althene said nothing.

Rachaela said, 'The Scarabae are always liable to watch us. I mean *my* Scarabae, at the house.'

'They might.'

'Now I'm carrying a child, and they've probably found out, the way they find out everything. And we've left them in the dark.'

'They're used to that, I imagine.'

'I shouldn't be having a baby.'

'So you've said. But you are.'

'I'm a coward. Selfish. That's why I didn't get rid of it. It's what would be done to *me*. I don't care about the child.'

'You don't know the child yet.'

'I knew Ruth.'

Althene said. 'Yes.' She bent to touch the dry soil of the red geraniums. It was Althene who watered the plants, Rachaela forgot.

'I dreamed about Ruth,' Rachaela said.

'Go on.'

'It was nothing. Egyptian. But she was interested in Ancient Egypt. God knows. Perhaps they all go back that far. They seem confused about their ages. If I credit any of them is three hundred years old then why not three thousand? They grow old, and then they get younger. Miranda was doing it. I don't know them. I don't know you.'

'I do my best to alter that,' said Althene. 'I tell you great amounts about myself.'

'Yes, your mother, and the house in Amsterdam. But your childhood sounds all wrong, doesn't it. One minute like the nineteen twenties, and then like something much earlier. Or is that your technique?'

'I feel very old, Rachaela, sometimes. And sometimes young. I began to feel young when I saw you first, at that window, glaring down at me. I felt myself wake up.'

'And set yourself to have me.'

'And succeeded. How clever I've been.'

'I still don't know you.'

'How dare you,' said Althene sweetly, 'suppose you could know me so quickly. It will take you many, many decades even to begin.'

'Do we have them? Many many decades?'

'We have, certainly, some cold wine in the refrigerator.'

Rachaela lifted the watering-can and made offerings to the parched flowers. Over the river, the art deco building let forth its soft chemical plume.

'Aren't I drinking too much for a pregnant woman?'

'A little wine is always good. And, you're Scarabae. You can drink what you like.'

'I'm half Scarabae.'

'It's enough.'

Along the mud flats, a man was walking slowly. His head was not turned towards the apartment. Behind him, leftwards, the sun westered, scaling metal ripples over the river like a fire.

Ruth . . . fire child.

Althene came back with two long green glasses of the white wine. As she emerged, the sun touched her face with Inca copper, and the curve of her breasts, that looked so real inside the amber silk shirt.

Rachaela felt a warm resinous stroke of desire.

She did not know any more, or care, what it was she wanted, Althene the woman, or her hidden maleness. In the dark, Rachaela could turn and smooth over the flat loins under their sheath of satin night garment, and find the creature sleeping, coiled shameless at the centre of this perfumed female icon. And it would raise its head, and next a beautiful woman would lie against her, sideways now for the comfort of the contorting pregnancy, and pin Rachaela through with the golden pin.

'Drink that. Shall we go to the restaurant below the bridge? They prepare a wonderful dish, a whole chicken baked with grapes.'

Unerringly, too, Althene sensed Rachaela's current wish for voyaging things, before matters inexorably changed, before she grew heavy and inert and wanted *only* little-girl buttered toast and tea before the comforting fire of summer's end.

The man had disappeared from the shore, and the chemical cloud shone bronze. Was the watching only her paranoia? Perhaps the cloud watched too. Perhaps the birds had binoculars.

In her eighth month, they moved. It was made very simple for them. Three courteous packers arrived to parcel up the books and objects, and the clothes. The flat had been furnished on Rachaela's arrival, and they had never utilized the lower floor. The plants were put in terracotta troughs and sailed out like angry galleons. The cats yowled and clawed their baskets. Juliet screamed imperiously.

Rachaela felt guilty. They had left the flat because of her – perhaps unreasonable, biologically induced – sense of watchers. They thought Juliet had mated with Jacob by now. Juliet too, pregnant, should have consideration.

But the cats liked the house on the hill.

The hill itself was preposterous, vertical. No one, unless very dedicated, could walk up it. Far below, soundless in distance, maroon buses passed along the town street.

A high wall guarded the house, and above it an equally vertical garden ran up to the building. Poplars of immense size topped a lawn rife with daisies. A stone bird-bath perched before the door. White, two-storeyed, and flat-roofed, the house had also lion-coloured shutters and a wooden door. There was no lock. A panel gave on a small bank of buttons. You pressed for entry, as with a safe.

And the windows were of bullet-proof glass, Althene casually said. With, here and there, stained glass on the inside. Two gorgeous women in the long window over the wide stair, red, ice green, and gold, Ceres and Persephone, perhaps, goddess mother and daughter, the woman's hair a long gold sheaf of wheat, and the paler daughter with an innocent armful of scarlet poppies. In the main room, the living room, a mediaeval Zodiac was set in at the upper casements, fire signs in rose, air in blue, earth saffron, water green.

Althene had not brought Rachaela to the house before moving day. Trust? It was like a Christmas morning, coming down to find the presents magically assembled by the tree – some fantasy Rachaela had never, as a child, realized.

'It's too large for us,' she said.

'We will fill it up.'

Skulls of old fawn bone emerged from Althene's crates, a globe (unscratched), of malachite. Books. A bronze Grecian statue of a boy in a garland. Wine was bought for the cellar. A washing machine of complex design, a dishwasher from outer space. 'Someone will come in to clean. A couple, I belive,' Althene said.

'*They* have arranged this?'

'Miranda.'

'But then they know we're here.'

'Not at all.'

Rachaela acceded, gave up.

It was a fact. She felt safer on the hill. She would look at the tiny buses from the window. Where were they going?

There was a minimum of furniture. They were left to choose, maybe, later. Yet there was a dreamy quality to the wide cases of rooms that had only flowing curtains (muted sky colours, milky emeralds), a chair and Chinese rug islanded on a polished floor, a wide bed adrift in sunny emptiness.

The autumn was mellow but brief. The poplars yellowed. The yew on the vertical drive came into olive-black prominence.

Rachaela observed herself. Her back did not even ache, this time. There was only heaviness.

She let Althene cosset her. Mulled wine in bed, the endless wholemeal toast with butter and strawberry jam which was now all she wanted, eating only from duty the succulent omelets and chicken breasts that the woman, Elizabeth, prepared. Elizabeth was not Scarabae. A plump Scot, with redder than red hair and a glorious accent, who installed a Hoover in the lockable cupboard opposite the stairs. Sometimes Elizabeth sang as she cleaned the two bathrooms, or made the bed. Lovely lullabye of a voice. *I am the one having the child. I am not the child.*

As she had always done, Althene handwashed her silken lingerie, and it hung in rainbow weeds in the second bathroom. Later she would iron the silks with a tiny iron. Rachaela gazed on the ritual, fascinated. *She is my mother.*

He is my mother.

Rachaela laughed.

'She finds me amusing, does she?' Althene said, standing in her tailored grey jeans and exquisite French sweater.

Does she love me? Rachaela thought. *Yes. How odd.*

The light melted down and down and the days grew short.

The man, Reg, mowed the lawn. A hundred feet away another imposing house stood blind-side on over the garden wall. No one could get close, to watch.

'Juliet is definitely due to become a mother,' said Althene, having expertly and tenderly tested Juliet's sleek black undercarriage.

'We two,' said Rachaela. She looked down at Juliet, who behaved just as she had always done, and now lay purring on Rachaela's abbreviated lap. But there were more than two of them in the chair. There were at least five – Rachaela and the baby, Juliet and her impending kittens – a sudden flash of utter delight passed through Rachaela.

It stunned her. She had felt what women were expected to feel – were coerced into feeling.

Behind the split second of joy came a deep depression.

* * *

On Sunday mornings you could hear the bells from the Saxon church down in the town. Rachaela stood in the October living room, where the sun would come in the late afternoon.

It was a clear day. The windows were bright, gleaming from Elizabeth's Friday attentions.

Rachaela looked up at the Zodiac.

Virgins in kirtles, scorpions with wicked tails, solemn bulls, twinned fish – and there the Scales, with its balanced cups, brazen on the sapphire glass. Libra.

Libra was glowing. Some strong sideways reflection of the sun, perhaps striking on a surface outside, pierced back through the balance like a flame.

Then the twisting, grasping pain came, violent and without warning.

Rachaela clutched at a chair in terror.

The time had come. Her time. Would it be like it was before? She was early . . . Surely the midwife had said – a false alarm? No. Oh no.

The pain redoubled, and Rachaela cried out. She experienced the motion of a wave going through her lower body, a wave of molten rock—

Then an easement came, and she went up quite steadily to the bathroom. When she emerged, she crossed into the bedroom and looked down the hill, where Althene had gone with Reg in the car, for groceries at Alldays, which stayed open on Sunday from eight a.m. to nine p.m.

All alone with the telephone.

Rachaela dialled the appropriate number.

There was no delay, no prevarication, no argument. Why had she expected one? The Scarabae had seen to everything. Even if, ironically, Althene, the mother-figure, was not here to assist.

Inside twenty minutes the midwife had arrived, and ushered Rachaela to the designated room, without flap or hesitation.

Kate Ames, the midwife, was one of those slender

15

women strong as a cart-horse. She radiated quiet enthusiasm.

'We're going to be very quick, Rachaela.'

Rachaela already knew that.

Kate Ames did not ludicrously tell her to push.

The pain was horrible, worse than she remembered. Or
then again, sometimes it did not seem so bad. She had
wanted Althene, and started to cry like a little girl, but the
pain had brought her round like a slap.

'What bad luck,' said Kate Ames, 'that your sister isn't
here. It's those queues. They go mad on Sundays, as if the
shop wasn't there the rest of the week.'

Five minutes later, when the malfunction to Reg's car
had been dismissed with Reg, and Althene was walking
up the vertical hill with two bags of shopping consisting
mostly of strawberry jam, the true child that had been
inside Rachaela's hard white belly, came out into the
smoking air of the third bedroom.

Rachaela was on a river.

She thought, *I know I am hallucinating. What was that stuff
she gave me? Is it that?*

The river was wide, brown as liquid honey. Duck
rose from a fringe of reeds. And then, in an oval of
soft light, Rachaela saw her baby hanging by a nail
of gold.

'It's a girl. And in full working order.'

Rachaela heard the child begin to cry, a mile away,
getting nearer.

'That's it. You have a weep, love,' said Kate Ames.
'You've been brilliant.' And to Rachaela, 'Just clean up
a bit, and then you can have a cup of tea. Are you ready
to hold her?'

I don't want to hold her. I don't want her.

'Give her to me,' said Rachaela – 'please – quickly—'

'There you go.'

The baby only cried softly after its first screech. It smelled
clean and faintly antiseptic.

16

Rachaela looked at the face. It was a cat. A cat wrapped up in a white shawl. It was Jacob. No, it was a baby.

'Yes, she's all there. Properly operational kid, that is.'

'What – what's this little mark?'

'Oh that. That's nothing. That will just fade.'

A tiny bluish whisper, like the palest bruise, left of the chest, just under the tiny unopened rose-bud of nipple.

Kate Ames was making Rachaela comfortable.

Far away, Rachaela heard the downstairs door open.

Too late.

Who are you?

The eyes of the baby were strange. Not dark, yet not blue. Silvery. And the head was orioled, like Juliet's black fur, with a glim of blondeness.

Is it peculiar? Another weird Scarabae baby.

In a minute, Althene, having seen the midwife's car on the drive by the bird-bath, would run up the stairs and rush in. And how would Rachaela greet her? A dulcet picture of dam and infant. Or the former image, the reluctant mother saddled with the weight of rendered life.

'She's stopped crying. Is she all right?'

'Oh, yes, she's fine. Perhaps you're going to be fortunate there. Some of them *are* quiet, you know.'

'My last . . . cried all the time.'

Kate Ames waxed serious. Naturally she knew Rachaela had given birth before, but not the fate of this mysterious and absent progeny. Kate Ames was a good woman. Rachaela's safe and uncomplex delivery of a correctly formed child had made her genuinely happy. She cheered up. She said, 'Well, who knows. She may be screaming blue murder in ten minutes' time.'

The child did not sleep. It could not see, they said, no focus yet to the eyes, that were like silken dead hydrangea flowers.

Then the door flew open.

Althene stood there. She was white, as pale as she looked sometimes after sex.

*But you are really a man. A man white-faced to find me here.
Yes I'm alive. And so is this.*

Your daughter, said Rachaela, but not aloud, to spare
Kate Ames.

And Kate Ames, beaming, said, 'Rachaela's been a
marvel. I don't even think we were an hour over it. A
perfect little girl.'

Althene's eyes went to the baby, and in Rachaela the
serpent uncoiled. *Love at first sight. I am going to be stupidly
and ridiculously and unworthily and torridly jealous. And we
are incestuous Scarabae. Christ knows, I have some cause.*

Chapter Three

ELIZABETH STARED OUT AT THE SNOW.
It was a massive fall, mitten-thick upon the trees, and in places piled up to the windows. Bags of nuts for the birds, which Reg had put up earlier, hung dead still. There was a great silence.

But inside, the faint strains of music seeped from the living room, and here, in the glistening kitchen, the oven popped faintly, giving off a wonderful aroma of baking cake.

'Oh, Mrs Day. I expect you'd like some coffee.'

Rachaela had never persuaded Elizabeth to use their first names, and in Elizabeth's world, seemingly, all women with children were Mrs, like Victorian cooks.

'Yes . . . Just instant. I'll make it, Elizabeth.'

'No, no. I've been dreaming. Well, I won't say dreaming. Worrying.'

Rachaela braced herself for another's troubles.

'What's wrong?'

'It's my sister's son. She's afraid he'll be called up. He's in the reserves. You don't think, do you.'

Rachaela did not. She did not know what Elizabeth meant. And then she recalled the dark shadow on the new year, the war. What could she say to comfort? Rachaela was ignorant of everyday affairs.

'Perhaps it won't come to that.'

'Well, the good Lord knows what it will come to.'
Elizabeth put the kettle on the gas, as if it were the last
kettle of the world. Although grammatically her speech
was only Anglicized, her lovely Scottish accent moulded
every word, giving each an extra savour, and potency.
'The hospitals could be packed with them, young men
badly burnt, and ruined. And their chests. I've seen, when
I was a girl, what mustard gas can do.'

Rachaela too looked out at the snow.

Reg and Elizabeth had somehow got the car up the
hill, and now they were delaying departure, dreading
probably the performance of descending. The car had been
temperamental any way, ever since the morning it broke
down outside Alldays. The Sunday Anna was born.

The coffee came, and Elizabeth allowed herself to sit at
the kitchen worktop. They ate oatmeal biscuits Elizabeth
had baked.

'But there, it's no good worrying, is it?' said Elizabeth.

'No, not really.'

'If only it were,' said Elizabeth. 'We could put the world
to rights in a tick.' She listened a moment to the Sibelius
symphony drifting over the hall. 'She likes her music, Mrs
Simon.'

'Yes.'

'And your little Anna.' Elizabeth sighed. She said, 'I
do lose track of time. It happens when you get to my
age. Sometimes I lie awake, just planning tomorrow's
shopping, and then I pop along to the toilet, and it's
half past two in the morning. Four hours, and it only
seemed like twenty minutes. But Reg, he sleeps like
an old dog.' She smiled. Elizabeth liked Reg, who was
effortlessly clever at all he did, monosyllabic, restful.
'And your little girl,' said Elizabeth. 'Is it three she
is now?'

'No,' Rachaela said smoothly. 'One year and a few
months. She's grown fast for her age.'

'And she's got a good head on her.'

Elizabeth made more coffee for Rachaela, who had drunk her mug dry without noticing.

Jelka, Juliet's daughter, came into the kitchen. She was a black cat without a dot of white, yellow-eyed like her sire. She stalked to the window and meowed to be let out.

'Oh, you won't like that, you won't,' said Elizabeth, but she went and opened the sash window (of bullet-proof glass) and Jelka leapt into the snow, vanishing at once up to her breast. The cat scrambled out and sprang into the stone urn that, in autumn, had held geraniums.

Juliet's children had been three in number, two of them black and white in a handsome but usual way, and Jelka like a coal. Juliet had produced the litter without drama the previous November, in one of the nests of newspaper Althene had left about to entice her. When they were old enough, the male and female had gone to Eric, Miranda and Sasha, as a gift. Althene had seen to this. Jelka, the witch's cat, cleaved to her mother. In time, she too would mate with Jacob, her father. Cats also, were intractably Scarabae.

But it had occurred to Rachaela that the cats now represented a unit like their own. A male, two females, consort and child.

It had been Emma who had said to her, after the birth of Ruth, 'You're missing all the best parts.' And Rachaela had taken care to miss as much of Ruth's babyhood as possible. Had anything really changed?

It was Althene now who had bottle-fed Anna; Rachaela – deliberately? – had not produced sufficient milk. It was Althene who, mostly, changed Anna's napkins. Everything was disposable. It was all quite easy. Besides, very quickly, Anna stopped being messy. By five months she had been able to use the bathroom, and had evinced a demanding desire to do so. At first supervised, and with a stool to climb up by, presently self-possessed and alone. Although they kept her in diapers, thereafter Anna did not have accidents.

21

Rachaela knew that was not normal. She knew from Ruth.

Anna had spoken her first word on Christmas Day. Not quite three months after her birth.

It might have been imagination. The eager parents misinterpreting a gurgle or burp. But then Anna spoke again. It was a name. Althene's name. Not quite correct. 'Althni,' she said.

And Althene picked Anna up and held her, and Anna smiled down, from this pinnacle, on the other mother, the woman-mother who did not love her but was quite kind. 'Rashla,' said Anna, generously.

By the age of six months, Anna could talk. Her speech was unformed, like that of someone with a mild, mellifluous impediment, but her syntax was correct. She did not speak in the quaint yet logical way of children, 'I runned', 'I is here'. No, she was exact. She *ran*. She *was*.

Althene began to teach Anna to read, and soon Anna could write in big unwieldy letters. She wrote a note to Juliet about Jelka. She seemed to think the cats, with whom she constantly played, and beside and amongst whom, when allowed, she would fall asleep in the *natural* way of an infant, could talk also, and read. It disappointed her, learning that Juliet could not.

Physically, she was a flawless child. Long-legged, slender, with the slightly protruding stomach of the evolving girl. Tall for her age. White skin. Her eyes a silky grey. Her hair white-blonde – no. Her hair, too, was white. It did not darken, became paler as it thickened. An ethereal child. Special.

On the left side of the breast, the little blue mark had faded but not gone away. A birthmark, then. That was all.

Anna was left-handed. She discarded her right hand, let it lie. As if it did not have anything much to do.

And was she beautiful? Too soon to tell.

No. Not too soon. She was beautiful in the way of the white-haired super-children of 1950s science fiction.

Already she had a dressing-up box, full of fantastic dresses stitched by Elizabeth from lengths of material Althene purchased. And of course the books stacked neatly up and up beside her mattress – she had graduated from the cot long ago. Anna did not yet read the books from the library they had made in the fourth bedroom. She read fantasy books suitable for a child – of ten. *Robin Hood, Atlantis, Greek Myths*; books too about wolves and tigers, ancient cities.

Althene acquired tapes of plays broadcast by the BBC on the obsolete Third Programme, Louis MacNeice, Dylan Thomas . . . Anna listened, bolt upright, her eyes wide. She could not understand them, surely, but they held her. She would ask for this one, that one, again. And music too. Anna liked music.

The Scarabae had named her.

Maybe, in those first minutes, holding her, Rachaela might have been compelled to stake a claim. Afterwards, she could recollect the emotion which swept over her, but she did not know what it was. And once Althene looked at the baby, the emotion shrivelled. Rachaela had renounced her child at once. It was no use.

If Althene guessed at Rachaela's reaction, she gave no sign. She treated Rachaela like a proper mother who, due perhaps to fatigue, or some unexplained other duty, could not spend as much time on Anna as she otherwise would have done.

And Althene, obviously, was mother and father both. A better bargain even than Emma.

It was after the cats were delivered to the Scarabae house. Althene had gone there in Reg's car, to the turreted masonry above the common. She was away ten hours. Returning, she brought two bottles of some extraordinary champagne that Eric had accorded them. And a box of chocolates ostensibly from the adopted girl, Tray. And the name.

That far they had called the baby The Child, the way

they frequently called each of the cats The Cat. It was not complacence, more the recognition of essence. For, still, then, Anna was a child.

'Miranda said something to me,' said Althene, as they sat before the fire Reg had laid, The Child on the sofa lying noiseless and alert between them.

'Something about your daughter,' said Rachaela.

Althene did not say, '*Our* daughter'. She said, 'Miranda asked if we would consider naming her for Anna.'

And at once the child rolled, looked up at Althene with her focussing eyes. It was not quite Christmas. As yet the fatal words had not been spoken (Althni, Rashla). Yet, it seemed she knew.

'*Anna*,' Rachaela said. 'You mean they want to name her for the dead. The dead old woman my former daughter killed.'

'They'd like us to honour Anna's memory.'

'It's like sticking a piece of a grave to her.'

'No. Only a few soft ashes.'

'Well.' Rachaela looked at Reg's nice domestic blaze of clean non-smoking coke. She thought of the first house which burned, and how Anna burned, and then she said, 'But it's putting the fire on her again.'

'Or putting out the fire,' said Althene.

'No. Oh, it doesn't matter. Call her what you want. She's yours.'

Althene said, at last, flatly, without evident purpose, 'Ours.' And then, 'They weren't insistent. We are not obliged.'

'Anna,' said Rachaela. And the child now looked at her. It was her name.

Despite this, although Anna spoke their names to them like a spell on Christmas Day in the morning, Anna had not declaimed her own name until her first birthday, last October. And then she set out, in her coiling, uncoordinated letters, ornamenting with the paints Althene had given her: I AM ANNA.

Elizabeth had thriftily drunk all her coffee and was now washing up the breakfast plates and her cake-making bowls.

Rachaela remembered that you dare not any longer lick the mixing bowl for fear of the mooted Salmonella in raw egg.

Outside the snow cracked, and a swathe fell from a tree. Jelka skidded under the urn, lashing her tail, and a bird flew bleakly, like the last bird, to the bags of nuts.

In the living room Anna lay in Althene's arm, and they listened to Sibelius' music of the Scandinavian ice.

And in the Gulf they got ready for Armageddon.

'I don't think she should have it.'

They stood in the slushy market, all around them the bright flags of clothing, stalls of tall green bottles, necklaces of crystal, clocks.

'Because it's the fur of a dead thing.'

'Not exactly.'

'Because someone will run out and lynch her. Rachaela, she doesn't want to wear it. Do you, Anna?'

'It's not for dressing-up,' Anna said.

From the rail of the stall, the fox-fur hung. Its face had become pointed, like a beak, its fur was dark, unfoxlike. From its pointed face, that seemed to Rachaela sad and wise, not pitiful, yet bereft, two orange glass eyes gazed out.

'Try to tell Rachaela,' said Althene, holding the child by her hand, 'why you want it.'

'It's my fox,' said Anna.

Rachaela looked down. They had dispensed with the baby-carry in which Althene had ported her; Anna preferred to walk. When she was tired, lagged, Althene simply picked her up. Any way, Anna was now too tall.

She looks four or five. Slim and small. The long white hair, with its roots of silver flushed like soft water into the transparent white of her temples.

A solemn little girl, who wanted a fox-fur as a toy.

'It's not a toy,' said Rachaela. 'They hunt them, ghastly people. And then they turn them into this.'

'My fox,' said Anna, again.

'Anna,' said Althene, 'what will you do with it?'

'I'll hold it,' said Anna. 'It will sit on my lap.'

'It's not a cat,' said Rachaela. 'It's not real.'

'Oh, no,' said Anna sensibly.

'For God's sake.'

Rachaela was angry. With the slush and the grey wind, the snivelling bare trees. With the images she had seen on television – an injured civilian rushed from the site of a scud attack, helpless on a stretcher, his anxious little dog sitting on his ribs. The birds, oiled black, also helpless, drowned in a shit not their own. A cat walking over a starving sunset city, shortly perhaps to receive a limited nuclear strike.

'Oh, have it then.' Rachaela heard her own harsh mother. She snapped up her head. 'No, I'm sorry. I'm sorry, Ruth. Yes, have it. Of course.'

Silence.

Rachaela looked at them. Her lover, her daughter. What had she said—

'Who is Ruth?' said Anna.

Oh Christ, is that what I said?

Althene, serious and rational, explaining: 'Ruth was Rachaela's other daughter. Ruth isn't alive now.'

'I'm sorry,' said Rachaela.

'It's all right,' said Anna. Her unformed voice – *Issall ride.* Like a drunk. But she was sober.

I've insulted her. Oh God, does she know how badly?

Rachaela felt faint.

The market, full of bustling people, colours, seemed to swarm to engulf her.

But Althene did not see. Althene said to Anna, 'It's just like that time yesterday, when I called you Rachaela, by mistake.'

'Oh, yes.'

'Now,' said Althene. And she lifted the serpent of fur with dangling paws. The stall keeper came back from his conversation and Bell's-laced tea at the adjacent stall.

'That's smashing now. Quite the vogue. It's all right, you see. Nineteen twenties that is. Killed before Friends of the Earth got going.'

'Are you sure?' inquired Althene.

'Eh? Go on. 'Course I am. Look good on you, that will.'

Althene laughed. She said, 'I prefer human skin.'

The marketeer grinned. Not widely enough.

He wrapped the fox in tissue paper, and they carried it away.

Anna named the fox Ursula.

No reason was given.

She slept with the fox in one protective arm and her white rabbit in the other.

'They called her the Vixen.'

'Ruth.'

'Yes.'

'An old pun. To denote female degeneracy. Cervix. Cer*vixen*.'

Rachaela said, 'From the womb.'

'There is an old brandy,' Althene said. 'They would cork it into the wombs of dead women, and so let it mature.'

'This bloody war,' said Rachaela. 'I remember the Cuba Crisis—'

'Ah. So you've noticed.'

'It seems to be out of control.'

Althene said, against her in the dark, 'It will be stopped.'

'What? *How?*'

Althene said nothing more.

Like a goddess, like a statue of cream flesh, she slept.

Rachaela lay in the darkness, and under her the world turned. As it had always done. As it always would?

Chapter Four

SHE LOVED TESCO'S. WAS IN love with Tesco's. She should, maybe, have married Tesco's. For marriage ideally promises to bring security and pleasure, excitement and contentment both. And these things Tesco's had always offered to Sharon Ferris, while her husband, Wayne, offered all the opposites.

The moment she walked in through the revolving doors, Sharon's heart instinctively lifted.

The cleanness and the sunny light, the pretty green and white striped awnings over the greengrocery, where vegetables and fruit lay like coloured playthings. And presently the scent of fresh bread, and the heavenly desserts, the cosmetics in their own elegant aisle, the chocolates.

However, since her last visit, a sombre angel had spread its wings over Sharon's magical rapport with shopping. For although she detested other housework, she had always liked to shop. This was because Sharon liked food. Not unreasonably. It was her one true remaining contact with the joy of living.

And Sharon was fat.

She had had problems ever since she started Andrew. And after his birth, the fat had not melted away, as somehow she had always thought it would. Constantly running round after her child in addition to running round after Wayne made Sharon very hungry. And so, Sharon ate. Snacks of crisps and bubbly drinks, cakes, bananas, and, when out, McDonald's.

And in the evenings, the big cooked dinners must be prepared for equally hungry but rod-slim Wayne. Steak and chips, lamb and roast potatoes, cherry tart, coffee ice-cream. And afterwards, when Wayne was out at the pub, or somewhere else, Sharon ate Mars bars and Whispers before the telly. They said the taste of chocolate sent a message to your brain that was like the stimulus of falling in love. Sharon had never noticed that. But at least chocolate did not get you pregnant.

She had conceived Andrew in a field by starlight. And as Wayne pushed inside her, hurting her, filling her with a strange sweet triumph, a line of poetry from school had come to Sharon over and over:

In fields of light, that warm to touch . . .

She had not told Wayne of the poetry, he would have sneered. She had had to tell him though, four months later, when she was beginning to blow up, not only her stomach, but all over, that she had his baby in her womb. Wayne had been going to dump Sharon. But Wayne's dad had threatened him and Wayne was still scared of his father. Men had a responsibility. Sharon would make a good wife. Sharon was the mother of Wayne's son.

They were married in a registry office and Sharon looked a sight, her pink dress already too tight for her, and her hat trying to blow off. Wayne was sullen and cocky by horrible turns.

It had not been an easy birth.

Wayne, again by turns, was annoyed with the baby, or proud of it. With Sharon, he remained only annoyed.

But Wayne was a TV repair man. They did not have to economize. Andrew was smartly dressed, and there was always plenty of food.

When Sharon had to start buying a forty-two C bra, she did become a bit worried. But she could not see what she should do. She was hungry, truly hungry, all the time, and if she had to wait for food, sometimes she felt sick and giddy. As Andrew grew, when he was at home, she would also share his little-boy lunches. Beefburgers and fries. Fish fingers and alphabetti spaghetti. Andrew, she thought, quite liked her. She liked Andrew. It was not his fault.

And he was an odd child. Sometimes he wanted books from the library, and once, when a piece of classical music came on the television, he sat enrapt, and his eyes were full of something – not tears, not thought – she did not know, and Andrew did not say.

So then she let him choose the odd classical CD at Woolworth's, even though Wayne jeered and called her a soppy cow.

Sometimes Andrew would come out with long, long words. At five, he had said to her, abruptly, 'Candelabra.'

'And what's that?' asked Sharon, who was genuinely unsure.

'A fing wiv canals in it,' said Andrew.

'What, like a river?'

Andrew looked lost.

She could see she had disappointed him then, just as she did his father. So she opened the freezer and got out the full-cream ices with chopped pecans.

Sharon's bright thick hair was cut very, and very unbecomingly, short. Someone had told her, she did not want to bother with it now, and this would make things simple. But now and then, when she caught sight of herself, Sharon wondered who she was. She had been a plump firm pretty eighteen-year-old, with a primrose mane dazzling to her waist, and she had been glad of her big breasts.

Somehow she did not associate the process of eating her meals, her comforts, with growing larger. Fat was a malignant sorcery. Although, she did see that when they had that war, and she had been so frightened, she had had an awful lot of chocolate. Sharon had been afraid of a scud-missile attack. Wayne had told her she was insane. This did not help, but the chocolate did, it calmed her. When the war ended she celebrated, really happy, with Andrew. They had double burgers and fries and banana splits.

Then, last month, she had had to go to the doctor with a painful swollen foot that made her chores extra difficult.

'It's a bad strain, Mrs Ferris. But you know why, don't you?'

'No,' said Sharon, honestly, embarrassed to have failed the doctor's test.

'You're too fat, I'm afraid. Much too fat. You're putting a strain on your feet, and goodness knows what sort of strain on your heart.'

Sharon and Wayne's doctor was about twenty-nine, slim and fit with lush auburn hair. Wayne always said he fancied the doctor. Her apple-blossom skin had never been tainted by make-up and her large black-lashed eyes mocked mascara. Nature had created the doctor in an impulse of beauty and health which probably nothing short of a wilful intake of cyanide could have damaged. Yet from this rostrum the doctor was inclined forcibly to assist others less lucky to try to attain her (impossible) heights.

'Here's a diet sheet, Mrs Ferris. Follow it, and come back in two weeks, and I'll weigh you again.'

Sharon looked at the diet sheet bemused. And this was the treatment she received for her hurt foot.

Ten days later, an elasticated support from Boots had cured Sharon's strain, and she had duly begun to diet. Sharon, all her life, had done what strong-minded people told her. Even to the extent of having sex with Wayne Ferris in a field.

But the diet was awkward. Now, instead of one big meal that Sharon could enjoy, Sharon had to make one big meal that she *would* have enjoyed but was not allowed, and one small meal that she hated and would presently, to the accompanying aromas of chips, pies and gateaux, try to consume.

All day she felt weak, as if she had the 'flu. Once she was actually sick, but perhaps that was good. Her stomach was sore from lettuce and carrot.

She had always dreaded salad. Hard-boiled eggs made her queasy, grilled fish tasted like cardboard. She did like fruit – cooked, with sugar and pastry.

Worst of all, she missed her chocolate. In the long nights while Wayne was out with the women he picked up when mending their TVs, Sharon ate raw apples and oranges until she got diarrhoea.

After two weeks she went back to the doctor.

The doctor did not remember why Sharon had come, but when Sharon humbly reminded her, the doctor weighed Sharon. 'Well, you haven't lost any weight yet, Mrs Ferris. Have you been sticking to the diet?' Sharon said that she had. The doctor frowned. 'Well, if you're sure. Sometimes it can take a few weeks before anything starts to happen.'

The doctor told Sharon she was on a plateau, but in fact Sharon was in a mild, prevailing hell. She did ask how long she would have to diet.

'Oh, you mustn't think of it as a diet, Mrs Ferris. When you're inclined to obesity, this has to be a way of life.'

'You mean I'll always have to eat salad and stuff?'

The doctor smiled. She told Sharon, as if it were lovely news which would please her, 'That's right, Mrs Ferris. If you stick to these foods, you can't go wrong.'

And so, when Sharon entered Tesco's with Andrew trotting by her side, her heart lifted – and fell into the abyss. She could look, but not touch. The touch that warmed . . .

Sharon wheeled the trolley bravely in among the salads.

When they were passing the hot bread, direct from some

hidden oven, and Sharon felt dizzy and her mouth filled with water, Andrew came out with one of his words.

'Melanic,' said Andrew.

'Pardon?'

'Melanic.'

'And what's that, Andy?'

Sharon stared at her child from a tower of flesh like a slender shaking prisoner in a window.

'Black,' said Andrew. *'Dark.'*

Looking at him, Sharon's fallen heart suddenly stirred.

He was six, and that morning he had had a dentist's appointment. It was only a check-up, and there was never anything to do. Yet Andrew did not like the dentist's. She had been the same as a child, and only got used to it after all the fillings. But, even though nervous, Andrew was controlled and well behaved. He had always been good, even when he was tiny.

He was not a cute child, but, when you looked at him, properly, he had a satisfying face, well proportioned already, and framed in black soft hair, not like Wayne's at all.

'Dark,' said Sharon. 'Mell-annic.' She tasted the word, literally tasted it, a dark slab of chocolate cake in her watering mouth.

Wayne would come in with the smell on him of other women. He made no real secret of what he did. Cheap, nasty scent, and sometimes expensive, nasty scent. He wore each one like an additional piece of clothing. Slept beside her, reeking. Dreaming of them. He never made love to Sharon. If he ever had.

She thought of the cafeteria here, in Tesco's, and how she had gone in and had a cream cake or a hot chocolate. Well, that was out. But they did do nice salads – not like the limp, wet, harsh things that were all she could conjure. Ham and coleslaw . . . that would not hurt. Not for once. And she could have a cup of tea with sugar. Who would know? And Andrew could eat something really exciting, a baked potato with cheese and beans. They deserved it, before the wait for the bus, and lugging the shopping up the road.

And then she turned and saw the cold case full of Weight Watchers meals, and all at once, in the desert, Sharon knew she was saved. Wayne could afford it. She would eat these. Look at them. Lasagne, spaghetti bolognaise – and so low in calories. Tesco's had not let her down.

'Just a minute, Andy,' she said absently, 'Mum won't be long.'

And she reached in her hands and took up the packets of her salvation, and tossed them, with an unconscious swash-buckling grace, into her trolley.

She was generous. Sharon had been able, at last, to be friendly to Sharon.

When she turned round, she saw Andy over by the fruit pies, and she thought, gentle now, *Yes, he'll like that for tea.* And she recalled the diet chocolate drink two aisles back.

But then she saw it was not, actually, Andy, but another child, older and not so interesting.

Sharon gazed about her.

Andrew was gone.

She felt a wave of irritation and then a long slow heave of panic. He was not a child who strayed.

She took hold of the trolley in a firm, business-like way, and marched up the aisle, and down another. And then up the second aisle and back into the first.

There were not many shoppers at this time of day, and few children, for it was not a school holiday.

Two small girls were playing with a woolly bear by the frozen peas, and Sharon asked them, 'Have you seen a little boy, about your age, in a blue pullover?'

The mother of the girls came up.

'Have you lost your boy? Oh, they are a nuisance.'

'Yes,' said Sharon.

Andrew was not a nuisance.

Andrew was her son.

Born from the sweet triumph of a starlit field.

Now she ran. And all at once she left her trolley, piled with the shining gold of hope, and empty-handed she raced, panting, up and down.

The banks of adored food passed like a glassy nightmare. The tints and shapes were wrong. Beauty had died.

Half an hour later Sharon found a woman in a tomato coat, one of the shop's attendants.

The woman was efficient and concerned, seeing Sharon's round fat face streaked with tears.

Over the Tannoy they alerted the shoppers to a missing child. A little boy in a blue jumper and jeans. Unfortunately, nobody seemed to have seen him. Not even the security cameras.

Later, they led her up into a sanctum of the store, and in a small warm room they brought her tea on a tray, and a plate of consolement, chocolate biscuits.

'Don't you worry, Mrs Ferris. The manager will call the police. It's just a precaution. Little Andrew's wandered off. They do, don't they.'

These people were so kind to her.

But she was alone.

Sharon reached for the chocolate biscuits and fed them slowly and regularly into her weeping mouth. It seemed they would colour her crying. Chocolate tears.

And as the water rolled down her face and the chocolate entered the forbidden gate of her lips, in the heart of her soul she knew she would never see Andrew again.

Chapter Five

In July, Elizabeth and Reg went for two weeks holiday in Glasgow.

The house soon fell into a flowery bloom of dustiness, through which Rachaela, Althene, Anna and the cats picked their differing ways.

Fascinated, Rachaela noted how quickly the top of the cooker darkened from spilled olive oil, and the sink from washing-up left overnight. She was not inclined to chores. Once she had kept her various domiciles in order. But that was before the corruption of servants.

Finally, the night prior to Elizabeth's return, Rachaela cleaned the kitchen. Althene did not ask her what she was doing. It was Anna who did that, Anna, just come from a conversation – in Dutch – with Althene. 'But Elizabeth will be here tomorrow.'

'I know,' Rachaela said, 'and it seemed unfair for her to come back to all this mess.'

'What mess?' said Anna.

'Yes, so I'm mad,' said Rachaela.

She did not look at Anna, and presently Anna went back to Althene. In the living room these two then watched a video of *The Ten Commandments*, a film Rachaela had once loved. But she did not want to watch it now. Her concentration flagged, as it did with music. She found she would stray into the room and turn on the TV. A habit had

36

formed after the war, of watching the news. She did not know why she did this. She could and would help no one whose sufferings were brought so cruelly to light.

The cooker was not pristine, but she had done her best.

In the morning, Elizabeth and Reg were, unusually, late.

The day was hot and dull, the sun pushing over the house, deep shadow in the hall.

When the knocker sounded, Rachaela went to answer the door.

'Here we are,' said Elizabeth, and Reg silently saluted Rachaela, passing round the house to the mower shed. One of Elizabeth's rare concessions to her heritage popped prettily from her mouth: 'We're a wee bit tardy. That old car. It's got a mind of—' Elizabeth halted. Something happened to her.

She did not lose her colour, and yet she turned to stone, and one stone hand went up to her lips.

Rachaela did not ask Elizabeth if she was ill, or what it was.

Rachaela merely turned, and beheld Anna, her daughter, passing through the steep shadow, from the kitchen to the living room.

Anna was dressed in one of the dresses Elizabeth had stitched for her. It was shorter now, only reaching a few inches below her knees, where it had trailed on the ground. It was perhaps also too tight. The dress was white and had a formless yet mediaeval air. Anna's hair floated to her hips, and fluttered like smoke as she moved.

Behind her, Rachaela heard Elizabeth say, like a beldame on a blasted heath, 'Awa' wi ye, my fair, awa' tae the hollo' hill.'

Rachaela glanced at Elizabeth and said crisply, 'That's an old ballad, is it? Or a charm? Do you think she'll go?'

'I'm – sorry, Mrs Day,' said Elizabeth. 'She gave me a turn.'

'Why's that?'

'I never realized – how she's grown. It *is* Anna?'

'Anna, say hallo to Elizabeth,' Rachaela said.

But Anna, who was normally polite, and sensitive to the presence of others, did not seem to hear.

Yes, she looked like some fey ghost haunting a Scottish castle, one of those white maidens who flung themselves from battlements when deprived of love.

And from Anna's right hand something dripped darkly, and made a shining trail along the floor . . .

'Just a minute, Elizabeth, excuse me—'

Rachaela walked after Anna as the girl glided into the main room.

There the glow of day enveloped her.

She shimmered, and grew actual.

'Anna!'

Anna turned. 'Yes, Rachaela?'

'What's happened to your hand?'

Anna looked down and lifted her right hand, rather as Elizabeth had done, automatically, and opened her fingers. Out fell two dissolving ice-cubes. They had come from the fridge which, last night, Rachaela had vigorously wiped with Jif.

'What are you doing, Anna?'

'I don't know,' Anna said. She appeared surprised but not dismayed. 'I think I meant to get some orange juice.'

'Then go and get it. Don't be stupid.'

Anna gazed up at her. She was still not so tall that she need not do that.

But of course Elizabeth had baulked. She had seen Anna so often it had not properly struck her, but two weeks away were enough. And even in two weeks, doubtless, changes had gone on.

Anna was too old. Much too old.

And I hate her. It's in my voice. My rival again. And this time I won't even have twelve years before she catches me up.

38

In the hall, Elizabeth had hung up her summer jacket, and now she was in the kitchen.

'My, isn't it clean, Mrs Day.'

She was cheerful and at ease, and already the filter jug was bubbling for the coffee, and on a table lay fruit and flour, and a hand-written recipe for home-made ice-cream.

'It must have startled you,' said Rachaela.

'Well,' Elizabeth shrugged. 'Just for a minute. But there. They shoot up now.'

'Some of them do.'

'What I said,' said Elizabeth. 'It's an old fairy song. "The Elvinbrod". The fairy people.'

'The hollow hill,' said Rachaela.

'Tam kissed the Fairy Queen on the lips and went under the hill,' said Elizabeth merrily, 'and he was gone a day. But when he came out he was seven years older.'

'That's what she's done, is it,' said Rachaela. 'Had a magic kiss.'

Elizabeth laughed.

Was she acting? Her eyes were open and innocent. But then, she and Reg must have known the Scarabae before this.

On the news that night there was a report of a little girl who had gone missing in Dyfed. She had been observed by friends cycling off into a disused railway tunnel, but she had never emerged on the far side. A fossil collector chipping away at the rocks there had not seen her, and though originally intensively questioned, the police had let him go.

There was something eerie as well as tragic in the story. Even the bicycle had disappeared.

'Maybe she was sucked down into a hollow hill,' Rachaela said, but Althene did not answer.

Althene held a letter in her hand. It had come that morning, with a Netherlands postmark.

'I have had this,' Althene said.

'Yes.'

'But you're not concerned as to the content.'

'It's your business.'

'If it's my business, Rachaela, it may also be yours. Are you interested in me at all?'

Rachaela shrugged.

'I think that we'll need to talk,' said Althene. 'But first, I must warn you about this. I'll have to go to Amsterdam. A few days only. I'm afraid I must go alone.'

'All right.'

'You don't want to know why?'

'It's up to you.'

'You are becoming,' Althene said, 'exasperating. You're forming yourself into it, like a creature into a chrysalis. What will hatch?'

'A beetle,' said Rachaela. 'A scarab.'

'Very well. I must go back to see what Sofie – what my mother is doing. They say she's behaving unwisely.'

'They?'

'The family.'

'*Your* Scarabae. The Europeans. And *they* decide you have to go.'

'Not precisely.'

'Then why do it? You loathe your mother, don't you? The bitch who beat you with a leather strap.'

'I don't love Sofie. I don't like her. But I feel loyalty to her.'

'Fathomless mystic Scarabae loyalty.'

Althene paused. She wore a dress the colour and nearly the texture of Sauterne, that left bare most of her hairless creamy lightly muscled arms, on the left of which hung one copper coil. She raised her head and the black jewellery of hair swung away.

'We had these dialogues,' she said, 'in the beginning.'

'But this,' said Rachaela, 'is another beginning.'

'Is it?'

40

'Your beginning with Anna.'

'I see. Anna is my daughter.'

'And what else?'

'No,' Althene said, 'we will discuss this when I've come back.'

'Will we.'

'Adamus,' Althene said, 'is dead.'

'Is he? Is Ruth dead?'

Althene said, 'Please, Rachaela. I have to attend to this other matter. My mother, you see, is unhinged.'

'And did you do that for her?'

Althene's black eyes with their blue rings – they flashed. She could kill as well as kiss. The magic kiss. What was she to Anna? Had Anna ever questioned? Father – mother – lover . . . not yet.

'As with your own mother,' Althene said quietly, 'she was driven mad by the attentions of my father.'

'He loved her and left her.'

'Substantially. Rather worse than that.'

'What did he do?'

'Something. I don't know. He got me on her. Isn't that enough.'

Rachaela said, 'I don't think so.'

'And now you are intrigued. Well, I'll tell you a story of my father, what I know of him. I saw him only once. Long ago.'

'How long? Was this in the fourteen hundreds perhaps? Earlier?'

Althene grimaced. She said, 'Suffice it to say our dresses swept the floor.'

'All right.'

'It was in the city, in Amsterdam. At the old house. I was playing in a lower room—'

'Describe it to me.'

'Why? It was a quite ordinary rich house. The floor had black diamonds on white. There was a tree, a hybrid orange in a pot, which had grown up through the ceiling.

It would produce hard green inedible fruit like lime-green boiled sweets. I was about twelve, playing with a kitten, and he came in. This man.'

'And how were you dressed, Althene? As a boy or as a girl?'

'You're perceptive.'

'No, you said dresses sweeping the floor.'

'Yes, then, I would bribe a maid to assist me. I would dress as a woman.'

'How were you dressed?'

'A little cap on my head and my hair down my back. Folded cloth over my breasts, which of course did not exist. A tight waist.'

'And he saw you.'

'Yes, he saw me. He looked tall to me, and then – then he must have been. Quite tall. He had jet black hair that fell, straight as a pen stroke, back from his face. A broad, high forehead. Blue eyes like jewels. He had a beautiful, goodly face. And he smiled. He didn't know my name, but he called to me and I went to him.'

'And this was your father.'

'The man who got me on Sofie, yes.'

'He was, naturally, Scarabae.'

'Naturally. He asked what my name was. I had another name I would use, a secret name. But I told him. Out of every pore of him there breathed a kind of aroma. It was danger and darkness.'

Rachaela bowed her head. 'I know.'

'Of course you do. But Adamus, to this man, was like a whisper to a battle song.'

'And Malach?' Rachaela suddenly said. 'What comparison would you make with Malach?'

'Oh, Malach,' Althene smiled. 'Malach is Malach.'

'Go on. What did your father do?'

'He petted me. Very civilly, decorously. He told me I was very beautiful and that he had heard of me, and that I must be his daughter. He called himself Cajanus. He asked my age. He stroked my face. And my mother came down the stair and she howled. Like a dog. It frightened me, but he only stood up. And he put me behind him, as if to protect me, and I had in that moment a fantasy that he would take me away and all manner of things would be well.'

'But he didn't.'

'Obviously not. My mother took him aside. They went upstairs. He turned and kissed his hand to me as he climbed up. The light of the windows caught in his eyes. Evidently, I've never forgotten.'

Rachaela thought, *Don't try and win me now by your pain.* Althene alarmed her, as at the start. Althene, it seemed, could always win.

'And your mother told your father you were not a delicious tender nubile little girl, but a beastly perverted little boy.'

'Oh, she did better than that.'

Althene looked into distance. How many centuries? The scene she had described, like a fantasy upon a Dutch painting, the floor, the kitten, the corrupted orange tree.

'What?'

'She had me brought, and shut the chamber door on us. The three of us. And then she stripped me with her bare hands. Quickly I was naked in front of him and he saw his mistake. I suppose he may have been embarrassed. His face closed like an eye. He was blind. He went straight out, but he had already left us. She laughed, and then she beat me.'

'You said she was excellent at that.'

'I've told you the story.'

Rachaela turned her head. 'I'm sorry.'

'Yes, I've never elsewhere had such shame. Never since. And never before. It was a baptism. But he.'

They sat in silence, and down below Anna had turned on the music centre and Shostakovich rose up through the house, the perfect music cue in the film of life.

'Do you have to go?' Rachaela said.

43

'If only to make you miss me, like before.'

'And Anna,' Rachaela said.

'You'll take care of Anna. Anna will be safe with you.'

'I may strip her naked and whip her.'

'You may learn to love her.'

'She isn't loveable. Not that way. Not as a mother's daughter.'

'How would you know?' Althene said, and her face was colder than a closing eye, farther away than Amsterdam.

A new car had been bought for Reg. Rachaela found out when Elizabeth thanked her. The Scarabae must have seen to it. It was a smooth, dark grey Citroën XM.

In this vehicle, a few days later, Althene was borne to the airport. Anna, but not Rachaela, went with her. And, in the evening, Reg drove Anna home, and as the Citroën purred away into the afterglow, Anna pushed the buttons on the door, and stepped into the house, alone.

Rachaela went out to meet her, reluctantly.

'Did you see the plane?'

'Oh, yes. And I watched it take off.'

'That's good. You can go and meet her when she comes back.'

'Will you come, then?'

'I might. I was tired today. I don't like long car drives.'

'Reg is happy with his car,' said Anna. She stood in the hall, patiently. Rachaela thought, *Am I, somehow, barring the way into the house?* Anna said, 'Did Jelka miss me?'

'Yes. She looked for you. I expect they'll all look for Althene.'

Anna said, 'What did Elizabeth leave for dinner?'

'Chicken and quiche and salad. And there's a cold trifle.'

Anna nodded.

Ruth would have wanted to eat at once. Ruth was always almost insatiably hungry. But Anna ate only normally, in fact rather frugally. She had probably only asked about the meal to be courteous, to ease the tension.

'Would you like tea, or a cold drink?'

'Just some water,' said Anna.

Rachaela went into the kitchen and took a bottle of carbonated water from the fridge. She poured it into one of the tall green wine glasses. Anna would drink a glass of white wine with dinner.

When you thought of it, of her age, that was absurd.

But Anna was not her age.

The evening passed calmly, but separately. Anna played with the cats and listened to Rachmaninov preludes on the music centre. Later she put on a video, *The Fugitive Kind*. Anna, unlike the Scarabae at the house on the common, liked older films.

Rachaela painted in the fifth bedroom, which she used as a studio. The painting was ineffectual, would not coalesce.

Althene had said she would be gone for six or seven days. Rachaela had not asked her anything further about the visit.

They had not been apart for three years, more. It must be a wrench. At least a vacancy . . . but then, they had already parted. Anna had parted them. No longer was Althene whole for Rachaela, not complete. She was divided, luminously and amorphously, into her dual nature. Her maleness, thought always invisible, save at its most intrinsic and momentary, had taken on a strong and threatening life.

And I don't like men, do I? I want them, but I don't like them. I never forget them, but I never love.

Adamus, in the church, kissing her mouth. And on the stair of the Dutch house, the one Althene called Cajanus, kissing his hand, the light in his jewel blue eyes.

Anna went to bed about ten o'clock.

Rachaela stole in presently, trying to be dutiful. To see

if Anna needed anything. But that was foolish. For Anna was not a baby. Even if she should have been.

And in any case, Anna was already quiescently and silently sleeping.

How have I accepted this? But then I haven't. It has simply occurred.

Yet, Anna was in so many ways, mentally, still so very young.

There in her arm Ursula the fox, who filled the bed with loose fur, and on the other side, the rabbit. How long had Ruth retained her bear? Until she was nine, ten? And then, there had been no cat, and here, as now, Jelka would lie on the pillow, black satin to compliment the wash of ice pale hair.

Was this room, this second bedroom of the grand shuttered house, like Ruth's area in the London flat?

In the dim influx of light from the hall, Rachaela stared about.

The walls decorated in pastel, the floor thick-carpeted in dark green. An old-fashioned carved wardrobe, and beside it, the carved chest that was the dressing-up box. Book shelves bricked in by books. A few ornaments, a shell, a bronze Libran scales with a fruit of amber marble in one dish. On the ground no dolls, but various toy animals carefully arranged for their own comfort. A kaleidoscope, paints – but no paintings on view. More books piled up. And there the mattress, its almond pillows and sheet, and the patchwork blanket folded off, and Jacob also in a nest there, sleeping before his nightly sortie to the garden.

She must miss Althene very much.

Had she cried, or tried not to cry, at the airport?

Ruth had always been rather repulsively controlled.

Until that last time, on the stairs. When they carried her up screaming. *Malach! Malach!*

Anna's hair was just like Malach's hair.

She could have been his daughter.

But she's mine.

Anna stirred in her sleep, and turned a little, and Jelka mewed. Anna opened her eyes, and as she reached to caress the cat, saw Rachaela.

Does she think I've crept in to smother her? The wicked step-mother?

'Hallo,' said Anna, 'did you want me?'

'Just to see you were all right.'

'Oh, yes. Thank you. I dreamed Althene was in Amsterdam, by the canal.'

'She will be by now.'

'I hope it's okay for her.'

'Yes.' How much had Althene confided to Anna? 'You'll miss her a great deal, but she'll soon be back.'

'I know,' said Anna.

And there before her, peaceful as the sleep which had gone before and now returned, Rachaela beheld the pure and utter trust of true love. Anna had not cried. Anna had no doubts. Althene loved her and Althene would come back to her.

But the world is never sure, Anna.

Unless, perhaps, for the Scarabae.

Rachaela went out and drew the door closed, as Anna preferred it. (Ruth had liked to be private.) Rachaela went down and opened another bottle of wine. She sat drinking from the cold glass in front of the cruel TV, watching news of the unsure world.

There were altered warnings in the doctors now, to go along with the old ones. *The Facts About Aids.* And on the tables were leaflets on the menopause, food sense, and child abuse. An attractive poster of drinks informed the waiting room that more than two small glasses of wine a day could seriously injure a woman's health. There were no warnings about BSE, radioactivity or aluminium in tap water. However, the No Smoking notices were enormous.

Rachaela thought, *I know more and it's made me angry. Or only facetious.*

The questionnaire she had had to fill in was like an application for a top-secret job. She had not completed every section. The receptionist did not seem to notice, but then she was rather busy talking to her colleague.

The panel of doctors had agreed to accept them, in the absence of their own doctor. After all, they were also entitled to National Health advice.

'Ms Day? Doctor Collins will see you now. Pink door.'

They got up, and Rachaela walked with Anna, neat in her fashionably short white dress, to the pink door.

Doctor Collins was about thirty years old, attractive and calm.

She held their questionnaire, which had come through a hatch, but barely glanced at it.

'How can I help you?'

'This is my daughter, Anna,' said Rachaela.

'Hallo, Anna,' said the doctor, smiling. From the movements of her hands and the inflexion of her voice, one could tell she would never be rough, except perhaps to save a life.

Anna did not speak. She waited.

Rachaela said, 'Anna's been having some problems. With her right hand. And could I ask you to examine her?'

'What seems to be the trouble?'

'It's a general problem,' said Rachaela, 'I don't know. I'd prefer a complete check-up.'

'Well, your daughter's at that age – we all go through it. Don't worry, Anna, I won't be doing anything to hurt. Just slip your top off.'

The doctor proceeded, very gently, politely, to test Anna's chest and heart. It seemed she had reacted to Rachaela and Anna's tension. But as the examination went on, the doctor began to look more and more serenely pleased. Rachaela recalled Kate Ames. Doctor Collins was delighted, because everything was in order.

Last of all, after the eyes and throat and ears, the doctor investigated Anna's right hand.

'There really isn't any cause for worry. You're left-handed, aren't you, Anna?'

'Yes.'

Anna had submitted gracefully.

Even to being naked, before the stranger, and the other stranger, her mother.

Rachaela had looked quickly, and away. Seen.

The doctor presently reiterated that Anna was in excellent health. Doctor Collins said she wished she saw all young girls this fit and well coordinated. Perhaps a little mild anaemia. But calcium and iron would see to that. It was not uncommon, after the onset of the menarche.

'She doesn't have periods,' said Rachaela.

'Oh? Really. Then I would definitely recommend a course of vitamins. It isn't that unusual. Sometimes worrying about it can delay it.'

They sat now in a conspiratorial ring.

Rachaela said, quietly and firmly, 'I'm afraid I didn't completely fill in your form.'

'Oh, don't worry. We can catch up on that.'

'How old, Doctor, would you say my daughter, is?'

Doctor Collins looked up again, and now lit a collusive smile at Anna.

'Well – let's see. Anna appears to be sixteen. Perhaps a well-developed fifteen?'

'My daughter, Doctor, is less than two years of age.'

Doctor Collins did not laugh. Something withdrew inside her clever, elegant face. She gazed hard at Rachaela. Then she said, 'Ms Day, I'm afraid I have a lot of patients waiting, but I think we should talk again. Perhaps you could call by tomorrow, after eleven-thirty, when Anna's at school. I can spend some time with you then.'

'All right,' Rachaela said. She stood up and took the prescription for calcium and iron, and she and Anna went out, leaving the doctor very serious at her desk. Rachaela, of course, had not given their real address.

Outside they walked speechless up the sunny street.

Cars passed. The large houses, with their gardens of shaped conifers and rose roses, summer spreading its last gold randomly; a leaf, a sill, a snoozing cat on a path.

'I know you want to say something to me, Anna.'

Anna said nothing.

'You must be furious. Upset. I'm very sorry. I apologize. But it's done.'

I stripped her naked. I whipped her with humiliation.

Anna said, 'Why did you?'

'Why did I take you to an unknown doctor and have you examined? Don't you know?'

'Because I've grown very quickly.'

'Yes, Anna. You've grown extremely quickly.'

'I thought I had,' said Anna. 'Sometimes I ached. Althene said . . .' Anna paused.

'She said it didn't matter? Yes?'

'She said I was different. She said we all are.'

'You're Scarabae.'

'Yes,' said Anna.

'I think I took you to that doctor to punish you, Anna, and that is very unfair, because it isn't your fault. Whoever the hell you are.'

'I'm Anna.'

'Are you?'

They walked. The street ended on the brink of a busy road, and here they stopped, in stasis, and faced each other, while everything else rushed by.

Will she soon be my height?

Anna, in her white short dress, a lovely girl of sixteen. And naked, so healthy, the doctor said. But Doctor Collins had not said beautiful. Like a dagger in the heart. While on Anna's left lovely breast, like a pale blue feather, the ghost of a real dagger, the memory of a knife?

'Someone threw you from a battlement,' Rachaela said, 'but I'm the castle you haunt. You're haunting *me*.'

Anna looked at her, no fear, no distress. More serene than Doctor Collins.

'Do you think that I'm Ruth?'

'Yes. What do *you* think?'

'I don't know.'

'*Don't* you?' Rachaela said, more questioningly, 'Don't you? Do you remember anything—'

'Oh, yes. But not that.'

'Then – what?'

'Places,' said Anna, musingly. 'But I can't paint them. Old rooms.'

'Do you remember him?'

'Who?'

'Malach.'

Anna looked into Rachaela's face and for a moment a tide moved behind her skin, colourless and emotionless, yet like a blush.

'Althene told me the name,' she said. 'I know the *name*.'

'What did she tell you about him?'

'Nothing much. That he'd been kind to her. That he had a lot of dogs. He lives in a castle.'

'Then haunt that one,' Rachaela said.

Anna suddenly began to cry. The water spilled from her silvery eyes as if from a bottomless vault of rain. Rachaela stared at her. Anna cried as she did. Anna was her daughter.

And Rachaela reached out, awkwardly, to touch Anna, but Anna only stood like a pillar of ice, ungiving, noiseless, crying, in the rushing street.

'I don't know what to do,' Rachaela said. 'Oh Christ.'

Anna said, clearly and softly, 'It will be over in a minute.'

And, in a minute, it was.

People squinted at them curiously as they walked on, the exquisite blonde girl brushing the rain from her cheeks, the beautiful black-haired woman, obviously too young to be her mother, walking by her, her fists clenched, her neck bowed. Lovers maybe? A little tiff.

Chapter Six

By TRAIN IT TOOK HALF an hour to get into London. At the station they found a taxi. The yellow afternoon went by, Madame Tussauds, the park, the river.

Anna did not seem apprehensive. She had enjoyed the train journey. And in the taxi she looked about. Like a child.

She wore another of her short white dresses, with pale purple and green flowers coined over it, green tights, and green flat shoes. At her throat was a tiny slender silver snake Althene had bought her. (Talisman?)

The taxi drove up the slope.

The common above, and the house with the tarot card windows, and turrets. The sun was westering over, adding a dramatic photographic filter of bronzy sheen to the sky.

Rachaela half turned to Anna. She meant to say, 'What do you think?' But Anna-Ruth had seen the house before. Only she did not remember.

Anna did look, but she had looked at everything.

They got out, and as Rachaela paid the driver, Anna stood on the driveway, gazing up.

The taxi reversed and rumbled off down the hill. A butterfly flew out of one of the hedges that were planted now in the gravel. And Anna held out her hand and the butterfly settled on it.

'Isn't it beautiful, Rachaela.'

'Yes. How did you do that?'

'What?'

'Never mind.'

Rachaela went cautiously to regard the butterfly. It was palest lemon, and its wings trembled with life. As suddenly as it had come to rest it lifted away and up into the trees beyond the house.

Rachaela knocked on the door. The green man face of the knocker glared at her above leafy lips. She had not telephoned them. The visit was to be a surprise.

A straight, not very tall, old man opened the door.

'Good afternoon, Michael.'

'Good afternoon, Miss Rachaela. Miss Anna.'

I should have known better. Of course, Althene has secretly kept them posted.

Anna said, 'Hallo, Michael.'

They went into the gracious hall with its pillars and waiting lamps. The stained-glass women were still in their windows, and the minstrels over the stairs. Down that stair Ruth had stolen with her golden razor. And up it, when the man lay dead in a riot of blood on the floor, Michael and Kei had dragged her.

But someone else was coming down.

They always knew, when one of their own had arrived.

'I'm sorry I didn't call, Eric. But I've brought Anna to see you.'

Did she imagine it, or was he taller? Straighter, more solid? Quite possibly. The Scarabae could do this, grow younger and more hale. His hair was a very dark grey, almost a muted black. His eyes were bright. In one hand he carried a large book from which dripped a black silk marker.

He reached the bottom of the staircase and came towards them. He took Rachaela's hand and touched his dry firm lips to it. To Anna, he bowed.

'My daughter by Althene,' Rachaela said. 'This is Eric.'

'I am glad you have come,' Eric said.

'Thank you,' Anna said, 'for your welcome.'

Not a flicker between them.

Does he not know, then? Or is it only rude to take umbrage at an old enemy reclad in a new skin?

They went into the white drawing room.

It had been thoroughly dusted, gleamed with polish. Flowers were in a stone bowl on a table, and by the television lay a scatter of twenty-five or thirty videos in gaudy cases. Books sat on the sofas. The room looked lived-in. *Alive.*

They too sat. Eric said, 'Michael will bring us something. Will you have tea, Rachaela? Anna?'

Anna said, 'Could I have coffee, please?'

'I'm afraid we don't keep it,' Eric said, regretfully.

'Then tea, thank you,' said Anna.

She was like a perfectly gorgeous nineteenth-century young girl, taken calling on a rich uncle by her chaperone.

Ruth had never been like that.

Anna was, in fact, not like Ruth. Though beautiful, it was an unlike beauty; though graceful, an alien grace. And Anna's remoteness, her unearthly quality, they were not the same as the clandestine demoniac locked silences of Ruth.

Eric opened his book and Rachaela saw a page with black lines ruled across one of the paragraphs. In the margin was a neat column of insectile and minute writing. Sylvian had ruled through all the books, at the last house, by the sea. But Sylvian had not made notes in them.

Eric said, 'I must amend. History – they've changed it.'

'They? Do you mean the Scarabae?' Rachaela said.

'The Scarabae . . . We are history. We are the truth.'

Rachaela glanced at Anna. 'Then Anna is the truth also.'

'Of course.'

Anna smiled. She smiled at Eric. And even the smile was not like Ruth's, which had been so wonderful. Anna's smile was like soft light.

Eric nodded, just as Anna had done.

He said, 'I'm afraid Miranda isn't here. She's always out now. She loves the city. But Sasha will come down. You must pardon Sasha,' he said, 'if she seems a little strained.'

Do you mean if she acknowledges who Anna really is?

'Why would Sasha be strained?' said Rachaela, flirtatiously.

'At our age,' Eric said, 'one must condone some eccentricity.'

Rachaela laughed. He was quite serious. He meant, when one is two hundred or five hundred years old . . .

They talked about films then, Eric and Anna. Their tastes were diametrically opposed. The house Scarabae liked violence, vivid action, and adventure, brutal killings and ruthless justice, adrenaline and startlement. Anna spoke of Vivien Leigh in *Caesar and Cleopatra* and *A Streetcar Named Desire*, Bogart's *Casablanca*, Olivier's *Hamlet*, Alec Guinness and *The Man in the White Suit*.

They found common ground with Claudette Colbert's *Cleopatra*. 'Inaccuracies don't always matter,' Eric said. 'It is the soul that counts. A delicious film.'

But Rachaela, her eyes irresistibly caught by the video covers on the carpet, thought, *How odd. Anna prefers black and white.*

Cheta and Michael brought tea in a blue porcelain pot and a service of blue and white china. There were plates of little cakes and candied fruit, and a small decanter of some colourless liqueur.

It was like the refreshment that had been served when Malach first brought Ruth to the house.

Where was Sasha? Would she refuse to come down?

Anna took one of the cakes, and a single piece of orange. She drank her tea black. Had she always?

From the stairs outside piped a young girlish, childish voice with a faint yet erroneous accent.

'I like strawberry best, Nan-Nan.'

Yes, that would be Tray, the daughter of the man, Nobbi, Ruth had fatally sliced in the neck. The adopted Scarabae daughter now, presumably. Her voice had altered. Less cockney and far less adult. She had been about twenty, and now would be twenty-two or twenty-three. But she had become, of course, nine or ten, maybe even younger, in those past moments of blood and screaming.

Would Tray – or Terentia, the Roman name they had given her – would *she* acknowledge who sat here now, in white, the demon-murderess? Or would that be out of the question?

Sasha and Terentia came into the doorway together, slender forms sliding through.

Sasha wore a contemporary damson dress suitable for a smart woman of eighty years, which is what she appeared to be. Her hair was no longer piled up, but becomingly cut and shaped, just touching her shoulders, a style too immature, that suited her.

Terentia-Tray wore sequined black, a yard of black hair coiling down, blue eyes wide and guileless. She carried her toy lion, the one they had bought her after Nobbi's death. It looked battered, like any loved toy, both of its ears resewn.

Sasha did not seem stressed. Unlike Terentia, her face was full of knowledge.

'Oh, look, Nan-Nan,' said Terentia, 'Cheta did me some strawberry ones.'

'Of course she did, dear,' said Sasha.

Miranda had been *Nan-Nan*, three years ago. But perhaps Miranda was now too youthful for the role. Sasha had replaced her.

The two women moved forward over the clean milky carpet. Anna had stood up, like a well-mannered young gallant.

Terentia looked at her, with childish interest, as if at another little girl, probably come to play with her.

Sasha raised a strange quiet scowl.

Then she fell on the carpet.

She was so light, so apparently fragile, there was scarcely any noise, but Terentia bent over her in panic – 'Nan-Nan! What is it?'

Eric rose and went to Sasha. Cheta kneeled beside the fallen woman. Then Michael came and carried her to one of the white sofas.

Sasha was laid down. She turned her head and looked at Eric with tired ancient eyes.

Eric held her hand.

The Scarabae could be unbearably touching. But they were not. They were old and strong and regenerative and deadly.

Rachaela glanced at Anna, who seemed grave but composed. Rachaela did not say anything.

Now Sasha was sitting up, and Terentia was sitting by her, holding her other hand.

'It's all right, dear,' said Sasha. 'Sasha's well again now.'

Terentia let her go and picked up again the plate of solace, the candied fruit. 'Have some, Nan-Nan.'

'Not for a moment. But you eat one for me.'

Terentia began to eat the candied strawberries, ungreedily, almost dutifully.

The two black and white cats, Juliet's children, had emerged through the door. They too sensed importance.

Anna called to them, and they came. She picked them up and sat down with them, beside Rachaela.

Cheta brought Sasha a glass of brandy from the cabinet.

Sasha said, 'You must excuse me, Rachaela. I'm a little frail today.'

And you've just seen Ruth again. Ruth who killed the original Anna by hammering a knitting needle through her heart.

'Yes. I understand, Sasha. And this is Anna.'

Sasha looked at Anna again.

Sasha said, 'Anna, how glad I am you came to see us. I hope I didn't frighten you.'

'No,' Anna said. 'I'm sorry you were ill.'

'Only for a second. I'm restored now.'

The conversation was not correct. It was not even stilted, save by the Scarabae way of talking, the foreign accent that was always inaudibly yet intrinsically there, the phonetics of steppes and cold mountains.

'Thank you,' Anna said, 'for my name.'

'Oh, my dear,' said Sasha, 'my dear—'

Eric said, 'It is a family name. Yours by right.'

Acidly, Rachaela said, 'Biblical names are always so apposite.'

Terentia said, quaintly, 'Do have a sweetie, Anna.'

Anna said, 'I've had some. They're nice, aren't they.'

'I like the strawberries best.'

Rachaela beheld them, the twenty-three-year-old with the toy lion on her lap, aged nine. And the two-year-old who was sixteen, holding two cats.

The key to the mystery came to Rachaela. Tray had become amnesiac to blot out the ghastly butchery of her father. And Ruth, reborn as Anna, had also become amnesiac, to blot out the very same thing and its consequences.

And the Scarabae? For them Anna was not Ruth. Or if she was, they could forgive if not forget.

After the tea, Eric showed Anna over the house. The green and white bathrooms, the ornate bedrooms with coloured windows. In his own chamber with the orange and chartreuse casements, he had carved a mask, as in the old days. It lay beside a half-formed head which now he was working on. It seemed the face was being assembled by consulting the contours of the mask.

Terentia followed Anna, obviously interested in her.

Sometimes Terentia would point something out. Anna was even allowed to cradle and admire the lion, which she did. But then, Anna too had her toys.

At some juncture Sasha disappeared. She returned when they were, about an hour later, at the brink of leaving.

She carried in her antique ringed hands a curious web. Threadbare, clustered with brittle husks that might have been dead petals or moths . . .

'It's very old. Anna. It's a shawl that Alice made. I would like you to have it.'

She put the relic into Anna's white hands, and Anna raised the shawl. Through its vortices of emptiness, fragments of idyllic crochet or unworldly knitting were revealed.

Carefully, Anna drew the shawl about her.

She became ancient, elemental.

Then she held out her arms and Sasha went into them. They held each other, Sasha and Anna. Then let go.

Eric kissed Anna's hand and bowed to Rachaela. Michael opened the door, and they passed out, into the folding wings of day.

'Would you like some coffee?'

'Yes, please.'

'It used to drive me mad,' Rachaela said, 'the way I couldn't get coffee in the Scarabae house. But then they let me have it.'

They went into the café, where early escapees from various jobs had gathered for omelettes and exotic toasts, wine and Perrier, before the public transport fight homeward.

Anna had coffee with cream and Rachaela a glass of white wine.

Near the bar, two ugly young-middle-aged men began noisily to 'display', shouting witticisms at the patient waitresses. Rachaela realized they were trying to attract Anna's attention.

They would, naturally. Anna shone with beauty.

And the shawl now safely in a green Harrods' bag Cheta had supplied. Anna only looked cunningly young.

Rachaela said, gently, 'Anna, how old are you? I mean, how old would you say you were?'

Anna frowned. (Was this awful surrogate un-mother going to start on her again.) But, graciously, Anna said, 'I'm quite old inside.' She smiled. 'But then, you are, Rachaela.'

'I'm forty-five . . . Am I? I can't remember.'

'I don't mean like that.'

The younger ugly man shouted jollily, 'Did you put the salad in the microwave?'

'Yes,' said the waitress, 'makes 'em nice and crisp.'

Anna grinned.

A true grin. She appeared like a handsome wicked boy when she did it.

'They want you to look at them,' said Rachaela.

Anna laughed now, and drank her coffee, not shy, flattered or contemptuous.

Why did I bring her here? Am I trying to get closer to her? Her beauty is daunting. Was Ruth as beautiful?

Rachaela thought, *Am I falling in love with my daughter?*

She said, 'Althene rang last night.'

'I know. I heard the phone.'

'I'm sorry, I thought you were asleep. I meant to say earlier . . . She'll be home tomorrow.'

Anna looked pleased, the way a child does. 'I hope it was okay.'

'I expect so.'

'Will you come to meet her?' said Anna.

'If you want.'

And now Anna was removed. She lowered her glowing platinum eyes, and her dark lashes – impossible for the albino that clearly she was – swept her cheek as in a romantic novel.

Anna wore no make-up. But her lips were drawn in tawny pink. A violet hinting accented her upper lids, and the thick dark charcoal lashes drew a line, too, round the exact shape of her iridescent eyes. The eyebrows were white, long and sleek, and never needing to be plucked. There was, Rachaela now knew, no hair on Anna's body save at the groin, where it bloomed like rich feathers of virgin snow. And yes, with Anna, one sank into these poetic descriptions.

I am in love with her.

She's mine, after all.

'We could go to the pictures tonight,' Rachaela said, rashly, an adolescent after a first date.

'What film is it?' sensibly, innocently inquired Anna.

'Something that would bore Eric. It's the specialist cinema. The silent *A Midsummer Night's Dream.*'

'Oh, yes,' said Anna, eager and sweet.

The sun was dropping on the lurid, declining city, over its soot and slime and wreckage, and the gilded heights that still protruded, like the funnels of a sinking ship. Red sun fire filled the café, and as the two women rose, the aging men peered after Anna with unconscious yearning masked as lust. What a looker, and the older bit was in no need of dusting, either. But, busy men, preoccupied, they had not moved fast enough. And besides there were the regular wives at home, waiting with cooked dinners and reminders of worries, the mortgage, the broken washing machine, the loss of hair and joy.

Chapter Seven

FARAN STOOD ON THE EXPENSIVE blue chair.
He was looking out, across the road, at the echoing autumnal park.

Behind him, the expensive blue flat lay still before the coming of the man and the woman.

In the burnished window glass, Faran could also glimpse, like a shadow, his own slim black seven-year-old self. He wore expensive blue jeans, and a black T-shirt with an elephant, which read, in red, IVORY IS NOT WHITE.

He liked the elephant. He had pictures of elephants which his mother had let him put up in his room. But the logo troubled him. He knew it meant that white-skinned villains had robbed elephants of their tusks. But then black men had done it too, his father had sorrowfully told him.

The world was being destroyed, said Faran's mother, by unscrupulous and stupid people. Soon nothing would be left. Faran would inherit a ruined earth.

He had had nightmares about it.

When he told them, they agreed. He had been sensible to have nightmares. Well done.

Both Cimmie and Wellington Objegbo, Faran's parents, spoke with extreme upper-class English accents. Sometimes, it was true, Cimmie would come out with a phrase of what she said was an African language. She designed

62

ethnic prints, using old methods of batik – which she said, although Javanese, had links to her genetic culture.

Cimmie was a pretty, slender woman, the colour of cocoa. Her hair was in short tight curls, despite the fact she could have grown it longer. She wore Western clothes and things she said were African as jewellery. She had earrings, for example, of buffalo horn. Apparently it did not matter if buffaloes were killed for this.

Wellington had a job with the government. He did not say much about it. Out of the flat he wore Savile Row suits and silk ties with the insignia of his school, and in winter, although Wellington was now over forty, and had some grey in his black hair, the old school scarf. Indoors, more often than not, Wellington wore jeans and went otherwise bare-chested. He had a marvellous body, and his dark muscular chest was his show-piece.

If Wellington went bare, especially when snow was on the park across the road, Cimmie could not leave him alone. They would disappear into the first bedroom for half an hour, several times a day, and soon Faran would hear his mother screaming. He had never been afraid. Somehow he knew that her screams had to do with pleasure, not pain.

They had told him early about sex. He had understood. Only when Cimmie added that he must marry a white girl had Faran been rather puzzled.

It turned out Cimmie and Wellington were racists. They did not like blacks. While being, conversely, fiercely fascist about their heritage, which they blamed previous whites for damaging, they had exclusively white friends. And when these white friends came to dinner, Cimmie cooked French dishes, with which they drank Italian and German wines and Swedish liqueurs.

The white friends, oddly, were also just as racist about their white colleagues, and sometimes it would almost develop into a row, once the four or six people were on to the tenth bottle of Hock: the whites shouting all whites should be shot, and the Objegbos howling that the blacks had rejected their honour and were worth nothing. On these nights, Faran, allowed to dine and sample the drink with the guests, went away to bed as soon as danger signals came visible. (His mother laughing too much, his father not enough.)

Faran, called for an African hero, was aware he did not know his parents.

He seemed to recognize a great deal in life, but he had never found them familiar.

In babyhood he was fond of Cimmie but he had not trusted her. From the age of two she left him regularly with (white) babysitters.

Over the past four years, Faran had also had tutors. There was the white Ms Baldwin, and the black Mr Thorpe. Why black Mr Thorpe had such a name Faran did not know. Cimmie said that doubtless he had *changed* his name. She treated Mr Thorpe with a studied swimming vagueness, while sitting over tea or wine with Ms Baldwin.

Faran found Ms Baldwin held his attention in arithmetic and geography, but Mr Thorpe, who taught history and English, filled Faran with happiness. Mr Thorpe was in his late fifties, very overweight, and of a beauty such as stars possess. He was blackly dark, as Faran was, and his eyes were like black lights. Others did not see Mr Thorpe as beautiful, but then, maybe they had not been able to look into his eyes.

Along with his subjects Mr Thorpe imparted myth and legend. He seemed cognizant of all cultures, impartially. His tales lifted the short fleece of Faran's head.

Once Mr Thorpe had been hungry, and Cimmie was out. Faran went into the white, white kitchen which the (black) cleaning lady made into a sort of Arctic heaven. Here Faran made Mr Thorpe a sandwich on wholemeal bread, of endive and cold chicken, pickle, beef tomato and mayonnaise. He added a large glass of chilled Gewürztraminer.

Mr Thorpe said, 'Oh, Faran. No, Faran.'

'My father's in Paris,' said Faran.

'All the more reason,' said Mr Thorpe, 'to desist.'

Faran sat and deliberately looked sad, until Mr Thorpe ate the sandwich, and drank half the wine.

Faran then drank the other half.

This seemed like a bonding. They were now wine brothers.

The gap in their ages did not deter Faran. He preferred the company of adults – in any case had been permitted to meet very few children. However, Faran did not count Cimmie and Wellington, their friends, or Ms Baldwin as adults. Mr Thorpe was, and some of the people he saw on TV, and some of the people he read about. Faran grasped that he, too, was older than he was.

And Mr Thorpe seemed to have done this as well.

Then came a phase when Mr Thorpe attempted to take Faran to museums, galleries, and even to see films. Cimmie had grudgingly allowed this. But when Wellington returned from Kuwait, he put a stop to it.

The implication, which Faran instantly deduced, was that Mr Thorpe might have a sexual interest in Faran.

Faran knew this was not so. But demonstrably he was a child. He did not get a vote.

Mr Thorpe vanished from Faran's clean, liberated, comfortable, arid life.

Now, at the window, Faran studied the park.

Cimmie sometimes took him for walks there, if they did not go shopping. Usually it was the latter. Designer coats with ragged images of black men wielding weapons, spiked jewellery, art materials, coffee-table books with wondrous photographs of velds, lions, and firelit Masai. T-shirts for Faran costing forty-two pounds each, displaying glorious-looking animals that were being destroyed in the rain-forests – so that every time he put them on Faran's heart cracked and his blood ran cold.

But the park was simple. Simple pleasure, without screams.

They would buy rolls and feed the ducks and the brown geese almost as tall as Faran with black velvet tongues. The two swans came like lords. Cimmie always told him swans mated for life. This was the ideal.

Faran recalled that unswan-like Wellington had once or twice strayed, for whenever Cimmie and Wellington had a quarrel, Cimmie would allude to Wellington's 'women'.

Now, cut off from Faran by the ferocious road, a tumult of cars, taxis, and buses, the park, like another world, dreamed in its auburn autumn foliage. Through the thinning leaves he caught the smoky glint of water. While below, in the ornate gateway, the man stood, looking up, as Faran had seen him do for several intermittent days.

He was a black man, rather fat, dressed in a quite fashionable but cheap raincoat. His head was bare, just as most men went bare-headed now.

Faran guessed he had five minutes left before tipsy Cimmie and Wellington erupted into the flat from their Savoy Grill lunch.

Faran lifted his arm and waved to the man.

And the man who, although he was not Mr Thorpe, so closely resembled him, lifted his own arm in the autumn gate, and waved in return.

Then Faran heard the lift.

He jumped off the chair and brushed its velvet seat. He put it back in alignment with the regimented other chairs. He strode to his bedroom, and the essay on European meat production Ms Baldwin had set him.

Chapter Eight

On Anna's second birthday, they went into London again, and again by train, because Anna said she had liked that. Anna looked sixteen still, sophisticated and self-contained, but she smiled. Her parents, the two beautiful young women probably taken for youthful aunts or family friends, sat with her in the carriage.

Ormolu autumn weather, woods full of crows. The houses gathered in procession as the capital swung towards them.

Anna had expressed a want for a black dress, and among Althene's presents, there the dress had been. Anna wore it now, and her black wool coat, and on her long legs black tights with golden suns. On her feet were ankle boots of silvery leather. She would need the boots for walking through the cemetery, the famous one which Anna had wished to see.

On Anna's left middle finger was the ring Rachaela had given her. A tourmaline in silver, the Libran jewel.

The morning had been marred only by a fight between Juliet and Jacob, who often attacked each other now . . . mimicking the general situation? Otherwise the day was planned: the cemetery, then dinner at one of the restaurants they had frequented before Anna's birth, a late film, something foreign with English and Dutch dialogue which

Rachaela had never heard of, and would not, entirely, understand. But Anna was apparently now bilingual. Even more versed than that, maybe, for now and then Rachaela had heard her singing, in a pure high soprano, snatches in French, and even Elizabeth's Gaelic lullabyes.

They left the train, walked through sunlight under the high hatched walls of the city.

They lunched in a wine bar – Anna's choice. Anna drank a glass of red Burgundy with her salad. Rachaela on her own got through a bottle of Mâcon.

I'm drinking too much, Scarabae or not.

They moved along the pavements in a loose-knit trio. People looked at them, and builders on a scaffolding nearly plummeted to the pavement in their efforts to evince enthusiasm. Occasionally, Althene and Anna stepped slightly ahead, but never for too long.

Rachaela wished she were alone with Althene. They could have gone to an opulent hotel, had afternoon tea, made love in some cream-laid room. They had not made love for several months. Rachaela had not wanted to. She had not wanted to since Anna. Or, was it only that she would not? She was on the pill. There was no excuse there—

And now, now her libido had been roused by the mushroom quiche or the wine, now there was Anna.

Better be careful though. Could it be Anna she wanted instead?

Anna, wholly female. Anna physically old enough to consent. And mentally young enough to see no harm.

Well I am confused.

Since Althene's return they had been *such* friends. We three.

Althene had said very little about her trip. Her mother, Sofie, had waxed contrasuggestive. There was not much one could do. The family were alerted and would take care of things. Malach was not referred to. To Althene, Rachaela had not said, *But Anna is Ruth.* Probably Althene knew everything there was to know.

And then again it could all be my own dear little insanity.

That Rachaela had taken Anna to an unknown doctor, Althene did not mention. Rachaela had not told her of this treat, and presumably neither had Anna. (*Keeping my shameful secrets safe?*) The call on the Scarabae was openly discussed. Althene had accepted it, without much comment, saying she was glad Anna had met Eric and Sasha, and going to gaze on the antique shawl, and asking after the cats. To Althene, Rachaela had said, when they were alone, 'I don't know if I took her there as a test or a penance.'

'It seems to have turned out to be neither.'

'Sasha fainted.'

'Sasha is old.'

'For now.'

Althene had said presently, 'But Anna liked her visit to them. She'll want to go back.'

'The grannies and granddads,' Rachaela said, remembering Ruth's words all those years and aeons ago. Rachaela had been jealous of Ruth too. Not wanting Adamus to have her, not wanting Ruth to have Adamus.

Rachaela had given Anna a CD of Benjamin Britten's piano concerto. Anna listened, as always, as if the spirit went out of her. 'Planets dancing,' she said at the end. It was what Rachaela had always thought:

They reached the imposing gateway of the cemetery about three. There were no guided tours that day, but after a moment of incomprehension, someone came apologizing, and let them go in alone, and unguarded, among the green and gold wilderness.

The child on the tomb . . .

Why was it so ominous?

Looking in through the closed and padlocked doors of the mausoleum, to the upright carving over the tomb-case. The young girl of marble, perhaps thirteen years old, turning her head almost modestly away from the wide-winged angel that had taken hold of her.

Did she not want to go wherever the flying thing meant to take her? Up, or down, into the hall of Death.

And the angel's face, by a fluke of the dim light coming in at the stone lattices of the doors, had been eclipsed like a moon in shadow. The angel was faceless, and terrible.

The cemetery was magical. Allowed to run to seed, rare, almost prehistoric plants had come up in it, and great oaks twined with ivy. Up from the massed grasses dog-roses sprang.

And from the wild garden pushed the stones of the dead, obelisks and pyramids, winged women, a lion who smiled on one side, frowned on the other, lying sleeping with folded paws and carven whiskers like those of the goddess Sekhmet. There were pillars too resembling the Egyptian sets of some mystical epic, and curving downsweeps of stone houses, on every porch a vanquished name, the lintels clad in briars and marked with the lambs' blood of berries.

Foxes ranged here by night, voles and hedgehogs. Now squirrels played along the paths, and dragonflies glinted over matted water green as frogs.

In places gardeners were at work on the upkeep of the cemetery. Only one had challenged them, politely. But Althene mentioned some name, and the man waved them on.

Rachaela turned from the mausoleum of the child, and there her own child was, up on a tomb of grey stone above the path.

The sun fragmented through the trees and lit her hair to a blizzard of gilded snow. Althene was beside her, saying something, pointing.

And then, out of the undergrowth, like a rough, rolled-up carpet somehow made to move, a badger came.

Its white head poked from its dark body like a snake, and it trundled to the spot where Anna stood, poised in amazement, and there it hesitated, blinded maybe by the sunshine, sensing proximity above it.

Now it will lay its head in her lap, Rachaela thought brutally. *The prototype timid woodland creature, as in myth and story, charmed by my uncanny daughter.*

But the badger only snuffed the air and bundled on, liquid and ungainly at once, back into the living wall of the garden.

'Oh,' said Anna.

Althene said, 'We were lucky to see him.'

One of the gardeners, a middle-aged man in a shabby overall, was coming up the avenue with his spade.

He nodded at Althene and Anna on the grave, climbing up to where they were.

'You don't often see those fellows out by day.'

Anna said, childish with ecstasy, 'It was a badger.'

'Yes it was,' agreed the man.

And he swung his shovel hilt foremost, with all the bulk of his weight behind it, into Althene's belly.

Like some strange preview of the weird film they had been due to attend, Rachaela saw Althene go unbelievably white and her body dip bonelessly forward and collapse, soundless, on to the couch of grass and stones. She was completely unconscious.

And then Anna stood alone, with the sun upon her like golden frost.

Another man had come from somewhere.

He glanced at Rachaela. 'Don't you move.'

The two men took Anna each by one of her arms. She was intensely shocked, like a being without mind or soul. They revolved her easily about, and then all three went down the slope behind the grave and the wild trees ate them up.

Rachaela started forward; her heart pounded like cannon or bombs detonating in her body. But she only reached Althene's fallen shape, only reached the grave. And here Rachaela stumbled, and it was as if time had ended, or never begun.

Chapter Nine

That summer had been uncomfortable.

Connor had been prepared for it to be, just like the preceding summer.

With Camillo.

The first spring they had kept mostly on an even keel, Camillo riding his new bike, an '89 limited Electraglide Classic, a black blaze straight from the oven of might, and Red up behind, helmed and matchless. Never a cross word.

As they drove north and west, Connor's legion picked up numbers, and finally they were twenty strong. Camillo's mercenary army. Sworn by unspoken oaths to stick to him, to bear him where he wanted to go.

As the land had greened, they had ridden the blossom route and over into castled Wales. Then, with the months, they veered to and from the coast, and in the heart of the season, rode east again and up into the dark hills of Derbyshire, riven with grey stone villages and old Roman footprints.

By then he was restive, Camillo. He would turn viciously on Red. Only words, always clever and cutting, that would have had another woman sick or angry or in tears. Tina sometimes cried, just to hear him. Christ, he had a tongue, Camillo, like the knife. Old sod. But then. He did not look so old any more. As the year aged he spasmodically youthened. Connor accepted it, but some of the others pulled away (that and Camillo's tongue), grasped other loyalties. The army diminished.

But Connor remembered that house where they had collected Camillo, and the woman, fifty-five if she was a day, but like a girl. And how these people at the house had a video on the TV months before that particular film was *on* video. Connor kept his cool.

Even the new bike had not bemused him. For Camillo had killed the earlier trike, scorched it out, and when they caught up with him, he removed the stuffed horse's head from the prow, and then cremated the trike at the roadside. Only, of course, it did not entirely burn or melt. They left it there like a nasty accident. And a few hours later, in some back room of a mechanic's, the new bike, the Electraglide Classic, had been served to Camillo from an unmarked van.

By the first summer, only Rose and Pig, and Pig's Tina, remained of the former battalion. Cardiff, having smashed his leg on the M1, had gone back to his grandmother's house in Birmingham. The bimbo, Lou, who had run off with them from the house, had absconded with another biker she met in a field where they had gone to listen to some music. Of the new battalion, the fourteen who stayed, Shiva was the best. Half Indian, he was the colour of a thunder cloud. He rode his machine like a demon on the wings of the storm, tied-back black hair three times longer than Connor's.

It was Shiva who had, perhaps, one night in a country pub, prompted Camillo's departure of the first summer.

Shiva had been talking to Rose about a Hindu god. Rose was very interested, asking questions. Shiva explained how families would shelter in the shrines and cook food there, making an offering, and then eating it to partake of the blessing. The heat of the offering flames was also inhaled for this reason.

Camillo, who had been sitting silent for fifty-nine minutes, said, 'And you breathe in the flame and blow it out again as hot air.'

Shiva shrugged. He was used, Connor thought, to the reactions of morons. And Camillo, their king, had just spoken like one.

Viv, Connor's black, white and yellow dog, pricked her one upstanding ear. The bikers, spread round four tables, did likewise. Only Viv did not look resigned. Camillo said to Red, 'Tell me something stunning about fire rituals.' He was always, insultingly, challenging her, her knowledge of history. In Derbyshire it had been, 'And which Roman commander was it that urinated here?'

Red, who was over with Tina and Josie, and Viv, said, 'Carthaginians burned children alive to the glory of Baal Melkart. Celtic women jumped through the bonfires to ensure the life in their wombs.'

'And Jehane d'Arc,' said Camillo, 'was roasted at the stake. And while you've a Lucifer to light your fag, smile boys that's the style.'

Shiva said, 'I like the Hindu gods.'

'All gods,' said Camillo, 'are crap. Shit. *Ca-ca.*'

Shiva said, 'For you, then.'

'Now you'll tell me,' said Camillo, 'they answer your prayers.'

'Yes,' said Shiva. 'Though I'm undeserving.'

'Except,' said Camillo, 'your prayer that I should fuck off.'

Shiva looked at Connor. Connor nodded. Shiva was behaving impeccably, it was the king who was at fault.

Connor said, 'There's a festival tomorrow, Camillo, Ludlow way. Do you want to go?'

'More of the music that roars?' said Camillo. 'I'm too old for all that.'

The stereo on the Electraglide poured out, all along the country tarmac and the shale, Iron Maiden, so the immature corn rocked on its stalks.

Red had not finished her chicken and chips. She was feeding Viv with most of it, and Viv beamed. Viv ignored Camillo. In the last month she had taken to being unresponsive to him. Camillo remained courteous to Viv. Perhaps he gauged, accurately, Connor's last straw.

Camillo reiterated, 'Poor doddery old man. Too old for all this.'

He looked, Connor thought now, in the smoky pub murk, about thirty. Some days he looked forty. Not much older, ever.

Basher had gone over to the juke, put in a couple of fifties, and out came The Eagles 'Hotel California', at full volume.

Camillo grinned. His eyes were old black murder.

He said, 'Does Red want to go to Ludlow?'

'I'd be willing.'

'Tell me about Ludlow.'

Red looked tired. There were little silver lines around her eyes. 'No. You're too old.'

'Oh,' said Camillo. '*Please*.'

'Sixteen thirties,' said Red, 'Milton's masque *Comus* was performed there.'

'Then you can go,' said Camillo, 'but I won't. I'm off somewhere.'

Red looked at her plate, and Viv licked Red's fingers unnecessarily hard, trying to comfort. In Connor's muscular body the heart thumped, and in his big belly the digesting meat-pie moved too. Camillo was disturbing him.

Red remarked, casually, 'You know, Camillo, I used to go to bed with a man of sixty. He was half crippled by arthritis, I couldn't even put my weight on him. But he was a beautiful lover, and he was a lovely man.'

'He died,' Camillo said, 'you told me.'

'But you won't die,' Red answered.

'Oh, I might. Poor decrepit old man.'

'You won't die and you are a selfish bloody cunt.' Red spoke levelly.

She stood up and went to the Ladies, and Tina and Josie marched after her.

Viv pattered over the table, licked Basher, Shiva and Rose, and sat down on Connor's knee.

Camillo said, 'We must part.'

Connor said nothing.

Camillo went to the bar and bought two rounds, so many drinks Basher and Rats had to go up and help bring them back.

When Red returned, she was yet dry-eyed and still. Connor looked at her with regret and hope, the sapphire irises and fresh rosy skin, the rust-copper hair.

But then Camillo said to her, 'You and I, fair lady.'

'Why?' said Red.

'Because you will fight.'

'Oh, I'll fight. Why should I?'

'Because I'd like it. Where shall we go?'

Red looked at Connor. Connor nodded.

That night, while they made their bivouac under the stars, Red rode away with Camillo on the Electraglide, a river of Iron Maiden vanishing into the dark. When it faded they heard, from the pub juke, Killing Joke: 'Love Like Blood'.

Early in the second summer, over a year later, one night drinking Carlsberg and blackcurrant with Josie, Basher, Connor and Viv, Red told them something about that time alone with Camillo.

They had biked through Scotland, and then down again, and crossed the Channel in the heaving infant winter. Neither Red nor Camillo had been ill, but all about them people vomited. The sound of the ship's engines, the thrust of the sea, the noises of tortured human throats erupting were the insignia of that crossing.

They wintered in Paris, in a luxury hotel, from whose

windows Notre Dame was visible like a sphynx upon the River Womb. They had champagne with every meal, champagne fit for decapitated kings, till Red hated it.

Through the late spring and the summer and the autumn, they ran across France. Black mountains and ruddy fields ruby with French filtered sun. Farm-houses from the 1800s, places where guillotines had rested in 1793, still marked by stone. Provincial squares, dove-cotes, villages rimmed by poplars, and blue-shuttered houses where jasmin grew, and sheep passed through the streets, and *l'après midi* vineyards made tunnels of jade.

Camillo would not speak French, although, in bathrooms, Red could hear him mutter it. In the villages he spoke what seemed to be Polish, waving his arms helplessly, to annoy.

They returned to England before the seas began to upend, and lived in a rented house in Highgate with twenty-five rooms. Camillo had sex with the two Spanish maids, as he had had sex with more than thirty French women in France.

'He never touched me,' Red informed them, 'after that night here, when I told him about Anthony – my tutor. Camillo would say, "I can't follow that, can I? Perhaps if I get crippled with something." He seemed to be inviting me to arrange it.' She did not say very much else that was intimate, only once, 'He sometimes talked about his mother in his sleep. In France. He used to do that in French, too. But simple childish French. *Maman, je t'aime*. He said his father killed her through lack of love.'

And Connor recalled how the woman at the old-young house (the night-eyed Morrigan, sex and death) had said white-haired Malach was Camillo's *father*. Malach, who looked like Camillo on his young days, thirty-seven, maybe.

Camillo had been gone, Red avowed, days and nights in London.

At the beginning of summer, he got word to Connor,

and Red and Camillo came back into Connor's world of black metal wheeled horses.

So, the second summer burgeoned, and was like something too tight, constricting them, the ten riders and their women, who had stayed together: Connor, Rose, Pig and Tina, Basher and Josie, Rats, Shiva, Whisper, Owl, Blick and Cathy, Jas and Ray. Triumph Bonnevilles, Norton Jubilees. There were more dogs as well, Meato the Mongrel Fiend, and Jezebel. And even the dogs felt it. Less fine than Viv, they would growl at Camillo, and only Rats' or Blick's hands on their collars could dissuade them. Even the bikes acted up.

Connor had given his allegiance, there was no turning back. If Camillo wanted his battalion, there it must be, ready.

But Camillo was, or was like, a vicious old man. He looked thirty-seven consistently now. White dreadlocks very long and woven with beads. Rings on firm brown hands. A face to turn a woman on, that was for sure. Black eyes like dead yet fiery seas.

He had kept the horse head. It was on the prow of the Electraglide and had been all over Provence and Brittany.

He moved, limber and strong, and one night Camillo seduced innocent silly little Tina, so Pig hit her and left her, and they had to take her to her mother's, where she stood on the doorstep crying as they rode away.

Damn Camillo. Old man. Evil rotten old bastard.

I could cut his bloody throat. But I'll have to stay true. So Connor said to his angry brain.

And *why* stay true? Because once Camillo had seemed breakable and ancient, coming down on to a beach by firelight. Crazy and lost, a valiant eccentric old fellow, like a character from a legend.

Connor was waiting for Camillo to do some truly awful thing, so that true loyalty might be pissed from the window.

But Camillo was insidious in the way of the crafty elderly mad. He laughed his high imbecile giggle, and turning in the brightness on some village street, the young girls gazed at him and blushed.

He did look like that white one, that Malach.

'Do you miss your son, at all,' Connor said one evening as they rode slow down a bumpy track into some town.

'I have no sons.'

'Oh, your dad then.'

Camillo did not glance. Camillo said, '*Mon père est mort.*'

Later on, Connor said to her, to Red, 'Did he say his daddy had died?'

'He said it. But who knows.'

She looked thinner, burned away, like the trike they had let Camillo cremate.

There were thin veils of grey in her hair, Connor had seen that day in the artist's sunlight. Connor looked at Red with desire, and leaning forward, gently kissed her lips. She did not resist. 'Thank you, Connor,' she said, 'you make me feel human again. But . . . you're too young for me.'

'Bugger it,' said Connor. 'Couldn't you wait?'

'I'll be old then, too,' she said. 'Not like *him*.'

Then they went into a pub.

There were fat stuffed fish in cases, beams, and no juke. But in a corner, the inglenook, probably, by the unlit summer hearth, an old man sat with an open book before him and a bottle of Bristol Cream. He would pour a glass and drink it slowly, steadily. Then fill the glass again.

He had white hair from old age, and his face was a panoply of wrinkles, fluted over fine hard bones.

'Look,' said Connor. 'He's old enough.'

Red looked.

She moved quietly across the pub, and stood over the old man, who raised his head and saw her. He smiled, for Red was a pleasing sight; then he glanced uneasily at the bikers. Connor went over, too, bowed and said, 'She was wondering what your book was.'

'Kipling short stories,' said the old man. He had a musical, resonant voice. He was strong.

'Can I buy you a drink,' said Connor.

'No,' said Red, 'let me.'

Connor retreated. He watched, surreptitiously, the real old man looking amused, musing, kind.

He left them to it, and so did Camillo. Camillo made no comment. It was Basher who did that. ' 'Ere, you're losing your bint, mate.'

And Cathy and Ray tittered. And Meato mounted Jezebel, to the consternation of some lady drinkers near-by.

Camillo said, 'Her father was fifty-seven when he conceived her. He died when he was seventy-two. She was fourteen. She's always looking for the wise old prat. I am not he.'

Connor realized Camillo did not speak as he had when Connor first knew him. There were glimpses of that sometimes. That was all. Camillo was now someone else. Connor said, 'Owl, I'll have some scrumpy.'

Meato left Jezebel in order to surprise Owl at the bar.

Chapter Ten

❧ SOMETIME BEFORE THE PUB CLOSED, Red's new old man went home. Red sat on the grass of the slope, where they had camped. 'I might stay. I'd have to go slowly. His wife died and he's still in love with her. Then again, she was twenty years younger than he is. Like my mother, leukaemia. A wicked shame.'

Connor thought it was like Red to be regretful of the old man's wife, even if her death offered a chance.

Or had the old man not gained Red's full attention?

However, presently she said, 'His name's Mark.'

She looked shy.

There might be a way out for her.

In the morning, about ten, a cheery woman came up to the camp from the pub and told them they could have breakfast in the pub garden. It was an ample fry-up, not greasy but appetizing, local sausages and bacon, market mushrooms, tomatoes from the house garden, eggs (free range), and fried home-made bread.

After the feast came the reckoning. Very mildly and pleadingly, the pub owner asked Connor if they would move their camp. It might otherwise scare off the regular customers.

For Red's sake, they did not go too far.

Above a cloud of pine woods, some forestry planting,

they emerged on a round and tufted hill. A few miles off were the frills of the town they had come through earlier. Below, in a valley smudged by the mist of a hazy day, an old gabled house, a mansion, lay above a drained pond with broken statues.

Connor and Viv, Rose, Blick and Shiva, went down with Cathy and Ray, to look. The others did not want to come, and Red was busy washing her hair with ten bottles of Evian and some Boots shampoo. (An optimistic sign.) Camillo lay asleep, like most of the others, and the dogs, in the sun. Camillo had told them they would get skin cancer. It had made him gleeful.

The mansion was only a shell in any case, partly roofless, with a huge inner area, its walls mysteriously white-washed. The wooden floor still held. A carved wooden stairway, strangely not yet pilfered, led up to nowhere.

Viv barked theatrically at daylight ghosts.

They returned to the camp. Red was drying her hair and reading a novel by Muriel Spark. Viv ran over to help.

'If you want to go back to that pub tonight, Rose and I can go with you. That won't frighten anybody.'

'I can go alone,' said Red.

'Well, Rose or Whisper will ride you over. I'll come and see if you want bringing back. It's open country.'

'I can take care of myself.'

'Yeah,' said Connor.

'Except in the matter of Camillo.'

When the afternoon was deepening, three or four vans and a couple of cars drove into the valley below, and pulled up on the gravel before the house.

The bikers' camp, concealed on their woody hill, watched with lazy interest.

The sun set in a daze of gold.

From the mansion's openwork roof supernatural rays began to wheel and spin, like trapped lightning.

' 'Ere,' said Basher, 'they're going to have a do.'

A thudding beat started up, and fell back instantly. Meato the Mongrel Fiend howled in horror.

'It's a festival,' said Cathy, pleased.

'No, a rave,' said Connor. 'We'd better clear out.'

Connor stood staring down at the valley. He felt uneasy. Music was one thing, but a rave was not about music. He remembered the night he and some girl had biked out to the standing stones at Calversham, and found a black box hidden in the bushes, swords and robes and chalices and a phial of amyl nitrate. They had taken off, he and the girl, pretty fast. Not that raves had anything to do with witchcraft. They just made him feel the same.

'Let's get the bikes,' Connor said.

Yet there was a lurid fascination in the view that held them there, the threatening gouts of bass and drum, over which no melody was audible, the flares of imprisoned lightning, now pink, now sick orange, now viper green.

As the dusk came out of the ground and the sky turned to a beautiful backdrop of blue and stars, like the fake sky of a planetarium, hordes of vehicles began to surge into the darkened valley.

Their white lights cut across, flamed, and died.

Connor thought, incongruously, of the ghost scene in Olivier's *Richard III.*

Viv quivered, and Connor picked her up.

'We'll be off. Whisper, you can circle round with Red later, to the pub.'

Then Camillo spoke.

'I want to go down there.'

Connor turned.

Camillo was standing in his I-am-a-poor-little-old-man pose, infantile and grotesque on a handsome man in his late thirties.

'Not good, Camillo.'

'Nah,' said Basher, 'bloody dick-heads.'

'A rave,' said Camillo. 'I want to see.'

Then he straightened. Became a man of thirty-seven.

Below, the swarm of Colt GTIs and Fiat Unos kept on gathering.

The beat was continuous now. The hill shook.

Viv whined.

'It'll be thirty quid at least, on the door,' said Blick. 'No booze. They don't drink or smoke, those fucking kids. It ain't healthy for them.'

Camillo said, 'I'm all a-tremble with excitement. Red, are you going with me?'

She was there in the shadow behind him. Her hair smelled of peaches. Ray put her hand on Red's arm. Red said to Camillo, 'It's a very bad set-up, Camillo.'

'Goody. Pack up my troubles. Do you think I'm too old?'

And Camillo started to walk down the hill, towards the beating house of lightnings.

'You can't let him get into that,' Red exclaimed. She sounded angry and alarmed, as if her baby meant to run out on the road.

Connor said, 'No. We can't stop him either. Shiva, what money have you got?'

'Enough, Connor.'

'Rose?'

'I can manage.'

'All right,' said Connor. 'We go in with him.'

There was a noise from the others, and Meato barked, appalled he could not surmount the deadly barking from below.

'Basher, take charge. Keep an eye out. If there's shit, I may need the lot of you.'

'Connor, you're fucking mad.'

Connor did not argue. He put Viv into Cathy's arms, and Viv snarled at him. 'No, baby,' said Connor, 'be nice to Cathy. You're my one and only.' Viv put down her upstanding ear to join the other ear that never went up. Cathy kissed Viv. Cathy looked nervous, the way she did when Blick got seriously pissed.

* * *

Into the valley of the rave . . .

Camillo was ahead of them.

His guard, Rose, Shiva and Red, with their captain, Connor, moved about ten paces behind.

The hill was dodgy, in the dark, outcrops, tussocks.

Ahead the *light*.

It hit the sky. Sheered, fragmented, spiked and burst.

Thud*rr*. Thud*rr*.

'It's like a migraine attack,' said Red. 'The kind that knocks out your vision. How do they stand it?' She took sunglasses from her pocket and put them on.

Connor thought, *She could have been sipping sherry with her Mark*. He thought maybe her Mark was there, in the pub, waiting for her. Feeling jilted and old. And Connor was sad, and enraged.

Fucking Camillo—

The pines crowded to the gravel and then there was the wodge of cars all around the basin with the statues.

A group of kids sprang out of a Mini and raced towards the doors of the mansion, now white, now blue, the gate of electric hell.

Camillo strode after them.

Then Connor and his lieutenants.

Connor said to Red, 'Do you want to stay outside?'

'I can't hear . . . No.' And Red went by him, up to Camillo.

'Ah, there she is. My chestnut mare.'

Camillo put his palm on her breast.

Red said, 'Do you want to go in? *Do* you?'

'Yum,' said Camillo. 'Let's see what the real young do.'

Inside, where the remains of an entrance was, loomed two big men, bouncers. They wore white shorts and Day-Glo tops. The lights wheeled, and changed them.

'All of you?' said one. 'You ain't dressed right. Yer gonner get all hot.'

'How much?' said Connor.

'How'd ya hear?'

'Flyer,' said Connor. 'Radio.'

'No bother,' said the other man, 'y'understand?'

Shiva stalked forward. He plonked down a wad of notes on the rickety wooden table.

The first bouncer counted them.

'Okay. Cheek or hand?'

'Hand.' Connor stuck his forward, and the second man sprayed him through a stencil with a black flower.

Camillo said, 'I want two.' He held out both hands. The bouncer only laughed. He did what Camillo asked.

Shiva had put one hundred and fifty pounds on the table.

They passed on, through the thick waves of bleeding sound, and the shot blood-sprays of the migrainous light.

There came a sharp menthol smell.

Cliv was sitting up on the bonnet of the Land Rover, just under the carved staircase that went nowhere.

He was comfortable, in charge. He had thought at first they could not get the Land Rover through, but they had done some work on a doorway, and managed it. Cliv liked heights.

Beside him was the silver ice-bucket packed with melting ice, and in it the bottle of white, full-cream milk. He would take a swig every so often, toast the dancers.

He had their sweets for them, too, in the vehicle. The white seeds of E, cheap tonight, only twelve pounds a tab.

Cliv had brown hair tied back in a short ponytail. He was growing his hair, but it took a long time. It might be worth getting extensions. He wore shorts, and his chest was bare. Something rather clever there. A zit had come up, dead centre between his large nipples. But Zephie had plastered the zit with skin-tinted Clearasil, and sprayed glitter over. It looked like a medallion.

About every forty-five minutes, Cliv would phone Zephie, on the car phone.

He would tell her what they would do, after the rave.

The dancers would be off to chill out. But Cliv and Zephie did not go for E.

Cliv found it arousing to tell Zephie what they would do. More arousing, possibly, than actually doing it—

He had had a pipe of crack before they opened the doors. And he would have another in an hour or so.

Crack gave you perspective. You could see where you could get to. No limits.

He gazed down into the hall of the mansion. It was a great sight.

The guy on the music knew how to keep it going, and the strobe lights whirled through every colour and shape, striking the whitewashed walls and veering off into the sky above. (Give God a thrill.) On the walls too were fractals, fantastic visions black and red, computer forms, twisted, tangled, splintered. Like a spiral staircase undone by an explosion. Like the Crown of Thorns.

Over behind the Land Rover was the bar. Bottles of cold Lucozade, juice, and French mineral water – that had been a laugh, the boys filling them up all afternoon, from the taps. They had watered the juice too.

But the kids needed a drink.

They danced like crazy.

They loved it. They loved each other. It was good for them.

Someone was pushing over through the dancers.

Cliv focused in the roil of lights.

'Hey, Hyreesh. Look.'

Cliv's bodyguard leant forward from the side of the vehicle. He was Indian, dark coffee in a suit, with naked feet. Zephie had said Hyreesh had brilliant feet, but Cliv could not see it. Hyreesh's fists were better.

Hyreesh said, 'Bikers.'

'Yes. What are they after?'

'Must've paid.'

Cliv stretched, and the Clearasil cracked on his pustule. He could be expansive, providing they were prepared to be friendly.

'Hi. As you know we've got some lovely stuff here. Only fifteen to you.'

'This is Ecstasy, is it?' said the oldest one.

He was about forty, but he had a weird face. White hair like a rock singer. The others were in leather too, and a tasty bird among them.

'It's *E*, mate,' said Cliv. 'Best in the home counties.'

'Give me some,' said the old boy.

Behind him one of the other bikers, with a big fat gut and longer hair than Cliv, clapped his hand on the man's shoulder.

'No, Camillo.'

The old boy shook him off. He looked happy already. He eased three fives out of his jacket with a stencilled hand ringed by silver, skulls and roses and swords. Cliv nodded, and Hyreesh took the money.

One of the bikers was a Pakistani too, Cliv deduced. His hair was down his stinking arse.

Cliv leaned round, and undid the Land Rover door, and Hyreesh brought out a white tab for the nutty old boy.

The rest looked at Cliv as though, instead of Santa Claus, he was the Devil. Both powerful guys.

Cliv said, 'Don't often see you people.'

They had all been shouting, pitching their voices over the music. And suddenly Cliv found this tiring.

Let them get on with it.

He watched them go off, back into the dancing crowd, and said to Hyreesh, 'Get Rhino. Tell him to tell them, watch out for that lot.'

Hyreesh signalled across the spoilt pseudo-orgasm of light.

Camillo did not swallow the tablet of Ecstasy.

He held it, contemplatively, and he said, 'White as cod.'

All around them, the dancers danced.

'Red,' Camillo cried, soft as a murmur, over the noise, 'what festival is this?'

'No,' she said.

'Yes. Tell me.'

Connor thought, *He's done this to her since the hour they met. Asking for history. But only a couple of lines.*

Red said to Camillo, 'Maybe the Dionysia, without the sex. Or the wine. Wanting to get close to the god. Or the frenzies of Cybele.'

'Ah,' said Camillo, 'castration.'

The air was furred with the scent of vapour rub and nasal inhalers. Nearby, a boy of seventeen, in long blue shorts and T-shirt, danced, waving and punching one arm, an inhaler stuck into each nostril by his free hand.

'Why?' said Camillo.

'It clears their heads,' said Rose.

'Pollution,' said Shiva.

Camillo turned, slipped into the slipstream. It was hopeless, in the fractal of the strobes, the mania of the beat that had no tune, immediately to follow. Camillo swam away.

He went to a girl of fifteen, with cropped shining hair. She wore a short white lycra skirt and a white lycra top that left bare her flat smooth midriff, save where tinsel tassels bounced.

She danced, and saw Camillo, and, dancing, clasped him in her arms. Her face was washed by light, virginal, potent and pure as the face of a saint.

'I love you,' she said. 'I love everyone. We're one.'

She held him, as she had held a hundred. There had been men at the rave who had felt her breasts, even handled her vulva, as she danced with them this way. But she had not minded. Love was love.

'What's your name?' said Camillo.

'My name's Love.'

'And who am I?'

'Love.'

'No,' said Camillo, moving with her like a black snake of leather.

'Yes. This is the truth. This is the reality.'

'Do you think you'll live?' Camillo asked.

'For ever,' said the girl.

'Who'd want to?'

The girl laughed. She was sweet, delicate, under her razored mop of hair, her waist fine as a strand.

'Don't be afraid,' she said. She kissed Camillo's mouth.

He drew away, like a snake.

'Little girl,' he said, *'petite mignonne*. Have you taken it? Are you in Ecstasy?'

She laughed again. 'Oh, yes.'

'You hunger for your entity, your group soul,' said Camillo. 'But you won't find it here.'

'Life, death, love,' said the girl.

'It eats your brains,' said Camillo. 'You're happy now. But later you'll be depressed. You'll be suicidal. And if you see God through a tablet, how can you find the cunt again? Do you think God loves you? Do you think you're love? You're lost, *ma belle*.'

She shook back her shining aura and looked at him through the torture of the strobe, which, to her, was enlightenment.

'Listen,' said Camillo. He drew her close, and whispered into her ear.

All about the dancers danced.

Their faces were lit, outside, inside. They raised their arms to the white heart of the strobe, like antique worshippers to the core of a sun.

Dionysos, Cybele . . .

The madness whereby to find the soul and free it from the shackles of the flesh.

Some embraced. As in the grave they could not. Some only laughed with happiness.

They were one.

Camillo, lips to the ear that had been corporeal such a little while, told her, carefully, strategically, what E would do to her. Alive. And dead.

She did not believe.

She slid away, and he brought her back.

Then, she believed him.

Red clipped Connor's arm. 'What's he doing? Oh, I can't stand this noise. The light – Connor—'

Connor said, 'Rose, take her out.'

'No,' Red sobbed. 'Damn him, what's he *said*?'

The girl in white had slithered to her knees. She was writhing on the ground. (The tassels bounced.) Dancers shied from her. Some bent near.

Camillo hovered in among them.

In that stroboscopic jigsaw of pastels, his black leather was hard and shining like a carapace. He drew them up. He spoke to them.

There was a sound. Under the beat of the beat-without-a-tune.

Like the earth moving, in pain.

Over the phone, Zephie sounded stupid. But she was not. She had a great body and gel-slicked hair, like a boy's. Red Revlon lips. Long pale eyes.

'And then I'll put the cream on you and I'll eat it, Zephie. But I'll mix a little something with the cream. And we'll kiss—'

'It ain't half noisy there,' said Zephie.

'It's always noisy,' said Cliv, righteously.

'No, I mean, it sounds like, well – what track is that?'

Cliv listened.

'Don't know, babes.'

'Well,' said Zephie.

Cliv had been off into the ruin of the mansion, with Hyreesh, while Rhino and Bobby took over the Land Rover. Hyreesh had lit a candle and Cliv had smoked a glass pipe, like something from a science lab, and risen up and up, until even Hyreesh looked good. Then, to be sensible, Cliv had a small chaser of smack, to level off.

When Cliv came back, he opened a new bottle of iced milk. After that he phoned Zephie again.

Zephie said, 'It sounds like howling.'

There had been a dog barking somewhere, when they drove in. Probably that. Was it?

Cliv *listened*.

Not in the way the girl in white had done, but, nevertheless, attentively.

And he heard.

'Jesus fucked. Zephie – I'll call you later.'

Outside the Land Rover, the fug of vapour rub and sweat and deodorant and hot damp lycra. Usual.

But another smell. Sour. Untraceable.

Had one of them freaked out? Like that guy at Cleathorpes. Hyreesh had carried him into the fields. They left him there for some lucky farmer to find. E sometimes . . . they could not take it.

He had been howling.

And now – now some of them were.

Spectacular strobe effects still blatted over, and the music still pounded through the floor. But the DJ was signalling, and huge Bobby was going across to him.

'What's up?'

Hyreesh grinned. He said, '*Doc*.'

Cliv looked blank. 'Come on, you brown git. What gives?'

Hyreesh composed his Asian face.

'They can't handle it.'

'There's something wrong with the stuff?'

'No.'

'Then what—'

Hyreesh said, 'Man, we're losing the plot.' He touched the little automatic at his crotch.

Cliv saw people lying on the floor.

He had seen that somewhere else. He tried to forget. When that IRA device went off. He had only been seventeen.

But it looked – like that.

Only there was no blood or puke. No glass. Only fractured light.

Cliv was responsible for the rave, its success or failure.

'Get the boys,' said Cliv. 'We're going to have to stop it.' He pointed at the music. 'Tell that bloke to pull the plug.'

One tear alters an ocean.

It was like that. For an ocean they had become, no man being an island, not here.

That was why they did it, as they tried to say, impatient that you did not cotton on, because you were too far gone in life to dare, or to credit.

They were young, and they knew. The young always know. They know more than they know. And life hammers it from them on the anvil of living.

The drug made them one. A group consciousness. And the joy was shared. The boundless energy and the mind-rocking beat that wove them together like the tiny creatures of the beating sea. Like the thunder of a heart common to all.

They danced. Hour after hour. Not needing to stop. Needing no other stimulant, alcohol to lift them, nicotine to calm.

They were one.

But then the poisoned tear was dropped into the golden water.

Since they were merged, what one felt was communicated to every other. The group soul, the entity. One had been wounded, and all of them were wounded.

Agony spread like napalm, burning not the skin but the psyche.

They lay howling, pausing only to draw breath to howl again.

'*Christ*,' said Cliv. 'What am I going to do?'

'We'll have to go down,' Basher said.

And Meato whined. Jezebel had gone under Owl's Jubilee.

The night was otherwise absurdly dumb.

The noise, the beating, had stopped. Abruptly. And the strobe lights flailed and coiled over like a broken wing, snapped off into the dark.

They felt deafened, blinded.

Owl said, 'I got my knife.'

Jas said, 'Let's take it slow.'

They mounted up, the women and animals left on the hill. Cathy was upset and Ray furious.

Viv would not be held. She sat in the grass, upright, ready.

And when the bikers started down the hill, she ran after. But not making a sound.

When they breached the gravel, between the pines and the cars, they slewed to a halt.

They could hear another noise now.

It was a crying, low and deep.

Such a sound, maybe, had risen from Egypt when the first born were taken. From Rotterdam, when the German bombs stopped falling.

'Christ, Christ, what is it?'

'Bad trip, man,' shouted Whisper.

They told him to shut up.

And as they went towards the mansion, from the blackened door, Camillo came, spry and fly, and after him the others.

In the very doorway a big bald man in shorts tried to tackle Connor. But Connor smashed him in the groin, and the big bald man dropped down. Another one appeared. He was dark, like Shiva. He *saw* Shiva, hesitated. The

94

unknown man had a gun, Connor was sure, a little, dangerous gun. But he turned away, went into the house again, as if they were invisible.

Everyone could see Red was weeping. Crystal ribbons ran out under her dark glasses.

Rose scratched the tattoo of a rose on his head.

Their hands were marked black as if with stigmata.

''Ere, Conn,' said Basher, 'do we go in?' Basher too had seen the man with the gun.

Connor said, 'We ride.'

Camillo said, 'And goodbye.'

Connor glanced at Camillo. 'Yes?'

'Yes. I manumit you. I'm off. And from the red-haired woman. She can remain. I've had enough of you. You're too like a *family*, Connor, you and your tribe.'

Red retreated from them. She leaned forward and retched into the gravel. Her vomit was starry in the absolute dark.

Connor thought, *Her urine is magma, her shit is gold. And she's off with an old man called Mark.*

But not with Camillo.

Camillo walked uphill now, away from them, towards his fabulous bike.

Viv came running. Connor caught her up. Oh God he loved her, she was the only one. She bit his ear in her love, because he lived. He could have bitten her back.

And behind them, from the house, the awful noises went on.

'Let's go.'

They climbed the hill, the bikes veering, the way they had descended. Rose was partly holding Red. She had thrown up the past. She had finally got sick of Camillo.

The sombre sky seemed scarred by the strobes.

They drove away from that place, and soon the softness of the summer night was there, scent of fields, horses, manure; stars like gems. Viv sat in the saddle-bag, with her goggles on, and Meato and Jezebel rode behind Owl and Rats. They were a fellowship.

Red travelled with Rose, her head down on his shoulder.

Tomorrow he would bring her back to the pub, and wait and see. Red would be safe with Rose.

But beyond the fields, where the world tipped towards the distant burning glare of the town, Camillo cut away. The Electraglide fuming and swerving, he took the vast concrete highway, off from the ageless starlit land and into the flat ochre heartlessness of the sodium lamps. And music boomed from the machine, and died. No more music. Camillo was gone.

Chapter Eleven

As RACHAELA KNEELED THERE, a cloud covered the sun.

Althene opened her eyes.

In shadow she said, 'I'm alive. You must go and find someone.'

Rachaela stood up. Althene turned her head and fluid came from her mouth, streaked scarlet.

'A telephone.' Althene coughed. 'Call the house.'

'Reg—' Rachaela said.

'No, Eric. Tell Eric. He will know – what to do.' Rachaela turned and Althene said, 'Don't speak to anyone of Anna.'

Rachaela thought, *Normally I would run distraught to the police. The mother of the kidnapped child. Or would I?*

She had always feared the police, not because she was a criminal, but because she trusted no one, certainly no one in uniform.

Althene said, '*Duizelig* —'

Rachaela ran along the path, between the green towers of grass and ivy and the grey graves.

Round a glory of tomb, in the dark under the cloud, a thin young man was pulling at a weed. A proper gardener? Rachaela ran to him.

'My sister—' she said, 'my sister's ill. I must use a phone—'

She must seem deranged, for he did not argue, took her to a tiny hut concealéd among the trees, gave her a portable phone. Probably he knew who she was, one of the three special visitors who had been allowed in.

Rachaela imagined Althene dead among the grasses.

The phone rang on. Then Michael answered. Surely Michael would do.

'Michael – Althene's – hurt. It's serious.'

Michael did not dither. He asked where they were. Then Eric came. Eric said only, 'There will be an ambulance in ten minutes.'

This seemed unlikely. Then Rachaela remembered that they were the Scarabae. She seemed always to have to re-remember this. *They – I—*

She wandered out of the hut and could not recall where Althene was.

Rachaela stood on the path, with her arms crossed over her body, and stared up into the tops of trees alight with birds and frittered sun. The clouds had gathered.

She should have run after them, the men with Anna. And then what? They would have struck her, too.

The thin young gardener appeared and said quietly, 'I've put a blanket over her. She keeps being sick. Did you phone? That's all right then.' He too seemed in the know, and led her back.

Althene was conscious and in terrible pain, held rigid against the physical onslaught as sometimes Rachaela had seen her in the throes of sex.

The young gardener went away.

Rachaela sat by Althene. 'What is it?'

'Something – has given way. Don't panic, Rachaela. I shall mend. Did you call Eric?'

'He said – an ambulance – how will you . . .? I mean, your clothes—'

'Oh,' Althene, even in pain, looked ironical, blasé. 'Don't worry, little girl. This is not your NHS.' And then she said, dimly, '*Mijn dochter—*' My daughter.

Do I even care about Anna now?
Oh God, make them hurry.
They had hurried.

A few minutes later two men came with a stretcher, incongruous, up through the ranks of the dead who no longer needed such things.

When they moved Althene, she cried out. A man's voice. Unmistakable.

But it was not going to be a problem, that.

The private hospital was soothing, attractive. Dove grey and cream-pink walls. Flowers everywhere.

In Althene's room, which had a private bath, the flowers banked to the pigeon-breast ceiling, white carnations, white roses, mauve lilies, lemon-curd chrysanthemums.

'It's not fortuitous,' Althene said, 'to send red and white flowers. Blood, and bandaging.'

And chrysanthemums mean death, Rachaela thought. *But then, not to the Scarabae.*

There had been a muttering, *peritonitis*. Then they had left it. They had told Rachaela her sister – although now, they must know Rachaela's sister was not a woman – was strong and had come through the surgery wonderfully. Now she had only to get well.

Quaint nurses in elegant uniforms, nurses not sick from lack of sleep, fluttered round Althene, flirting. Did they all know?

Althene, by the fourth day, wore dark purple silk, soft make-up, her hair brushed, perfume. Her face was not sunken any more, only pale.

Rachaela was not afraid for her, but of her.

They did not talk of Anna, not until that fourth day.

It was Althene who began.

'You've brought me grapes. How apposite.'

'I'm sorry. I didn't know. But I thought you'd like the colour.'

'Of course I do. We'll eat grapes and drink wine.

In one week's time. And then. Then I must think of Anna.'

Rachaela said, 'You instructed me not to tell them.'

'Yes. Not yet.'

'But—'

'Obviously,' Althene said, 'you are devastated. So concerned.'

Rachaela threw back her head. She stared at Althene as she had stared at the trees above the cemetery.

'What do you want? I'm *terrified*.'

'Because she was stolen.'

'Why?' Rachaela said.

Althene turned her head on the petal pink pillow. 'Someone wished to have her. I should have thought of this. Stupidly I did not. It's my error, Rachaela.'

'Who *wished* it? Who's taken her? Why? What will you do?'

'So many questions. I don't know.' Althene hesitated. She said, 'Malach . . . will be told.'

'She's *yours*,' Rachaela said.

'And yours.'

'Yours and mine, then. Not his. He pushed her away.'

'And someone else has netted her in.'

Rachaela said, 'I can't stand this. I can't, Althene. I'm lost.'

Althene said: '*Mijn dochter is zoek.*'

'Your *daughter's* lost. Yes.'

'No, more than that I've lost her,' Althene said. She closed her eyes as she had in the grass of pain. 'I mean she has lost herself.'

'How? She had no choice.'

'Perhaps.'

'Althene—'

'Listen, my beautiful one, go away. You come here and sit, and you're no use to me, Rachaela. Go home. You'll be more comfortable. I'm well. I'll soon be with you.'

'I've tried—'

'It's not enough to try.' Althene looked through her. 'I must sleep now.'

'I'll come back—'

'No. Do as I say. Go home. To the house on the hill.'

'And what shall I tell them? Elizabeth, Reg—'

'What does it matter?'

Rachaela said, 'They'll want to know.'

'Say I have had appendicitis. Anna has gone to stay with her friend . . . in France.'

Rachaela dug her long, unpainted nails into her palms. 'Her little two-year-old friend who looks seventeen. You're sending *me* away like a naughty child.'

'You are a naughty child.'

Rachaela thought, *What do I feel now? Nothing. Nothing.*

She went home, by car.

The driver was chatty but not intrusive. She created for him a pack of lies. Her husband, whose city job she did not understand, and – oddly – her two daughters at grammer school.

He announced she looked too young for that.

She said he had made her day.

When they reached the town, she got him to drop her off near the supermarket. Dinner for her strapping family.

She gazed in at the women who shopped.

As she walked up the hill, the heavy overnight bag in her hand, she talked to herself, and soon she was out of breath. When she came to the wall of the house, she leaned there, and looked back the way she had come.

So far. And so far still to go.

The house was polished and airy, Elizabeth had kept up her attentions. A smoked-salmon salad and a gâteau were in the fridge, and two bottles of Californian white wine. Someone had wired ahead.

Rachaela went up into her bedroom, her bedroom with Althene, after the fourth glass.

She stripped, and looked at her unmarked girl's body in the mirror.

At six, she phoned the hospital, but Althene, doing excellently, was asleep.

Tell her I love her, Rachaela thought but did not say. *Tell her I am alone.*

She watched a TV film about a woman who wanted children and could not have them.

Rachaela laughed. She laughed until she cried.

It was someone from the hospital who phoned Rachaela on Friday morning, at ten a.m. Althene had discharged herself and was coming home.

Rachaela felt peculiar, like a young Victorian virgin whose fiancé was sent back from the front. *Fluttery*, that was it.

She had been still in bed. Now she showered and dressed, powdered her face, made up her eyes and lips. There was not much time. Althene would be travelling, too, by car.

At eleven, Rachaela ate half a piece of bread, and tried to drink some coffee, and could not. Instead she took the uncorked last glass of wine, the single refugee from the previous night's two bottles, and drank that.

It did not really steady her. Her heart beat lightly and very fast.

The car arrived at noon. It was a Rolls. Ah, yes, it always was, was it not. The Scarabae car of rescue and escape.

Rachaela did not spy from the window.

She went across the living room and stood on the Chinese carpet.

Should she run to the door as it opened? And careful of the bandaging, fling her arms about her paramour?

She heard the door open.

In the hall, Althene's footsteps were not quite right. Obviously, recuperating, she was not wearing high heels.

A bag went down on the floor.

Then the not-right steps crossed the hall, and someone

walked into the soft-lit living room to which the sun did not come until later.

A pang, so violent as to be painful, twanged like a string inside Rachaela's chest cavity, descending, twisting her stomach and bowel.

If she had still been holding the glass (refilled from a new bottle), she would melodramatically have dropped it. Luckily for the rug, she was not.

Who was it? Who was *he*? This man.

Adamus . . .

Ruth's father.

The first love. The first demon.

He said, 'I didn't mean to upset you. I'm sorry.'

Rachaela heard herself say, 'It's all right. It's just – I've never seen you like this, have I?'

And she did not follow what she said.

For the man was young, handsome, very pale. He wore black trousers and a black shirt. His black hair was not very short, only pulled back and tied, so the length of it hung down his back.

Yes. Adamus.

A family resemblance, then. They all looked like each other. Even Rachaela. Even Althene. Althene dressed as what, physically, she had always been. A man.

'I should have forewarned you,' Althene said. 'Sit down.'

'Don't be silly. I'm not going to swoon. You just surprised me. It's very effective.'

Althene shrugged. 'There have been those who would have preferred it.'

'Well, it's up to you, isn't it,' Rachaela said. She sounded arch, idiotic.

Althene's hair, of course, even tied in so severe and masculine a way, had a waviness to it. Not like Adamus. Her face was not really his face.

But it was a fact, Rachaela had never seen her like this. For even in bed, there were the silks and lace, the breasts, the fount of tresses, touches of powder for the night. The perfume of a beautiful woman.

Althene crossed the room. Lean and lightly muscular, it was easy to make out the ribs of the bandaging. Althene – he – sat on the sofa.

'If you needn't, I must.'

'Can I get you something,' Rachaela said.

'Not yet. Let me explain.'

'It isn't necessary.'

'Naturally it is. Please hear me out.'

Rachaela stood on the rug. 'Yes, then.'

'I have to look for Anna. I have to – to seek out various people. And to do it, it will be simpler, like this.'

'Anna,' Rachaela said.

'Anna. The little two-year-old girl who appears to be seventeen.'

'Do you know where to look?'

'Perhaps. I don't know.'

'And what role do I play in all this?'

'I'm afraid it would be better if you merely wait. That's hard, I know.'

Rachaela said, 'That, I take it, is cynicism.'

Althene – he – looked at her obliquely. The way Adamus had been used to do. Cold priest. But that was not Althene. Or never until now.

'Your self-obsession, Rachaela, never fails to intrigue me. I'm trying to console you. Even if you're jealous of Anna, she's your possession. And someone has stolen her. You'll be left alone. You'll have to wait. Weeks may go by without news of her, or of me. I realize this is unpleasant. A thankless position. But it's all I offer you.'

'Well, I suppose I deserve it.'

'And, added to your self-obsession, a guilt complex.'

'Don't analyse me. It's already bad enough.'

'That's true,' Althene said. And then, 'Would you get me some water? It's all I want.'

'From the tap? Or can I open a bottle of celebratory Perrier?'

'I would prefer it still.'

'Like life? We'd all prefer life to be still. Yet here we are, aslosh with horrid waves of accident and treachery.'

Althene got up.

For a man she was not so very tall, yet taller than Rachaela. And built on a larger scale. The face of bones, the hair. Even the hands, on which, now, a faint male down had begun. No rings.

'I want you to hold me,' Rachaela said.

'Then I'll hold you.'

'But it isn't you.'

'Yes. I would always be me. A law of physics.'

'Your arms,' Rachaela said, 'are already full to bursting, with Anna.'

'I don't want Anna as my lover.'

'Are you sure, Althene?'

'Perfectly sure.'

'You look like him now. Maybe she'll like that. When you find her.'

'If I find her.'

'Or Malach will find her. Rivals?'

'Rachaela, I'm very tired. All these iron nails being thrust home are tiring me worse.'

'In the vampire coffin,' Rachaela said. 'At least, you never drank my blood, the way he did.'

Althene said, 'Nor you mine. Let's leave this now.'

She – he – went out of the room, and in the kitchen the water was poured.

Rachaela, so intent, had forgotten to do this. Unforgivable.

More lush fuel for the guilt complex.

They slept in their bed. Or, Althene slept, in exhausted silence. Rachaela watched.

When the light began to seep around the edges of

the curtains, Rachaela put her hand on Althene's neck, quietly, not to disturb.

What would it be like to make love with him? With *him*?

Thrilling? Dreadful? The same?

I'll never know.

Rachaela went down into the lower house, and sat on the floor by the sofa and drank some wine.

The light came blue, and outside the dark-fronded poplars stirred with birds.

She had once said to Althene, *I love you. Don't leave me.*

But in space, their hands had parted. Now they fell away from each other, separately, into the abyss.

It was very sad, but she did not feel it yet.

Not quite yet.

Chapter Twelve

It was a rainy gusty day, but Cimmie was dressed like summer, in a turquoise blue dress, gold earrings and bone bracelets. She was in a sunny mood also, because she was going shopping, and to the hairdresser's to have her two inches of hair cropped back to one.

'Don't eat any of that cake until Ms Baldwin comes. Then you can have a piece if she has one.'

Faran concurred. He was always responsible. Since the age of five they had been able to leave him alone in the flat. He was not the type of child to stick scissors into his ear or set the place on fire with matches.

The cake was left over from a dinner party the evening before, black grapes and walnuts with cream.

Cimmie and Wellington had made love three times during the night, waking Faran with their noises.

After Cimmie had gone, Faran went into his room and got the geography books, and his arithmetic exercise, and laid them out on the oak table.

Then he went to the window with a chair.

Over the rushing road, the park rushed only with diagonal rain.

The fat man was there too, in the gateway.

But it was no use waving. The man would not see him through the rain.

Faran reached out to the ebony lampstand on the low pedestal by the window. He switched the lamp on, off, on, off. Perhaps that would do. It was better than nothing. It must be uncomfortable, just standing there, in the rain.

Faran went back to the table, replaced the chair, and sat down on it to wait.

Half an hour after, he was still waiting.

Ms Baldwin was never late. She knew the geography of the city and the mathematic of time, and there was no margin left for mistakes.

So it was peculiar.

Faran did not worry about Ms Baldwin, however. Although he did not wish her ill, he did not like her. She would have to take care of herself.

Finally he left the table and went to look in the refrigerator at the cake. But he was not hungry.

Just then the rain stopped and a bright glass-edged ray of sun struck through the windows.

Faran went back to the window, to see if the man in the gateway was relieved.

The man looked just as he always did, the cheap mac, his glowing blackness. But he waved at Faran.

Faran, on the chair, waved back.

And then, the man in the park gateway beckoned.

It was a brief, but not an obscure gesture.

Evidently the man did not grasp that Faran must not leave the flat.

Faran shook his head, regretfully.

He climbed down, and returned to the oak table and went over his essay on Scandinavian fishing.

About ten past four, when Ms Baldwin had still omitted to manifest, Faran pushed the books along the table.

The sun streamed through the flat, lighting up the Objegbo treasures, the baskets, and statues of elephants and lions, and Cimmie's batik prints and splintery masks on the walls.

108

Faran looked about him, at the big room. The sun was cruel.

He went and gazed in at his room. There were pictures of animals on the swarthy yellow paint, he liked the animals. But his 'toys' were all clever devices to help him learn, puzzles and tests. They had not wanted him to have a bear. The books were lessons, too. A novel based on some children who had been at Nagasaki when the atomic bomb was delivered, others concerning the slave trade, and ten-year-old Jewish refugees in 1940.

The sun lanced in.

Faran felt a burst of impatience at Ms Baldwin, who should have been here. Her grim company was preferable to this sudden dense frustration.

Actually, Ms Baldwin was not at fault, only trapped in a blacked-out tube with several hundred other distressed passengers. She had been very unlucky. This line was the only one affected by a power failure all week.

Faran opened the door of his father's study, looked, came out. Then the guest room, kept ready for tipsy guests, who last night had after all gone to their home. Then his parents' bedroom.

There were ethnic cotton prints cast across the bed, whose seven pillows were of zebra-striped linen. A spear with a crimson tassel hung above, rather as the cricket bat hung above his father's desk.

Faran frowned.

On his mother's dressing table squatted bottles of Chanel and a face cream in a white and gold box, formulated for black women, costing thirty-five pounds.

It dissatisfied him. And her clothes in the little dressing room. And the scent of her left behind, peppery, attractive, and alien.

Just as Ms Baldwin was recrossing her legs for the fiftieth time and wiping the nervous sweat off her palms, hoping she would not be stupid and faint, Faran stalked back to the window and saw the man was still there.

Then Faran went into the kitchen and took out the cake and carved off a big, generous slice. He put this into one of the polythene bags kept for food, and was sorry when the cream squashed into the walnuts. But it would taste all right. He removed a silver dessert fork from its box and dipped up two lavender and blue paper napkins from the drawer.

Carrying everything carefully, Faran let himself out of the flat.

He allowed the door to shut, for Cimmie would be home by five-thirty, and even if the man in the park got bored with Faran, Faran could always come back and sit in the foyer of the flats.

Faran had been told, from the earliest age, that he must never speak to strangers. That he must *never* have anything to do with unknown men.

But then. One of Cimmie and Wellington's prized white male friends had once cornered Faran in the kitchen, and, the new cold Riesling in one hand, put the other on Faran's genitals. 'Soon be a man,' jovially had said the guest. 'Let go,' said Faran. The man did so, and laughed. 'Only teasing.' And, besides, black Mr Thorpe had been suspected, accused, of perverse paedophile desires, things as distant from him as the earth from Andromeda.

In any case, it was the *known* who were the strangers. Although he could not quite have put this concept into words, Faran gripped it.

If he had been reliable all these years, perhaps it had been because there was no other option.

Outside the elegant apartment block, the pavement was wet, and the buildings resembled damp newspaper. Crossing the road was not such a challenge. The traffic had slowed and lessened as it occasionally did.

Faran, having looked both ways, ran lightly over and up to the park gate.

The man smiled at him.

'Hallo, Faran. It's good to meet you.'

110

It was not bizarre that the stranger knew his name. It was, somehow, logical.

'I brought you a piece of cake.'

'Why, Faran, how kind. Thank you.' And the man accepted the squash of cake and, there in the gate, began to eat it with obvious enjoyment, plying the silver fork.

Faran watched. He said, 'Who are you?'

'Call me Danny,' said the man. 'I hoped you'd come down. I guess you'd like to see Mr Thorpe, wouldn't you?'

Faran said, with intent truth, 'Yes.'

'Then I'll take you there.'

They walked into the park, and the man wiped his round face on the napkins, screwed them up and tossed them, with the empty polythene and the rich man's fork, into a rubbish bin.

Faran watched this. It did not disturb him. He sensed, already, something . . . like a distant song.

But he said, 'I'll have to be back by half past five.'

'Don't worry,' said Danny, 'about a thing.'

On the road that ran through the park, at the verge, was a pale grey Montego. Danny unlocked the car, and they got in. As he did so, Danny took off his mackintosh. He had on a smart brown suit and a tie like a knife of pale blue water.

He drove well, and Faran sat back, belted into the front seat, looking out at everything.

Beyond the park, the streets streamed up through the rainy after-smoke and the sunshine.

They moved down among the inner tendons of London, where the vast stores rose, lit with colours, and far up the forgotten and overlooked architecture crenellated the sky.

Faran saw young girls, black and white and tawny and brown, girls with long hair and short, glamorous and dull, and men with umbrellas, and dogs on leads. He saw doorways full of people who seemed to be invalids, wrapped in blankets.

111

Before a great hotel, with stone women up above, and plants in urns, the car pulled up.

The doorman touched his hat to Danny.

'They're in the lounge, sir. Waiting for you, young man.'

Inside, the hotel was maroon and sage, scored with gold. Enormous fruit bowls of flowers reminded Faran of cornucopia.

Over the dark green carpet, Mr Thorpe was sitting on a plush settee with a very pretty, plump, black young woman.

Faran did not run forward.

For a moment, he was awed. But the awe warmed him.

Mr Thorpe was wearing a suit even more smart than Danny's, and certainly more beautiful than any of Wellington Objegbo's. It was a sort of fulvous grey, and the line of it did not either bulge upon or disguise Mr Thorpe's bulk, but instead made it into something statuesque, important. Mr Thorpe looked like a great statesman. And he held out his manicured hand to Faran.

Faran went to him. He took Mr Thorpe's hand. He felt happy, as if he had met his father. Except that Wellington had never induced this feeling.

'I've missed you, Faran,' said Mr Thorpe.

'Have you? I did too.'

And then Mr Thorpe leaned down and kissed Faran weightlessly on the cheek. After that he indicated the lady. 'This is Estelle.'

Estelle laughed. She looked full of laughter. She wore a sugar pink two-piece and a long pink-and-black fringed scarf. She was very plump, very, very pretty. In her ears were silver rings. She smelled of some light and frivolous flowery scent.

She too held out her hand and asked Faran for a kiss.

He kissed her, in turn, on the rosy sable of her cheek. She said, 'You are gallant, monsieur.'

Faran liked this. She had meant it. She had a French accent.

They went up then, Mr Thorpe and Estelle and Faran, in a mirrored, gilded lift, and so came to a mirrored corridor and a suite of rooms in honey and orchid.

Here there was a sumptuous hotel tea. A myriad of tiny sandwiches filled with cucumber, Brie, salmon, hot toasted muffins, cream cakes, chocolate eclairs and raspberry slices.

Faran was hungry after all.

He did say, as Estelle poured the tea from the golden and silver pot, 'I'll have to call my mother.'

Mr Thorpe said, 'It has been seen to.'

'Does she mind?' said Faran. Mr Thorpe smiled. 'It's just that she might.'

'It will be taken care of. Don't worry, Faran. You're not worried, are you?'

Faran said, slowly, 'No.' He was not. He was not remotely concerned.

Cimmie seemed light years off across the galaxy.

She always had.

Estelle said, 'We're going to see a film, Faran. What shall I wear? Green or red?'

'Red, please,' said Faran. 'It will look good.'

Estelle giggled. 'Yes. For you, then. Red.'

'What film is it?' Faran asked.

Mr Thorpe said, 'An old film. I've told you of it. *King Kong*.'

Faran thought about this. Cimmie had said that *King Kong* was a travesty. It demeaned black people.

Faran wanted to see it.

While they waited for Estelle to change her immaculate clothes, Mr Thorpe talked to Faran in the old way, as if there had been no gap. He also drank a whisky, and Faran had a coke.

Estelle, when she returned, looked incredible in burgundy red, and they went down again.

Danny drove a new car. Faran did not know what make it was, but it was large and roomy. It was also left-hand drive, and had French number plates.

When they were getting out, in the cinema car-park, a white man came up to them, a beggar. Cimmie would have ignored him, but Danny put some money into his hand.

'My mother says,' said Faran, as the man went away, 'they spend it on drugs and drink.' He uttered this on a reflex.

'Perhaps. Or on food and shelter. That is their choice,' said Mr Thorpe. 'There have always been beggars. At the gates of Rome, at the gates of Hell.'

Faran recalled the invalids in blankets. They were the homeless.

The world was a terrible place, he knew. People suffered in it. Sometimes the pall of pain was like a thundercloud. But yet, not now.

They went into the cinema, and took their seats for *King Kong*.

The foolish things about the film did not count. It was, Faran believed, wonderful. Wonderful and appalling.

The giant ape filled him with love. It was a marvellous and extraordinary creature, transcending its knowledge and nature, until, when it had been tortured and corrupted, it turned, and became then godlike in its rage.

At the end, when Kong, destroyed by the wasps of planes, died, Faran wept.

Mr Thorpe held his hand.

It was beauty killed the beast.

Faran talked about the film all the way back in the car, and in the suite of the hotel, Mr Thorpe said, 'Greatness is nearly always feared, Faran. And genius is capable of being wounded.'

They had dinner in the room. Estelle, it turned out, was a vegetarian, but she was one in a lovely, easy way. Mr Thorpe had sole with limes and radishes, and Faran a hot chicken salad. They drank wine, Estelle and

Mr Thorpe, but Faran preferred juice, although wine was offered.

He did wonder vaguely what had caused Cimmie's change of heart. Perhaps she had found out Mr Thorpe was wealthy.

When they had reached the dessert and they were all eating strawberries, Faran did say, 'When do I have to go back?'

Mr Thorpe stopped eating.

'Now Faran. I will tell you. You needn't go back at all.'

And this startled Faran. Because nothing sweet had ever lasted.

Mr Thorpe said, 'Do you believe, Faran, that I would never harm you.'

'Yes.'

'Then, you must trust me a little. Presently I'll tell you something. Can you wait?'

'No,' said Faran, 'but I will.'

Estelle laughed again. She said, '*Pikanini induna.*' Obviously, not French. Some African language. But she looked so charming and friendly, he did not mind.

When the meal was over, Mr Thorpe sat down with Faran on a couch.

'I should like,' said Mr Thorpe, 'to send you to some people. They are your friends.'

Honestly, Faran said, 'I don't have any friends.' He paused, and added, 'Except for you.'

'These are people,' said Mr Thorpe, 'who knew you – long ago. Friends who knew of you, before you were born.'

Faran said, puzzled, 'But how?'

'Only they can explain it to you. But they want you, Faran. You're theirs.'

Faran looked down at the floral carpet.

'What will happen?'

'It's very simple. In the morning someone will come, someone nice. You'll go with them. You'll fly in a plane.'

115

'A plane? Where?'

'Somewhere far off. First, you must want to go.'

'I don't know,' Faran said.

Mr Thorpe stood up. 'Come with me.'

Faran accompanied him, and walked into another room of the suite. Mr Thorpe opened a black leather folder. He took out a photograph, and gave it to Faran.

'Here is the woman,' Mr Thorpe said, 'the woman who wants you to go to her.'

It was a colour photograph, excellently produced, probably ten by eight in size.

Faran held it under the chandelier, and looked.

The woman was not posed, she merely sat before the camera, and her eyes had come to meet it, without reserve or favour, still as deep night.

She wore a black garment, a dress, but here and there a point of something glittered, like spent rain, upon it. Her long white hands were folded, and the nails were a dense matt red. She wore one ring, an oval, not shining.

Her face. Broad brow and long eyebrows, and long eyes, almond-shaped these, and midnight black, that put out the dress and the ring. A long nose, like that of a great cat. Lips not thin, nor full, *soft* red . . . like – the line came from somewhere – like pomegranate.

Faran felt all his blood flow up and down his body, meeting and knotting at his centre.

Now and then he had had a faint stirring there, in the slender finger of his boy's penis. But now he engorged, royal and burning he came up, rock hard and ready and it hurt him.

The sight of the woman hurt him.

'Her name,' said Mr Thorpe, 'is Lilith.'

Faran began to cry again, the water flowed out of him, and as it did so the frightening erection faded as if drawn off. He held the photograph away, so that his tears should not spoil it.

*   *   *

116

Cimmie had said he must marry a white girl.

And, oddly, it seemed he was.

It was a cathedral. Vast spiderwebs of stone. Windows like cut-open fruits.

He stood with her before an altar, and above the gold crosses, the forms of saints.

She was at his side, in the colours of her house. Burgundy red, and on her divine skull, over the black silk of her hair, a chaplet of red roses.

He had already possessed her. In her father's garden. But then, maybe he was not her father. White flowers there. She was not a virgin. But she clung to him.

He put the dark gold ring upon her finger.

He was black, black as jet, taller than she. He could snap her waist in his hands. He would die for her.

'You are so gallant.'

And then he was on a river, and the river was browner than beer. He saw her in her little house of reeds with columns of alabaster. She sat at the boat's centre. At the centre of his loins.

He went to her. She wore the vulture crown.

He was not black. An Arab? He kissed her mouth.

And then, under the eaves, in smoulder of candle- and hearth-fire, a narrow room with low ceiling, beams, and painted between them the little flowers.

His hand like coal upon her breast like snow.

The firelight flickered on the flowers and the beams.

She was an owl. An owl made of blossoms.

She sat astride him. He burst in the core of her.

And then she held him, like a child.

'Come back to me,' she said, 'come back to me.'

Mouth red as pomegranate, eyes black as night. Hair the night river flowing to the cataract.

A small town. They stood in the place behind the house.

'They will kill us.'

He said, 'Don't leave me.'

117

'Then come with me. I'll lose you,' she said.

A cock crowed and the sun rose and he and she, they went to their beds. They did not like the day.

She wore red when she married him. Her blood had marked the sheet. Yet, she was not a virgin . . .

In the black of the hotel, Faran woke and sat up.

The hotel was not silent. It hummed and purred, it was full of gadgets, and modern. But, he had been away.

Mr Thorpe had said, *Perhaps you will remember her.*

Faran knew her, the woman, Lilith. But could not remember—

And then the dreams.

They had seemed gothic, mediaeval, and also Eastern, and the last, a cold place, to the north. And he had been a man.

But she. She was a constant.

His mother.

Faran checked. Seven years old, in the hotel's murmuring electric dark, he knew. His love.

And so he could forget the other two, the man and the woman. Forget it all.

In the morning he would say to Mr Thorpe, *I'll go.*

And thus, and so, he could go back to her.

Chapter Thirteen

ANNA LAY ON HER SIDE.

The girl was leaning over her.

'Anna? Good. We'll be landing in another fifteen minutes. Do you wish for the lavatory?'

'Yes,' Anna said. She sat up, and her head felt weightless.

The girl helped Anna to her feet, and then guided her up the cabin aisle to the tiny toilet. Anna was allowed to shut and bolt the door.

Presumably, it could be broken down, if needful.

If Anna became abruptly difficult, uncooperative.

Anna used the lavatory, then washed her hands and face. In the mirror, her familiar pallor. Shadows under her eyes.

She stayed in thought for a moment. But no thought would truly come.

They had given her a drug, at the house. It had affected her. But she would have had to acknowledge, any way, that there was nothing she could do, save accept.

In the seconds after Althene collapsed, when the men dressed as gardeners drew Anna away, she had been shocked, almost nerveless.

They led her swiftly down through the cemetery, which passed in a green blur, pierced by graves. Then into a kind

119

of alley under the trees, and out of a tiny gate from which wire netting had been pulled away.

Outside was a blue Lada, into which they put her, not pushing, not hurting, but irresistible.

The engine did not sound like that of an ordinary car.

They started off, very fast.

One man sat in the back with her, and the other with the driver at the front. The man in the back was decorous. He did not touch her during the journey.

As they came out into a high street of shops and other normal things, Anna snapped awake.

'What are you doing?' she said.

'Please don't fret,' said the man sitting in front. 'You won't be harmed. We didn't hurt you, did we?'

'No. Why have you taken me?'

'Someone wants to see you, Anna.'

She accepted the first thing, that they knew her name.

She said, 'Why?'

'Only they can tell you that.'

She said, 'Who?'

'It's family,' the other man said, the one beside her.

Family was Eric, Sasha. Holland, even. Why would they do it this way?

'Scarabae?' she said.

'That's right,' said the man sitting by her.

Anna still thought like a child. She was a child, almost, about ten or eleven some of the time, then six or seven. Then much older.

But Anna thought something like: *They're lying. Yet it's true.*

After they had driven on in silence, with only the buzz of the specialized engine, for nearly an hour, they pulled into the high-walled grounds of a big house.

It was not like the Scarabae house at the common. It had glass doors and long windows, uncurtained.

Inside, when they had conducted her, politely, in, Anna

saw the house was empty. A few pieces of furniture under dust-sheets, bare floors, the gardens overgrown.

A girl, about twenty, entered. She was fashionably but conservatively dressed in a suit, her black skirt half an inch below her slim knees. She had short black hair and no make-up but for red lipstick. She looked European, and indeed spoke in Spanish to the man who followed her. Anna did not know Spanish.

The man was large, like the two spurious gardeners, but he wore a dark suit. Inside the jacket was a gun.

The girl came to Anna. 'Is there anything you need?'

'I'd like to go home.'

'But that's where you're going.'

Anna said, 'I mean to my—' Anna hesitated. She said flatly, 'My parents.'

'I'm afraid you must come with us first,' said the girl. 'You will be comfortable. Your relatives are eager to see you.'

It could not be Eric. Surely not Holland.

Other Scarabae existed, Anna knew this.

Anna accepted, now, the second lesson, that they would only tell her so much.

Then they had a picnic in the bare room, some cold lobster and rolls – which Anna did not like or eat – some coffee.

The drug was apparently in the coffee.

Suddenly the walls of the room seemed to swell out. The world grew greater, and Anna was in a tube of crystal balanced on the wide floor. She felt not sleepy but boneless. She raised her hands, to see if she could, with an effort.

'Don't be afraid,' said the Spanish girl. 'It's to help you relax. It will wear off soon.'

But it did not wear off, and when they walked her out to the next car, Anna found it hard to move. The suited man held her arm.

Outside it was now dark, evening.

Anna tried to say, 'Please let me go.'

But she could not control her lips as she could not control her limbs. It occurred to her that this was what it had been like as awareness came to her in the first year of her life. When she had had the words but not the coordination, and Althene had been there to catch her, prompt her, assist, persuade.

Anna wanted to cry. What had happened to Althene? Would Rachaela help her?

But it was no use. Even emotion would not come.

Anna seemed to see everything from a long way off, some height or depth, but she was used to the amorphous perspective of time if not to the disturbance of vision.

So then she accepted all of it, and got into the car.

It was a limousine with polarized windows and diplomatic plates.

The gardeners had left them. The chauffeur, too, was armed. They drove to the airport.

By then, she was in a waking dream, and since they put her in a handsome wheelchair, it was easy to be will-less.

They did not go among the crowds, but through a deserted corridor and a small room where some official spoke to the suited man in French. After this there were further corridors, walkways, and an ascent into the plane, a torpedo of power, all vacant, but for them.

A stewardess in another suit, cream with pink piping, brought them drinks, more sandwiches. They were belted in, Anna by the red-lipped girl.

'Taste your wine,' she said. 'It will be a long flight.'

Anna did not ask how long, and she would never know. After she had sipped the wine, rollers of sleep came in on her.

They had taken off, for Red-lips was undoing Anna's seat-belt. Red-lips encouraged Anna to lie down on the three seats, cushions under her head. Anna slept with the roar of the jet, in a womb of steel and sky.

* * *

The landing was bumpy. Anna had already looked from the window. She saw an extraordinary view, bare brown mountains carved from hardened fudge, cut by white roads and distant spoons of salt. They came down in a desert.

When they alighted from the plane, there was a singing in the ears, not the drug, a new type of silence.

A natural flatness had provided an expansive runway. They were in an arena, held by brown rocks. Above, a golden sky, blue only at its apex.

Another plane, a twin to the jet, rested about a hundred yards away. It looked white to Anna, with markings that made no sense, for the heat caused them to vibrate, and she did not care.

Two covered jeeps stood alongside the runway. They were the colour of brown sand, with machete mounts on their sides, radio ariels stuck up like silver antennae, and mounted M60s pointed out from their backs like cannon.

There were also what Anna took to be soldiers, informally dressed in the universal brown. Ruger P85s in their shirts.

They were fit and agile, these men, young, and some good-looking.

Two of them came over to greet the red-lipped girl and the man. One spoke in French. He said something about a delay. Then, he half turned to Anna, glanced at her under his lashes. Anna said, '*Comment allez-vous, monsieur?*' Her speech was still slurred, but not impossibly.

He smiled. He nodded. '*Très bien, mademoiselle. Enchanté de faire votre connaissance.*'

Anna said, in English, 'What gun is that?'

And in English, touching the long shape of the M16, he told her.

Anna said, 'Where is this place?'

'The desert, mademoiselle.'

The suited man said, 'How long must we wait?'

Then they spoke in Spanish.

Anna stared about her at the brown mountains. They did not seem so far away as perhaps they were, and she had been able to speak. The drug they had given her was less. But that would not pose any awkwardness. They could always give her another dose.

Besides, where could she run to, now?

The soldier conducted them into the shade of a brown awning. Presently, from a portable kitchen, some more food was brought, hamburgers in buns with a hot sauce, bottles of Perrier.

Anna ate. She was hungry.

Red-lips did not eat all her bun. Of course, she would watch her figure.

After the meal – breakfast, lunch, whatever it was – Anna slept again on a mattress under the awning.

She dreamed as she always did. Of fragments, voices, rooms, mazes, sounds.

When she woke up, there were more hamburgers, tortillas, and fruit.

A sunset began. It was unearthly, the way only things of the earth can be. Flaming boulders of cloud stacked over a sea green screen that sank, in radioactive bands of topaz, iris and mauve, among the rocks.

Across the scrub that edged the basin of their arena, lizards went scuttling. Red-lips pointed out the trail of a snake that had passed near them, undetected.

The delay was over, and they went to the second plane.

In the cabin, Red-lips handed Anna a pill.

'It will help you sleep again. Otherwise, so boring. I'll take one too. I hate long flights.'

She proved it by swallowing her sleeping pill before Anna's eyes. Or pretending to.

But Anna did not take the pill.

She watched from the window as the jet surged up into the stars, and later there were the stars of cities below. But blackness came, and she slept any way.

124

She dreamed a man stood before her in a tunnel of the dark. His hair was white as her own and clotted him round. His eyes were like jewels.

Something moved in Anna.

Her heart, perhaps. Or something more profound.

They refuelled somewhere. She smelled the oils pumping into the plane. It sucked the tubes dry, a vampire.

Perhaps a day came and went. Or not. Maybe Red-lips had coaxed a somnolent Anna to take the sleeping pill. It was gone.

And then again, the girl was leaning over her. 'We will be landing in fifteen minutes.'

Again, Anna visited the lavatory. She had not bathed, it seemed to her, for weeks. She wanted to wash her hair and clean her teeth.

It was strange. She would have thought the Scarabae, so attentive as they had always seemed in Althene's tales, in Rachaela's mutterings, would have provided such items as toothbrushes, even shampoo—

Then they were down.

Cloud had obscured the windows. Anna had not seen very much, until the plain appeared.

Hills far off, not like the mountains of the desert. Hills clad in wind-bitten turf.

And the blown sky.

When the doors were opened, it was cold.

'Where is this?' she said.

Red-lips said, 'The tip of the world.'

Anna said no more.

There was a long hut, and in it a primitive but operational shower that ran scalding hot. Soap and shampoo were provided, toothbrush and paste of an American brand. Nothing more.

Anna found, outside the shower cubicle, a pile of clothing. They had told her she must put it on.

There were thermal undergarments, a one-piece jump-suit in dark blue, a fleece waistcoat, a parka, pants, insulating bands for the neck, head, wrists, ankles, thermal socks, and boots, a hood and hat, a jacket packed solid as if already filled with flesh.

Outside, amid the windy landscape, a beast of a plane, a black Ilyushin-76, bulked on the runway.

Another man came to Anna. He was dressed very much as she was, but he had a gun across his shoulder.

'Miss Anna. Will you board the transport, please?'

She went with him.

Red-lips and the other man were gone.

Across the air-field, against the watered sky and the hills, a little stone thing stood up. It reminded her of the cemetery. A tomb? The statue of a child-girl, classical . . . Her face was cold and unkind and at her feet someone had laid a sheath of blood red flowers.

The plane had no windows.

Undersea muddy light.

A little boy, who had been sitting in the aisle, playing with a giant woolly llama, looked up at Anna. He too was dressed as she was, but his clothes were miniscule and rosy.

'I'm Andy.' He corrected himself: 'Andrew.'

Anna looked at him. Still a child, and always a mature woman, she did not respond to his youngness, or his pleasing face.

She liked the llama. It was a pale soft ashy shade, with tassels on its neck that had bits of mirror in them.

'Where are we going, Andrew?'

'Are you going too? All right,' said Andrew, thoughtfully. 'We're going to my Uncle Kay—' Andrew broke off, as if trying to add something to the name, but not able to.

'Why?' said Anna, although she knew it was no use.

'It'll be great,' said Andrew.

He had a South London accent, but not consistently. His hair was feathery dark.

'Why?'

'I've had a great time,' said Andrew. 'I watched funny telly, and they played me music. And I've got this llama, he's brilliant. I drink wine now.' Then he said, 'Albescent.' And then, 'Snow-White.'

The man in the matching clothes came into the plane. He told them they should sit down now in the seats and fasten their belts. He would see to Andrew's belt. And the llama too, since Andrew desired the llama to be safely belted in.

It was not a long journey. Not far, now.

'My Uncle Kay has a huge house,' said Andrew. 'Mum's coming, later.'

The Ilyushin rose like a heavy can of clanking metal, and they the belted peas inside.

'Forty-five minues is all,' said the escort. 'Then another little flight. Half an hour, perhaps.'

Someone came with lemonade and cookies.

They plunged down in a place of snow. Across a slide of water, ships of ice sailed blue-green across the green-blue sky.

The little boy made snow balls, but did not throw them.

'The summer is coming,' said the man, smiling into the burning kiss of the cold.

Anna thought, *whither thou goest I will go*. Who had said that?

The sky throbbed. The snow-white snow stretched, soul-less, away and away and away.

Chapter Fourteen

THE CEMETERY WAS PLANTED WITH cedars, holly, conifers. Its ambience, even at the onset of winter, was dark green. Laurels grew in tubs along the paths, speckled with glassy yellow. The graves were dark iron or toothily clean and white, streaked only faintly with weather. Brown statues kneeled in ivy.

Roman was sweeping up the leaves of the birches, and overhead, revealed by the trees' bareness, hung enormous abandoned nests, blot-black on the flat sky.

Roman came to a marble grave. *Hier rust Magdalena Einer.* Roman stopped, and checked that the big china dog was in his right place, guarding dead Magdalena. The dog had a sad but not a tragic look. He understood his duty. Roman leaned down and touched his head. 'Good friend.'

Roman was seventy years of age. He appeared to be fifty, but for his eyes. Held in the long taut stone-brown mask of his face, they were the colour of the wooden instrument he played. Unlike the dog, Roman's face had tragedy in it. Not an expression. The tragedy had formed the flesh.

Leaving Magdelena's tomb, Roman passed down the gravel, and stopped again, to watch a red squirrel investigating under a bush.

The death garden was full of life. In spring, there were also flowers, daffodils, pansies, tulips, pots of hydrangeas.

The squirrel finished and flew up a tree, lighter than a bird.

Roman went on. Behind the cedars, where the cemetery folded over to the river, the tall reeds stood petrified to umber already by the cold. He leaned his broom on a moss-grown trunk.

Roman took a packet of Gauloise from his coat, and lit a cigarette with a match. He smoked, looking over the reflecting water, in which, now, a little breakage of rain began to fall.

The man soon came along the bank; it was the one called Vonk. Vonk was fat and seemed dirty, although he was not. His unshaven pig's face broke into a smile.

'Roman. You devil.'

Roman shrugged. His Dutch had always remained heavily accented, and he spoke little. As he stretched out his hand to take the envelope from Vonk, the tattoo on Roman's hand pulled with the dried skin. They had done it when he was young.

'For him?' said Roman.

'For him. For the Prince.'

'He is not,' said Roman.

Vonk shrugged now.

That was all: Vonk went off along the bank, whistling.

Roman retrieved his broom and crushed the cigarette in the bank. He walked back into the cemetery, and there stored the broom in the building by the naked stone goddess. Here he located also his bicycle, and wheeled it out.

From the top of the basket he took a flapping dun raincoat, and pulled a beret on to his long head. In her waterproof, the hurdy-gurdy lay now alone.

She would be a bitch today. The rain. His *vrouw*, as the bagpipes were a man. Nut brown, made from old furniture, her strings and wheel, her keys in their box. Bitch.

Roman got on the bicycle.

Under the raincoat, in which he had carefully stored the unmarked envelope, his feet were just visible plodding on the pedals.

He swung, like an old bent-wheeled moth, out of the death garden, up the picturesque slope, by the river and the poles of the trees with yellowing leaves. Towards the concrete bridge.

A dog barked on a boat.

At the back of the sea, in front of the half-circle of her canals, Atlantis, Amstelredam, the city of Amsterdam.

His bicycle one of a million others, Roman wove through the coiling tram-lines.

Down the straight streets between the banked shops, the French cafés, the bars, under the bannered signs (*cineac*, Marlboro). The dainty dark tower of the Vestertoven was playing its music-box tune, *Waar de blanke top der duinen*.

Roman pedalled through on to the grid of canals, bumping over the cobbles. Late florist flowers were on the pavements under bare trees smelling of smoke. The bridges made their immemorial O's of reflection. Water buses honked.

Then off the grid, dancing with the yellow trams, and so out alone on to the ruled wet highways running from the city.

The deluge poured now. The roads like the canals.

Cars sped by, angel-winged with spray.

A pink glare was in the sky over the level green of wintering grassland.

Roman's back was hunched up, and before him the hurdy-gurdy lay wrapped in her basket like a portion of severed body.

Some kilometres out, Roman turned away along a veering, tree-columned lane.

The Prince.

It irritated Roman when Vonk or the others said that. But it was only their respect.

And what was the Prince to Roman? A demon – maybe.

That first image. Roman would never mislay it, and saw it now, stamping on the pedals through the gasping wet.

Fire then, not water. A wall of burning houses, and a shape rising up, black on ruby red, from the corpse of a German soldier.

He had thought, Roman, one of them had murdered its own, for the figure wore a German uniform, that of some high-ranking officer. But then the man, the killer, spoke to Roman, in the purest Dutch. And from the collar of the coat, in which he had tucked it, slid one amazing snake of death-white hair.

It was how he would do it. Prey on them, under cover first of the fires they had created, and later in the cloak of their night. One by one, like a leopard, he took them. They would think him theirs. His German was flawless. He seemed to them Aryan, the perfect type, white-blond, blue-eyed. He would soothe, even fondle. Then he broke their necks, or tore out their throats.

He would vanish at once. That night he took Roman with him.

And that was the beginning of their association, if such it could be termed.

Other lanes slanted off from the first. The grassy fields lay all around, dotted with impervious wet black-and-white cows. Ditches of water sliced between, hung with willows.

Then the chestnuts gathered. And behind these, the pines.

A magpie, matching the cows, sat arguing with the rain on a bough.

Roman pedalled under an old crumbling stone arch with a notice on it warning that there was no entry.

On the far side he pushed up through the wood, and emerged on the tabled pasture before the castle.

Kraaienslot.

To uphold its name, a murder of crows was circling over it, beating against the rain.

Four round towers, their turrets, and the conical cap of the gatehouse, aching blue against the storm. Walls that in summer or autumn had a mellow painterly glow, now blocks of shadow, and the window-places skull-eyed. Behind, half a mile off over the castle's shoulder, the ghost of the windmill called Mina was visible, before the pines resumed.

Surrounding Kraaienslot was a wide moat, alchemically bubbling. On calm days, two or three piebald, red-beaked ducks would swim there. No ducks today. Never any drawbridge. No way across.

Roman put his bicycle against a mature tree, out of the rain, and lifted his *vrouw* from the basket.

At the wood's edge jutted a tree stump, with ivy growing on it. It had not been tampered with since last year's spring.

Roman knelt by the stump and felt under the ivy for the concealed button. He pressed, and a small shudder shook through the wood as the inner weight was shifted aside. Easily then, Roman lifted the hollow stump-head off the opening to the tunnel. A cunning Swiss design.

When he was down on the steps, where the dim overhead electric light began, he drew the stump back into place.

Carrying his musical instrument, Roman walked along the tunnel, whose walls dripped and whose floor was always paved with liquid from the moat.

It took three minutes to reach the other flight of stairs, where occluded daylight came in from the iron gate above. The automatic lights switched off.

Roman climbed out of the tunnel, slipping a little, and pushed wide the gate.

A burnt-black dog sat there, like Cerberus, some unsocial breed. He recalled it slightly. It wore a collar of leather with knobs of silver.

'You are his dog,' said Roman in Polish. Then he said, in Dutch, for probably the dog was not familiar with Polish, '*I* am his dog.'

The dog simply sat, and regarded him.

It made no aggressive move, and he went by.

The courtyard of the castle was cobbled, and in the middle was a well, surmounted by a sort of iron bird cage.

On all sides, high, the oblong windows, arched over at the tops, leaded-blind, gazed sightless down.

The main chambers were to the back, where the stairway was with the carved stone crows.

Aloft, the living crows had begun to fight.

An inky feather floated to the earth.

Bad omen.

The rain had eased.

Roman detached the hurdy-gurdy from her packaging. He sat by the wall.

The instrument gleamed under a mist of damp. She would have a damp voice, contralto, today.

She and her kind had been banned in the sixteenth and seventeenth centuries. Turning her handle turned the brain.

Roman started to turn the handle.

He tuned her by the notes of the city's trams, and the noises of the streets.

Resting her on his knees, he rotated her with his right hand, and depressed with his left hand her sliding keys.

The drone of her was deadly, hoarse, yet after all divine. She knew where she had come.

He played an old tune, perhaps a thousand years of age. *My love, you are leaving*.

Yes, she was sounding like a siren, like an enchantress, Circe . . .

The bitch. It was not for her husband. But for *him*. The demon.

The black dog had waddled close, like a barrel on legs. It seemed to enjoy the music. Its coat was coarse velour, but there were scars below the collar, as if another dog had once assaulted it.

Roman played on.

The usual madness came from his *vrouw*.

And then he heard the door flung wide above.

Chapter Fifteen

STANDING ON THE STAIR, MALACH beckoned. Roman ceased playing, and the *vrouw* gave a stuttering groan, a woman stopped before she could come. Carrying her, Roman ascended, and followed Malach into the great square room, the black dog padding after.

'Don't let Kraai worry you. He's gentle enough now.'

Roman glanced back at the dog – Crow – called for the castle.

'I remember him, Mijnheer. He was fierce then.'

'He's still a fighter. But not with my friends.'

Roman bowed.

He set the hurdy-gurdy down neatly on the large table of heavily polished wood. A carpet lay across it, old red, and on this sat a pewter plate and a tall goblet of green glass from the sixteenth century. The castle itself went back, Roman believed, to the 1300s.

The room was high, the ceiling crossed by a huge, black, mother beam, from which depended a brass orb, stemmed with candles. Even so, there was electric light, if rarely used.

The black-and-white floor was very clean. The ancient cabinets and the painted chest showing Venus and Mercury, in fourteenth-century Dutch garments, shone like molasses.

There were swords on the white walls, and one seventeenth-century painting, of a strange field, that disturbed Roman always, for heads were being harvested from it.

Few objects littered the room otherwise. A burnished globe was on the wooden overhang of the fireplace, which was itself tiled with blue and white animals, goats and boars and hares. Brass candlesticks, glittering, ranged there with the thick white candles in them.

One of the wolfhounds lay on a green velvet window-seat, before the window that looked, through small squared panes of soft white, smoky blue and glaucous green, out to the windmill Mina, and the pines.

Malach crossed to a cabinet, opened it, and poured Roman a glass of French brandy.

A faultless host, and so dangerous.

The scent of limitless things was on Malach, and now too he seemed more lively.

That spring, the last time, he had been like something dying. Roman had wondered. They did die, Malach's kind, although it took more than age to do it. Pain, sometimes, pain of the soul, the very sort that killed ordinary men.

Malach's beauty too would have made Roman laugh, if he had not been Malach.

Such a face was absurd. Yet it was a true face, carven out and set with those icy scorched-blue eyes. He wore shabby modern clothes, once very expensive, shirt, pants, shoes, nothing for the era of time or the cold which jointly filled the castle at the breath of winter. And his winter hair poured over him. The hair of women could not match it. Except, of course, *their* women. Scarabae women.

'Another brandy?'

'Thank you, Mijnheer. But I must give you this.'

Roman held out the envelope.

'Sit, please,' Malach said.

He went to the window where the dog lay, and absently

136

smoothed the creature's head. It was Enki, the paler hound. Kraai the crow jumped up on the seat. Malach caressed him too. The rings on Malach's left hand flashed as he slit the manilla.

He read, in silence.

Then he turned. There seemed to be no change.

'You must have your brandy now.'

He filled up Roman's glass – costly warped grey crystal some hundreds of years old.

Through the other door then came the rest of the dogs. Oskar the second wolfhound, Tarash and Firs, the two ruffed wolf-like mongrels.

They went to Malach and stood about him. Enki came also. The crow dog was the last to realize. Then he sprang down and joined them. They were Malach's guard, powerless, but formed ready to defend, to slay, to console.

Something terrible, then, the news. They would know.

His hand on the brandy had been steady. Malach had not paled. But yet, his face had drawn in on the bones. In the light of the cold grand room, where once counsels had been held and judgements given, he had that look of age *they* had only when their appearance was young. A thousand years. A skull with white hair and frozen eyes.

Malach walked, easily, through the dogs, to the chest. Took the black key from its hook and unlocked the antique lock. He removed a handful of money, many fifty-guilder notes.

'This is too much, Mijnheer. Always – too much—'

'No. It's my pleasure.'

The notes were chilled from Malach's hand, or only from the winter castle.

Roman must go now. The long journey back. Sometimes Malach would invite him to remain. They would eat, drink wine. *She* would be played. *She* would purr, and the dogs would lie on their feet before the firelight, or in the honey-dust of summer evening.

But not today.

Roman said, 'I am at your service. If you need.'
'I know it. Thank you. Go carefully.'
Roman went away.

He moved through his fortress of crows, a thought in its stony brain-case. The dogs followed, its feral dreams.

He saw the wooden chairs, sternly carved, the tapestries of maidens and knights, the cupboards with secret locks. On walls plaques of polished granite, a mediaeval woman's face, her lips rouged, a headdress like segments of an apple.

Stone floors, and the floors of black-and-white chessboards. The hooded fireplace of the other great room, with its pig-roaster and iron chains, flanked by caryatids of marble, their faces chipped, then stroked over again by time. In the corridor were the glass cases, old china in palest blue, like sea mixed with milk, funeral fans, a doll's house of evil black-clad dolls. Glasses of bloody green. Old books bound in leather, with clasps of bronze torn by rubies.

In the bedchamber, the box of a bed, its inner ceiling painted with birds, crows feeding on cherries, and fish for fertility, and a white dog for faithfulness.

Beyond that place, the other room, kept for a woman.

The bed curtains here were of damask, the pillows covered with embroidery. Nearby, the painted cradle.

Bed, cradle, empty.

This room smelled of powdery flowers, herbs. On the wall were a golden sun and a silver moon.

Through the armoury he went, too, where the chainmail hung, the maces nick-named *Goodnight*, and the spiritless robot metal men of the armour.

The dogs paced after.

Sometimes Firs or Kraai ran to sniff at something. They were the youngest.

The others were stiff, concentrated.

Below in the red stone-flagged kitchen, the copper

kettles and warming-pans and china bowls. And the modern refrigerator, where Jutka would leave for him cooked chickens and hams, smoked fish, a little cheese, and wine. The beer kegs lined up against the wall. And on a plate lay the winter berries she had brought.

Jutka was old, and lived in an exquisite modern house across the pastures. Her garden in summer was like a garland; the house, narcissus yellow edged in white icing.

Jutka would come regularly, but when Malach was walking in the trees with his dogs, or sleeping. Then, silently, she worked upon the castle, mopping its floors, polishing its wood.

She baked bread and brought it, like a woman of old, in a broad basket. Her husband hefted the beer and wine.

It had been in their family for centuries; service to the castle.

Having reached the kitchen, Malach fed the dogs with meat.

Enki whined.

'Yes, I am going away for tonight.'

Then Kraai whined, and Oskar turned and licked Kraai. Kraai came from under the earth, up from the pit. And now Malach must go down again, into Hell.

A door led from the kitchen into the subway that Jutka used, going under the moat as the other passage did, and so up into the sombre water garden on the farther bank.

The garden had been someone's pride, once, but they were long dead. Clipped hedges and trees, an orchard, a channel of water. Now the evergreens grew together, over the water, closing it with drowned emerald. The orchard Malach had outlived. It too was dead, but for one tree, a ruined quince, that produced, every three or five years, some black and bitter travesty of fruits.

A snake wall held espaliers, bare as bones.

Here Malach unlocked the door to the world beyond. The world he did not want and seldom visited.

139

Shimmer from the rain clad the woods and pastures. Mina the windmill rose like an anthill crossed by sails.

Malach walked away, back towards the wooded road where, in a hidden barn, the car waited, topped up and gleaming from the ministrations of Jutka's husband.

It was dark there, under the pines. Malach raised his head and shouted, without words or thought, at the branches and the endless sky.

Crows cawed. From the road came the rush of vehicles. Malach touched the button in the barn wall.

The city by night. Filigree towers, warm windows. The lamps, the red neons. Against the deepening sky were arrayed the two-dimensional façades, cut-outs of intricate architecture. The tram-lines glowed. Pewter perished in the canals and fire reflected there.

Bolivian musicians were playing in the square. He listened to their music, and when they had played and came, graciously, for money, he too gave them guilders.

Then he went into the bar. He drank beer, then Jenever. He ordered two extra glasses of the spicy gin, which he did not drink.

Over the small bar were battered copper pots, a bull's head, and skulls with horns. Terracotta bottles stood under the red-and-yellow windows. He ate an Israeli orange from a basket.

Beyond the bar, in the long street called for a queen, where the trams rattled, he sat down under windows of red and green that had lost their light.

A goat's head of wood was on this wall, rimmed by wooden grapes and lilies.

She would have liked that, liked the horned skulls.

He sat by the fireplace, obscured by black and white tiles with pictures of churches, harbours, castles.

An auburn dachshund came to look at him, but would not stay.

Malach ordered their meal.

For him, the baked tuna and the creamed potatoes. For her, the green pea-soup with smoked sausage, the shrimps, the *haché* with apple. And to follow, little pancakes with sugar.

They had two bottles of a white wine brought from under the street.

She did not, obviously, touch her meal, or drink her wine, as she had not drunk her Jenever.

She was not there.

The waiter came. He asked if everything had been satisfactory.

Malach assented.

The waiter said, 'She isn't joining you?'

'No.'

Malach took the flower from the table. A white last rose.

He bore it away with him, when he had paid for their meal, into the brilliance of the night.

Where the street narrowed, the engorged neons offered many things. Malach passed inside the light.

'Ah, good evening. Would you care to see the show?'

'The Jewess,' Malach said.

The man's face altered.

'Is she expecting you?'

'She'll see me.'

'Go up. I warn you, no trouble.'

Malach laughed shortly.

He went up the stair, thin and twisted as a child's broken spine.

When he knocked, he heard her. She rasped, her clothing, her lungs.

'Who?'

'Malach.'

The door was opened.

The room was filthy and it stank. One half-open window looked out, as if desperate, upon the street with its lit signs of girls, beer, hot dogs, and Indonesian cuisine.

Among the muffled furniture, lay plates with sticky, reeking crumbs on them, and tall lager glasses with the dregs of wine. He handed her the rose.

'You burn,' she said. 'Always you burn. Sit there. Your fire will consume my chamber.'

'No, my darling. Only me.'

'*Not* only you, you devil.' She spoke in Yiddish a moment, as if to compose herself. She said, 'But I like to look at you.'

Malach said, 'Honour me. Look.'

The Jewess laughed in turn.

She was hideous. Fat and crumpled, as if the food she gorged on trampled her in its progress through her body. Her fat face, ringed by chins, sank on her swollen, drooping dugs. Even her eyes, dark as the wood of ancient, polished cupboards, were sunk in pouches of waxen flesh. She was a great psychic. He had used her before. Indeed he recalled when she had been young, a waist like a wand and black hair to her hips, which hair now frayed down like dry grizzled straw.

'What do you want, my *wit minnaar*? Do you want my blood at last? Drink me, a shit on you, and make me a girl again.'

'You're too useful, lady,' Malach said.

The Jewess lifted her fat shoulders in their greasy, shapeless jumper. 'Then?'

'I told you about the woman.'

'Your lost love, lost all over again.'

'I left her,' he said, 'and she died.'

'Died of love? We all die of love for you, Beautiful.'

'No,' he said. 'A knife through her heart. I told you then.'

'Yes. I remember. I saw her. A woman killed her. Do you want that woman now?'

'You said, she would come back.'

142

'Into another body?' said the Jewess. She reached for a left-over glass of stale wine, and drank, smacking her lips.

'She did so.' He said, 'Her name's Anna.'

'Well,' said the Jewess.

Malach said, 'Now someone has taken her.'

'Before you were ready to do it? Oh, you should have hurried, Whiteness. You should have had her, quick.'

'She was a child,' he said.

'*No*,' said the abominable witch. '*No*. She grew up. She ran towards you.'

'Tell me where she is,' he said, 'or I'll break your neck.'

The Jewess assumed vast dignity. 'You don't harm women. I fear nothing from you. Sham. Impostor.'

Malach said, 'There's money here.'

'I want your blood,' she said. 'Like the last time. It didn't work for me. But maybe it will.'

Malach said, idly, 'Perhaps. When I know.'

He flexed his wrist, held it out. Withdrew it.

The Jewess got up and moved, cumbersome, to her cluttered table. The tarot was there, the Khartis, a quartz sphere, a ouija board. *Paraphernalia*.

She pushed them aside and leaned forward, her foul hair smoking in the cobwebs and muck.

'Ah,' she said. 'Aah.'

He did not speak.

She said, 'You'll let me drink from your vein for a whole minute?'

'If you want. My blood will poison you.'

'You're not so rotten as that, my Prince. Listen. Her hair is white, like yours.'

'I know. Someone has told me.'

'Well, now, beloved. Her hair has covered over the hills.' The witch snatched a coated bottle up. 'Here's white brandy. Will you have *ice*?'

Chapter Sixteen

ALTHOUGH IT WAS NOT REALLY the time of year for it, there was a khamsin blowing, as could happen, the wind of fifty days. The windows were fast shut and the blinds pulled down, yet everywhere in the tarnished luxury of the hotel room, fine grit had gathered. He had swept it from the desk with irritation. And, over the insectile stirring of the fan, sometimes he heard his daughter cough from her bedroom.

He wished she would be quiet.

Paul-Luc Lebas completed his notes in his careful, closed hand-writing and impeccably grammatical French. He shut the calf-skin binding of the book and reached for his attaché case.

Outside, the almost ceaseless uproar of the city went on. Shouts, imprecations, cars and carts competing, the laughter of donkeys. Up in the narrow streets alongside the hotel, fruit sellers and pedlars of sweets, bangles and sexual perversion, still squatted, hopefully cackling and calling. Along the corniche above the river, vehicles drove and the evening populace walked. The racket would not let up until the last hours before dawn. Even the flail of the desert, Set's scorpion wind, could not quell it.

Paul-Luc Lebas unlocked the case and reached into the secret compartment. He drew out the map.

He spread it before him, on the desk.

It was no bigger than a photograph, a snap, the paper not strong, nor local. It had been made about 1900 he supposed. It was not a fake, but then, European and so young, that scarcely mattered. Either it showed truth – or a lie.

He had been excited at first, in his cool way. Then he doubted. But there had always been stories . . .

Paul-Luc had dabbled in archeology for twenty years. He had attended the sites of other men's triumphs, always making enemies there, not especially through his jealousy, but merely because he believed in total discipline, had a dedicated contempt for Arab workers (scum), and would trust no one, nor do anything that did not seem reasonable and mathematical.

Now this chance had come his way, expensively enough bought. The seller had promptly disappeared with his French francs and American dollars. (What else could one expect of scum?)

Paul-Luc, travelling with his little daughter, brought them inland.

It was a nuisance, dealing with the child. But, when she was older, she would have profited from all this, and he foresaw a time when she might even be useful, a secretary he could burden with esoteric knowledge hidden from others.

It would be pleasant too, once she had been trained, to have a woman on hand to type his manuscripts, the articles and criticisms he wrote on literature and the classical theatre. She would need to learn Latin too, however, and perhaps Greek, even something of hieroglyphics. And women were so poor at these languages. Even Berenice's English was halting although she was almost seven, and had been learning for two years.

Paul-Luc studied the map avariciously.

Tomorrow—

The boat was ready, a dreadful thing with unstable bathroom facilities, and the cabin floor damp from the bilge. But the journey would not be long.

Then again, this damnable wind, coming out of season. They were superstitious, the filthy Arabs. They might refuse to travel in it, or demand higher rates of pay.

A small soft thump came from Berenice's room, audible even over the howling cacophony of the streets.

That child. What was she doing?

Paul-Luc rose and crossed the fabulous, slightly threadbare carpet, woven on steep looms to the south. The hotel was unfashionable and excellent. In summer too it did not resort to unhealthy air-conditioning. Paul-Luc always patronized it.

He knocked sharply on Berenice's door.

After a pause, the small voice: 'Yes, Papa?'

'What are you up to, Berenice?'

'Nothing, Papa.'

'I shall come in.'

He walked into the bedroom.

The fan was off, she had said its motion frightened her at night, like a huge fly. But then it was not particularly warm at this season, only the wind had brought a closeness to the air.

Berenice sat on the side of her bed, the provisional netting pushed away.

She had been named for a queen. Unfortunately.

When Marthe, that she-wolf, had produced her, he had selected the name for their baby. She should have grown into it.

But she was a plain child, even sometimes she looked to him ugly. Marthe had been chic, pretty. But this had not served him well either, for three years ago Marthe had left him. She made only a feeble attempt to secure her daughter, which he quashed. They had not heard of Marthe since.

Berenice had a pudgy face, and her left eye was far narrower than her right, something which Colette had declared made a face more interesting, but Paul-Luc had no time for Colette, either. Berenice, also, was short-legged

146

and her stomach was always swollen up like a little bal-
loon. Her hair was long but very fine. He made sure she
brushed it thoroughly, but it was stringy, no adornment,
and muddy in colour. He was able to have no pride in her.

'Why are you not in bed?'

'I'm sorry, Papa.'

'You're a bad girl. You know you must go to sleep.
Tomorrow we rise early.'

'Yes, Papa.'

'Get into bed. Hurry up.'

She scrambled her way back under the sheet in her
miniature white nightgown.

No toy shared the pillow. She had had a woolly cat, a
disgraceful grubby hideousness, but a chambermaid at the
previous hotel had apparently stolen the beast for her own
deprived brat. Paul-Luc made a scene, to no avail. It was
embarrassing to have to make a scene, any way, on such
a matter. The maid, obviously, denied everything.

Berenice, of course, had snivelled. But when he told
her to stop, she did so. She did at least always obey him
instantly. He had never struck her. He had never struck
her physically.

'Now compose yourself. Recite your English lesson to
yourself. I've told you before, it will help you to remember
it, and calm you for sleep.'

'Yes, Papa.'

She assayed a funny little unconscious gesture. Towards
the side of the bed vacant of her stolen toy.

Unwillingly he recognized this.

In the first nights after Marthe had gone, he too . . . But
he was not a fool, or a weakling. Marthe was a slut. Sometimes, in extremity, he had even informed their daughter
of the fact. At least, unlovely as she was, she would not
have open to her the opportunity of faithlessness.

Berenice wriggled on to her side. Her ill-plaited hair lay
on the pillow like a rat's tail. 'Goodnight, Papa.'

*   *   *

147

Down in the dining room the fans did not turn.

The long windows looked towards the river. Veiled in dust, it shone intermittently at the lights from the corniche, like oil in mist.

Paul-Luc sat at the marble table with its fringed shawls, and picked at the menu. He would dine lightly and drink French bottled water, the sort that had not been filled up from the Nile – these despicable scum.

The mosque lamps of the restaurant burned through their frets, each with a reddish dust-halo. Above the traffic, Set's khamsin growled in gusts.

The area was almost empty. He scanned it, bored.

And then the Frenchman's attention was abruptly caught.

At a table across the room, where one of the huge green palms sailed from its brass tub to the pillar, a youngish woman sat. A European.

She was perhaps unnaturally but elegantly blonde, with wide dark eyes and a thin, transparently tanned face. She wore a blonde linen suit, to go with her hair, and under that a knitted silk sweater for the evening chill that had not come. Two silver drops trembled from her ear-lobes. He could not see her legs beneath the table, but doubtless they too were good and clad in sheer nylons.

Seeing him look, she raised her cloudy glass of absinthe.

A spare but flattering acknowledgement.

It did not occur to him to respond, not yet.

He thought, perhaps she would still be here when they returned from the desert. If not, naturally, he was indifferent.

The child would be awkward, but then he could simply leave Berenice in her room. It had happened elsewhere.

The blonde did not appear cheap or easy. She had an aristocratic air, of which two hundred years of republicanism had not dispelled the magic.

He had not greeted her, but he glanced sideways again, as he toyed with the menu.

She still observed him (let her, he was worth a look), and then, unflurried, away.

She had style. Not French, but French-Swiss, perhaps, or a travelled Norwegian.

The waiter came in his clown's crimson hat, and Paul-Luc pointed out to him one of the French dishes on the menu. He said, 'Recommend it to Madame.'

'She has ordered couscous, monsieur.'

'That then is her misery.'

Chapter Seventeen

LIFE, CLICHÉD, CHANGED AFTER ALTHENE was gone. Rachaela slept through the days. She woke in the late afternoon, or sunset. The clocks had gone back, but only the messages of the TV had finally alerted her. Then she altered some of the clocks to the correct time. Others remained on summer time, out by the salutory hour.

Elizabeth and Reg, having the code of the door now, came and went as they had always done. Sometimes Elizabeth, with the Hoover on the stairs, woke Rachaela for a moment. But there were not many carpets.

She left Elizabeth notes. She said she had the 'flu. Later, she simply pointed out to Elizabeth that the cake had been wonderful, or that one of Jelka or Jacob or Juliet's toys had gone down into some inaccesible part, could Reg retrieve it? Or she asked for more coffee or wine or cat food.

Althene had left a store of cash, and Rachaela's bank account stayed always full. Rachaela realized she would eventually have to go down to the bank and draw some money for the purpose of paying Elizabeth and Reg. But not yet.

Sometimes Rachaela walked round the garden in the twilight. It was overgrown, although it had no statues. Not really properly Scarabae.

Otherwise Rachaela did not go out.

The cats, always movable beasts, slept with her through the days, using the window to the garden if necessary, climbing down through the tree, going off to Elizabeth afterwards.

Sometimes Juliet sat with Rachaela by night, on the floor of the living room. Juliet drank a saucer of cream or Carnation milk. (Rachaela drank a bottle of wine, glass by glass. Later, through the night, usually, another.) Jacob crept, voyaging through the grass outside.

Jacob and Juliet did not fight any more. Jelka was the most disturbed. She had grown rather wild, flying up the walls of the garden and on to the roof of the house. She yowled at the moon, and battled any other strange cat who approached. Sometimes her father.

Did she miss Anna?

Do I?

Althene has gone to find Anna. But she – he – won't find Anna. Althene will never come back.

Was this Rachaela's paranoia?

Or had she ever been paranoid? Was it not all true – the fears of watchers – they must truly have been there.

And so doubtless she was correct in the matter of Althene.

Rachaela had lost her already, any way. Althene had become a man.

I was alone before. Thirty odd years. I liked it.

She recalled her private, makeshift, careless existence. She had had her own routines. Washing her hair every third day, shaving her pearly legs, going to the launderette when she must, cooking her neat little barren meals, her weekly bottle of wine spread over two or three days.

I am no longer she. The she I was.

Rachaela ate now the meals Elizabeth left, and on the days Elizabeth did not come, Rachaela ate mounds of hot buttered toast, wedges of Brie and Cheddar, tinned puddings running with treacle.

She did not alter physically, herself. Like the un-tampered-with clocks. No ignored imposed hour lessened her. Her skin was clear, her waist slender. No hair grew after all on her legs. Perhaps all the cruel shaving had destroyed it. The hair on her head, unshampooed for five or six days, did not become greasy.

She changed her bed once a week, washed out her lingerie and tights. That was all.

She drank pale pink wine and looked at the TV through rosé-coloured spectacles.

She did not feel unhappy, desperate, angry; not bereft.

She felt . . . unreal.

A ghost, she padded about the house at three in the morning – hour of the wolf, of the shadow. Juliet, sometimes Jacob, might go with her.

She glanced into Anna's room.

Elizabeth had made the bed. Ursula the fox lay on it, wrapped about the white rabbit for comfort.

Sometimes Jelka slept here too, curled into the fox and the rabbit that must hold, for her, the faint perfume of lost love.

Sometimes Rachaela would lie on the floor of the living room with the cushion under her head, and play Prokofiev, Tchaikovsky, Rachmaninov. But her concentration could never cling now to the stairs of the music. Certain gorgeous phrases, golden melodies, filled her for a moment, but then again she slipped away.

When she played the music she found she thought, for some reason, of her mother, of the life before the Scarabae. Dull, often unpleasing, memories.

Then again one night when she had watched a late-night horror movie, at four in the morning, going into the library-bedroom, she had wondered if she would find a black-haired man hanging from a rope. A wave of terror had gone through her. She saw the vengeful shade of Ruth slinking through the trees with a burning torch, to destroy the house and cook Rachaela in it.

But Ruth could not be a shade. Ruth had come back in the flesh.

One night too Rachaela fell asleep over her third bottle of Sauvignon, and was unconscious until nine in the morning.

When she came out of the shower and had dressed, and towelled her hair, she heard Elizabeth come in.

Rachaela went down from a peculiar curiosity, to see what Elizabeth looked like now, and what Elizabeth would do.

Elizabeth jumped slightly.

But she looked otherwise the same, aglow with hair.

'How are you, Mrs Day?'

Rachaela said she was fine. She wandered to the fridge, but Elizabeth was before her. Elizabeth made grilled ham and poached eggs and spread with butter the bread she had baked the night before.

They ate this together at the kitchen table, and the three cats, as if content, ate their portions of egg, then played with catnip mice under the sunlit windows.

'You mustn't take it too hard,' Elizabeth said. 'Reg left me once. But he came back.'

Rachaela said, 'Oh, so you think that's what has happened.'

Elizabeth blushed.

'It's none of my business, but then. I told myself I'd let you know.'

Rachaela thought, *Does she suppose Althene and I were female lovers or does she know too that Althene's male?*

Rachaela said, 'It's nice of you. But I'd say the situation is rather different.'

'Well, wait and see.'

Elizabeth changed Rachaela's bed-linen today.

Rachaela sat before the mirror and made up her face; powder and blusher, eyeshadow, mascara, and lipstick.

'I might go out.'

'It would do you good.' said Elizabeth, piling up the bed pillows around Juliet, who had decided to nest there.

Another cliché. Elizabeth's simple homely TV-soap words had given Rachaela back a sense of proper womanly purpose and human hope.

Rachaela laughed.

On impulse she went down the hill, skirted the town and walked into the station. She bought a ticket to London.

She knew London.

What in hell had she been doing out here?

In the train she sat and thought about the last journey. Anna and Althene.

The Scarabae were in London.

But she would not visit the Scarabae.

She knew what she would do. They had made her rich. There was enough money to escape.

She would look in estate agents' windows. A flat, big enough for herself and her three dependants, Juliet, Jacob and Jelka.

When she got off the train she went into a wine bar with cucumber glass in the windows, and late-lunch, expense-account and half-drunk lovers lingering at the tables.

Rachaela ordered pasta with cheese and mushrooms, and a bottle of Verdicchio.

After this she went into another bar and had two glasses of a dry rough red. Here a man tried to pick her up. What would she have done years ago? Shunned him? Run away, pushed him off? She said, 'How lovely. I charge a hundred pounds. Is that all right?'

'Christ,' he said. He went red as the wine and slunk out, smelling of sudden sweat under Fabergé.

What would she have done if he had agreed? Gone to the Ladies and climbed, still Ruth-like slim after her gorgements of treacle pudding, through the lavatory window?

She walked about the streets. She looked in the estate

154

agents' windows. The flats were startlingly costly, and she could afford them all.

But she was not ready to decide.

Here and there she went into a bar, even a pub, and bought a couple of drinks. No more pick-ups.

The streets were filthy, the buildings coated with dirt and time. Glimpses came of white columns, cranes, girders, high stone ornaments, cold-killed geraniums in baskets. Pigeons picked among the moving feet. She felt a stab of pity, their precarious lives. She turned away along streets of houses.

A sunset began to come, the astonishing vivid tint of tinned apricots, syrupy twilight.

By then she had found a park or heath, she was not sure, and gone up a dark green hill.

Here, against the liquid glass shell of sky, kites were flying. A sort of quiet club had gathered, persons who had ascended from below to watch the end of another day.

Far down, as if on an island, the tallest towers of the city banked, a science fiction scene or modernized set-piece from *Metropolis*. As the sky's brilliance dimmed, pale orange, the lamps of the world started to burn. And soon the wooded hill was ringed in a lariat of lights.

'Anna!' someone cried.

Rachaela turned. Was she afraid or only amazed?

But it was an ordinary child running to its sane, adoring mother.

Rachaela sat on a seat, in the ashes of the day.

She missed the three cats, abruptly, so much that tears stood in her eyes.

She would have to go back now. All that way.

She left the hill and found a pub, and had a double brandy.

Then, in the posh area below the heath, she located a car firm prepared to drive her out to the house on the hill.

Thank God, the driver was silent.

She thought over what she had done. She had done

nothing. Achieved nothing. Only two bursts of feeling, for the pigeons and for the cats.

Two nights later, after dark, somebody knocked on the house door. Jacob bounded to open it, and of course did not.

Rachaela thought, *Some dangerous assailant? A man with an axe?* Or, someone from them, from the Scarabae.

When Rachaela reached the door, Jacob ran off.

She opened it. Unwise. Perhaps.

Outside, a small child, a girl, dressed all in trailing black. She wore a white mask that covered half her face, and her mouth was crayoned, inexpertly, red. She grinned, and in the mouth were yellow fangs bought from some novelty shop.

A vampire.

A little girl vampire, all alone.

'Yes?' Rachaela said, dumbfounded.

'Trick or treat?'

It was Hallowe'en, and the customs of America had come among them all. Even up the vertical hill.

Down beyond the poplars, someone stirred. An adult accompanying the vampiress, in case.

And yet, Rachaela could yank her in. Slam the door. Do murder, worse—

'It had better be a treat then, hadn't it?'

Rachaela, regardless – the adult might still have an axe – left the door wide.

She went into the kitchen and took some of Elizabeth's chocolate biscuits from the jar, poured a glass of red wine, drew two pound coins from the change bowl on the table.

These things she bore back to the patient vampire.

'Mind you don't break your fangs on the biscuits.' She sounded like Elizabeth. 'Have a sip of that, then give it to your daddy.'

The little vampire was happy. Too happy to be polite,

she bolted down the drive and the wine glinted in the hall light.

A hoarse, frozen male voice called up a thank you.

I could have poisoned both of them.

I could have lured them in and drunk their blood.

She closed the door, and the following dusk, found the glass set neatly on the bird-bath, half full. Not a drinker. Not a Scarabae. A mundane, difficult, easy life.

Chapter Eighteen

IN THE DELICATELY CUT-OUT LINE of slate and dove-coloured houses, one house was a dark warm pink. It shone, in the last of the bleak day, down into the canal, like a warm sun.

How misleading.

It was a cold house, for when she had had it internally modernized three decades before, Sofie had not wished for central heating. Electric fires lit her rooms, but other rooms, and the stairs, were glaciers.

Some charm had been left the house, inside. Some of the floors sloped, the ceilings, the stairs themselves were eccentric and tortuous, though carpeted in thick black pile. But the walls were painted red, mauve, there were large modern paintings like broken eggs and slashed arteries – she would never have admitted *that*, or to the use of extreme colour. The house was 'up to date' – she used the English expression.

The young man left the car, and stood on the cobble-stones as the vehicle drove off. Bare trees clawed after the vanished summer. Soon enough it would freeze. There would be skaters on the canals.

Amsterdam smelled of cold, car fumes, some vague whisper of the sea.

When he had gone up the blunt steps, he put down his bag, and rang the bell.

He waited, immobile. Sofie's servant, Grete, would take a while to come. She was old and obstreperous. She gossiped to Sofie alone, and sometimes broke things. Sofie would laugh. She could always buy more.

Then there was audible a kind of heavy immanence, not Grete's, and the door sprang open.

A man was there. He wore jeans, a checkered pullover, and a leather coat. Quite tall, thickly built, muscle losing tone. A mop-head of long-short yellowish hair. The face had features, but that was all, culminating in two small light eyes.

'Hi. Who're you?'

An American.

The visitor said, 'Where is Sofie?'

'Sofie? Uh, Sofie. Here she comes now.'

The other man looked past the bulk in the door, over the black carpeted hallway with its bronze statue of a twisted intestine. Sofie stood on the stair.

She said, 'Johanon. Why have you come back?'

'I will tell you later.'

She was surprised, but she knew who he was. No doubt, no faltering, though she had not seen him like this for a lifetime. More. Her son. Her son who had come to her last in women's clothes, and with women's cosmetics on his face. She had called him Johanon then, also. The name she had given him at the first. He had long ago ceased to tell her it was not a name he used. She had never *never* fallen, stooped into his filth to call him *Althene*.

'Won't you speak in front of Bus, then?'

'No, Mother.'

'You must. Bus is my companion.'

Johanon looked at Bus. Bus found some problem in meeting the cold black eyes, but he was armed, Bus, quite well. Sofie had just put the weapon in his hands.

'Oh, so *you're* the faggot, huh?'

'Get out of my way.'

Bus involuntarily stepped back. Then he swaggered.

159

'Sure, baby, sure. Don't want ya to chip a nail.'

Sofie, composed, retained her height.

She was a small woman, with the body of a voluptuous dancer, large breasted, with dainty bony hands, a slim flexible throat. She appeared to be thirty, thirty-one. Her shoulder-length hair was expertly bleached and streaked. Her eyes, a pale green-blue, were rounded. An owl with a snake's neck. She wore a plain modern navy dress and a piece of contemporary jewellery, a sort of collection of talons in silver, on her wrist.

'Why is he still here?' Johanon said, in Dutch.

She said, 'Please talk English, Johanon. Bus doesn't speak Dutch.'

'Does he speak English then?'

Sofie made a face. Her round eyes became more round.

'Bus is my friend,' she said in English.

'They wanted you,' said Johanon, in English, 'to choose another friend.'

'Hey, hey,' said Bus.

Sofie said, 'Come into the salon.'

They went up, Sofie, Johanon, Bus. Bus whistled tune-lessly and made little gestures, as if checking himself from pinching Johanon's bottom.

The salon was on the first floor, a big room with two scarlet walls, one peach, and one black. An 'up-to-date' chandelier hung down, owl-taloned like the bracelet.

Bus threw himself on to a black leather couch with diamond-shaped neon-yellow cushions.

The electric fire was burning, a strange shape with a black-marble surround. There were spotlights picking out sculptures, a single hot-house lily in a vase like a drain.

'Sit down,' Sofie said. She sat beside Bus, and reached out and took his hand. He allowed this, chuckling.

Then Sofie screamed. She screamed for Grete.

'Jesus, for a little gal, you've sure got a big voice.'

Johanon sat in a stainless-steel chair.

The room was not 'up to date'. It was by now historical.

'Well, Johanon, what do you want?'

'To speak to you alone, Mother.'

'I've said you can't. I want Bus here.'

'This isn't about the family. At least, it has nothing to do with your relationship with this man.'

'Hey, hey,' said Bus.

Sofie said, 'They've tried to poison me with lies. They must leave me alone.'

'This family,' said Bus. 'It's these old – uh – *vampires*, huh?' He smiled. His teeth were good strong caps.

Johanon said nothing.

Grete came in. She glared at Johanon. Did *she* recognize him? Perhaps not.

'*Ja*,' said Grete.

'Bring us tea.'

'You got a beer?' asked Bus.

'And some cold beer for Bus.'

'*Ja*,' said Grete.

She peered at Johanon, and then her brows went up. She had fathomed it. If Sofie was an owl, Grete was a fat vulture. She turned and plodded out.

'No, but tell me, Pussy,' said Bus to Johanon, 'about these Scarabae.' He pronounced it wrongly, Scara*bye*.

Johanon sat still. He looked at Bus, but Bus would not be caught. His slimy eyes slid off.

'*I've* told you the truth of it,' Sofie said, 'they're hundreds of years old. They live on blood and unkindness. I have only half their corrupt genes. But I'm older than I look.'

'You look just great, honey.'

'Oh, but that's a family trait. I've never assaulted you, Bus, have I?'

'Wouldn't let ya, baby.'

Sofie said insistently, 'I've never *tried*, Bus.'

Johanon said, 'Yes, Mother. I know you've told him all these interesting tales of the family. I know too about the ring you gave him which he pawned on the Amstelstraat. And how the family got it back. I know too he spreads your stories all over the junk areas of the city, where he goes for the porn and the girls, and in the cafés where he smokes dope with other Americans. You met by night. That is excusable, perhaps. The rest, not. But we've had this conversation before.'

'I oughta tell you, ass-hole—' said Bus.

'You ought to tell me you are leaving.'

Bus got up. He flexed his softening body.

He came and stood over Johanon.

'Wanta try me, sweet-cakes?'

Sofie said, 'Bus, stay here with me.'

'Sure, sure. I guess this feller ain't gonna do nothing but yap.'

Bus swung off around the room. He paused by a steel cabinet. Inside were three priceless matted convolutions.

Johanon said in Dutch, 'Sofie, I'm here to talk about my father.'

Sofie's face became a colourless plate. Even her eyes seemed to lose their dye. She brought up her hands and held her neck. She cried out, 'Bus – Bus – don't leave me.'

And Bus looked round again, and at Johanon.

'Hey, you just wanta make trouble. Well I have an idea.' Bus smiled, 'Why don't you go blow out your ass.'

'Get rid of him,' Johanon said in Dutch.

Sofie got up, and ran out of the room. Her soft satin shoes made no sound on the carpet, she was only gone.

Bus shrugged.

He sidled back across the room, sat down on the leather sofa.

'Kind of hysterical, your mom. That's why she likes me. Needs me. Let's keep this friendly. She looks good for her age. What is she, forty-six? Great surgery. We get on fine.'

Johanon stood up.

Bus licked his lips and rose also.

'Hey.'

162

'Do let's keep it friendly,' said Johanon, 'since she would prefer it. There is the door.'

Bus leaned forward. He said very low, 'Why don't ya just go up and do *your* famous thing, like she told me. Put your dress on. Go on. I'd like to see ya. I bet you look real good as a dame. Let your hair down. A bit of lip rouge and mascara – fish-nets—'

Johanon's left hand took Bus back-handed across the centre of the face. Bus rolled and blood burst from his nose like thick raspberry juice.

'Uh Jesus – uh Christ—'

'Now get out. Keep away three days. I'll be gone by then. What the two of you do after that is your affair.'

'Uh, my loving nose – you broke it—' Bus kneeled sobbing on the black carpet, into which the raspberry blood plopped invisibly.

Grete entered. She looked at Bus, then came around him and plumped the tray of silver octagonal tea service and iced beer, rattling, on a table.

Bus said, 'I want a fucking doctor.'

Grete grinned. She stayed still. '*Ja*.'

Johanon said, 'She will dislike it if I kill you, American. But I will kill you. Now I know her carpet won't show the blood.'

Bus looked up around his running doughnut of a nose. He was scared.

Grete cackled. '*Ja*,' she said.

Bus got up. He stumbled out. Unlike Sofie, they heard his crashing rumbling descent, and then the thud of the door, which shook through the old standing wood of the house frame.

He left the tray of tea and beer, and walked up through the cold pink house, up to the curled stem of corridor with her bedroom in it.

At the door, Johanon said her name.

'No,' she said, behind it.

'Then I'll wait in your salon.'

'Go away. You frightened *him* away. I want my friend, my Bus.'

'He isn't yours, Mother. He belongs to several. He gives them your money and the jewels you had no right to part with.'

'They were mine!'

'To keep. To give among the Scarabae.'

'Go to hell, you foul monster. You – *thing*—'

'Sofie, I'd go away gladly. But there are questions I must ask.'

'No, no.'

He descended the house again, and drank the tea in the salon. Grete stood in the corner, under the lily in the drain, like a dummy.

'Will you get the attic room ready. The room she gives me.'

'*Ja.*'

Grete did not move, and then she came across, and lifted up one of the two cans of beer that had been meant for Bus. Ice had turned to water. She raised the can and drank it down.

She clumped out.

There had not been so much Sofie could, or could see how to, do to the attic. The ceiling sloped to windows that gazed across the darkening canal. (Lamps, fireflies in the water, flickering on the slope above his head.)

Above Johanon's head.

The room was white, and freezing. The bed had not been seen to. A mattress, one pillow without a case.

She had lost interest in this high place, and so she had put her son here.

He lay on the bed, in the bloom of the dark, and watched water-lamp-light ripple above.

His body had not entirely recovered from the blow that had burst his appendix and perforated a small part of his colon. It would do so. But still, he was not as strong as he would come to be.

He lay and looked up.

It was worse than that.

Althene – she – was his armour, his soul externalized, and put upon him like an iron flower.

That poor lily – Althene would have plucked it out, set it in some frosted green bottle. But he was not Althene, not now.

Sofie would grow calm.

She had been very savage. Usually after her savagery, she became soft, amenable sometimes.

Poor bloody bitch.

Tired, he closed his eyes and slept a little.

At about nine, Sofie scratched on the door.

'Johanon – will you come down and eat with me? No, not Grete's cooking. I've sent out. An Italian meal.'

He told her he would, and went into the bathroom that led from the attic bedchamber. There were no towels, no soap. He used what he had brought with him, brushed his teeth.

He let down his black hair, not looking, and bound it back again, off his face.

Always, in some form, with a parent the child becomes again a child, be he thirty or three-hundred years of age.

'Courage,' he said. One of Althene's stances blossomed, and he put it aside. He would not think of her, or of Rachaela, or of Anna, at any depth. There was not the time.

Sofie was in the dining room.

It was a small area, windowless. It had been a great closet. Now it was done in magenta with a gargoyle of a glass table resting on a hunched column of brass.

The meal though was simple but aromatic; fresh rolls, spaghetti and sauces with basil and walnuts, spinach pancakes, amber cheeses, and a large decanter of red wine uncomfortably made like a pair of buttocks. Once in the tubular glasses this mattered less. It was a good wine, very drinkable.

Sofie wore an evening dress. She would. But she looked beautiful, perhaps, her hair brushed up, and the white gown off her shoulders, showing a few inches of bosom, which Althene, naturally, could never do.

But Sofie was not sparring with him.

No, she had attained her apologetic, rationally minded stage.

She toasted him in Latin, an old wish: 'May a goddess sit at your side.'

He bowed. He said in Dutch, 'Wear your garland, fair lady, roses and the vine.'

They ate in silence, save when she said how impossible Grete's culinary efforts were, and spoke of a terrible day when Grete had burnt a piece of pork, and the house had filled with the stench, and even on the canal those in boats had looked up. He laughed.

When they had reached the cheeses and some fresh figs, she said, 'Please try to understand about the American.'

'I'll attempt to.'

'Yes, he's deceived me. But – I'm lonely. And the family—'

'You hate them. Or you distrust them.'

It was Rachaela. Half Scarabae, Sofie was this too. She had spent her extended life running to them and rushing away.

'Well, they don't always treat me well. This business. I was angry with you when you were here last. Bringing you to me, my own son, to make me change my ways. But I'll get rid of him. Yes. I will.'

Then she looked at him through the ruby lorgnette of the wine, coquettishly. 'But I admire you now. You're a man, now. Has she done this, your lover?'

'No, Mother. Something else.'

'Well, it's good, Johanon. *Good.*'

He did not say anything, and she did not press.

She only said again, after a while, 'Bus bores me. I shall get rid of him.'

After the meal, Grete came in, her fat-ringed neck thrust forward, and cleared it all, and set down Jenever, brandy, tea, and little sweets in silver paper.

When she was gone, he said, 'I don't want to hurt you.'

'Oh, don't you?' It was said without challenge, only wonderingly.

'Sofie, I never would.'

'No. I'm glad. Sometimes I've been afraid.'

'Sofie, I need your help now. I must – I have to ask you to speak of him.'

'Of whom?' she asked, innocent, a little girl.

The little girl who could make him back into a little boy, nine years old, shivering with anguish, struck by rods – no, he must not think of this.

Times change, as well as fly.

'Sofie, I mean Cajanus. The man you told me fathered me.'

She dropped her eyes and gripped her hands about her square glass of brandy.

'Please. No, no.'

'My daughter was stolen. Anna. I told you about my daughter. And, from what I've learned – I believe now – *he* took her. But I know nothing of him. Where he is – some stories. We search for him and only high dark walls are there, I can't find him. And I want him, Mother. *Give* him to me.'

She darted up a glance with a sparkle of her turquoise eyes.

She said, 'You'd make me do it.'

'I have to make you do it.'

'Why?'

'A clue, Mother. A way through the labyrinth.'

'But – it was – hundreds – so many years ago—'

He reached across and took her small thirty-year-old hand.

'It's all I have. Don't deny me.'

'I can't.'

'Sofie, you are Scarabae.'

'No. I reject them.'

'You can't, Sofie.' He said softly, 'Your beauty is Scarabae. Your youth. *Tell* me.'

She said, 'Very well. But first I must go out for a moment. I promise, I'll come back.'

It was her immemorial way of excusing herself for some bodily function.

He nodded, and let her go.

He wondered if she would leap into her bedroom and lock the door. Only her bedroom had such a lock.

Somehow he did have faith she would come back. If only because he would not leave her alone until she had answered him. It was harsh. But it was needful. They were all on the rack.

He took one of the little sweets and opened the silver petals. Dark chocolate with a centre of kirsch and almonds. He put it down. There was nothing sweet in what must be done now.

She came back, Sofie, five minutes later. She bore in her hand two long red goblets of French *fin de siècle* design, and a little red crystal flask.

'Look, you'll like this better. It's Armagnac, but I know you detest my glasses.'

She put the goblets and the flask down. She said, 'I had to hide these from Bus. He's a – what does he say? – a *cretin*, he knows nothing. But he asks people. Do you know a Turk almost bought the jasper seal-ring – before the family sent their agents to recover it? The Turk was very shocked. He had me delivered one hundred orchids. They died in a day. The house was too cold—'

She pushed a glass towards Johanon, and filled it, and filled her own. She lifted the red glass and sipped. She said, 'Rather bitter. But then, that's appropriate.'

He drew his own glass near but did not drink.

He waited.

'Do you remember him?' she said. 'Cajanus?'

'Yes. It was a memorable day.'

She lowered her eyes again. 'Don't blame me.'

'No. Go on.'

'He had come to me, those years before, out of darkness. I was alone. And in the night, a man rode to the door. He had obtained their authority – *Scarabae*. Or he'd gained it.'

'I understand.'

'He dined with me. Oh, not like this. Do you recall . . . of course you do. The old table made from an oak tree – and he ate rabbits. But I ate them too. We drank Rhenish wine. He was—' She looked about as if, now, only her vision tried to abscond and failed. She said, 'He was handsome.'

Sofie did not drink. She laid her hands on the table, loose, and empty.

'He wooed me. He said he was married to a woman who couldn't bear him sons. He said he would divorce her. He was so gentle. His voice. There was – a kind of hesitation in it, so musical, as if he made the words into velvet before he let them fall.'

'He had black hair,' said Johanon, 'and blue eyes.'

'Yes. He seemed tall. But now – Bus would be taller. You also.'

'Perhaps he's grown. We do grow.'

She shook her head. She said, 'Let me turn away from you. I can't say this to your face.'

Then she turned. She turned her head.

She said, 'He seduced me. With words and poetry, and by caressive touches. I longed for him. And one night he came to my chamber.'

Johanon waited.

Sofie said, 'He told me he was old. One of the oldest of us. He said I mustn't call him Cajanus, but Cain. I laughed. Was his name like the name in the Bible. *He* laughed then. He didn't answer me. Then he made love to me.'

Sofie rose. She walked across to the magenta wall and stood facing it.

'He was loving, until the candle burned down. And then in the dark, in the dark, the dark—'

Johanon waited.

Sofie his mother said, 'He tossed me on my face and lay on me. I couldn't move. He took me like a tiger. A manic love. He rent me, bruised me – inside – my back – scored down to the bone. I screamed and he tore out my hair and stuffed my mouth with it. He drank my blood. He was like the Devil, icy cold. Or scalding hot. I don't know when he went away. I thought I had died of it. They found me. The Scarabae took care of me. Yes, Scarabae. I'm strong, as they are. I lived. I had the scars on my back for one hundred and thirty-three years. All gone now. But they're there. On my spirit. That is what he did. Cajanus. *Cain.*'

Johanon waited. He said, 'Where did he go to?'

'I don't know. I know nothing.'

'Didn't he speak to you of any place?'

Sofie bellowed at the wall, '*Don't you care what he did to me?*'

'Yes. I care. Let me find him.'

'He told me nothing,' she said. 'Only of his wife, that he would leave for me. He went away. Drink,' she said, 'drink to my destruction. *Drink.*'

Johanon took up the goblet of Armagnac and swallowed it. It was bitter, as she had said.

'And then,' she said, 'I was with child. I brought you out. Four days I was at the work. *Four days, four nights.*'

'I know, Sofie, I know.'

'You *man*. You ape a woman. What do you know of women? You *man*.'

'Sofie, I didn't mean to distress you.'

'No, nor when you split my womb. His bastard. Blood and muck from his rotted, scalding seed.'

She whirled back. Her face was mad again. Now she did

not shout: she said, 'Go to bed. Grete's prepared the room. Take the Armagnac.'

'No, thank you.'

And then she picked up the red crystal flask and flung it at the wall.

Like blood on black, it did not mark, it was only wet, like tears.

When he reached the attic, it seemed to him he must speak to her again, and she would be calmer, and maybe recollect – but no, she would not. All she had she gave him.

How she must have longed to thrust this bouquet of thorns into his hands. (Why hold back?)

Johanon felt exhausted, ears whining, nauseous, deathly. The white attic that had no true light or heat wheeled slowly, and he half fell down on the sparse, now-sheeted bed.

The ceiling pulsed with the lights below, and now they were like blood. A white bloodied wheel . . .

Yes, he thought. His mother, of course, had put something in his glass. Had successfully murdered him at last.

And from the pit of his heart it came, a shameful sinking ease, that he could do no more.

Chapter Nineteen

SET'S BREATH DIED IN THE night.
So much for the fifty day wind.

The water was quite low, and as they pushed upstream, the suburbs of the city, under a briary of TV aerials, hid the great tombs that lay along the desert of the east bank.

Red brickyards followed, with sandal boats at their quays, palms like green tarantulas, acacias. Sometimes women had come to the water in the cool morning. They filled aluminium pots and plastic buckets from the grey-brown fluid of the Nile.

It was easy to believe this sluggish stained tinfoil water had once been turned to blood.

But an eruption had done that, not the fury of God.

Lebas, an atheist, stood complacently on the afternoon deck. He watched the silt-built banks drift by, the acacias, the women. Once a noisy motorbike outpaced them. They were going slowly. The Arabs who manned the boat were of course lazy scoundrels, dirty, shiftless, villainous. And their normal ill-feeling towards a Westerner had been augmented by the war. The city had been notable for a dearth of tourists. But that was a blessing. Paul-Luc loathed also the Americans – uncouth, the English – constipated and soul-less, the Germans – beasts.

Berenice he had put in the cabin and instructed to remain

there. Arabs were not to be trusted around a child, and besides she tended to infernal sore throats, and the day was cold. She had her English and literature lessons to do and, slower even than the boat, that would occupy her until dinner time.

Lunch had been execrable. Rice and some slop. At least the boat kept going. They were refusing to travel by night, but he would insist. They said it was illegal.

He thought about the map. He knew now exactly where they must dock, and where he must ride out across the desert. His agent had promised the donkeys would be waiting at the village, but you could not be sure, sure of nothing in this country.

He glanced at the captain in the wheel-house.

This benighted race the descendants of Ancient Egypt.

Then, for a second, he recalled the blonde woman in the hotel restaurant. She had left before he did. Her legs were as alluring as he had predicted, in sleek blonde stockings and high-heeled sandals.

Then he forgot her, thinking of the map again. Of what the map showed.

There had been a slight earth tremor. Finding some fault, it had dislodged hill rock and quantities of sand. This had happened before, apparently, at the turn of the century, but then the natives, the very peasants, had gone out, it seemed, and covered up the spot. This time, no one had, as yet, done so. Modern life overwhelmed honour, or fear. For, as with all these graves of the old world, an air of the superstitious and the uncanny hung about the burial place.

It was a rock tomb, out in the low hills, beyond the village with the name that meant Dove. Unusual, in any case, to find this type of tomb in just this area.

It could be a hoax. Paul-Luc Lebas had enemies . . .

But he could not risk losing such a chance, if it were genuine. If it were – it would make his name. Not since that gaudy, over-publicized tomb of the boy-king,

Tutankhamun – oh, he could remember the exhibition in Paris in the '60s. He had eschewed it.

No. Here was something wholly original. Unique. Mysterious.

He turned, and saw Berenice had come up on deck.

'Go back,' he shouted. 'There's nothing to see, the water's too low.'

She whined, 'Papa, the cabin's stuffy.'

'Never mind. Go in.'

The sunset was like fire and the Nile changed to blood. The winter-parched flower they called the Nile Rose turned purple, black.

More slop for dinner. Paul-Luc swallowed a couple of penicillin tablets.

The stars came through like daggers, so bright. These stars, if not quite the same, had blazed above the land of Lower Egypt. And now the god journeyed through the hell beneath the earth in his boat, the night-Nile of death, from which Khepri would raise him with the dawn—

Moved, Paul-Luc wrote two or three lines of poetry in his notebook.

The boat had been persuaded to go on, illegally or not.

It sailed past villages like dreams of the ancient time, russet window cracks and smoke lifting, but then another village would appear, neon lit, with a water tower and the TV aerials bristling. Pedlars from night markets ran to the bank, offering the boat unripe bananas, tiny oranges. A single woman rose like a ghost, an antique jar upon her head. The lights of the boat picked out her inky garment, then she vanished among the palms.

If he went to sleep probably the boat would moor. But he was tired now, and tomorrow was another early start.

Berenice was sleeping on her bunk, rolled into four blankets like a worm. She snored a little, congested. He hoped this would not disturb him.

*   *   *

Muezzins woke him, singing from their sky-scanning towers, at the town where the boat had tied up.

Lebas cursed them.

The dark was barely opening.

But day came in a wash, and Khepri lifted the sun disc into the air.

Berenice murmured in her sleep.

'What? What are you saying?'

She whispered, in French, 'Out of dark he arises, conqueror of the night.'

But still he did not catch the phrase.

He said, 'Clear your throat and speak properly.'

She said, 'I don't know, Papa. I – forget.'

Outside, on the morning river, a great two-masted sandal passed, laid with white limestone blocks from the quarries farther south.

Paul-Luc argued with his captain. He did not want to spend time at the town where, any way, they should not have tied up. The river police, the captain explained, had told them that they must, or be fined.

Paul-Luc swore.

They went on, up-river.

He had once visited the vast pyramid above the city, but not gone very close. He had taken the child. As night came, there, the neoned metropolis glared emerald green, yellow and white, creating a surreal sky, and the floodlit mound inflated to a giant triangle of broken biscuit.

Paul-Luc had experienced contempt. He would not enter such a spectacle. His times of doing that were done.

When they reached the village named Dove, the day was going. Not red that night, but fulvous. Wild duck flew across the vast orb of the sun. There were ten-feet-tall reeds around a stubborn little island in the channel. Not papyrus, some other more common thing.

The village itself was a dustbin of mud-brick hovels, with patches of fields, sugar cane, maize, beans, and clover.

175

Tortured-looking fig trees huddled together. There was no water tower. And yet street lighting had come here, up on wires, and from some of the desperate roofs the plague of aerials poked forth.

They slept on the boat, woken now and then by the laughter of their sailors playing cards and smoking hookahs with the villagers.

When the sun came, he told Berenice she must stay below.

'But, Papa, you said—'

'I know what I said. We're late. It will be a nasty ride. If I find this place, once we begin, I'll come back for you.'

'Will you?'

He glanced at her. The horrible food, this morning a sort of porridge affair, seemed to suit her. Her face was pale but fresh, and her gaze had widened. So he glimpsed, unknowing, how her odd eyes would be effective in adult life, bright grey and starred with golden freckles, alluring eyes of differing shape, that each held separate thoughts.

Did she doubt him? If he said he would do something, it should be done.

'Berenice, don't be stupid. Attend to your lessons. Stay in the cabin. I'll be back before sunset.'

Berenice wilted. 'Yes, Papa.'

He got off the boat and walked along a street. Women emerged from hovels with their tin jars. They came out like rats.

Near the street's end an Arab stood in white galabia and turban.

'Monsieur Lebas? I hope you have had a good journey.' The man spoke in excellent French.

'Foul. What a trial. Are the donkeys ready, and the men?'

'The men will meet us at the site. And the donkeys are ready.'

As he uttered, as if conjured, a donkey moved across the end of the street between two leaning ochre houses. On its back was tied a large colour television weighted by a piece of pumice.

Lebas stared.

And then, as if to try him further, a woman in blue veils followed the donkey, on her head what seemed to be a Swedish microwave oven.

'What—?'

'It's of no importance, monsieur. Wealth comes and goes in these places.'

Their two animals were under a palm, held ready by a small, mostly naked boy.

Paul-Luc stared out across the clutter of hovels, the dismal fields with their shallow irrigation ditches, to the powder brown stretch of the desert. The hills rose on its flank, looking too near, lions' backs, under the warmthless blue sky.

As they rode, they did not speak. The Arab had attempted a little polite conversation, but desisted. Lebas was the master, and the pay-master.

The donkey, evidently, had fleas.

They kept the rounded hills over to their left, and the pointed hill to their right.

The sun was hard, like glass.

Lebas drank from his Evian bottle.

It took two hours (sweat, contrary dryness, dry winds), and then they were there.

A solitary palm stood like a burnt column fringed with fronds, and beside it the four men he had hired sat smoking and drinking coffee, under an awning.

They got up as he approached, and salaamed. At least, then, they knew their place, or made believe to. A small heap of tools lay on plastic sacks.

'Ask them if they were questioned.'

'They all speak French, monsieur.'

One of the four, a man with three very white front teeth, spoke up. 'No one noticed us, monsieur. We've been coming out for a week or so. They think,' he grinned more widely, 'we know a place with boys, and pretend to go into the desert.'

The other men laughed.

Paul-Luc, disgusted, made no comment.

'Well then,' he said.

'I will show monsieur,' said the three-toothed man. 'We have cleared a little sand.'

Feeling oddly reluctant, Paul-Luc swung off the donkey; he was stiff and at pains not to display it.

Three-teeth oozed over the ground towards the slope of the nearest hill, now only about twenty-five feet away.

Lebas went after.

The man slipped round the mass of rock, which had in it veins of white and pink, ambled up almost on all fours, disappeared around the face, and called, winningly, '*Here*, monsieur.'

Lebas touched the pistol in his jacket.

But that was nonsense. The money could only come to them from the city at his order.

He climbed, unwieldy, round the rock.

Ah God – that nonexistent God – *it was there*.

The sand mounted the hill like a sheath – foolishly he was reminded of his daughter in her furl of blankets – but there, above, the cut oblong of red door stood from the hill.

It was a ruddy granite, smooth as a pearl—

Here and there, small vortices, some damage from the quakes, the last or the most recent – very little.

Above the sand, on the door, the incised shoulders of a man, who had the head of a scarab beetle – Khepri. Just as the map had told him.

'You! Go back and fetch the men. They must brush off all this sand.'

Three-teeth slid down the hill as if he had skates on his backside, and was gone.

Deftly, softly, unwisely, Paul-Luc reached up and fanned at the powders of the desert.

The flat carven breast of an Egyptian man-god appeared.

Then, Lebas looked up.

There were scarabs, the sign of resurrection, around the top of the door. They were bizarre. Beetles with wings and also with human legs and arms. He studied the hieroglyphs. Twenty-first Dynasty, probably, they were the usual ones. *None must enter here. Beware.* Let the vile Arabs beware. The warning might mean that poison had been incorporated in the mortar at the joins of the door. As the door was forced, bane showered out. He had told his workers, via the agent, they must acquire surgical masks and gloves, which might protect them.

He lost interest in that. For this – what was this? The picture writing ran clear—

A papyrus leaf, a kite, the cord-measure for one hundred, a symbol that had to do with the Underworld . . .

He put it together, his lips working.

The phonetic sound *Khau.* The sound that could mean shame, or a vessel from the altar, or the crown of a king – but this . . . was *Darkness.*

Khau-Khepra.

The darkness, then, of the scarab god. He that raised the sun. (And, punned from other words, something that must be filled.)

From the upright lintel of the door, the writing proceeded. Lebas took time over it. He took care.

It read: *I am the one that came out of the desert. I am the blue-eyed—*

The writing stopped, in a masonry graze that had erased it.

Blue-eyed? No. There were barbarians, of course, but the Egyptians did not generate blue eyes. Not until Alexander's Greeks had come among them. Some earlier infiltrator then. Risen high enough to gain this tomb.

Lebas thought of Joseph, the Hebrew who had brought his people into Egypt, a time of prosperity and then despair, enslaved, until the ten plagues freed them (wealth comes and goes)—

But Joseph would not be here, would not be termed *Darkness*.

Paul-Luc looked up over the actual door, and in the scored rock above, he saw, faintly, the hieroglyphs that spelled *Ukha na*. There was a gap between them.

Yet, something made him step away.

He turned, and the Arab workers had grouped obediently down the slope.

'Clear the sand.'

'Monsieur,' said the one who had met him in the street of Dove, 'may we first finish with our coffee?'

'No you may not. Come up now, and brush away the sand.'

Three-teeth said, 'It's the time for prayer. We may not labour yet.'

Lebas felt a gouging of rage. He cursed them in their own language, terrible curses that he saw offended. He finished, 'Do as I say.'

For this tomb was a find indeed. He would not be cheated.

And then, the camel glided around the rock, like a honey-coloured prehistoric sheep, and poised itself below, dripping tassels. On its back sat a beautiful woman with blonde hair. She wore white trousers and shirt, and a straw hat with a long, floating white-green scarf.

She called to Paul-Luc.

'Monsieur Lebas. Forgive this intrusion.'

She spoke the French of France.

He gaped at her.

She said, 'Or, dear monsieur, simply graciously forgive *me*.'

Chapter Twenty

How HAD SHE COME HERE? The train from the city, to some town up ahead, then riding back? Or all the way, somehow so fleet, on the camel? For whom was she working? With whom was she in league? His foes? Some museum?

Fifty-seven years old, he felt childish.

He did not like it.

He said, coldly, 'Explain yourself.'

'I will, Monsieur Lebas. A moment.'

She spoke to the camel in Arabic and it kneeled, its proud sheep-rabbit's face a study in enviable distance. The woman came gracefully off its back.

The Arabs clustered round and she smiled, and put some money into the hands of the man in the white galabia. In their own tongue, again, she requested that they lift the hamper off the animal. They did so. Then, they melted away, and beyond the rock, as they went, he heard their male laughter.

'I insist—' he said.

'Oh,' she said, 'I'm very embarrassed.' She lowered her large fine eyes. 'But I must confess.'

'Confess what? How did you know of this place?'

'I didn't, monsieur. I had – someone discover where you were going. A little bribery. I followed you. You know, in this land, they can learn anything, and will sell – anything.'

'Are you French?' he rapped.

'I wouldn't presume to claim so much.' (His shoulders went back. He accepted the accolade, despite himself.) 'Perhaps a little.'

'Then why this interest in me, and in my whereabouts?'

She looked at him. And then, prettily, she blushed. Or seemed to. She said, 'You make me very shy, monsieur. But I must be truthful. You see through me. You give no quarter.'

'Well?'

'I saw you at the hotel. And then – you were gone. I set myself to discover you. Have I been very terrible?'

'You've been bloodily impertinent. Do you know what *this* is?' He waved his arm at the door behind him.

She looked, considered, and said quietly, 'I believe so.'

'Then you understand a need for secrecy.'

She said, softly, but he heard her, 'Well, you must silence me. The best way to stop a mouth . . . a kiss.'

Paul-Luc glared at her, and yet, he was aroused. She had used an ambiguous phrase. The kiss might mean more . . . than a kiss.

'This is absurd,' he said.

'Then let me placate you. I promise, I won't betray this place. You alone found it. I'm an admirer of yours, Monsieur Lebas. I always read your columns, on *Antigone*, on *Electra*, *The Bacchae*, Petronius. Long before I saw you, I knew about you. And then—' She smiled again. 'And then, dare I say? The lightning struck.'

He was lost for words. But no longer childish.

She was quite, quite spectacular. About thirty-five. Slim, nearly boyish. Exactly of a type he liked – Marthe had been of this sort. But Marthe had never read his writings. The sun lit this one's hair to angelic floss.

'I shall call you Medée,' he said, 'a cunning witch.'

She laughed. She indicated the hamper.

'I've brought you a feast. If you'll be my Jason.'

'I'm far too old for that.'

'You?' Her eyes were like warm dark flowers. 'Ah, monsieur.'

Then she opened the lid of the hamper, and he saw the golden unleavened bread, one of the few foods of Egypt he cared for, and Russian caviare on ice, and coppery duck breasts wrapped about mahogany dates. Two bottles of light red claret rested in coolers. She said, 'You don't believe in the snobbery of wine, I know. You'll find these tastes complementary.'

'I hate the stupidity of wine drinkers,' he said. 'I seldom drink.'

'But now, with me?'

He laughed. 'Who can resist Medée? But what's your name?'

'*Call* me Medée,' she said. 'Until you know me. Names are magic.'

'But you know mine.'

'You're special to me.'

He said, 'You expend too much flattery upon me, madame.'

'So. I'll say no more. All that's needful is said.'

She sat down, careless, on the sand, and even through the white trousers he saw the lines of her slim, firm thighs and calves. Her hands were small, narrow, lightly tanned. The hands of a French woman of the south. She had very white teeth, and today no liptstick, so the tawny plum of her mouth was revealed. *A kiss.*

He sat beside her, and she deferred at once to him, spreading a white napkin, offering him the wine to open, as she polished, with another white cloth, his glass.

The ice was intriguing. Where had she got it? From Dove . . .? Well, if TV had come there, why not refrigeration? Why not caviare and claret.

Women had sometimes pursued him in the past. Never so boldly or with such finesse. He had to admit he enjoyed it. And, it had been almost a year, cumbered with Berenice, since he had allowed himself a dalliance. This woman was in love with him. He could secure her, his Medée. (And why not Medée? The ancient Greeks had been a golden race, unlike the oily black-haired wretches who had kidnapped their islands.) She would be loyal. She could help him. Perhaps that impossible rarity, like a unicorn, an intelligent woman.

They ate. He was hungry, but she was spare with her meal, fastidiously toying with her fork amid the food, assuming little bites, liking them, not captivated. More enamoured of him. Perhaps, despite her sophistication, in awe of him, and a touch nervous.

He did not mind this. Nor did she.

He imagined her, sitting at his feet, in some cool room, her small ringless hand upon his shoe.

He tried the wine. It was excellent. Light yet mature, an exact accessory to the fish-eggs, and the richness of the duck.

He said, 'I've waited some months to be sure of this tomb.'

'I know,' she murmured. 'I've found out.'

'Inquisitive little creature. But what do you know of it?'

'I have heard of this burial place. It's rumoured.'

'Perhaps you know more than I do.'

She laughed at the idea. She refilled his glass but not her own. He was pleased to note she drank, too, abstemiously. Not like Marthe with her passion for Cognac in chambers cloudy with cigarette smoke—

'I know a little. Who they say it is. The body in the tomb.'

Down the slope, the camel stood peaceably, as if sleeping.

Paul-Luc, expanded by wine, relaxed, quickened a fraction. It was true, she might, with her woman's curiosity, have stumbled across facts, or symbols of facts, he had been denied.

'Well, tell me, blonde Medée.'

'A sorcerer perhaps. Named Khau. Darkness. A man with blue eyes, feared greatly, his corpse brought away from Men-Nefer, the White City, and buried here. Maybe a second burial. Prestigious, performed from terror.'

'And this is a novel by that charlatan Rider Haggard. That's what it sounds like now.'

'Oh, do you consider Monsieur Haggard a charlatan?'

He said dismissively, 'If you had studied where I have, so would you.'

And she, charmingly, 'Ah, but for a woman, monsieur, a writer of great allure.'

The wine had gone to his head. Lebas did not wonder if a hint of irony had crept into her tone. He was fascinated by her mouth, more than what it said.

Beyond the rock, silence. The bloody debased Arabs had slunk far away. Would it be conceivable he might even, in a little while, possess her here?

His own readiness startled him, but he did not mind it.

He said, 'And this Khau, this sorcerer, what do you know about him?'

'Something,' she said.

'Then tell me.'

'He was a king, but they expunged all trace of him from the temples and the walls of Memphis. In revulsion his body was flung first into a pit for crocodiles to devour. But later the bones were brought here. Even dead, he held them, even nameless, with no chance of immortality. *Neshenti* – Fury of Set. That's written too, on the door of his tomb. Or so they say.'

'The great mysterious *They*,' said Lebas. Mellow, he leaned on the slope, where the sand packed against the foot of the grave of Khau-Khepra, the blue-eyed. Something stuck into his back, he did not care.

'Oh, it's imbecilic, of course,' she said. She filled his glass. 'Shall I tell you the rest?'

He said, smiling, 'My Scheherazade, not my Medée.'

'He, the Lord Khau, was the instrument of God. As were his people. The Tale of the Lost Tribe of Israel . . . In the story they are lost before the Exodus. Lost, and called back, to assist the prince-prophet Moses, the boy left in the reeds for the priests of the sun.'

Paul-Luc corrected her, 'Pharoah's daughter.'

'No, there the story is mislaid. It was a custom at Memphis – Men-Nefer – to put out the unwanted children of the peasants in baskets of mud, among the papyrus, for the priests to choose from. Some children were taken into the temples. Some left in the river. The mud cradles melted away and the Nile sucked them down. But Moses was chosen. Have you never heard, monsieur, how some of the old texts call certain of the temples "Son of Pharoah" and "Pharoah's Daughter"?'

He nodded. Perhaps he had. He was sleepy yet sweet with desire. The hard knob of rock was nearly comfortable in his back. In a while he would draw her close. But let her go on with her game. Her voice was musical. The sun felt warm now, and old, like the ancient disc, the Aten, giver of health and joy.

'Pharoah resisted the plea of Moses, as you know, to let go his slaves, the Hebrews. And so ten plagues descended on the city.'

'The Nile to blood,' he said. 'It's all explainable—'

'Oh, yes. Everything is, monsieur. But the *story*, monsieur, the *story* has it that when the first three plagues had been unsuccessful – the plague of water changed to blood, of frogs falling on the land, the plague of lice – a fourth plague was summoned.'

Paul-Luc Lebas closed his eyes. He felt elated, pure, as if some religious ecstasy had captured him. The wine. Well, why not. He saw against the lids of his eyes, red from the old gold beaten bowl of sun, her pictures.

'A wind came, the hot scorpion wind of the desert.' She said: 'The dust thrashed against the city. The sun was dull.'

And from the dust, the wind out of the desert waste, they came. There was no true name for them.

'The Torah,' she said, 'instructs that they were *Arov* – this term is disputed by scholars. Wild beasts, say some. Others tell us that flies came upon the city of Pharaoh. Or snakes. And others say that they were, the Arov, blood-suckers. *Scarabs.*'

From the desert, haloed by dust, the plague walked on bare narrow feet that did not feel the furnace heat of the sand. Their robes were black. Their hair was black, blowing about their faces. Their eyes were like the drawings on the walls of tombs, almonds painted in by a black rim, the iris black as an orb of night.

Scarabs. The Arov.

'They entered the streets, and the wind covered them over like a cloak. The sun-bird was snared in a net of shadow. For *they* did not like the sun.'

They crept into the palaces and the hovels of the city. They were – she told him – too marvellous to resist.

And there they sucked human blood.

They tore out throats, they fastened their teeth into necks, they drained dry Men-Nefer, whose white walls, deadened with shade, were then splashed by red.

And the river ran scarlet, as before, from the dead thrown into it.

'Vampires?' he queried. Amused. But his voice, slurred, annoyed him.

'Yes, monsieur. Delicious vampires. Lovely until the moment of attack. In Men-Nefer some of the citizens died of shock, and some of the blood that was lost. Some of not giving in, killed. And the streets were dyed with red, and the river was red, and the sun was red too, in the black day sky.'

He saw it. It was horrible, and fair.

He meant to say, 'And then what?'

'It wasn't enough. The king, the Pharaoh, was obdurate. And so other plagues fell upon Men-Nefer. The diseases that the vampire Arov had brought with their bites. Hail that flamed. Locusts that ate the crops. And then – Darkness came. Darkness which could be *touched*.'

Paul-Luc felt the hardness under the sand, as if it had grown into him. Some arcane buggery. It came to him that a ledge of the tomb itself was pressing into his flesh. He should move away. Uncover it carefully.

He could say: Now you'll tell me that the – what would it be – ninth plague, this Darkness, was Khau-Khepra. Your sorcerer king.

As if he had, she said, 'He came among them, like his people, from the desert. The Egyptians thought he was Set himself, riding on an ass, with black hair. His eyes were like lapis-lazuli, the sky at dusk, kindled with the dawn star.'

Paul-Luc did not reply or move.

She said, 'You'll say, but what of the tenth plague. I'll answer you. Khau took away their first born. He robbed them of their children.'

Paul-Luc did not move. He thought, *This thing. Under my back.*

He realized she had stood up. She was like, now, a white shadow, rimmed by the ancient sun. So bright. Yet – dark.

'He took away their children and left the city bereft.'

Paul-Luc did not move.

She said, 'And then he returned into the desert, with his tribe, his Scarab people, and the children of Men-Nefer. And only the Hebrew race were safe, for they had marked the lintels of their doors – with blood.'

Paul-Luc did not move.

She said, 'The Angel of Death is another, an apt, name for him. Monsieur.'

She waited then, and looked at Paul-Luc Lebas, who sat with his back against the sand of the hill. His glass rested in his fingers, on his knee. His eyes looked out, as if fixed on her pictures still.

But by now the thing, with which she had wiped his glass, had killed him.

She kicked him at last in the side, and he went over and rolled down the slope, right down, into the sand below.

(The camel snorted, a farting, scoffing noise.)

On the skin of the man's back, under his jacket, was an impression of the hieroglyphs cut out on the door, mirror-wise: *Neshenti*.

The woman turned and called, in Arabic.

The men were waiting. Now they would cover up the tomb and seal it close. And in the village of Dove their reward was already in position, the satellite TV dishes, placed high on the mud walls of their huts.

Berenice had been afraid.

Not at first, while she had heard the crew of her father's boat playing music, shouting to each other, and other noises from the village, goats and typewriters.

But now silence had come, and when, finally, she disobeyed, and went up on to the deck, no one was there. The men had left the boat. The wheel-house was empty. And on the streets of the village, nothing moved.

The sky was overcast too, thick with something like a smoked lens.

It was, as it had been in the city, chilly but close.

She went to the side and looked down into the water. It was not as she recalled – but what did she mean?

She had some memory, from a film or book no doubt, of a beer-clear Nile, massed only with hippopotami. But this was muddy, sickly, destitute. She mourned for it.

And then she looked up, at the high bank with its figs and muddled houses, and beyond, the vague ghost of brownness that must be desert.

He did not like her, she knew, her father. He had only kept her because her mother was insane and a slut. Perhaps he had grown tired of Berenice now. Her stupidity, which irritated him so. Her appearance.

She started to cry.

And strangely, as she wept, it seemed to her that others wept with her, demons of the land and water. Women had wept here for so many centuries. Their tears had filled the Nile.

She was curled on her bunk in her blankets, half asleep, half unconscious, in the shadow of nightfall, when the lady came in.

The lady wore white and had wonderful golden hair. Berenice had seen her in the hotel.

'Don't be frightened, little one. It's all right. Poor little girl. There.'

Berenice sat up.

'Where's Papa?'

'He's had to go on to another village. So I've come to look after you for a while. You won't mind, will you?'

Berenice only stared.

The lady was beautiful. Beautiful like someone else, long ago. And she smiled at Berenice, a true smile, which there is, never, ever any mistaking. The smile of possessive desire.

Chapter Twenty-One

THEY HAD GONE BACK TO living in the trees. To living in what had been recycled from trees: cardboard boxes.

Along the desert of grey cement, the bashes stood, leaned, the tents of the fallen. Scaffolding and poles and tarpaulins nicked from building sites, bakers' trays once warm with new bread, now cold. Tin drums, old dustbins. And the cardboard boxes, marked Electrolux, Cape grapes, dog food.

Here and there a fire burning. A dog, who had perhaps never eaten dog food, scratching, getting ready for the day's ham and egging.

Against the black undersides of buildings as indifferent as cliffs, others lay, or sat up now, in sleeping bags, combing the hair out of their eyes with yellow fingers.

Not far off, the liquid-metal river with its embankments of sphinxes and obelisks. All around the city of steel and stone, under which lay crypts, plague pits, seventeenth-century Roman baths, and temples to Mithras, investor of light.

Light limped up the winter day.

And heads raised to the smell of food as the American woman, who always came on Monday mornings, rain or shine, moved down the line of bashes, boxes and bags.

The American brought a trolley, and on it cooked-sausages in soft rolls, cartons of juice, apple pies (an irony?), bananas, thermoses of coffee to pour into little plastic cups.

She was herself about seventy, slim and neat in her dark grey coat and hair, with a lined, powdered, pretty and grieving face. Her name was Adoreen, she had told the ones who asked. She looked sadder than they, for she had not accepted their lot.

'Here you are, honey,' she said. She had, still, despite four decades in London, a soft New York accent. 'Take this too. You don't like apple, honey? Well, I have a strawberry one here.'

And the voices, rusty with pavement-found tabs and Carlsberg dregs from bins, rusty with the frost of the twenty degrees Fahrenheit of the past night, thanked her, fawned on her, or were indifferent as the cliffs to this angel of the morning.

'God bless yer, darlin'.'

'Yeah. Ta.'

'Hnph.'

Adoreen went on around the curve of the emplacement, down to the dim tunnel formed by Eastern House and the Thurlough Centre.

'Hi, honey. How are you today?'

'I'm fine,' said Lix, sitting up in her sleeping bag, blue eyes sharp as broken blue glass.

'Here you are,' said Adoreen, delivering the goodies. Lix took them. No need to comb back this hair, for Lix's hair was cut short to a quarter inch; she did it regularly in the public lavatory with the mirror, using her little scissors, which she had also once stuck in an attacker's hand.

Lix bit into the apple pie.

'Lovely.'

'I'm glad,' said Adoreen. And she went to the man lying about five feet away in his blanket. He did not stir.

Lix said, 'I think he's dead.'

'Oh lord,' said Adoreen. Her sweet face fell with utter distress. She withdrew her gentle hand from him.

Lix went on eating as Adoreen leaned over the dead man, mummified hard by cold as if to a pale black stick. The police car would cruise by later, and find him. Nothing more to do.

Adoreen went on with her trolley, turning the edge of Eastern House, out into grim daylight.

Lix swallowed the last crumbs and licked her lips. She drank the juice from the carton, warming alternate hands on the plastic cup of coffee.

The dead man lying near stayed quiet.

Then a shadow fell across the other opening of the tunnel. Pigs already? No. Lix sat carefully still. Three old men, old dossers, were coming along the narrow way. She recognized one of them, Two Hats. He was drinking from a bottle of facial cleanser, doubtless thieved, treating it like a fine old brandy. The other one at the back Lix had seen here and there, begging on the pavements, smoking down by the river.

The one at the front was wrong.

He was younger. About forty-five, forty-eight. That could mean perhaps he was in his thirties. The wrongness was not that.

He wore a belted coat, stiff with muck. Like the others, his skin had the wooden look, like a carved mask, ingrained by filth and weather. Black eyes pierced it, too solid, too wet and bright.

He too had cut his hair short, but in jagged cockatoo tufts. The hair was white.

They came near now, loomed over Lix with the familiar stink of old unwashed clothes, smoke and spillages, the sour fried-egg smell of human dirt.

'Look, a deader,' said Two Hats. He cackled. Crouching down he prized open the corpse's mouth. 'I want his teeth.' He took them, wiped them on his sleeve, and slipped them in a pocket.

Above Lix, the white-haired man said, 'And *I* want his eye.'

Two Hats cackled again.

Lix sat still. From the corner of vision, she saw the younger man bend over the body and pop an eye out of its socket. It gleamed fiercely and cleanly. It was real glass.

'That's nice, that is,' said Two Hats.

He and the other one riffled through the corpse's blanket and pockets, discovering things, discarding them.

Lix finished her coffee. There might be trouble, and she must put it inside her, where they could not get at it.

The man with white hair was staring down at her.

He said suddenly, 'And what about *your* eyes?'

Lix slid out of her bag and stood up on it.

But he only said, 'They're very blue, aren't they?'

She said, 'Fuck off.'

'And you don't speak like the others,' he said. 'I heard you talking to the American. A nice middle-class accent.'

Lix ducked, and gathered up her bag and the mildewed cushion she kept under her head. She stuffed them into the duffel bag.

Abruptly he giggled. It was a high, thin soprano noise. It reminded her of a demented horse, a sort of . . . nightmare.

She took her duffel bag and slung it on, and walked off. He followed.

They walked out, shoulder to shoulder, on to the busy pavement, where office workers were rushing now to get to their valuable sought-after dull jobs, up stairs into halls of computers, wracked by migraine and RSI.

Lix slipped away, but the man kept with her.

Her would-be suitors were not usually so adept. The other two were following now as well, sharing the cleanser.

At the corner was the old public lavatory. Lix went sideways, into the Ladies.

Antique protocol would probably stay him now.

Presumably it did. He did not go after her.

But half an hour later, when she came out, there he still was, sitting by a flight of office steps, holding out his hand now and then to the oblivious passing pedestrian traffic.

The other two men were on the other side of the steps. They had been joined by Janice, with her mongrel dish-mop dog.

Along the pavement patrolled the sandwich-board man. The placards ran from his chin and the base of his skull, turning him to a sort of house of cards. Between his lips an always unlighted fag. The words on his boards, carefully inscribed, read: THE END IS NIGH. He passed solemnly.

Lix walked after him, acknowledging only Janice.

Her pursuer did not bother now, why should he?

The short day evaporated slowly.

On the street time was meaningless, only dawn and dusk caught attention, and the encroachment of neon night.

In the alleys a homeless boy of sixteen was stabbed, and from this place they ebbed away.

The ones with dogs did better. Women peered down and said, 'Please feed the dog, won't you?' Fifty pence, a fiver.

Like a warning, they were. What you could come to. It was easy. Lose your job, lose your house, lose your family. The gates to Hell stand open night and day . . .

In the evening the soup kitchens garnered them in. Clad in marigold yellow the tribe of Hare Krishna brought them hot spicy food, and a lone lawyer in a suit went up and down with rolls and juice and tea.

The ancient river pulled them too, its tidal rhythm, more life than death.

Along the bleak ribbed mud, under the arches of the Smokie, they lit bonfires, blobs of orange light sewn on the lower dark.

He came to her fire, where she was sitting with the others, in the dark night.

195

Sparks went up, and he said, 'I want to fuck you.'

'So what,' said Lix.

Like an elderly man, sitting beside her, he said, 'How old do you think I am?'

She said nothing. She sat looking into the flexible flames.

Janice said, 'You're only thirty, darlin'. Look, me dog likes 'im.'

And the white-haired man fondled the dish-mop dog who, that day, had brought Janice ten pounds.

The man did not stink. Smelled of nothing but mud and cold and night. The river, as if he had been in it.

Lix stole half a glance at him. It was as though he made her do it, for she did not care.

'I'm old,' he said to Lix. Behind him, Two Hats and the other one were ambling up. She recalled the second man's name, Vinegar Tom, for he carried his favourite drink, a bottle of turned white wine.

Lix watched the fire.

Ashy dug the white-haired one in the ribs. 'Camillo, you see them corks floating in the water? Know why?'

White-Hair – Camillo – said, 'No.'

They passed their box. It was a bucket filled with red and white wine, Heineken, Pepsi, and a quarter bottle of White Satin gin found in a litter bin.

In went the plastic cups. They drank, Lix and Camillo too.

Ashy said, 'Them corks is from the bottles of the drowned. I seen it once. Young girl she was. She comes from Vauxhall Bridge and down. Long black hair to her arse, face like a shop-window doll. In this tight black dress halfway up her bum, and high-heeled boots. And she had this bottle of Margorks—'

'How do you know?' said Camillo.

'I seen.'

'And I bet,' said Camillo, '*she* knows how to pronounce it—' But Lix took no notice.

Ashy said, 'She wades out, and the tide's coming in. She

gets in the water like a bath. And she lies on it, floating, drinking the wine. And when she's drunk it all, she sinks under. She's gone. And the bottle's floating now, and the cork. I seen her after she was dead,' said Ashy. 'The chem-i-call polloo-shun in the water's washed all the dye out of her hair. Her hair was only mousy brown. And her skin was green.'

'Ophelia,' said Camillo, 'with Margaux.'

'But no willow,' said Lix. She did not know why she had responded to him. But she had. He said, 'She's dead then.' But Lix would not speak to him.

Janice said, 'I could go to me sister, but it's her hubby. He won't leave me alone.'

They mused in silence a while, and the cold stood like steel rods up through the air of night, up as high as the street-lamps on the bridges. There civilization went on, buses, and people in true clothes. But for how much longer?

Vinegar Tom burped.

Camillo said, 'Come over there with me, Blue-eyes.'

Lix said, 'All right, if you must.' She got up. But Camillo only laughed. The high-pitched horse giggle. She sat down. He said, 'How old am I? Am I twelve? Am I three hundred?'

She drank from the box and said, 'Love like Blood.'

'Oh, yes,' said Camillo. 'I know that song.'

'My son was playing it,' she said.

That was all.

The tide pushed against the muddy shore, and away up in the air things hooted, shouted and growled.

Two Hats said, 'There's an old shell near here, under the arches. Like a big metal egg. I seed it coming down. It'll go off one day. Germans dropped it. Bang.'

They gazed into the fire. Fire was eternal. There had always been fires. The world would end in fire, maybe. (The end is nigh?)

Camillo put his arm about Lix. She let him. He put his white head on her shoulder. He said, 'You're like my mother, Blue-eyes.'

197

Chapter Twenty-Two

PERHAPS THERE HAD BEEN OTHER rooms like it, once. Or were there still? A strange room, having nothing plain. Full of images, objects, and painted companions.

On the walls were stripes of tall green reeds, in places cupped by lotuses, white and pink and pigeon blue. Through the reeds stalked heron, ibis. Above, on blueness, flew kingfishers checkered black and white. There were fowlers in the reeds, ochre men casting nets, and tawny cats crouched to retrieve the shot birds bowmen would bring down.

Above all, was the sun. The sun was formed of real gold, old, scratched to softness, still dully shining. And inset on its face a black-kohled eye.

The ceiling of the room was dark blue, and in parts the heads of the papyrus reeds had spread out across it.

The floor was veined red stone, polished and scratched like the sun.

Inside a box of half-transparent whitish curtains, that the lamplight turned to cool yellow, a bed stood on gold cat's feet. It sloped a little, the head with its coiled crimson bolster some four or five inches higher than the foot. (She had slept balancing on a hillside.)

Before the bed was a golden footstool, cat clawed. The bed and the stool were covered with blood red silky stuff.

To one side stood a table that was shaped altogether like a long cat, this one black but with golden eyes and ears. Mirrors were set on the table, boxes and bottles of milky green glass, and creamy alabaster. The lamps on their tall stands were also alabaster, and burned with a filmy rich glow, now topaz, now red.

It was mostly, almost, authentic. The raised, round marble bath even, although a faucet – a golden crocodile – opened into it. The mirrors were wrong, of course. In such an apartment they would not have had looking-glass. It had not been invented yet.

The styles were also mixed. Possibly that jar was Greek, that comb – Roman? And the warmth too was contrived . . . while behind that painted door, where the painted handmaiden stood in her golden earrings, was an ornate lavatory, like the easement of some great Eastern lord. But modern. With a modern means to flush, cabinets of modern paper and soap, a wash-basin that had not a crocodile but dolphins.

The meal had not been Egyptian, either, neither ancient nor contemporary, so far as it was feasible to tell. Although there were concessions, black figs and green grapes on a silver dish. Otherwise it was a breast of chicken, lean, and pale in taste, with a garnish of beans and rice. There was also a bottle of mineral water with a name she did not recognize. The goblet was lop-sided, of dark, flawed olive glass. Roman – or contrived to resemble a Roman goblet.

Probably most of it was contrivance, for very little was actually antique. Made only years, or decades, before. Although the painted walls seemed older, faded in spots, minutely cracked, and here and there some miniscule bald area or refurbishment that did not quite match the rest.

There was a faint sound too in the room, an electric humming, which was nearly hypnotic. It ran all through this place. The noise of a generator.

In the end she would be used to it. Not hear it any more. How long would this take? And then, how long would she remain?

Anna stood still in the white dress they had brought her, the two women. The dress was like a sleeveless garment of classical Homeric Greece – yet its drapery and folds were pre-arranged. It had – she had laughed on seeing it – a zipper.

When the smaller second plane had landed, ladybird-red in the ice waste, she and the little boy had been conducted outside by their guardian or guard.

The woman had said, before, that they were at the "tip of the world". Here surely was World's End.

The whiteness went away on all sides, as it had at the other stop, and yet this whiteness was more final, more absolute. There was no far vista of half-frozen sea, no castled icebergs drifting on its glass.

The sky was bright, opalescent, greenish blue, like no other sky Anna had seen.

The little boy said, 'It's summer, isn't it. The sun never goes down.'

'Almost right,' said the man.

Then something dark appeared on the white, not as if coming out of the distance, but more as if it had merged into being on touching the green crystal air.

In fact the air was like a freezing wall.

'Put on your face mask,' the man said, 'Miss Anna.'

He too had known her name.

But she was utterly powerless now.

They were going to the child's uncle's mansion, Uncle Kay, as if in a fairy tale. The Snow Queen, it seemed, had been subdued by Kay after all, and now he had inherited everything. Was there an Auntie Gerda? Did Hans Andersen preside?

The darkness was a sled, pulled by a running huffing furry wave of dogs. They were like black and white faced wolves, absurdly pretty and savage together. The sled stopped. The dogs wagged their tails.

Andrew, the child, ran forward, toting his llama, calling, 'Wolf! Wolf!'

The man stayed him.

'Best not. They may bite.'

But then the rider of the sled, dressed as they were for the cold, faceless (unlike the dogs), in mask and hood, threw off an anchor into the snow to hold the team, and jumped down. He said to the little boy, 'It's all right. You can meet the leader.' And he conducted Andrew to the foremost panda-coloured wolf, and the wolf permitted Andrew to caress his handsome, dangerous head.

'They *are* half wolf,' said the man from the plane. 'It gives their nice nature.'

The dog weighed about a hundred pounds. He rubbed against the child's hand. Then Anna too went to the dog and touched through her glove his lush barrel of fur and oil and vital meat.

They were put in the sled, and the man from the plane sat with them.

The other man drew back the anchor and turned the dogs, some of whom had urinated into the ice, causing it to steam. The urine smelled of fish, even through the face mask.

The sled started away.

'Is it far?' asked the child.

'Not far.'

But it was.

Or was it only that it seemed far because the journey was apparently changeless?

The crystalline sky, the white rush of ice and snow. No landmarks. Nothing.

This was not the end of the world, but another planet.

At last – but when? – a sort of night fell. It was preceded by a turquoise sunset, when a blue sun seemed to sink away. And after this the sky was still like crystal, but now navy blue, with some banks of luminous clouds visible in it.

Andrew looked up at vagrant stars.

He said, 'Sagittarius.' And then, perhaps not so incongruously, 'Mum's Gemini.' And then, 'She'll come soon. But she won't like the cold.'

It was true, the cold was terrible, who could like it? It was so ceaseless, remorseless. Often Anna shut her eyes to close it out, but then, she looked again. This land made her look at it.

They went more slowly in the dark, but they did not stop. She had expected that they would.

Remnants of the drugs given to her, or only stress, caused her to fall eventually asleep, and when she woke the plane-man was supporting her against his body. She moved away, disturbed. She had felt no prolonged masculine physical proximity, save her father-mother's, Althene. Memory made her want to cry. And, as had happened when she had cried before, it seemed to her she had never been able to cry until that moment. That to cry was limitless, yet soon over. Meaningless. All tears spent.

Dawn was coming.

It was like green amber, and against the blows of it, over the carpet of the ice, she beheld the heads of three mountains, white as individual deaths, yet outlined as if drawn in by thick pencil – the protrusions of bare and ancient rock.

The mountains smoked.

'Is it—' she said.

The plane-man said, 'Volcanoes.' Then he said, 'But not on any map.'

They drove in through hills of whiteness and, rising, the snow sheered away from the runners like wings. Andrew's llama grew frosty. The dogs gave a sudden concerted howl as the sun rose on a column of light.

Above, blue ice-falls glistened.

And then, the ultimate peak appeared.

At once, she knew, and the child also, although no one had told them – and Andrew waved his arm and raised the llama to see. 'That's where *Uncle* lives.'

It was incredible. A mountain, that was in the shape

of the most antique and mummified of tombs, a white pyramid, cloven with steps of dark rock, towered into a sky that now was mazarine blue. And as they came up between the slopes of ice, Anna saw below the pyramid, reflecting it, a river of glass.

'But the water should be frozen,' she said aloud.

'Further off it is. Not here. The heat from the generator,' said the man.

The base of the pyramid, on the desert of snow, above the liquid river, was black.

Anna expected to see an Egyptian boat, with tilted sail and upraised prow, gliding on the river.

But there were no boats, and no sign of life but their own. It might only have been some freak of nature.

The dogs, eager and grunting now, recognizing and glad the haul was coming to an end, galloped down and down into the valley beneath the mountain, and so beside the cold blue river, in which slates of white ice lay like scales, and then away, to where the freezing had come back, and here they crossed, and so went into a tunnel like the hollow of a glacier.

The dogs barked, and phantom dogs barked back.

A door of steel, very tall, like something in a factory, opaque from cold, barred their way.

She had never really seen anything like this. Not in life. Not in dreams. Surely, never in memory. But then she did not know what she had seen. Someone had brought her here. Someone who remembered her, who knew her as she did not know herself.

The door would open and they would go in.

Or would the door stay shut?

The door opened on blackness. The gate into Death or Hell . . . Black Dis – the Underworld.

And then, staring, you perceived there was a faint flavour of light visible inside. The generator of Hades had supplied electric lamps.

*   *   *

It was not magical, or esoteric, the first interior.

It was metal, with trackways, the gut of the primitive factory suggested by the steel door, that smelled of rubber, paraffin, ozone. But quickly they were removed from this, as if she should not have seen it, or the boy.

The new heat was nearly unbearable and, in a type of alley, some of their outer garments were taken off by a woman.

The dogs had run the sled one way, and the woman, who was in dark ordinary clothing, a sort of uniform, put Anna and Andrew and the llama into a lift. The woman pressed the buttons.

The lift did not rise into the mountain. It *descended*.

But of course. Hell lay below.

When the doors opened they were in another place. It was so strange that Anna smiled, as later the zipper would make her laugh.

Another woman stood in a corridor, and she and it were out of time. At least, in another time.

The corridor was not metal, and was warm with light that was not made in lamps, but was fire. Torches burned above, and they had a scent, of incense, very sweet, smoky and intimate. It was like the smell of Christmas, the tree and the candles and the perfume Althene wore, mingling. And *not* like this.

The woman, pallid on the hot glow, wore a white wrapped skirt, pleated and Egyptian, instantly recognizable. One breast was bare, and round her neck was the Egyptian collar, blades of gold, and red beads. Her hair was either cut to or hidden in an indigo clump, a wig perhaps, that just touched her shoulders.

She crossed her hands over her bosom and bowed from the waist.

Anna and the little boy stepped out of the lift, and heard the doors closed, and the lift drawn away. It seemed unwise to look back, for such a dichotomy of scenes might produce an explosion.

The woman did not speak. She gestured them forward once. Then turned.

'We've got to go with her,' said Andrew impatiently when Anna did not move. 'Come on.'

He was not dismayed.

But then, it was only like walking into a great film set, or better, maybe, into the world of dreams.

The corridor went on some way, and there began to be paintings on the walls. Blue hippopotami, and black jackals – Tauret, Anpu-Anubis. Picture-writing, hieroglyphs, fans and eyes, trees and suns.

Presently there was a succession of doors, which the woman opened, as if in the Bible, by knocking on them.

Presumably they were automatic, for at first no one was behind them. Then the doors were opened by pairs of men, in linen tunics, with shaven heads. They looked, as did the woman, like extras in the film. For they were not especially Egyptian, or even Eastern, in appearance. Their bodies were pale. They had, she saw, black eyes. Black, black, *old* eyes, veiled over, as if blind. And Anna thought of Michael, the servant in the Scarabae house in London.

These too were Scarabae.

The corridors went on, and other corridors opened away from them. All painted, and with torches.

Then came a corridor with lamps of alabaster – she knew these from books, their cream material blushing red from the fire inside them. They were on stands of bronze, as in the books, again.

And at last there were doors that were opened into a wide space, a relief after the narrowness, and the oppression of fire-lit heat.

It was a court or yard, and at the centre lay a stone tank. Alabaster flame-light glinted in dark water. Lilies grew, or were they lotuses?

There were four statues. Anubis in black obsidian, and Bast, the cat goddess, in green, but there a Roman hero slaying a snake of white marble, and there a white goddess, lightly coloured over, Greek possibly, with long carved tinted curls.

Anna looked up. The court, which might have been expected to be open to the sky, obviously was not. Instead there was a mosaic in the ceiling. This, unlike the other things, looked very old, and was partly broken. It showed a chariot race.

Aside from the entry point, two separate black doors led elsewhere. A second woman, dressed for Egypt, came forward and held out her hand to Andrew.

The little boy went with her at once. He only said, 'This is my llama. He's wet. But he's washable. It's all right.'

And the woman said, 'Yes, Master Andrew.'

As in the best American epic, they had all spoken in English, and now rather unsuitably: *Master Andrew*.

But Andrew and his llama and the other handmaiden were gone through a door. And now the first woman led Anna to the farther door, which gave this time at a simple touch.

In the short corridor beyond stood an Egyptian statue of a man or god, Anna did not know. It held a spear crossed over its hard, flat body. It was old as time. It *stank* of ages.

The woman moved around it to another door, and on the door was a clay tablet.

'I will break the seal,' said the woman.

Anna stood, watching. And for the first time in a long while, she felt the tourmaline ring Rachaela had given her, on her left middle finger.

Then the woman struck the tablet and it broke.

The door gave on to an apartment fashioned perfectly for the film. An ebony chair, a round bath, a bed in gilded curtains.

'Here's your room, Miss Anna. There are two servants to attend to you, who will arrive shortly. Anything you wish.'

The woman had an accent, but surely not of ancient

Egypt. Her eyes were not dark, but greenish – yet glazed over, dusty. Michael's eyes. Worse than Michael's eyes.

Later, the two women entered.

They bowed before her, as the other one had, hands crossed on their bared breasts.

Anna had seen no naked breasts save her own. Rachaela – reticent. Althene – Althene's breasts had been fashioned and were not flesh.

These women had black eyes and black hair to their shoulders. They gave names: Mesit, Shesat.

'You're Egyptians,' she said.

They only looked at her.

Anna sighed and looked away.

They had brought her, the Egyptians, a pot of coffee and some dainty sandwiches. Ham, they seemed to be.

And she laughed, then, as with the zipper.

In the morning – was it morning or night? – after she woke, on the sloping bed, they came, the women, and bathed her. She let them for the strange foolish reason that, less than two years ago she had been a baby, an infant, and then she had been bathed. They also washed and combed her hair, and clipped on to the ends little silver beads. Then they put on her the dress, the Greek, zippered dress, over white silk knickers and bra with Paris labels.

And Anna thought, *Cecil B. De Mille insisted even the underclothes were authentic.*

It was not a film set. It was a new world composed of a hundred different times. As convenient.

The furniture was recent because otherwise it would collapse. The statues were new to replace older ones which had been subtracted or lost. And, in places, was utter *ancience.*

And here was she, Anna. Save that, this morning or evening, Mesit – who looked just like Shesat, as if they were twins, and maybe they were, why not? – called Anna by another name.

207

Chapter Twenty-Three

THERE WAS A DREAM.

It happened after the dress and the meal of chicken.

She had sat in the ebony chair and put up her feet, now in sandals trimmed by silver and red stones, on the crouching lion stool.

Anna had thought, again, *Here I am*.

But she slept. Upright and silent, like a dead queen in a chair at Alexandria.

The River was golden with the weight of barges.

The sun glistered on the water and on oars tipped by gold and scarlet and blue. They rowed downstream.

Under the green awning, as if in spring reeds, the girl Ankhet waited, in marvel and terror, afraid to move.

The priestess sat in the centre of the boat on an upright seat of gold and ivory. Like a queen. But she was more.

Ankhet had seen statues, drawn downriver. She did not move. A girl with a fan kept the heat and the stinging insects of the River from her.

The River seemed invincible now, its liquid muscles towing the three barges. And the soldiers, in their kilts of metal, stood outside the awning, silently enduring the sky, Ra's power.

Above, the gong gave the stroke to the oars.

The maidens sang. They were bare-breasted, like goddesses.

Their song was curious, and seemed to make no sense, consisting of disjointed words.

Spring, spring. The birth, the swelling.

We. The lion mother.

Mother and queen.

We, spring, the cat, we . . .

On and on.

Ankhet trembled. They had brought her from her village. She had known nothing else. But now—

Her fear rose and fell. Like the oars.

And scaled backs showed in the river and sank. Flights of birds shot like arrows from the straight green reeds.

Spring, spring, gold and silver.

A great curve was coming in the bank. The oarsmaster stilled the gong. The oars lifted, like wings. In the forward boat, as in this one, and the one behind.

They had stopped, only the muscles of the River still tugging at them. They drifted.

And coming about the River's curve, Ankhet saw the baskets floating at the edge of the reeds, and in every basket a baby lay. Some slept and some wept and kicked. They were secured by straps not to fall into the River. Brown burnished babies like dolls.

'There,' said the priestess. And she pointed with a golden finger. Her nail was long and blue.

One of the soldiers moved along the boat and shouted to the boat ahead. 'That one. There.'

Another soldier on the forward boat hastened to excavate from the River the indicated basket. Its child did not cry or sleep, it lay wide awake. It was, from the look of it, scarcely two months old.

'That's all. We will take no other,' said the priestess.

The soldier on her boat shouted to the forward barge, 'No other.'

Then the oarsmaster bawled, and the oars went down with a heavy silken splash.

They moved vigorously again, and passed the crying,

bundled babies, like turtles in the River, and moved on between the barricades of the green reeds.

The lioness, silver and gold . . .

Ankhet was six or seven. To her the babies had looked very young; unreal. She did not care about them. She knew the custom.

That male would be destined for the temple of Ptah, the Artisan and Maker. (The rest would drown. Or perhaps other women, barren, would fish them out.)

He did not cry.

But, nor did she.

'The Lady Nefertun says you will stand up. At the next bend we approach the City.'

All the maidens had risen. They raised also their arms, so their breasts and their singing lifted to a joyous quivering clash.

The River was bronzen with the westering sun, and a haze lay on the banks, the farther of which was smudged away.

They rounded the shoreline, and Ankhet, standing in the boat of the Lady Nefertun, the priestess, saw before her the City, a shining bank on the air, formed of incredible slopes, but dimmed by distance and the light.

This City was an island. It was white as nothing in the world.

Men-Nefer.

Nefertun, rising from her chair, raised now her own arms, before the sinking sun.

And Ankhet rose too from the ebony chair, and lifted her hands – and woke.

Here I am.

The room looked almost crude, its youth.

She tasted the name on her tongue.

'Men-Nefer.'

White Walls. *'Beautiful'*.

And as if they had waited for her to finish dreaming, the woman Shesat walked in at her door.

'You will come with me, Lady Ankhet.' (The new name. *Lady* not *Miss*.)

But it was a question.

Anna said, 'Do they call this house White Walls?'

The woman Shesat looked blank.

It was the easiest solution, merely to go with her.

She would never be able to find her way in these corridors, unless someone led her, as Shesat did.

The walls were sand-coloured, painted, flicked by lamp-fire.

And then came a stretch of darkness. The passage had opened into a huge stone vestibule. It was like the entry to a palace or temple. Black stone pillars rose, and the ceiling was a mile off. The floor shone below.

They threaded through.

And so, after black dark, an oblong of rosy red darkness.

It was the opening to another enormous hall.

'I mustn't go further,' said Shesat.

'Why not?'

'This is the central place. Unless I serve here, I can't go in.'

'What is it?'

'The Hall of Nuit.'

And Shesat pointed upwards.

Anna looked. It was astonishing, even after all the other astonishments.

The ceiling was a great curved sheet of iron, and over it stretched the goddess of the Beginning, Nuit, the sky. She was purely Egyptian, her face in profile, black in the iron height, but on her forehead was a star of gold, that gleamed. And on her breast were the golden sun and the golden moon, the crescent and disc together on her belly. And her lower limbs too, where they were lost in the distance of the further wall – how many hundred feet away – were also scattered with tiny stars.

211

As in the myth, she touched the earth with foot and hand, arched over Heaven.

Enormous columns of cornelian red went up to her, and the cupped flames burned near their tops, making them into crimson candles that reflected in the glimmering shadow of the polished floor.

And there were flowers too set in the floor, that sparkled. Jewels? It might be. Green jasper winked, blue glass paste, milky crystal.

All these gems glittering were like points of fire, like a sea of fireflies.

Anna looked up again at the curve of Nuit. The gold lights of lamps hung also out of her belly, her stars.

'You must go on,' said Shesat.

But it would be terrible to step alone into that burning vastness, under the giantess above.

And in the shade behind the pillars, things stood and watched.

Anna did not move.

And Shesat said, 'She waits.'

'Who?'

'The Mother.'

Then Shesat turned round and flitted back into the dark of the dark vestibule.

There was nothing to be done. You could stay still or walk forward.

Anna walked out on to the floor of reflection and lights, resembling a river.

No, it was not like a film set.

She trod over the jewels, and they went out and blinked up again, like undamaged eyes.

The candle pillars were so huge. Perhaps six or seven people could have ringed them round.

Anna's water-mirrored image slid under her. And behind and between the pillars she saw the old gods standing. Groups in black granite, Isis crowned with the moon, Osiris diademed by a reed, the hawk-headed child

Horus on his mother's hip. And there Nephthys, and Set, who was shown with the head of a bizarre hog, on which the red light wetly flickered.

There were others she could not identify. Some were primitive and ancient, cyphers, and here and there was one depicted in a modelled Greek style.

Some beasts were present too. An Assyrian lion, a cobra. And in a cave of blackness a Greek sphynx, crouched, yellow white as a bone. Her breasts were broken, but not her taloned paws.

The Hall went on for ever.

Under Nuit's loins, Anna passed the god of the burial place, Sokar, his falcon head grosser, unlike that of the Horus child, and surmounted by a beetle shape. And then Sekhmet loomed up, a stone woman with a cup of gold in her hand, and a golden lion's mask.

Beyond Sekhmet was a wide hollow alcove, and the last darkness, which was blue.

A distant window had been cut in the pulsing blood-womb of the Hall. An aquamarine window, the colour of the glass paste flowers, luminous and blind.

Steps ran up to it; she could just make them out in the vagueness beyond the lamps.

Something sat there, raised up against the blue window. It too was dark.

And then a pair of other things, which were dark and also very pale, padded out across the incoherent space.

As the first one morphed into the lamplight, it became visible, impossibly, like a ghost.

A tiger, full grown, a length of ten foot at least. It was an albino.

On the cream coat were brownish stripes. And the eyes were like the window and the glass paste and all painfully blue things.

It snarled softly, but it was, entirely, softness. The vast pads had not unsheathed – like the sphynx, like the goddess Sekhmet – its claws.

The other one emerged after it, slightly smaller, a clearer icier white, milk not cream, the stripes harder, nearly black. Its eyes were as piercingly, achingly, blue.

Anna stretched out her hands, and let the tigers nose her, if they would.

Their heads came to her breast.

When they had smelled her, she touched them. The whiter one shied away, shaking itself. The other stayed, and she felt its rough brisk fur. Its breath was slightly fishy. With its teeth it could have removed her arm. It had a collar of silver with deep sapphire stones. The whiter one had black stones in a collar of gold.

Then both animals turned from Anna, and trotted back towards the stairs that led up to the blue window.

And the figure sitting there stretched out its own arms, and caressed them.

The tigers lay down, under the chair where the shadow sat.

The shadow did not speak.

Anna walked towards it.

The window was quite large, about six feet across, oval in construction.

Outside, a glacial cavern of the ice – or, was it water *under* the ice? So still, so cold, so empty, one could not tell.

And against the blue radiation, the shadow was mostly only that.

Yet there was the impression of another goddess.

Anna also did not speak.

The shadow, which was a woman, kept her silence.

On the stair a white-banded tail thumped heavily, once, twice.

And then the hands of the woman – pale like the tiger fur, darkened only by a ring – moved. And flame flashed out like lightning between them.

How inappropriate. She must have struck a match. However, it only appeared to be magic.

A low lamp of alabaster smeared up its curdled fire.

It struck the woman on her right side, and on the left was the aquamarine shade.

Yes. She was Sekhmet, Sekhmet the woman, for she had the face of a lioness, the low broad brow, and long feline nose, the humanized smooth mouth, coloured transparent red. Her eyes were long and black in wings of faint leaden paint. Her black hair fell to her shoulders, cut in the way of Egypt, and with small gold buds caught in it.

Her dress was not Egyptian. It fitted her slenderness closely, covered her arms like gloves. A deep white V was open at its front, and here on a chain of embers, golden and green beads, hung a yellowish scarab pendant with wings of faded black and gold.

The woman looked at Anna in the light.

She had made the light to look by, not to be seen.

Her nails were opaque red. Sekhmet's claws dipped into blood? And pomegranate on her lips—

The woman spoke. Her voice was low, and sombre, lit by nothing, let alone a lamp.

'You're Anna. But he has given you a new name. Did they tell you? Ankhet Persephone. The child of life, stolen and brought down into the Underworld.'

'I'm called Anna.'

'Not any more.'

'Yes.'

'You're stubborn,' said the woman. 'He'll like that. Or are you only frightened?'

'Of course,' Anna said. 'Anyone would be.'

'Would they? I've forgotten what fear is. What is it?'

Anna said nothing, and the woman went on looking at her. She was beautiful in the same way that her pendant was. Flawless and untouchable. Perhaps hard, or only seeming so, brittle under the chalcedony shell.

'They called you the Mother,' said Anna.

'And these are my children,' said the woman. She indicated the two tigers. 'You understand quite well how long we can live.'

215

'Do I?'

'Of course. Or else we die and come back. As you have done.' Anna lowered her head. 'Embarrassed by reincarnation?' said the woman. She said, 'We're obscene, evidently. Our kind. And we are the oldest. Ankhet, Ankhet Persephone. Don't you remember?'

'No. Why,' said Anna, 'don't you speak in Ancient Egyptian?'

'Or the Semitic tongues, or mediaeval Russian, or the French of the eighteenth century. I've forgotten them all, like fear. I remember my childhood,' said the woman. 'I played in the mud, and my sister brought me little coloured animals she made, hippopotami and crocodiles. And I remember three rivers.'

She said something then in a language Anna had never heard. It was glaucous, guttural and knife-edged together, with the rhythm of water.

The woman said, in ordinary English, 'We've learnt your speech, you, the others. What else. My name is Lilith. Have you heard that name? There is a demoness in Babylonian and Hebrew writings . . . and elsewhere, and in alchemy, who bears this name. There are other versions. Lilith will be the easiest.'

Anna said, 'Do I call you that?'

'Yes. But we'll seldom meet.'

'What do you want?' said Anna.

'Nothing. Although—' the woman called Lilith gazed through Anna, far away. 'He says that someone is coming to me. One of the children. He told me this. But perhaps he lied. The boy is for him. And you are for him.'

'For whom? Who is he?'

'My lord,' said Lilith. A still little smile lifted the rim of her mouth. But not very much. She had forgotten also how to smile, it was a reflex. 'Already he'll have seen you, watched you. And when he wants, he'll appear to you, like the god. Suddenly. Yes, you have everything to fear.'

'This man – called Kay.'

Lilith laughed aloud. It was a cool mechanical sound. The creamy tiger rose and she put her hand with the ring upon its head, which was thickly ruffed. She dug her fingers into its fur.

'Is that what the boy child called him? Well, he has many names. He was a pharaoh once. Does that impress you?'

'I don't believe it's true.'

'Yes. A sorcerer and a pharaoh. Set's night. The bringer of darkness and loss. He has a black stone in his apartment. On it is a phrase in Roman Latin. *Tenebrae sum*. What have you been taught? Do you understand?'

'I know what it means.'

Lilith moved, a whisper; she crouched forward like the Greek sphinx. 'What does it mean, then? Say it.'

Anna said, slowly, 'Darkness, I.'

'That is him.' She paused. 'Or, all of us. What do *you* remember, Anna-Ankhet?'

'Nothing.'

'How old are you?'

'I don't know. Seventeen.'

'No. Two years of age. He watched you long before you were taken. Before you were born. He knows everything about you.'

'He knows who I am? Who I really am?'

'Maybe not. Or perhaps. He'll seem to know. And you're so small and slim. He'll be pleased with you. His height, you see. He's lived so long. He was tall, once.'

The whiter tiger turned its head, and then the darker one.

In the blueness of the window came a motion.

Lilith too turned to see, away from Anna.

And something passed through the vivid soul-less tiger's eye of the blue. But Anna could not make out what.

'I sit here very often,' said Lilith. 'Months go by. But today something swam through the water. A fish or a seal. Or something older. To honour you, do you think?'

'Why has he had me brought here, this man?'

'Why do you suppose?'

Anna thought. It was what had happened to her mother – to Rachaela. The same. She had guessed almost immediately. She said nothing.

Lilith rose.

Possibly she herself was tall, but then, it might be an effect of light or perspective.

She came down the steps and passed Anna like a night breeze, and the two tigers paced after her in their collars of silver and gold.

'Stay or go as you want,' said Lilith.

'I don't know how to find my way,' Anna replied.

'Stay then. This is the heart of his world.'

The lamp-fire curtained Lilith, and as she moved by the lion goddess, a ray of gold sprang out on her like a blow.

Anna walked up the steps. She looked at the black chair with its lion's arms on which Lilith had sat. There was a perfume where she had been, smoky, tarnished, dry as certain wines.

In the blue of the window, nothing was.

A handful of days went by, in Anna's room – her flat, as she called it to herself.

She had been struck by then by a sinister simplicity. Coming down from Lilith's alcove, going back across the jewellery floor of the Hall, Anna had seen Mesit standing on the threshold, presumably attending on Anna's wish to leave. Mesit had conducted her back to the 'flat'.

And it was all like this.

All – simple. Straightforward.

Meals came three times a day, as in an accustomed, well-regulated household. Rachaela and Althene's house had been able to operate like this under the care of Elizabeth. Although on days when Elizabeth was not there, it had not. These meals were Westernized – and *simple*. Chicken, fish, vegetables, pasta, bread. Seldom potatoes. Coffee and tea. And always, now, a glass of red wine on the middle and final tray. Anna had simply been acknowledged as an adult. As if at a party.

Books also came, carried in by male porters, chaperoned by one of the women. The books were in boxes packed with straw. It was apparently to be Anna's pleasure to unearth them, and partly it was. They were mostly novels, contemporary novels, of various times. No historical works. But there were a few volumes about animals, lions and elephants and foxes. Some of these were duplicates of books Anna had had in England.

When she asked for music, Shesat said that nothing like that had been arranged. Simple again, this dearth.

In what was presumably the morning, and at night, they bathed her.

They were decorous. Only once, when the jar of soap slipped from Mesit's hands and Anna caught it, did the women giggle. When Anna did not laugh, they desisted.

They brought fresh clothes every day. The underclothes and dresses were identical. All the bras and pants had Paris labels. All the dresses were without labels, but had zips. On the fourth evening, Anna marked her dress with a tiny cut – they had given her nail scissors and other accessories – at the hem. Two days after, it reappeared. The dresses then were not limitless; two or three of them only.

Sometimes Anna went out through her own corridor, past the dark stone guardian, into the courtyard with the four mixed statues. Shesat had told her that these were Bastet, Anpu, Hercules and Astarte. There were supposed to be fish in the pool, but she saw none.

There was no prohibition on her leaving the court and going into the passageways. Except, of course, that she would get lost. And so, she did not do it.

One day, after the middle meal, Anna was in the courtyard, and the boy, Andrew, came in, led by a male slave.

Andrew said to her casually, 'Hallo.'

Anna said, 'Where have you been?'

'With Uncle,' said Andrew. (Was that still his name?)

Ridiculously, or ominously, or *simply*, Andrew had been dressed for Uncle Kay's pyramid. Andrew wore a close-fitting top of brown material, and a white gaufred kilt, belted by gold. Round his chest was a light gold collar. He had a gold wristlet. His head had been shaved, leaving a cluster of dark hair on the right side, into which gold wire was coiled.

He was now a tiny prince – the son of Rameses perhaps, from De Mille's *Ten Commandments*. He did not seem disconcerted or delighted at this dressing-up. Did not seem to notice.

And he had been 'with Uncle'.

'What's your uncle like?' said Anna.

'Oh, he's brill,' said Andrew, at his most South London.

Then, not interested in the girl, he walked on, and the servant let him in through the other door.

Did Andrew still think 'mum' would come? Perhaps he no longer cared.

Anna stared in at the fishless tank.

When she went back to her flat, she began to investigate for spy holes. For 'Kay' watched and had watched her, watched her even before she was born.

Rachaela had been taken by the Scarabae to their house, brought there for the one called Adamus. And Rachaela had conceived the child of Adamus, as planned.

Anna did not recollect either Rachaela or Althene telling her this.

Somehow, nevertheless, Ruth had haunted Anna's childhood. Ruth, and Rachaela's seduction by the first Scarabae male.

For Adamus was the first, Althene the second. Third stood Malach, the unknown one, whose hair, like Anna's, was white. Fourth now came this other. The watcher. Darkness.

She had put the ebony chair against the painted wall and was searching along the tops of painted hunters and reeds for the aperture where an eye might look through.

Things were simple here, and so there would be just such a simple hole.

And then, standing on a chair, a last terrible simplicity occurred to her.

She had heard nothing, no sound, no movement of the door, let alone a footstep, or a polite alerting cough.

Yet she turned.

From her vantage, she looked down into the room.

He was there.

He was in the room with her.

Standing quite still.

The man who had had her brought here.

Anna jumped lightly, cat-like, down from her chair. Evidently elevation was not of paramount importance. She wanted firm ground under her feet.

Standing on this ground then, she found that he was – as the woman had seemed to predict – taller than she. But not by very much, a few inches.

His build was, for his height, broad, yet compact. He wore a long dark tunic that reached his booted ankles. Everything was plain, even the belt that shaped the garment to his waist, leather with a clasp of dull silver.

His hair was midnight black, thick, rushing hair, with the sheen on it of plumage. It poured round his face, going down his back to below the level of the belt.

And from the hair looked the face, on its column of throat.

He seemed perhaps forty years of age. A forty that was fit and honed, skin and muscle streamlined and taut as those of a far younger man.

The nose was short and the mouth long, the forehead wide, like a book. The eyes ruled the face. Large and set like jewels in carving. Bluer than the bluest eyes of Lilith's tiger children. He might have fathered them. He was like a tiger too. A black tiger, the essence of some ancient night.

Of all the new and old and mingled things of this

underworld of his, he was the core, the foundation. The Greek sphynx, that maybe Alexander had paused to look on, was a baby to this one. And the fresh-made ebony chair, formed in some clever shop in AD 1920 or 1970, that, by him, was scarred and worn and nearly defunct.

All times and no time. The woman had had a touch of it, but she was so motionless – frozen – a wonderful spider hung for ever in her web of dreams.

Did he dream? Or did he only *live*.

The long mouth moved in a gentle, friendly smile. It was very charming, almost – innocent.

He spoke to her.

He had the most beautiful voice she had ever heard, with a curious, halting cadence, as if thought was in every word.

'Anna,' he said.

Not Ankhet, although he had made the others say only that. Anna.

And then, 'I've brought you a present.'

And she saw he held out, in his cunning craftsman's hands, which looked as if they might have fashioned it, an exquisite cup of jade-blue faience. A standing girl in the Egyptian manner was its stem. On either side a duck's head rose from the bowl. The rim was cut with a design of leaves, perhaps convolvulus.

She did not take it.

'For you,' he said. 'It's very old. Quite precious. Look, I'll leave it here.' And he set it on a table.

He did not seem impatient, irked, surprised, amused. There was nothing threatening.

Then he said, 'My name is Cain.'

When he did this, a vast thunder, totally silent and without reverberation, seemed to go through the room, and through Anna's body. Why? It was only a name from the Bible. The Scarabae seemed quite partial to those.

Anna replied, 'The little boy said you were called Kay.'

'Yes. But he didn't understand.'

'And I'm supposed to be called Ankhet Persephone. But you don't.'

'I need not. The others must. That's how you must be known to them.'

'I prefer Anna. It's my name.'

'Then I'll call you Anna.'

She said, 'Thank you for the cup. May I use it?'

'Of course. It's yours.'

'Suppose,' she said, 'I broke it.'

'I'd bring you another. But it wouldn't be the same.'

Anna went to her chair and sat down.

He continued to stand. He was, apparently, utterly at ease. But obviously, if he had lived so very long, he was accustomed to all things, life and death, grief and rage and love, sitting and standing up.

She said quietly, 'You won't let me go.'

'Do you want to leave so desperately?'

'I'm a prisoner.'

'Not at all. My guest.'

'I was brought here for you,' she said.

'To be my joy,' he said. 'And already, you are.'

She lowered her eyes.

Then she heard him say a sort of poem to her. The hesitation in his voice was more pronounced. He might have been translating, into English.

'She is one among millions. Her beauty is greater. See, she is like the morning star rising at a festival. Burning white, bright of skin, with beautiful eyes for seeing, and fruited lips for talk and kisses.'

Anna blushed.

It startled her. She felt the blood race through her body.

He said, 'Like fire lifting in the alabaster. I think that you are the loveliest woman in the world, Anna. But then, I've thought so before.'

And the blood withered. She paled.

She looked straight at him, into the blue of his eyes that

promised everything and revealed nothing, like the surface of the sea.

'It's the Scarabae thing, isn't it? We live for hundreds of years, or we come back – we reincarnate.'

'Here you are,' he said. Just what she had said to herself.

'Who was I?'

'Yourself.'

'Was I that other one – *Ruth*?'

'Oh,' he said, 'Ruth. The little murderess. Sekhmet the Lady of Time, bringer of fire. If you were, don't mind it.'

'I don't remember,' she said.

'Remember other things. That will be easy, here.'

'But if it's true – if I was *Ruth*. I'd have to begin there.'

'No,' he said. 'Ruth was an error. A woman mad with pain stabbed Ruth through the breast and left her in a dark wet wood.'

'And Malach?' said Anna. She did not know, or examine, why she summoned that name.

But Cain, the lord of the mountain, the god of Hades, Darkness, Cain frowned, for one second.

He said, soft as the brush of his hair would feel, surely, running over her wrist, if he had taken her hand, 'Forget Malach. He is the past.'

'Then tell me about him.'

Cain smiled again. 'No, Anna. Never. Now you must concentrate on me.'

Chapter Twenty-Four

MIRANDA GAZED INTO THE FACE of a putrescent monster, whose inch-long teeth dripped blood. Softly, she laughed, somewhere in her throat. But under her coat of malvaceous wool, Miranda shivered. Not in fear.

Bonanza Videos was strung with Christmas tinsel. Tiny lights winked and glittered in the tiny tree on the counter.

The rather fat young man had followed Miranda from the counter into the store.

'That one's quite good. Weak ending though.'

'Why?' Miranda asked.

'They blow it up with dynamite. You can't do that to a vampire.'

'No?'

'Well, you're a connoisseur like me. It has to be a stake, or fire, doesn't it?'

Miranda lowered her eyes. Her lashes, so long and thick and black, beautifully seeped in Boots No 7 (who did not experiment on animals), lay on the damask cheeks.

She was not a girl, did not look one. About thirty-nine, maybe forty, the young man thought. But God, she was sexy. And mysterious, too.

He saved the vampire movies for her. She just loved them.

She would have been good in one, come to that. Her

shoulder-length black hair, with a wisp of grey, in dark lingerie, and red, red nails. Such white teeth.

She was called Miranda. She had told him. She had flirted with him. He did not feel fat then, he felt real.

'Well, I'll take it any way. And the one you saved.'

They walked back to the counter. He said, as he had before, 'Go on, I bet you're an actress.'

'No,' she said.

Rich husband, he thought. Lonely? No, no such luck.

She seemed contained, fulfilled. Full. Like a woman pregant . . . with herself.

The slim young man, the one who came in for animal videos, and travel documentaries, was standing at the counter. The fat young man had never liked him, this slim one with his dark eyes.

The fat young man beheld the slim young man dark-eyeing Miranda.

'Good afternoon, sir. Did you like the film on India?'

'Yes,' said the slim young man.

'The thing I can't stand,' said the fat one, 'is those ghastly American voice-overs.'

'I turn the sound off,' said the other.

Miranda produced some pound coins from the pocket of her elegant coat. She did not have a bag, although her boots, of russet leather, were immaculate.

An hour ago she had been in the heart of the city, drinking champagne cocktails in a gloomy smart hotel. A piano had played, and Miranda had sipped the drinks away. She had paid for those from her pocket also.

She did not like handbags. They impeded her. She liked, however, to cross her long slim legs in the russet boots, with the glimpse of purple lycra stocking. Men looked at Miranda. As she stood in freezing Trafalgar Square, an Indian gentleman had come to her. He was a head shorter than Miranda, who was not tall, and he had a gold tooth. He offered her a flat in Knightsbridge. Miranda, with a seductive laugh, declined.

The taxi had brought her back to the London village. But she had not been quite ready to go home to the house.

She felt so young now. Skittish, was it? *Zalotna.*

She had seen the young man before, the slim one.

He was quiet, scholarly. She imagined him in a dark tower, ringed by books. Handsome. Yes, he was.

She took the videos in her narrow pale hands, of which the nails were manicured but not red, decorated with rings, one of which had known the courts of sixteenth-century Italy.

She watched the vampire videos secretly in her room.

Porn.

They amused her. She was not yet aroused. Not quite ready. Yet.

'Excuse me,' said the dark, slim young man, at the door. 'You dropped this.'

'Did I?' She knew she had not, it was a twenty-pence piece. Miranda only carried notes, pounds, jettisoned anything smaller. It occurred to her he was mean, or careful, would not waste more on her.

'Yes, I saw it fall. Not much,' he admitted, 'but it all adds up.'

She accepted the coin. 'Does it.'

He held the door for her.

Miranda walked into the cold brittle street. Mauve sunfall lay across the house-tops, thin as glass. It matched her, considerably.

'You go that way. So do I.'

He's lying again, Miranda thought. *What fun.*

They walked up through the houses, towards the common, large houses with timbered masks, looming out over wide lawns turning grey. A lighted window flashed on.

'House there,' he said. 'I do their garden.'

'Oh, you're a gardener.'

Jesus Christ had been mistaken for a gardener.

But this one said, 'My name's Sam.'

'Yes? I'm Miranda.'

'You live in that big house, don't you? The fantastic house with coloured windows.'

'Yes.'

'I saw you come out once,' he said.

'Did you?'

'Beautiful architecture,' he said.

She smiled. *Does he mean me?*

He walked beside her. She thought, *Am I ready now?* But she knew she was not.

And then the beautiful house appeared above them up the slope, beyond the other houses, against the wild trees.

The sky was starting to flame behind it.

He said, 'It's like something from a film.'

'Is it?'

'I don't suppose,' he said, 'you need someone for the garden? I'm good. And I don't overcharge. It's a fiddle, you see. I avoid the tax man.'

Miranda said, 'How old are you?'

He looked furtive, or only shy.

'Twenty-three.'

She thought, *I shall be twenty-three soon.*

She said, 'Perhaps we do need someone.'

They walked across the quiet road, and up into the drive.

And there, at the house front, was a great bike, a Harley Shovelhead, black and solid as a sculpture. Someone stood beside it, who straightened up. He had jet black hair tied back. Solid as the bike, his stomach was a barrel, and the rest of him tense and hard, like steel.

'Who's there?' she said.

The young man with her flexed himself. 'What is it?'

And then the other man spoke from the aura of the Shovelhead. 'You won't remember me. I was with your Camillo. But he isn't here.'

And out of the shadow came a soft little bark.

'Connor,' Miranda said, 'and Viv.'

*   *   *

228

They sat in the gold and white room, drinking pink Alsace wine, Miranda, Connor, and Viv.

There was no one else, except the oldish man, who Connor remembered, and who had brought the two bottles, and gone away. The boy who had been with Miranda had gone away too, into the twilight like a young wolf. Connor had caught the words 'Garden' and 'Tomorrow', but he was not really interested. Was this boy Miranda's fancy? Maybe. Connor did not think much of him, though. Surely she would have more taste?

Her hair was cut shorter, and it was darker. And she was considerably younger, too, than when he had seen her last. That did not startle him; that she had had her hair cut surprised him more.

She had not told him anything much. Camillo had not been to the house. He had already learned this from the oldish woman who answered the door – Cheta? Miranda called the old-man-who-was-not Michael, as before. The others Connor recalled were absent, the man, Eric, the woman, Sasha, and the pretty, stupid young girl . . . Tray.

He was gone too, of course. Malach. *White-Hair* – Camillo's *father*.

'But you're alone,' Miranda said, when they were nearing the end of the first bottle.

'So I am.' They fell by the wayside. No, not quite true. One did. The rest had only scattered. Red went first, to her man at the pub, Mark. She was to help him with some research, or something. The sort of excuse people make who do not yet feel permitted to be together. Basher went somewhere less esoteric, and Josie, Cathy and Rats. Shiva had gone to his mother's house. His Hindu father had died and now the white woman was alone with her three daughters. Shiva had become the head of the house. He did not seem resentful. 'I'll marry,' he said, 'make some girl happy. My mother's very orthodox, though, she keeps all the festivals. She used to scold daddyji for not being devout.'

Pig went away, and Whisper. Cardiff had come back.

And so, that night in the northern hills.

'His leg, you see,' said Connor, 'wasn't much good. He had it broken, didn't ride for months. Like horses, perhaps. You need the control.'

He opened the new bottle.

Miranda sat in her mauve dress, listening and very still.

So, Connor told her of the great, black, wet road, and how Cardiff, full of beer and loud with farts – although Connor omitted this – went racing some unseen phantom rider away up the slickness of the dark.

They came behind him, and in a curious lit pane, like a mirror, that did not exist, for there were no street-lamps (possibly only a trick of memory), Connor beheld Cardiff take the bend with the fractured rhythm of a lost charioteer. Saw Cardiff and his bike leap high in a moment of senseless glory, the flight before the fall.

Both hit a tree, the bike and Cardiff, head-on.

And then they both slewed back and lay together on the road.

As Connor and Owl rushed up to Cardiff, dismounted and stood over him, they saw that, although the helmet had protected his skull, his neck was nearly severed from his body. He was dead, yet from his frame there issued one last saluting flatulence, miraculous and terrible in the suddenly silent night.

Then the dog Meato, who was with them yet, began a raw appalling howling. Viv kept quiet.

Ray said something about the police.

The others ignored this.

They carried Cardiff's ruined corpse, and the cadaver of his bike, away over the lone lorn hillsides, up to some old beacon place.

There they burned Cardiff and the bike. The flames burst up to the sky above and sang with the crack of bones.

A week later Connor and Owl went to Cardiff's grand-mother's house in Birmingham, and gave her what things of Cardiff's they had been able to rescue from his mess, and clean.

She did not cry. She was a dry-eyed old woman who had probably seen it all twice over. She said they were good boys to come and tell her, as if Cardiff had been detained at school. She gave them black tea and plum cake they forced down, like a wake, sitting in the front room of her ancient terraced house that had survived the war, and her husband's cancer, and now stood mute above the shade of Cardiff's dying and unspoken final fart.

Miranda sighed.

Connor said, 'The Dance of Death.'

Miranda said, 'I'm sorry.'

Camillo had scorned them for being a family, the army of bikers. Now Miranda commiserated with Connor, the bereaved.

They drank.

Connor rose. 'I must be off.'

He wished he could ask her again to ride with him, but they had been speaking of the death of riders.

And Miranda said, 'Come and visit me, when you're passing.' A strange little formal silly unsuitable phrase that gave him hope.

'I'm off to Scotland. In the spring – you won't want me.'

'Well, you must try, and see.'

Viv licked round the last of her wine in the white china bowl that might be some sort of precious Chinese object. Viv smiled at Miranda, and Miranda scooped her up on to the expensive skirt, and kissed Viv's brow, between the up and down ears.

'Goodnight,' said Connor.

He longed to escape, desired to stay.

But the night was outside. The world, with its threats of destruction and collapse. How much longer did they have, to ride and drink and sing and kiss?

Well, at least until the spring.

231

When the door was closed upon Connor and Viv, and the Shovelhead started up its power of roaring, Miranda went away to her room, with the films of vampires in her Christmas carrier bag from Bonanza Videos.

Chapter Twenty-Five

JUST INSIDE THE DOOR . . .
Rachaela stood there.
She was changed.

Her hair was shorter and blonde, her eyes were greenish.

Not Rachaela.

He tried to speak to her. But her name, which he had now, would not come out. *Sofie—*

'Are you awake?' she said.

She spoke in Dutch, and for a moment too, he could not follow it. He had been thinking in English. Or Latin. Something.

'Johanon,' she said. 'Answer me at once.'

'I'm – here.'

'Good. Then it's time for your medicine.'

He said, or attempted to say, 'Have I been ill?' But of course he had. Something had been hurt inside him when they took Anna. But no, that was England. He had healed.

He thought, *This is wrong*. And he moved slightly and he remembered, how he had been – Althene. But he had travelled here as a man. It was meant to make everything easier.

Sofie said, 'Bus came back at noon, but I sent him away. We don't want Bus, do we? We want to be alone.'

Johanon felt, on his male and breastless body, the night-dress of sheer silk. It was familiar and in error. Nothing of his mother's would fit him, he was too big. Somewhere she had found a nightdress of silk for a large slim woman.

He turned his head. His hair was soft and loose all across the pillow. It – he – smelled of Christian Dior.

'How long—' he said, clearly.

'Oh, a night, a day. I gave you something.'

'I know you did. Why?'

'To make you better.' Sofie was insane, and he had always known, and now insane Sofie had drugged him. She came closer. 'And I gave you a little injection. Bus showed me once. Quite safe.'

'In God's name what?'

'Just something so you can relax. It's pleasant. I like it.'

The room moved gently, like a lazy ship half becalmed. *Don't enrage her. Don't alarm her.*

'All right, Sofie. I slept well.'

'Do you like the silk thing? I ordered three or four for you. I know you prefer it. I recall, in the old house . . . how you used to dress.'

'Yes, Mother. You stopped me.'

'But you were so *clever*, Johanon, as a child. You bribed the maids to help you. And then you'd go about the house in petticoats and cap—'

'Yes, Mother.'

'They used to tell you, didn't they, when I'd come down. And then you used to hide. You wanted to so much,' Sofie said, tenderly, 'to be a little girl. Even if I beat you.'

There was no answer from the bed.

Sofie said helpfully, reassuringly, 'I'll give you your medicine now, and then we'll see to your face and nails. Make you lovely.'

Johanon held down words. Images.

Was this revenge? Was it only madness?

He tried a little, to see how his body responded. It barely did. In his bladder he felt the dull premonition of pain.

'I'm afraid I need the bathroom, Mother.'

'No,' she said, 'we won't worry about that.'

'But,' he said, 'I may piss your nice sheets.'

'They're not nice sheets,' she said. 'I don't care.'

So, she meant him to lie in his own filth. Perhaps, when she was gone, he would be able to reach the bathroom. It seemed unlikely.

'Here you are,' she said. She bent near. She smelled of some cheap, sweet scent, something probably the American, Bus, had given her. There was a small glass in her hand.

'What is it, Mother?'

'Something delicious.'

'What?'

She said, rationally, 'Either you drink it, Johanon, or I'll inject it between your toes, like last time.'

He tried to take the glass, which would give him a measure of control, but he could not make his hand, or neck, or body obey.

She put the glass to his lips.

It was in wine, whatever it was.

He let a lot dribble out, as if he could not help it. Actually he could not.

Sofie giggled like a girl.

'It's all right.' She said in English with an American accent, 'I mixed it strong.'

He lay back, and waited, and a fearful euphoria swept up on him, and then a wave of numbing delirious unconcern. The ship cast off. He was at sea.

Sofie swam through the bright air, which perhaps was that of late afternoon, a day or a month after he had come up here from their dinner, when she had poisoned him in the red-glass goblet.

Something shone in Sofie's hand.

'Do you recollect when you first got hold of it? The magic potion for your face. That man brought it, didn't he, from the Americas. It took the hair away. A *secret*.

But the Scarabae can get anything.' She leaned even closer than ever and he smelled her clean devil's breath. 'But now there's a little stubble, isn't there. And some hair on your hands and arms and legs. Not what you like.'

'It doesn't matter,' he said.

She must have heard.

'Oh, but yes. I want us to be happy. And I can make you happy now. Look.'

In one hand was a brush ruffled with foam.

In the other a cut-throat razor.

'Just keep very still, darling,' she said.

Chapter Twenty-Six

He REMEMBERED A HYMN HIS mother – an atheist – had especially hated, although where she had heard it he did not know. The words were mysterious. There is a green hill far away, without a city wall. Why wall a hill?

Yet, here, there was such a hill, green and lush, walled in by far high ruins.

Faran thought of Cimmie, his mother, briefly, looking at the hill. But it was like the fire-flies that came with the dark. A sparkle, then gone.

The children lived in a sort of bungalow place of yellowish plaster, under the semi-tropical hill. If they wanted, they could be taken to see the ruins, and Faran had gone. But the little girl, Berenice, had not wanted to. Berenice was always sad.

Clouds sometimes garlanded the hilltop, and mountains farther off often vanished and might not have been there. The sky was blue and vast, and huge birds hung in it like beings of dark paper.

Berenice had said something about a lost people, a people killed, exterminated, and Faran, confused, had thought she meant the Jews. Cimmie, who was anti-Semitic, had nevertheless frequently alluded to the Nazi persecution. But Berenice did not mean the Jews. She spoke of a people with golden skins hung by gold, and ink-black hair, who had worshipped the sun.

The Greek boy had laughed at her. Her English was not good.

Faran had told him to shut up. Berenice knew a great deal.

There were only six of them, including Faran and Berenice. The other boys were Greek and Swedish, and one came from Canada and spoke French. There was another girl from Wales.

They did not really like each other, had nothing in common. Their ages varied between six and nine. The Canadian and Faran were the oldest boys. All had some English, but Berenice, who should have done best with the French Canadian – she was Parisian – would talk only to Faran.

This was a responsibility. He did not truly want to bother with her.

He was thinking all the time of the woman. The woman in the picture Mr Thorpe had shown him, before the long journey out here. Faran had not dreamed of her again. At least, he had, but so incoherently he could not recapture it. He felt a strong thread of excitement in him, almost terror. She was not his mother, yet in a way, he thought of her like that.

Berenice was only frightened.

From what he could gather, her father had been unkind, not only an idiot but cold and harsh. She was timid, yet clever. She had wonderful cool eyes flecked by Inca gold. Each eye seemed intent on a different thought.

They had cut her hair, shoulder-length, and they washed it every day. It was fine as floss, but full of lights.

The adults who did these things, saw to their hygiene and comforts and expeditions, and some rudimentary though quite interesting lessons, were stoically helpful always, and smiling.

Faran did not like them, or trust them. After Mr Thorpe he had felt a grim, angry alarm. But then, some things must be taken on trust.

Besides, it was too late. Faran had shown he did not give a damn about Cimmie and Wellington. He was to be taken to the woman with the face of a lioness. The woman named Lilith.

His memories of her he had filed away. He was not prepared for them. Yet the beauty of the first rush of dreams, never repeated, kept some part of him at least in thrall.

He was secretly afraid poor little Berenice had a sort of crush on him. And Berenice meant nothing.

Faran was the only black child. But then they were all different. Perversely, although they did not much like each other, they were in some quite definable manner, similar. Precocious children, not necessarily coy or absurdly intelligent, but *old*. They were old children. Ancients in restricted moulds, chafing, irritated, or distraught.

The Greek was the worst. He had nightmares. He dreamed of soldiers and battles, murders, fights. And though each child had its own sleeping room, the wails of the Greek, Christos, sometimes woke them all. Then the Welsh child, Linnet, would cry – she was nine – and the Swede, Jan, would shout in Russian, and Pierre, the Canadian, boiled with silence. Berenice stayed hunched in her bed. Only·once had Faran caught the sounds of her weeping, and that was in the compound or garden or whatever it was supposed to be, behind the house.

'What is it? Do you miss your mummy – *maman*?'

'I – my cat.'

'Oh. yes. Well I should. What sort of cat was it?'

'No, was only – a doll. Someone stealed her.'

'Oh shit,' said Faran. 'That's foul.'

Then, thinking about it, he tried to explain to Berenice that, although the cat would miss her too, it would have a great time, being fussed over. If they stole it they must really have wanted it.

Tiny things – humming birds? – flew against the flowers.

Berenice calmed. 'Do you think she go happy?' asked Berenice.

'Toys forget,' said Faran. 'They have to, like animals.'

Probably it was a mistake, for after this, Berenice came to look at him in a special, haunted, docile way.

But he felt sorry for her; she had, after all, put the toy cat first.

The Welsh girl was nasty. She kicked you if you did not watch out. She refused to speak English, although she could. The adults spoke, presumably, in Welsh to her.

They had all been here too long.

Faran had spoken to one of the adults, the red-lipped woman.

'When are we going on?'

'Are we going on somewhere?' she asked brightly.

'You know we are. *We* know.'

'How do you know?'

He thought, she of all of them tried to treat them like children.

He said, 'I know I'm going to meet Lilith.'

'Ah,' said the girl. She sucked in her breath. She said, 'It is to be. But there has to be a little wait.'

'Why?'

'You're to meet him, too. The man who will have charge of you.'

'Who's that?'

'Wait and see,' she said.

Faran looked up at her. He knew, as so often, that she was younger than he, though mature over him by fifteen years, and taller by two feet. He said stubbornly, 'Mr Thorpe said—'

'Now you're here,' she said, 'do you wish to go to see the temple?'

'Yes, all right. But—'

'You must be patient.' Suddenly she looked at him in a sort of fearful respect. 'Please,' she said. 'You're special.

I'm only following orders. I don't *know* when they'll call for you. You know it's very cold there?'

'Yes.' The oblique lessons had informed them all of this, among other oddities.

'Well, enjoy the sun while you can. This is the land of the sun. It's *night* there for weeks and weeks. They – like the dark.'

'Then, I shall,' he said. Then he said again, 'Who is the man, this man we have to go to?'

'Señor Cain,' she said. Then she laughed as if ashamed.

And Faran felt an intimation of jealousy.

Cain – for some reason the name made him think of the dark kola men had sold on the mountain track, in the thin shrill air as they descended, by the private bus, to this house. A dark name. Or was it a sort of pun that misled him, co-*caine*. The drug that killed.

A shade fell, chill and unanswered. Faran turned. Only Berenice was there. They must have given her a new toy cat, for she now held one carefully in her arm. She was too old for toys. But then she was too old also, like all of them, to be a child.

'Come and see the sun temple, Berenice.'

Berenice held the woolly cat to her face and asked it caringly if it would like to see the temple.

'They have pumas on leads,' said Berenice, 'the Inca. Do you think are any still?'

'Ghosts, maybe.'

'Yes,' she said. She laughed. Something lighted up in her. Well, then. If Lilith had Señor Cain, Faran had, substitutionally, Berenice.

Chapter Twenty~Seven

THE PLANE HAD LANDED. IT had stayed down only thirteen minutes. The pilot wanted to be away from that place.

On either side of the brown runway, jungle lay like tapestry, green as paint, humming and buzzing, electric, live: spotted cats and snakes, monkeys, types of parakeet. As if nothing could eradicate it.

On the field, the man waited, in his sand-coloured clothes. Blind white, his hair lay over them. He was still as a stone.

Cicadas scratched.

Then the jungle moved.

Six men, sprung like the dragon's teeth. They ran, khaki and green, with camouflage-mottled, unshaven faces.

The leader reached Malach. The leader was a Brit, tall and heavy with muscle, with ginger in his overgrown wavy hair. And a ripe Glock 17 coming out of him like ectoplasm, pressed tight to Malach's forehead.

Malach said, in English, 'Good morning.'

'Shut up. Who are you?'

'No one you know.'

The mercenary pushed on the gun harder and Malach moved his head. The soldier said, 'Watch yourself. Put your hands up on your fucking noddle.'

'No,' Malach said.

There was another sound. It was not cicadas, but the noise of a jeep.

The mercenaries who guarded the strip turned their heads. The Brit with the Glock did not look.

'Now you're forrit, cunt.'

Malach smiled.

Out of the first jeep came the plump young man with slicked-back hair, sunglasses, a five-hundred-dollar silk T-shirt that mimicked the purple-green of the jungle. His driver, the beautiful woman in khaki, walked beside him.

The mercenaries waited now.

The woman walked straight across to the man with the Glock. She was also beautifully made up, her hair tied back like a dancer's.

She struck the Brit hard across his stubble.

He reeled.

The mercenaries fell back.

The plump man came to Malach, turning his T-shirt shoulder to the forest and the men alike. He bowed, then held out his hand. Malach shook it. The man spoke in Spanish.

'Will you come up to the house, señor? We have chilled drinks, and a wonderful whisky from Scotland.'

'Thank you, no. Where's my transport?'

'Five minutes, señor. They were delayed. Forgive the . . . nuisance.'

The woman looked at Malach openly.

When he met her eyes, she smiled.

Malach did not smile.

The second jeep came, soldiers with SA 80's.

At the edge of the forest, the first men cowered. The Brit looked sick. Where the woman had struck him was a welt. She wore a ring.

A grunt jumped out of the second jeep, and ran over. He stood behind the plump man.

'Can my people send something down to you, señor?'

'No. Just let my transport through.'

'Señor. I am distressed. We are honoured.'

Malach glanced at the woman. The plump man said, 'Anything you wish, señor.'

'Thank you. No.'

The woman frowned. She was very beautiful, golden, strong as a jaguar.

She walked behind her owner, back to the jeep. The grunt followed.

The young man wiped the sweat from his plump face. In English he said, 'You don't know why we must? Eh, Rosa?'

'No.'

He said, '*Scarabae*.'

Under her beauty and her make-up, Rosa's face went flat, like ironed paper. She licked her lips, and jumped into the driver's seat, eager to be off.

Chapter Twenty-Eight

WOMEN CAME IN.

Not her women – Shesat, Mesit. Nevertheless, by gesture, they intimated she would be theirs – or they hers. Did they not, then, speak English?

Anna consented, for there was nothing else to be done. She knew what this was for, he had told her. He had not remained with her for long.

The bath was as usual, but now there were heavy scents mixed in it – cypress, perhaps, cedarwood. They laved perfume over her from narrow, hard, smooth hands. They touched all of her, except the hidden places between her thighs.

When it was done, she was dressed, and now the dress was Egyptian. Gaufred white linen, tight, so tight on the thighs and legs she must take little, *little* steps. Across her bosom a cross of pleats, and a chitinous cape over her shoulders and upper arms, like wings.

One led her to the table shaped like a cat, and here they made up her face.

There was an unguent that smelled of honey, and over this a fine transparent powder, applied with brushes, but if they were modern or antique, she was not quick enough to see – she had had to close her eyes.

Upon her lids they put soft blueness. And then they painted in the dark green, certainly, of malachite, which, ground upon palettes, now was like fine dark cream.

They put on her lashes mascara. No. The Egyptians had not had mascara.

Her hair last of all they bound up tight on her head, and strangely this stirred a sort of memory, but what it was Anna did not know. Had Althene ever bound her hair? Rachaela? Or – as Ruth – then—

Over her head they slipped a wig of darkest blue tresses, plaited many times and twined with golden discs and miniature shells.

On her breast the women lowered, two of them, a collar of gold and green stones, conceivably jasper. This they fastened at her back, and a butterfly of green paste hung on her spine.

An inch below her waist they clasped a girdle of gold with beads of red and green and blue.

On her feet, gold sandals, with a broad band at the ankle embroidered gold with flowers.

They painted her toenails then, and the nails of her hands, a dull rich gold. And at the corner of each eye, they set a tiny golden sequin.

Anna stood up, and through the gauzy linen she saw the rose glimmer of her own nipples, although not the smoky mark on her left breast. The smoke was below, white, the nub of her sex. Not concealed now by French undergarments. She wondered if he had lied to her. He had spoken only of a great dinner.

Bracelets of gold.

A woman offered Anna a pot of rouge.

This one said, clearly, *'Pour les lèvres.'*

Anna took the pot – alabaster, formed like a grasshopper – and put a trace of the soft red on her mouth.

In the contemporary mirrors, how beautiful she looked.

Anna saw only that she was now an Egyptian.

A hundred lamps must be hanging, lighted like yellow stars, from the goddess-ceiling of the Hall of Nuit.

In the priceless floor they reflected with a mad loveliness.

There were lights too before the clusters of gods, the Isis group, the family of Set. Before Sekhmet with her gold puss-face. The blue water window shone beyond, dim as one more submerged jewel. No one was there.

The platform had been put into the centre of the enormous space, under the starry belly of Nuit.

Two chairs, unoccupied, stood up on it. They were both of black metal, perhaps iron. Lions' masks of gold were on the arms, and the feet were the hoofs of golden bulls. Two low tables rested in front of them, white in contrast to the black, and flowers floated in bowls of water, and golden sockets floated flame, and cups of faience, like the one he had given her, but also white, and black, waited for drink.

A Lilliputian green glacier lay on the second table by the black cup. Was it an emerald? It was huge, polished not cut, bleeding soft green light.

There were other low tables set about below the platform, and round them on low stools and chairs sat people. A company.

They were garbed in bleached linen and in jewellery. The men were shaven headed, some of them, others massively wigged. The women were wigged in hair of darkest green and blue.

These people laughed and talked easily and artfully, like diners in a fashionable West End restaurant.

They paid no attention, beyond the slightest occasional glance, as Anna was led by her attendant to a single plate of alabaster table below the three steps of the platform.

It was an Egyptian feast.

There was a coming and going, of the slave people. The women were bare-breasted with a single brace of gold holding up their transparent skirts. Over the pubic hair of one or two, faintly visible through the linen, was a mesh of beads.

Flowers were everywhere. Flames.

A scent of perfume, and wine.

A priest-figure strode between the crimson stalks of the pillars. His head was a shaven nut, and a spotted leopard-skin – was it real? – hung along his right side. He bore a ladle of perfume or oil or alcohol to Isis under her moon. He poured the fluid before her, touching his lips with his right hand, then bowing low.

The guests did not pay attention.

The offering steamed in the firelight under the goddess's knee.

Mesit was beside Anna now.

Mesit leaned forward with a bluish, exquisitely lopsided glass jug, something from a museum . . .

'Shall I fill your cup, lady?'

'What is it?'

'This is a French red wine. Or there is another from America. Or you may want Ksantha, the yellow wine diluted with honey.'

Anna held out the pastel cup on the table. It had dancers on its sides, naked and smiling.

'I'll have this. Thank you,' she added.

Mesit swayed like a vine and was gone.

Anna looked about at the sea of distances, flames, and unknown persons laughing.

She did not show fear.

The wine was hoarse and dry.

Someone laughed, loudly.

Anna glanced up. A shower of tiny sparks fluttered from a lamp in Nuit's girdle, and failed before they reached halfway down the tall height of air.

Another slave had come.

She said, 'Permit me.'

And when Anna did not resist, the slave dropped scent into her blue wig from a conical flash like a pepper-pot.

Anna remembered seeing these pots or cones in the reproductions of tomb paintings, set on the heads of feasters, taken for domes of scented wax. It was a symbol, of course. The symbol for scent at the feast, and so of pleasure. As the filled spilled cup was the symbol of love-making.

Music began to play.

It was old, reedy, breathless. Small bells, flutes, a harp with an acid twang.

Anna had never heard such music. Or had she?

The musicians were half seen among the pillars. They looked, yes, like the ones in the tomb paintings. But something else was happening. A soft, feral disturbance. She turned her head, and saw that now *they* came. The master and mistress, lord and lady of the feast. The Woman. The Man.

Lilith.

Cain.

Other men and women rose from their tables, and, perhaps defensively, Anna rose.

She watched them walk through the red shadows, across the flowery floor. Someone had strewn lilies, or lotuses, the bloom of the land of death.

Lilith crushed flowers with her feet, and the pads of the two albino tigers, which walked on either side of her, crushed them again. She too wore gaufred linen, but it was black. Through the smoulder of it were glimpses of a pale, firm serpent body. Opacity at her loins. On her head was a golden head-dress that hid her hair, flashing and spitting with brilliance.

He walked by her, beyond the darker of the two big cats. He had not apparently succumbed to the dynastic mood. His long robe was dark red – the marriage colour of the Scarabae, Althene had said, in a time before this.

But his collar was Egyptian, sumptuous. Silver, more precious than gold, and cornelian, with blocks of orange jasper, a scarab of turquoise. On every finger he had a ring of gold. Three on the third finger of the left hand.

He smiled graciously. He seemed benign, rational, as if this preposterous and gorgeous, and in any case anomalous and unmatched, scene was simply normal and correct.

As he passed by Anna, he stared at her.

The light from her little table caught his eyes.

They were like velvet. Midnight blue. Tranquil. He said nothing.

Together, these two called Lilith, Cain, went up the steps of their dais.

The woman seated herself, and a milky scrawl of tigers curled about her legs.

Cain stood. He raised his hand, and the music lessened.

His voice was more beautiful than the music, and better tuned.

'May he, who is life-in-death, bless this meal. May any malign thing fall upon me, your father. Let me take it from you. All who eat in my house shall be safe.'

Cain's guests – captives – what were they? – raised their cups. They drank.

He had spoken in English. Had they understood?

The music sprinkled out again and Cain sat on his iron chair, and lifted the sombre cup, already filled, and sipped.

He did not look at her again, the girl re-named Ankhet Persephone.

Did she wish that he would?

When the food began to come, it seemed peculiar to Anna. It was like food from a wine bar, but served another way.

Shesat had approached, and rinsed Anna's hands with perfumed water. Other attendants waited on the other guests. They laughed so much. The wine, perhaps. (And a shallow stemmed bowl had been set for Anna, of the Ksantha, a thick white vintage flavoured with honey, and diluted with what, for all she knew, was Evian.)

Cain's servants passed with censors, and the food aroma pushed between layers of this musk.

Hot, in wide dishes bound with gold and gems, there were white shoots and beans cooked with spice, and pieces of palest melon mixed with the bulbs of small onions. Striated leeks appeared, and then porcelain containers filled with a bright red mush of lentils. These were all carried from table to table. One dipped the spears of bread in the lentils, and ate.

Fish arrived fried to darkness, blond and pink flesh crisped. There were also meats, none of which Anna recognized, and which she did not take. She did pick out the fat, cloyed smell of roasted goose.

Figs and dates came on salvers under leaves of thin bronze that might have been edible. Honey was poured over them and on the round reddish grapes. Sweets that looked like floury fruit.

The process of eating went on and on. New dishes, endless. Sickening variety.

She tired of it.

She knew this too was a custom. Not even as modern as the prolonged Scarabae meals at the houses, which had been mentioned to her.

She did not mean to look up at him, to see if and what he ate or drank.

Only suddenly Anna heard one of the tigers softly growl, and Lilith's low dark voice murmured above her. 'No. Let him take it. See, here's yours.'

Lilith fed the white cats from her dish.

Anna glanced, fleetingly. And the green light glimpsed – so that for an instant she allowed herself – and saw him. He was viewing his feast, like Nero, through the lens of the green gem. Sapphire eye to emerald eye.

Anna removed her gaze, and as if to partner her, the lights sank. How? It was the way in which lighting was dulled in a bar.

Something was brought into the dim pond of the Hall.

Anna saw it, too, a huge dark and golden thing that came lumbering slowly in through the smoke and glow, like a monster in an old tale . . . Like the Mummy.

It *was* a mummy, a mummy-case. Huge, three men

supported it as it rode upright on a slender, wheeled sled. Flowers were showered about the image, which was black, encrusted by gold and studded by scarlet glinting stones. The face was painted olive, under an enamelled heavy wig. Its calm, dead, thoughtful eyes, shaped with black like two long fishes, stared over every head into the ceiling, the belly of the goddess.

Anna heard him rise, the brush of his long tunic. The chink of some goblet put down.

'See what we shall become.' His voice sprang out. His tone was intimate, despite the English doughy words, the distance he spread them. 'We must love and live, for life is never long enough.'

And they were laughing again, his people, standing up, those that were not now too drunk, rolling there over the tables of flowers and sunken lamps.

'See what we will become!' She made it out. Some of them did speak English, and others something else.

They laughed, and laughed.

And he laughed too, briefly, as if they had pleased him.

The mummy-case was drawn past Anna.

Lotus flowers were heaped against it, they had, periodically, to be moved so it could. A web of incense burned into the air before its loaf-shaped body.

'Make it an offering,' he said, above her, and only for her. 'A cake, Ankhet.'

And so she picked up one of the actually gilded cakes she did not want, and dropped it down on the sled among the flowers.

The mummy-case was tugged away.

One of the wheels squeaked, like a mouse complaining.

Then she saw a child was being led between the tables and the drunks, the way the mummy had come.

It was the boy, Andrew.

He wore his child-pharaoh clothes, and gold was all over him, and from the lock they had left of his hair, hung a silver crocodile with eyes of sea green.

252

Cain was still standing above her.

She heard but did not see that he stretched out one hand to the boy.

Andrew smiled, and went up the steps to the platform eagerly.

Cain spoke to them all again, 'Here is my nephew. Harpokrates.'

So that was the new name.

The tables applauded.

After death had made an appearance, the promise of new life.

Uncle Cain had put his hand on Andrew-Harpokrates' shoulder.

'Look about at them,' he said. 'Look straight into their eyes. You must learn to do this.'

'Yes, Uncle Kay.' Then Anna heard the little boy say, 'Can I stroke that woman's tigers?'

'Ask her. Call her Lilith-Eset.'

'Lily Is It,' said Andrew-Harpokrates, 'can I?'

And Lilith must have nodded, something, for Anna heard the boy go over and then his quick breathing as he patted and rubbed the striped albino fur.

'Aren't they tame?' he asked.

Lilith said, 'They know only human things. Apart from their mother, who died. Now they can't breed. There will be no more.'

'What're their names?'

'They have no names. Need no names.'

'They're brill,' said Harpokrates.

One of the tigers purred. Probably the swarthier, more friendly one.

'Ankhet,' he said. 'Now you must come up to me.'

'Must I.'

'Of course. They must see you.'

'Why?'

'You're mine,' he said.

Then she did turn and look at him.

Who had said this to her? Someone had said this.

You are mine. Until death. Until the sun dies in the River under the world. Mine.

She did not try to resist him. His eyes, which went directly in through her own and seemed to touch, quite gently, the back of her brain, were not to be denied. Anna did not waste her strength in fruitless struggle. Had she ever?

She went up the steps and he took her hand, and beyond him the dark queen of all mythology sat in her black chair, her head a sunburst from which a snake stood up on her forehead. And at her sandalled feet the child had laid his cheek on a purring tiger's flank.

But Cain held Anna's hand and he spoke to them.

'Here is my daughter's daughter, Ankhet Persephone.'

They caroused to her. Even the most inebriated made sure that they did.

She said to him, 'Am I?'

'What, Ankhet?'

'Your daughter's daughter.'

'Yes.'

'Rachaela,' said Anna, doubtfully.

'No,' said Cain, with the softest scorn. 'Your *father-mother*. Althene.'

'But—'

'She is a man,' he said. 'But I know. I honour her with her own lie. Daughter, not son.'

'Then you're my – grandfather.'

'Yes, if you like. Do you think I'll do?'

She gazed out, as he had, and the mummy had, over the feasters, and overhead gold dripped from Nuit like tears.

'Anna,' he said, 'like a little goddess already. Who has ever told you how beautiful you are.'

She thought, *Someone, once.* But it was not Althene, who had alluded to beauty only as fact. No, this other – who had it been? – had valued her beauty as a wonder. As this one did?

'Eset, when she rises with the new moon, Isis to the Greeks, mother, sister. Ra's daughter.'

Anna said blankly, remembering something else, 'I bet you say that to all the girls.'

He laughed, truly, properly, now. Not his actor's laugh. It came from the pit of his lungs.

'Oh, you,' he said. '*You*. You white vixen. You devil of a girl. Were you made for me?'

His hand was warm, close, dry and – *good*. It felt full of power, electricity and youth.

Her grandfather.

She pulled her hand from his, and looked instead back at the black chess Queen of Night, Lilith.

Lilith did not seem to notice them.

And he said, 'We'll go away.' And then something in another language, like the sound of birds.

Lilith had lowered her white lids stained with shade. She reached for her cup, and the paler tiger rose and shook itself.

'Come with me,' he said to Anna.

'Where?'

'It's dawn. Do you like the sun?'

'Yes.'

'That's wise. We'll go into the sun.'

He led her down the steps. Only Andrew-Harpokrates squinted sleepily after them.

Those at the tables who could, got up.

'Who are they?' she said.

'These people? No one,' he said. 'Only you and I.'

They went from the red gleam of sinking fires into the darkness of the portico.

Venus was in the dawn sky, like a blazing pin.

Sastrugi, waves of snow such as the sea would leave on a beach, the action of winds, folded the shore.

The sky was blue chrysoprase, so clear. So terrible. As if the air had gone yet left a colour.

Above, the white pyramid with its soaked, brackish base.

And under them, the River.

She had imagined an Egyptian boat, with lotus prow and triangular sail. Now here one was, they in it.

The boat was lit with gold, and shone in the water. The sail was palest blue, like the horizon, or the ice.

Ice scales drifted away before them, not hippopotami.

It was so still. Not a sound beyond the whisper of the oar.

Was Greek Charon the boatman, that servant-slave in his padded, modern, wool-lined clothing?

They sat in the pillared cabin, but they too were clothed for the bitter freezing of this outer world, swathed as she had been for her journey here. The garments were warm and thorough, black in colour. She had been dressed in a steel cell in the mountain. He too, presumably, but that had remained invisible. He must always be a magician, coming and going magically, changing his garments behind a veil . . . a magician or a whore.

Over the functional suits, further sorcery, he had spread for them a mantle of black velvet, timeless.

All his rings were gone.

The air, the water, rippled in slow motion.

'Is it beautiful to you?' he said.

'Yes. Aren't there any birds?'

'Too cold, my dove.'

She said, 'Why do you want me?'

'You are,' he said. 'Hasn't anyone ever wanted you, Anna, for yourself?'

'I don't know,' she said.

'Then no one has.'

Inside the edge of the mantle and the fur lining of the hood, his face, which had no protective covering of any sort, was matt and carved with thin architectural lines, like pencil strokes. His eyes were more blue than anything, the sky, the ice, the reflections of the river.

'This is Egypt then,' she said.

'Yes, my child. In a way.'

'I dreamed of a river.'

'But that,' he said, 'would have been Nil-eh. The blue one, the lotus.'

'The Nile,' she said.

'If you wish.'

'Would you still want me,' she said, 'if I'd killed some-one?'

'Have you?'

'I . . . don't know.'

'Kill whom you must, Anna. I should want you. If it was you.'

'Who am I?'

'Oh.' He drew in breath, and let it go, gazing up at the sky. His breath was a cloud of white. Tiny crystals formed in it, fell. 'You are the Beginning, Anna.'

'But I want to know.'

'You must give me time.'

She looked at him again. He had asked her for some-thing.

Cain put his arm about her, the girl, and the boat plied on over the icy river.

'Long ago,' he said, 'we were so young.'

'You called me a child.'

'You're my child.'

'No.'

'Yes. Mine.'

Mine echoed from inside her brain.

His arm was warm, as if great fires burned in him against the cold.

Anna half closed her eyes. It was like a dream.

He said, 'You and I have died. You and I have lived. I can love you like no other.'

'Lilith,' she said, dreamily.

'Lilith is my shadow. You're my morning.'

Something flew over the sky.

'You said there weren't any birds.'

'Sometimes a plane. Generally they avoid this area.'

'Why do you want me?' she said again.

'Do I want you?' he asked. His voice was playful. He looked, she thought, very young, innocent, happy, at peace. No one in the world but they. He lifted aside, carefully, the thin film of her outdoor mask. The cold came. He sent the cold away. He kissed her lips, quietly, without any thrust of sex, like warm snow falling, like a mother. Like the first father she had ever had.

Chapter Twenty-Nine

HARPOKRATES' MOTHER, SHARON FERRIS, CAME down the narrow, carpeted stairs and faced the front door. She did not like the door any more. But then, she did not like anything much.

Perhaps she need not answer. Usually they went away then. Only the Jehovah's Witnesses were always persistent, ringing over and over on Sunday morning, as Sharon lay alone in the double bed under the duvet, eating Smarties. The duvet had not been changed for six weeks, perhaps longer. It had chocolate on it. It smelled of chocolate. That helped.

But this was a week day, was it? And early afternoon. And the doorbell went off again, for the fifth time.

You had to do what people wanted. You even had to open your door, if they were really insistent. You had to say, 'No, thank you. I'm sorry. I don't believe in God.' But they only went when you cried and said, 'I've lost my little boy.' And then, too, one had started forward, talking about the consolation of Jesus. But the old woman had abruptly laid her hand on his arm, and they drew back. Until the following Sunday.

Sharon went, barefoot, to the door. And opened it.

'Oh. Good afternoon. Is Mrs Ferris in?'

Sharon said, because you had to be truthful, 'I'm Mrs Ferris.'

259

'Oh! Oh, Mrs Ferris. Well.'

And all at once Sharon knew who this was.

It was revealed to Sharon, since never before had she seen this person look so utterly taken aback. It was the family doctor. The one Wayne had fancied. Slim and blossomy, with auburn hair, in a smart, tight-belted coat.

'Doctor,' said Sharon. She did not ask the doctor in. It was not strength or bad manners, simply that Sharon was, and had been for some while, somewhere else.

'My goodness, Mrs Ferris. Well I remember I put you on a diet. A diet, Mrs Ferris. I didn't mean you were supposed to starve yourself.'

Sharon thought about this, vaguely. It was strange, because she could just recall the diet, which had lasted less than a month, and had not worked, and she had *starved*.

'Any way, congratulations, Mrs Ferris. Yes.'

Sharon stared at the doctor.

The doctor said, 'But that's not why I'm here. May I come in?'

'Oh. Yes.'

Sharon stood aside, and the doctor moved gracefully forward into the house. Her unpowdered, shineless, poreless nose wrinkled briefly. The Ferris home smelled. Unwashed dishes, unemptied bins, dust on radiator heat turned up too high.

They went into Sharon's living room. Some dead flowers stood in a vase, adding to the odours. Everywhere lay tights in balls, Kleenex packets, crisp wrappers on the unwood table, a plate with congealed sauce. Bits and pieces of life, as if life had broken.

The doctor did not comment. She sat in an armchair where some toys were sitting before her. She squashed them, and Sharon said, 'Don't sit there. Sorry. Could you sit on the other chair.'

So the doctor got up, with a look, and sat on the other chair that had only an old newspaper in it, and two empty bottles of lemonade by its side.

'You've let things go, Sharon,' said the doctor, adopting Sharon's name as if this made things nicer.

'Yes, I have a bit.'

'Well that's not the way, you know.'

Sharon glanced at her, and off again. Sharon sat down on the couch, and opened a box of Matchmakers. She offered it to the doctor, and the doctor shook her head sternly.

'You shouldn't eat those, Sharon. You'll put all your weight back on.'

Sharon slipped three mint chocolates into her mouth. The familiar gentleness came up into her brain, down into her solar plexus. She introduced another three.

The doctor said, 'I know some bad things have happened, Sharon. But you have to think of what you've got. There are so many terrible things in the world. You have your health and strength. What about the unfortunates who haven't? What, Sharon, about your husband?'

'Wayne?'

'Yes, Sharon.'

'Oh,' said Sharon.

'I'm afraid, Sharon, you've behaved very, very badly. In fact, I've been asked to talk to you about it.'

Sharon lay back, and held the Matchmakers to her full but proportionate bosom. She attended as the doctor went on, and on. It was a far-away noise.

Sharon's hair had grown to her shoulders. She had not washed it for a long while. Perhaps she had not washed it since – since that week. If the colour had been visible, it would have been rich, like lemon curd.

The weight had fallen from her like a series of clown's coats. Like a trick.

It was months ago, that day Andrew disappeared in Tesco's and no one could find him.

The police had done their best. She had sensed them losing interest. Wayne had shouted at her over and over, but all that was a sort of illusion that continued on a kind of screen. Like the TV she watched, not taking in very much. Colours and sounds, sometimes too bright or loud.

She still cooked Wayne's dinners, she could recall doing that, but he hardly ever came in for them. He preferred the company of other women all the time now. Andrew's loss was her fault. *His* son. She was a useless fucking stupid mare.

When Wayne did not come, Sharon ate both dinners. She ate all the time. Beef pies and waffles, eggs and chips with lashings of brown sauce, jam tarts, buns and eclairs, and Cadbury's chocolate, seven or eight bars a day, fudge, marshmallows, and at night she had Ovaltine, all night long, because she only slept now and then.

She lay and thought of Andrew, her mouth full of sweetness, her belly soothed and full.

And the fat streamed off Sharon. Something had changed in her. She grew slim as the models in the magazines which once she had bought and worriedly studied, seeing beings from another planet. She grew slim and then slight. Little pearly bones showed at her hips and her face was like a sculpture.

But the police stopped calling on her, asking her things, they stopped telling her to hope.

She had stopped any way. No, she had never started.

One hot evening, when she was cooking shepherd's pie, with a raspberry cheesecake defrosting on the worktop, a policeman did come.

He was one she had never seen before, and just behind him was a policewoman. Both had frowns of sorrow.

They were afraid it was her husband.

She looked at them. Her husband was Wayne. What had happened, had he finally left her, and for some reason the police had to come and tell her so?

It turned out not to be that.

Wayne had that morning been repairing the TV of a well-off, attractive brunette in a flat by the park, when something blew up and threw Wayne ten foot across the room into a tastefully papered wall.

The brunette, who had gone to make coffee, came running, and there was Wayne, cross-eyed and dribbling on her Axminster.

The current had fused something in the television, and also, more permanently, in the brain of Wayne Ferris.

They took Sharon directly to the hospital, and just before they had, Sharon did something silly. She took up one of her son's small bears, and put it in her bag. She realized presently this was a mistake, for it was not Andrew she was going to see.

Wayne was out of intensive care, and he was having a lot of tests. He lay washed, and already unshaven, cross-eyed on a bank of hard white pillows. The room smelled of industrial disinfectant, and wee. So did Wayne.

Sharon looked at him. He meant nothing.

Presently she was summoned to somebody's office, and here the somebody was, a handsome Indian doctor, who told her that, unfortunately, there was not much chance that Wayne would ever be any better than he was today. He could breathe, and sleep and swallow, but, although he could also urinate and defecate, this would have to be with assistance, and sometimes it would occur spontaneously. He would need feeding, washing. He was like a baby.

Sharon did not think Wayne was at all like a baby. She thought he was like a grown man who had never done much for himself, and now had to be helped even to take a crap. She did not use quite those words, even in her own head. She did not really think anything much about it.

But she went to the Ladies, and there in a cubicle she took out and kissed Andrew's bear. Then they went home.

Weeks after, during which time many sorties had been made on Sharon by many people, Wayne's mother took Wayne into her semi, and installed him in the guest room. Here he lay in bed all day, spontaneously shitting and pissing, watching TV.

Wayne's mother's husband had left her two years before, for a woman in Brighton. But now she had Wayne.

She made extended furious phone calls to Sharon. Wayne's mother told Sharon she was an evil, wicked wretch.

Sharon went to bed and drank Ovaltine and ate Galaxy. She too watched TV.

She had always known she would never see Andrew again. Now perhaps she would not have to see Wayne.

But here was the doctor woman. She was making elegant, controlled little gestures. She did not say Sharon was a fucking useless mare, or a wicked and evil parasite. But she did say Sharon had a responsibility.

'I've told Mrs Ferris,' said the doctor confusingly, 'that you'll go to see her today. This evening. Now you will, won't you, Sharon?'

'Yes, all right.'

Sharon had always done what the strong-minded told her to do.

She looked across at the panda and the bears and the dragon in the other chair. They were composed. It struck Sharon that if Wayne's mother was 'Mrs Ferris', then who was Sharon? And she recollected her unmarried name, Timberlake. She had always liked it. Sharon Timberlake. Sharon and Andrew Timberlake. She sighed.

'And you'll go tonight? Perhaps now, Sharon. I can give you a lift. Perhaps you should comb your hair first.'

'Yes,' said Sharon.

Mrs Ferris's house was on a corner. The day was dark already, and under the umber sky, the Ferris front window was a raw-yolk yellow.

She let them in at once, as if she had been lying in wait behind the door, but the doctor would not stay.

'I'm afraid I have to get on to surgery. But I'm sure you can both sort this out.' *Two grown women*, the doctor implied, from the high place of her excellence. She had never shirked a duty – but then, she liked the power that duty gave her, over others. No inner searching had ever disturbed her health or her skin. She left, and there they were.

In the front room everything was as Sharon remembered. The pus-coloured curtains with brown flowers, the brown and red walls, carpet and sofa, all with differing patterns. There were glass gazelles and ashtrays not for use, and over the gas fire a plate showing a painted little boy in an engine-driver's outfit too big for him. Mrs Ferris liked little boys. She had liked Andrew, although she had sometimes been bothered he was not boisterous enough.

There were photographs of Andrew everywhere, and of Wayne, too, as a child. Pushed behind a vase of regularly dusted artificial flowers was a picture of Wayne's wedding day, Sharon in her bursting dress and Mr Ferris Senior in his suit, obscured for ever by two large blowsy daffodils.

'Well. At last,' said Mrs Ferris. 'You'd better come up and see him.'

Sharon did not want to, but she could not be *that* truthful. So she followed Mrs Ferris upstairs to the spare room.

This was pink, and in the doll bed sat Wayne.

His eyes had uncrossed. He was gawping at a children's programme on the small TV set.

'I keep him clean,' said Mrs Ferris, as if she were offering Wayne for sale. 'I feed him regular. You won't find nothing wrong.'

'No,' said Sharon.

'So when are you going to take him on, Sharon, eh? It's high time. I know you had the shock over Andy, but you've got to pull yourself together. I can't deal with all this at my time of life, and with his rotten father leaving me. I tell you now, I'm sick and tired as well of paying your mortgage from the insurance money. You've got to take charge of it, Sharon, and the bills.'

Sharon watched Wayne.

A sudden sick, fruity smell oozed from the bed.

'Oh my God,' said Mrs Ferris. 'Oh my God. What I've had to put up with.'

Sharon went out while Mrs Ferris saw to Wayne, even though Mrs Ferris screamed down the stairs at her.

Back in the lounge, Sharon tried not to look at the photos of Andrew. She had put all her own away.

When Mrs Ferris came down, she was pale and angry, bristling like some stinging insect.

'I won't have no more of it,' she said. 'A great strapping girl like you. You'll have to see to him.'

Sharon said, 'He didn't like me.' She was not sure why she said this obvious and irrelevant thing. Wayne had not liked his mother either.

'Didn't like you? Should have left him alone then, shouldn't you, you little tart. Getting yourself in the family way and forcing him into marriage. Not that Andy wasn't lovely. But you couldn't even keep hold of *him*, could you.'

In Mrs Ferris's world, little boys were all right. They could not do without you. But Andrew had escaped.

Sharon took a Mars bar out of her bag. She offered it to Mrs Ferris.

'My God, look at you. You're a chockyhollic. You're mad.'

Mrs Ferris strode to a mirror and began to powder her face unevenly, and scratch a brush through her short grey hair.

'Any way, madam, I'm going out now. I'm going to the late shops. So you can just stay here and see to your husband. And when I come back, we'll sort it out. When you're having him. Do I make myself plain?'

She had made herself very plain, with the brush and powder at least.

Sharon said, 'Yes, Mum.'

'And don't call me that. You've got no right now. You've got a mother of your own, even if she is a useless fool.'

Sharon thought, dimly, of her mother. Her mother had

266

not approved of Sharon's pregnancy. She had sat through the wedding as if she was in pain, and soon after Andrew was born, Sharon's mother moved away to Yorkshire.

She had spoken to her mother, last Christmas, on the phone, and Andrew had spoken too. But Sharon's mother did not like children.

Sharon said, 'Sorry.' She put the Mars wrapper into her bag, and wished she had brought one of Andrew's toys, but the doctor would have seen.

Presently Mrs Ferris put on her coat and took her shopper, and slammed out.

Sharon stood under the yolk of light.

Andrew was dead.

It was as if she had only just begun to know.

She did not cry. She had stopped crying after the first two months. She felt as if the world was far away. She went to Mrs Ferris's kitchen, and in the white Jiffed fridge was a packet of bakewell tarts. Sharon ate only one.

Then she climbed up again to her husband.

He had not altered in twenty minutes. Yet what a change there had been. And he, who had smelled of the perfumes of other women, stank now of faeces and the disinfectant used in open graves.

Sharon regarded him, as if he might abruptly rouse, turn to her, and tell her how thick she was, how badly she ran his house, that she had lost his son. But Wayne only went on watching TV.

So Sharon crossed to the TV and pushed in the button of a vacant channel, and the picture vanished, and there instead was a white and blue world of falling snow.

Then she went down the house and let herself out of the front door.

During the evening, as Sharon packed, the phone sometimes insistently rang.

She did not answer it, and at last she took the receiver

off and left it hanging there. The phone whined like a mosquito. And grew silent. Was it always so simple?

There was not much to put into the big blue bag.

Most of her clothes did not fit. She selected a few loose T-shirts and jumpers, a skirt that had been hers before Andrew's birth and which, for some reason, had been overlooked when Wayne threw out all her slimmer clothes and told her to take them to Oxfam.

She had already, somewhere, bought two smaller bras, and some cotton pants, and some tights.

There was almost nothing from the house she wanted, except Andrew's CDs, which she had let him buy with Wayne's money. She had never listened to them, Rachmaninov, Stravinsky – the very names astonished her. But there. And she took all his toy animals. The four bears, the panda, the dragon, the snake, the mouse and the chicken. She arranged them carefully on her clothes, so they would be comfortable.

She packed chocolate too.

She put in her sponge bag, which she had employed on holidays, and this made her think a little of the bath and of her hair, but she was not primed for them.

She went to bed, and after her first Ovaltine, she slept.

In the morning there was some post on the mat. Normally she did not bother with it, particularly the brown, official-looking envelopes, another of which was now there.

However, through the door had been thrust also a selection of gifts. A new try-out chocolate bar, a sample of herbal shampoo, a tiny card of scent.

Sharon went into the bathroom, eating the bar, and next showered, and washed her hair with the shampoo. And then she rubbed the scent on to herself.

In the bedroom, clad in baggy jeans and floppy jumper, she made up her face, as she had long ago.

Now she had eyes again, and a mouth.

Who was she?

She was Sharon Timberlake.

Sharon Timberlake knew of the English seaside. Wayne had never wanted to go there. He had liked Spain, the hot beaches where she had not wished to show her fat body. But Sharon had in her heart little towns along the shore, ripe budding fields (they had always gone late in the year, her father's job, while he was alive). They had curious cranky names, and in her memory she found and chose one.

It would be another place now. But never mind.

Sharon stepped over the official letter – some demand for something – and went out.

She did not remember to close the door.

On the mat, the letter waited. It waited a great while.

It was from an imposing company, and a title that sounded impressive. Someone had heard of Sharon's loss of her son. Someone commiserated. He could do nothing. And yet, he would like her to have, gratis, some money. If it would help. She must not be insulted. He felt for her so much.

Other letters like this had gone . . . here and there.

The mysterious company. The titled man.

To Wales, to London – Cimmie and Wellington lighting up, thinking perhaps of some *real* black child they could buy now from Africa – and elsewhere far and wide. An island off Greece, Toronto in Canada, Gothenburg in Sweden. *Not* to Paris.

But here the letter lay,. and as the door hung open, the winter rain blew in on it, and ate it away.

As the train ran through the muddy landscape, Sharon thought with wonder of her money.

She had gone to the building society and drawn some. Her father had started that account when she was a child. Now, with interest, she had found she had almost five thousand pounds. And you could take two hundred and fifty pounds a day. It was hers. It was Sharon Timberlake's.

As dusk fell like rain, Sharon got out of the mechanical worm, and walked down into a town she recalled and which, very oddly, had not changed so very much.

They had built up the promenade it was true, but there were still ways to reach the shore, where the sea lay growling like an albino tiger, under the rising winter moon.

Sharon found a bed-and-breakfast that, in the morning, would do her bacon and egg, fried bread, tomatoes and mushrooms, toast and marmalade. And in the neat and not-pink room, by the kettle, were sachets of tea and coffee and sugar and chocolate, and little cartons of cream. All over the town they sold tasty fish and chips.

By night, she walked out unafraid, ignoring the invitations from the pizza restaurant, where later she would eat to her soul's content.

She took Andrew's smallest bear down to look at the sea.

As she stood there, on the silver beach, she beheld the fish-smelling waters of the earth, which came so playfully, so black and silken, and lay down before her, and then ran away.

A little snow was falling. Like the TV. Like a kiss.

Sharon Timberlake looked out upon the earth, and found it good.

And when she turned back for the hot lights of the world, for a vast pizza with cheese and ham and sausage and peppers, for a gâteau and ice-cream, Sharon found a shell, like the gold of the moon, lying at her feet.

She picked it up.

She held it to the ear of the bear, who listened.

Then to her own.

She heard the rhythm of life, not broken, a plaintive fearlesslness whistling far away, much nearer than the heart.

Chapter Thirty

WITH A MUCH LOUDER WHISTLING, the other shell had fallen.

It was not a shell, either.

It was a mine.

Some came down silently through the red and black of that blitz night in 1940. This one sang.

It dropped through layers of already crushed and crumbled paving, and down then through the sandwich-like fillings of concrete, rubble, pipes and bricks, into a perfect space below.

Another mine, which dropped and exploded nearby, covered its tracks.

In the warren of its pit, the singing mine buzzed.

The end of the buzzing would be a detonation. Something, some fault or fate, distracted it. The buzz stopped midway.

Like a giant metal bee it lay there, about eight feet long by three feet in diameter. Sleeping.

The city settled round it.

When Lix saw Camillo again he was playing with Janice's dish-mop dog outside the Pakistani cash-and-carry.

The owner had brought out some past-the-sell-by-date mince pies, and Janice and the dog had been eating these.

271

'How I've missed you,' Camillo said to Lix.

Janice waddled over on her bunyons and handed Lix a pie.

Lix took it and ate it slowly, carefully.

Camillo said, 'She doesn't remember our night of love.'

'Oh, did you have one?' asked Janice. She broke into a sudden creaky rendition of Novello's *Glamorous Night*, hitting, surprisingly, a very high top note. 'Used to sing in the canteen,' said Janice. Whatever that meant.

Camillo said, 'The sun will set in half an hour.'

Lix did not respond. There had not, of course, been a night of love. Camillo had left her, those weeks before, on the river beach by the spitting fire, and gone off with Vinegar Tom and Two Hats scrambling after.

Lix looked along the drab street, grey as the heavy sky. Only the cash-and-carry was bright, lit inappropriately by paper-chains and green glitter, to please the Indian's Western customers.

This was how Lix saw Christmas now, with her blue eyes, in the windows of shops, in Trafalgar Square, where the great tree rose as if to bless the maelstrom below.

Christmas once removed. For *ever* removed.

A young Indian girl came out of the store. She wore a red wool coat over a red and purple sari. She carried two bags crammed with shopping.

Eyeing Camillo and the women nervously, she hurried up the street.

'It's the way they looks at you,' said Janice.

'As if you were dirt,' said Camillo helpfully. 'We are.'

He watched the slender dark girl cross the road, and turn down where, behind the grey buildings, Two Hats and Vinegar Tom had gone to investigate the dustbins.

There was a dim crash.

''Ere,' said Janice. Her dog barked.

Lix thought, *I used to be wary of people like me. I gave people like me money, and tried not to look.*

From the turn-off the Indian girl had backed out again.

After her pranced Two Hats, waving aloft a sprig of mistletoe filched from somewhere.

'Giss a kiss!' howled Two Hats. He was high on the cheap aftershave which Vinegar Tom had shared with him.

The Indian girl stood at bay, her large eyes larger with terror.

Lix felt no pity, only a faint compunction, as if she had left the gas on and ought to go back to see to it. She did not move.

'Bloody fuckin' pigs!' shouted Vinegar Tom storming forth into the street. 'Moved all the bins, Celts! Can't call the place yer own.'

The Indian girl dropped her shopping, both bags, on the road. She cried shrilly: 'Take it! Take it!' And ran past them and away, her long plait of hair slapping her on the back, whipping her on.

Startled, Two Hats peered at the collapsed bags.

Some eggs had come out and broken, vivid on the pavement. An egg broke in the sky, also, yolk of sinking sun piercing abruptly through cloud.

'See if her pursey's in there,' said Vinegar Tom, squatting workman-like over the bags.

But the Indian girl had callously kept that. She had left them only packets of lentils, broken eggs, spice and wholemeal bread, five peppers and a cauliflower.

The Pakistani owner had stepped from the shop. He stood sorrowfully gazing at them.

'I feed you, and see this, now, how you pay me back. Scaring off my customers.'

'Sorry, luv,' said Janice. 'Me friends don't mean nothing.'

Camillo said, 'It's so hard being a foreigner, isn't it.' The Indian man blinked. 'An outcaste. A pariah.'

'I was born here,' irritatedly said the Indian, 'in 1943. Wandsworth.'

Camillo laughed, high and horse-like, and the Indian went back into his shop and banged the door.

'You don't want to insult him,' said Janice. 'He give me dog a packet of ham.'

'Dogs and ham are vile to him,' said Camillo.

'No they ain't. He's a nice enough bloke.'

Two Hats stood in the middle of the street eating unbuttered wholemeal bread.

'You didn't believe me, did ya,' he said, 'about the shell.'

'Someone could've ate them eggs,' said Janice.

'Like an egg,' said Two Hats. 'I see it come down. I know where it is.' He hiccuped, swivelled, and puked up the bread and aftershave in one simple gush. Straightening, he seemed unaffected. He wiped his lips with his sleeve and said, 'Want to see it, do you, Camillo?'

'The bomb due to go bang. Might do. Tempt me.'

Vinegar Tom said, 'Let's go to the kitchen first. It's Heinz night.'

Lix thought, *An evening of gourmet pleasure. The soup kitchen by the bridge, and afterwards a stroll along the Strand to see a mine.*

She thought, *I'm thinking the way he talks. Camillo.*

The club picked up more of its members at the soup kitchen. Ashy and Pug and black Arthur, pale young Kirstie, who tagged along, two or three others.

Full of floury, watered-down beef broth, they wandered to the artery of the hypnotic river.

Two Hats led the way, he and Vinegar Tom dancing on the sands like the Owl and the Pussy-Cat. (They had found some turned wine.)

The night was very, terribly cold, and Janice, and next Kirstie, began to whine about making a fire. But no one would stop. 'There were plenty of fire in the war,' said Pug.

'I weren't born yesterday,' snapped Janice.

The river uncoiled, tide lowered, black glass. There was no moon. Only the orange street-lamps burned above in the other world up the banks.

They came into a sort of special wasteland, where the shore seemed extremely wide and long. One bridge hung in the air behind them on a kind of mist that was rising from the ground. The bridge looked miles off. Ahead was darkness, with the high ghost tips of buildings, none of which looked real or known, painted out in luminous white.

Among the arches was a huge pile of masonry and junk. A hulk of something was there, perhaps an old boat, and even parts of a car seemed to have been thrown down.

They got through it, all but Janice and Kirstie, and the dog, who all sat at the entrance and would go no further. Kirstie said it reminded her of bad dreams she had.

Two Hats pushed metal lids and long rotten laths of wood aside with a proprietory violence.

Then they were in, under the platform of London, for they heard and felt the vibration of it up above.

There was a black channel, dripping with the stench of a cold jungle. Bones lay on the ground, rat carcasses, dogs, bits of human things too, doubtless.

'I come in here to sleep once,' said Two Hats. 'I never slept a wink.'

Camillo said, 'And then you found the bomb, which you recalled from long ago, descending just here.'

'Mebbe,' said Two Hats, enigmatically.

A thick echo took their voices, splashing them on the walls, as if to make a note, like a customer-check in a shop door, registering who went in and out.

Old crates lay in the channel, too. It was the entry to a tomb.

Then, beyond a smashed wall, plastered over once by timbers, now come down, they found, ill-met by match-light, a brick tunnel, arched and bold, its ceiling lost in darkness.

The floor was wreathed by metal pipes, exact, which resounded when struck. Some were large, and others twelve inches around. Cast iron, their joints were tight as crinkled elbows, felt, barely seen. Lines, skeins, of British Telecom cables ran around them, like leaden worms of hair.

The stink now was the excrement of the mud, or the poisoned river itself. Then the floor was gone. It had given way. They passaged down.

Something rose before them, and they struck their matches feverishly.

'I got a candle,' said Pug.

Black Arthur cackled. 'We know where that's bin.'

But they lit the candle. And by its thin choosy light, they saw Two Hats' metallic egg, green with moss, stained black, trickled by light like tears.

'Is it a bomb?'

'It's a bomb.'

Pilgrims, they stood before the altar. In silence.

Then Vinegar Tom sprayed a little of the wine upon the slope of it. And now it was wet and it shone.

'Told you,' said Two Hats. He paused and said, 'It sung as it come down.'

'What'dit sing? "Knees up Muvver Brown"?'

'Like the sea,' said Two Hats. In the candleshine he was a mystic. He had led them here, to his secret Holy.

'Well, Camillo,' said Pug. 'Why didn't it go orff?'

'It died,' Camillo said. He smiled. 'Or it's asleep.'

He darted forward suddenly and struck the mine a massive blow with a bit of rock he had, somewhere, picked up.

'Watch it!' cried Arthur.

'How long has it been here?' Camillo said.

'1940,' said Two Hats, reverently. His eyes sparkled. He drank Vinegar Tom's communion wine.

'Older than that Paki geezer,' said Vinegar Tom.

Camillo struck the case of the mine again. Then he

leaned and set his face against it, as if in kindness. 'Not a sound. It's quiet. Doesn't care.'

Lix climbed over the pipes and put her hands on the mine's chill husk. She did not know why. She was not afraid. So long since *she* had cared. She fought to survive on a reflex, for she had no fear of death. She had seen death. After it had been done to you, nothing mattered.

'Come on,' said Camillo. He kicked the egg of death.

Lix gave a shout. She too struck the egg with her fists, grazing and bruising them. She kneed it. Hurting herself, and it?

After that the others stumbled over.

Passing the two bottles, they jabbed and thumped. Now and then they would lay an ear to it. It was silent as they had been.

Camillo pulled Lix away from the bomb.

'That's enough.'

'Why?' she said.

'I've never seen you happy before.'

'I'm not happy. What's happy?'

'Come on. Let me make you sad again. Then you remind me of my mother.'

In a frenzy, the derelict men bashed at the dead bomb. Pug pushed Lix aside and she half fell. With adamant strength Camillo caught her, and hauled her away.

He pulled her back, along the channel.

She felt all at once near to tears. She did not want to go. But she would not resist, no more protests. She walked now at his side.

When they had climbed out over the debris at the channel's mouth, they found Janice and Kirstie standing in horror at the river's brink.

Wild noises reverberated from the innards of the concrete, roars magnified, the swiping and kicking raised to an orchestral crescendo.

'This way,' Camillo said. He leaned down and scooped

up the quivering dish-mop dog, which licked his face uncertainly.

They ran then, the four of them, Janice run-hobbling, along the beach.

'Why are we running?' gasped Kirstie.

'It's so good for you,' said Camillo.

'I got a stitch.'

They ran.

The phantom bridge swam nearer like a vast spangled bird on outstretched wings.

They were under the shadow of the bridge, and its traffic noises drifted down.

They stopped.

'Will it go up?' said Kirstie.

'What?'

'The bomb thing.'

'There's nothing,' said Camillo.

Janice sat on the shore. Hot now, she wiped her face. The dog, put down, leaped about her.

Kirstie started to cry.

Camillo drew Lix against him.

'Why don't you smell bad?' he said. 'You're too clean.'

'I wash. In the public lavatories.'

'Stop it. I want you to smell bad. It's the proper smell.'

Lix said nothing, Camillo kissed her non-existent hair.

'My mother had blue eyes.'

'Fuck your mother.'

'Oh, I might have done. But she died.'

'Yes, they do die, don't they.'

The river whispered to the shore that it was coming back. High on the bridge a girl screamed, but it was drink not fear.

'Who died?' said Camillo.

'Piss off.'

'Tell me.'

'Everyone.'

'No. We're here.'

278

'What do *you* matter?' she said.

'Poor old man,' said Camillo, 'nobody wants him.'

Lix shoved him away.

She turned, and saw back along the beach the merry bashing party emerging like black ants from the aperture under the city. Very fast.

They exploded out. They waved their arms, and she heard their squeals.

'Oh, goody,' said Camillo.

Lix began to count them off. Black Arthur and Pug were first, she knew them well enough to tell them even over the distance. Then the three men she knew only by sight, in their woolly hats. And then Vinegar Tom, who fell on his face on the ground.

Then the scene changed. It went scarlet, and then a cone of white burst out on it like a snowball, ringed by mauve and green.

Lix felt a blow in her chest. She found herself flat on her back, and Camillo sprawled over her, and she had a mad memory of films she had laughed at, where some muscular hero cast himself over the heroine to save her. Something whined across and dashed into the river. And then all the water was flashing and bubbling like oil in a frying pan.

The noise seemed to come hours later, a long choked growl.

Lix's ears started to sing.

She turned her head, and a bee-swarm of *bits* flew over her face, just missing her, and even a chunk of wood went into the water with a crash.

After this, a deafened silence.

Lix sat up, pushing Camillo away. He laughed.

She saw Janice lying on her dog in a passionate paraphrase of the hero position. The dog, also unhurt, was howling. Kirstie, unhurt, was shrieking.

As sounds came back into Lix's ears, she took in the other evidence, that was visual.

All the men were lying on the shore, but for black Arthur and Pug, who danced there now, not like an Owl or a Pussy-Cat, in strips of clothing and no trousers. The blast had ripped their nether clothes from them, and Arthur was covering himself with one hand even as he yelled in panic.

The red light burned on, but there was no other light. The buildings farther down had vanished. The bridge was only a bulk of night sidelit by fire. Not a lamp burning. Not a scream above.

For a moment Lix was going to run back, to where the men lay, and Arthur and Pug were dancing. But then the impulse faded.

Camillo said, 'I want you to marry me.'

Janice said, 'I thought it was the end of the world.'

Up on the bridge, the sandwich-board man, whose placard said the END was NIGH, had been tossed off his feet. He lay, full length, uncomfy on his board, and vapours of fire came down.

It had never occurred to him that the world's fire end might only refer to its inevitable dash, centuries hence, into the sun.

He had gone deaf from the noise, and he saw the sky was red. With some sponge-like joy, he held out his never-lit cigarette, and lit it at the falling embers.

In the Beehive, Connor had been eating lasagne and chips, and drinking beer, when there was a distant roar and all the lights went out. A bomb?

In the sticky black, he heard a scared woman say, 'It's like *Quatermass.*'

But in *Quatermass* the dialogue, Connor thought, would have been better.

He stroked Viv, and she snuggled up to him. He fed her chips. Someone brought candles to the bar, and suddenly it was Victorian London, with girls in mini-skirts, and tattooed men, and that lurker by the men's toilet door who had already tried to interest Connor in an illegal substance.

The candlelight also, however, made him think of Miranda. He saw her on some candlelit floor in some vast room, in a high tower, above the sea. But he was going north tomorrow.

In reality, Miranda was at the top of the Scarabae house, where she had climbed with the two black-and-white cats.

She looked out towards the sea of London, which normally was a panorama of lights. Tonight a swathe of the lights had died on a breath of sound like a prestigious cough.

Miranda had been watching *Blood from the Tomb*. At the vital moment, the instant of blood-drinking, this sound of the world had distracted her.

The cats had toyed and hunted round her up the house, and now both sat on the attic sill, gazing out as she did.

But to the cats, the sudden dark meant nothing, nothing at all.

Rachaela, as she was opening her third bottle of the night, sitting on the floor before the television, heard of the blackout of sections of the capital on the news. A suspected terrorist bomb.

It made her think, without prologue, of her demon daughter, of Ruth, the fire-raiser and murderess. And then, quite as irrationally, of Uncle Camillo.

But then these things swirled off from Rachaela, in the empty cave of the house. Swirled off like Althene's uncommunicating silence, and the disappearance of Anna; like all things.

Wine can conquer all.

She drank. As usual, there were several more bottles ready in the fridge.

Chapter Thirty-One

WHILE HE WAITED BY SOFIE's black door, Bus had space to watch three vehicles pass on the canal. She was a long time coming down. Or Grete, for that matter. Somehow he knew Sofie, not Grete, would eventually open the door.

He was right.

'Hi, honey-bun,' said Bus.

Sofie was crazy, he had always known that, nuts. But also she was always immaculate. Today, Sofie was a mess. She wore a pair of old slacks, with powdery marks down them, and a skimpy jumper with a little hole up by her collar-bone, like an ornament. No other jewellery, and no make-up. Had she even combed her hair? Her blue-green eyes looked nuttier and older. She goggled at him.

'What do you want?'

'To see you, baby. To see my girl.'

'Not now, Bus.'

'But honey, you wouldn't turn me away. I mean, I came by before and Grete said you couldn't see me. That was bad, Sofie. No way to treat a guy.'

'Grete's gone,' said Sofie, randomly.

Bus was again surprised. 'How d'ya mean?'

'I sent her away. To her sister in Utrecht.'

'Why d'ya do that, honey?'

Sofie said, 'I'm sorry, Bus. You must go.'

He squared up, towering over her with his big ungainly, manly frame. 'Nope. I guess I won't. I want to see my girl.'

Then Sofie glanced anxiously out at the street.

In the cold, cold day, the water still looked like the ice it had been a month ago and might presently be again. The bare trees stood rigid, afraid to move. A man walked his dog over the bridge.

'Come in then,' she said, 'quickly. Just for a moment.'

'That's it, honey,' said Bus, and ambled into the cold, cold house.

She took him into the salon, up the stairs.

'Please wait here, Bus. I don't want you to go out of the room.'

'What goes on, huh? What are you up to?'

'Just do as I say, please, Bus. I've got something for you. I'll bring it. But you must stay here.'

Bus shrugged. He sat on the leather sofa. The fire was not on and the house, as usual, seemed more frigid than the city outside.

He heard her patter away.

What game was she playing now?

He stayed put, more from inertia than a wish to please. And in any case, now she was not very long.

'Look, Bus. I want you to have this. There won't be any trouble this time.'

'What is it?'

She held out the object under his nose.

It was a ring, made for a small and slender finger. In gold was set a skull of yellowish white material, and in its eyes were chips of sapphire, and chips of diamond spiked its teeth.

'That's weird,' said Bus.

'It's very old. Seventeenth century. It's made of bone.'

'You mean ivory?'

'No. Human.'

'Get away,' said Bus, frivolously.

283

'There won't be any trouble for you, Bus,' Sofie repeated. 'They never knew I had it.'

'The family.'

'The family. It's very valuable.'

'How much?'

'I can't say. Perhaps priceless . . .'

'Well, I'll check it out.'

'Yes, Bus. Go and check the ring. Go now.'

'I find this hurtful,' said Bus, 'you pushing me off like this. You got some other guy upstairs?'

Sofie laughed abruptly. She looked like an insane owl. 'No, Bus.'

'Well, I guess you dames gotta have your secrets. But you know ol' Bus'll think it through. You know I'll figure out what you're up to, huh?' Bus paused. He said, 'Where's the faggot?'

Sofie tensed. 'My son has gone.'

'Oh, yeah? When'd he go?'

'Last week,' she said.

Bus thought that this then was the answer. The fairy was upstairs, and Sofie and the fairy were up to something. Maybe the fairy had an interesting habit, something less legal than drugs or buggery. But it was best to let it rest, for now, lull her. When she got excited, she could be a pain.

'Okay, sweets. I'll leave you alone. But I'll be back. Can't go too long without I see my girl.'

She let him out into the streets of Amsterdam with furtive, mouse-like movements.

After the door shut, he stood and looked up at her pink house. There was no clue. No lights in the dullness, not even drawn curtains. The attic attracted his eye for some reason, but nothing was there. At least, nothing he could see.

The yellow east-bound tram, waving its feelers, picked up Bus and bore him through the afternoon.

At the Zwartkerk, a man got on and went to sit in the

rear of the tram. He was young, twenty-three or -four with a few prickles coming through his milky cheeks. He wore a brown leather jacket and a square cap.

After a minute, Bus heaved himself up and went back into the tram, sitting down across from the man.

'I wondered if you still did the run, Sparky.'

'I still do it.'

Sparky was the name the Americans had for the young man, unable to pronounce his real name, or at least the name he had been used to give.

Sparky smelled of the icy street, and of Gauloise.

He sat impervious, looking straight ahead as the tram rattled on in its organized career. Sparky rode the tram every third or fourth day, getting on at the Zwartkerk and off at the Rubbish Market. Those that knew, knew.

'Got this,' said Bus. 'Like to know what ya think.'

Sparky held out his hand. His nails were very clean, and rather long. He took the skull ring. Looked at it without comment.

'Well?'

'Where did you get this?'

'Same place the other thing. She says, no problem.'

'She says.'

'Well. Give me something for it and you can take it. Ask around. I know I can trust you, Sparky.'

'Of course. Here then.'

Sparky passed Bus a brown envelope from inside his coat, for Sparky always travelled well prepared. The junks knew better than to mug him.

Bus quickly fingered through the envelope; more than a thousand guilders.

'So you think it's worth something, huh? More tomorrow, yeah?'

'If we like it.'

'You'll be on the tram.'

'I will be on the tram.'

They rambled over the serpent coils and the tram hissed

in by the Rubbish Market, where books were sold. Pea-green Telecom boxes shone out of a deepening gloom, as unlike the mood of Bus as could be.

A crowd of women and elderly men got into the tram and Sparky slipped through them and away.

Bus pushed the money envelope into his own leather jacket.

Bus let himself get high. He sat for an hour drinking Grolsch and smoking some good, good stuff, lavish to himself.

It was not just the ring. The more he smoked and drank, the more Bus could see that something new and useful was lying on the line for him. Sofie had got herself into some kind of mad fix. For Christ's sakes, maybe she had even killed the fairy, and had the body stowed. She would need Bus's help, and when he had helped her, she would need to keep Bus quiet. Because Bus would have pangs of conscience. It had happened before.

He was on a winning streak.

When he had had enough marijuana, for the time being, Bus went to a bar where they did a meaty sizzling hamburger. Here he found a spaced-out English girl, about nineteen, slim and leggy, with dyed black hair and a black-and-white-striped zebra skirt that amused him.

The girl told Bus, in a vague yet concentrated way, that she had some beautiful stuff at her place, the place where she was staying, and Bus gathered it was stronger stuff than the smoking variety.

When they left the bar, the sun had only just set, and the sky was a blank lavender over the city, the buildings darkening, the waters like silver foil, cut with red and yellow neons.

The girl led Bus down a couple of back streets, and then they came out again at the tree-lined canal-side, and she said some blurred touristy things that made Bus laugh.

They stopped after this and lit up a joint.

As they were doing it, Bus became aware of one of the million cyclists of Amsterdam pedalling along the cobbles towards them.

The man looked, of all things, like a crow, his dun overcoat flapping around him, as the cycle precariously jounced and wobbled. In the basket at the front rose something large and long, like a portion of meat.

Bus watched, amused again.

The girl drew on the magic cigarette with slitted eyes.

Then the bicycle swerved level and something happened.

Bus caught a flare of a long, bony, wooden face, surmounted by a black beret, and then the cycle seemed to unbalance, and Bus thought it was going to crash right into him. He saw the rider's stick-like arm, which seemed too long, flail out, and realized it would catch him in the chest.

'Hey!' reprimanded Bus.

Roman, the hurdy-gurdy player, who served Malach, but also the family of the Scarabae, slewed his hand forward regardless, and with the big knife in it, cut Bus's throat clean through to the spinal column.

Before any fluid jetted, swinging in his arm again, the cyclist was gone.

The girl sprang back to avoid the blood.

Bus reeled on the path, gazing at her, gargling.

The girl, who had earlier noticed the envelope in his jacket, darted quickly to him and pulled it out. As she leapt back a second time, and ran, Bus circled calmly over and dropped into the canal with a puffy splash. The water closed over him swiftly, leaving only one red oily circle, turning black.

Chapter Thirty-Two

THE STORM.

Under heaps and cloaks of living fur, the man lay, holding his soul against the agony of the night.

The dogs, too, whined, growled, burrowed deeper.

There is a whiteness which is a darkness. This they had. Snow mixed with black nothingness. No moon. No stars.

Sometimes he spoke to them, gently, and they responded, wagging their tails under the hillocks of ice that had fallen on them.

They held him close, their paws under his hooded, goggled and masked face. Their bodies packed against his.

Set came with the storm. *Came* in all senses. Arrival, climax. But that was the hot desert. This, the white desert. Yet.

White wickedness thrust and strafed them.

They were a mound, a tiny mountain. The snow, blustered against them, made a wall.

The dogs were silent now. And he, Malach, knitted into their skein of living warmth. Silent too.

Her hair had covered over the hills . . .

He had been some time, searching.

Then, finding.

She. Anna. Ruth. None of these. *Herself. She.*

And after this, the journey, the ships and planes, hot

places, mercenaries, guns, and chilled lemonade. And the
last plane. The ice. And then the Russians, met in the
green twilight on the snow. *Dobroye utra*, they politely
said, laughing at him in their blue and black.

They had brought the dog-team. He took and mastered
it. The leader, one hundred and ten pounds, was almost
black. He loved the dog, as if he had found again a brother.
They had fought in the snow, and he bit the dog, through
its double coat of fur and oil. Then, it was his.

At night, under the black sky luminous as a saucer of
radium, stars and stars. Sagittarius the Archer. The Eagle.

They drew near.

And so, the storm.

The *storm*.

The dogs howled and ran together. He banked with
them. No tent. No covering beyond the thermal clothes,
mask, the lenses over the eyes. For the dogs, only fur.

Malach, whose hair was also white as these hills. The
dogs were his warriors.

The two females came slithering to him in the night. He
held them, their faces pressed to his. So sweet, their meaty
sullen breath.

It was love that kept him alive.

Had it always, then, been love?

In the morning, an emerald sky, drifts of whiteness, like
cotton-wool pulled through eternity.

The dogs howled and barked. The other tumult was
over.

The dogs pissed in the snow, which steamed.

He fed them bricks of food.

The sled was wood, with plastic runners, and he dug it
out, the female dogs, and his dog, helping him.

He consulted the sextant.

Then he called to them, arrayed in their line before the
sled. They were tired. He used a voice from his heart, and
their white tails wagged.

Whatever was done to him, they would be well treated. They were precious as silver, in the place to which they went.

As the sled drew him forward, faceless, he beheld the dish shape of the world go up on the turquoise air.

But he was like the shape of Man. Universal, and for always. Straight and lean. Under the hood the stream of white hair. His eyes hidden by the polarized goggles. And his heart, from which he had spoken, hidden by the swords of years.

Chapter Thirty-Three

EVENING CAME TO THE BRIGHT city, and the procession moved with it, under the sinking coppery sun.

There was such a sea of light in the air, the tops of buildings and of sunbeam obelisks capped by gold, catching and flashing back the net of sunlight.

Over the River, birds wheeled lazily, with honey wings.

But the shadow of the advent of night passed softly through the streets.

Out of the shadow, every sistrum raised into the air spangled and sparkled, and the head of the great white fan, borne before the image of Sekhmet the Lioness, dipped and burned up. The goddess too was marvellously luminous. She stood on her sled in an open house of green and red and gold. She was of pinkish stone, smooth as water, her face golden, a golden collar on her naked breasts, a golden apron over her pleated skirt of yellowish linen.

Behind Sekhmet the goddess, on a gilded litter, rode the human Sekhmet.

Like the goddess, she was clothed in yellow linen, her breasts bare, high and round with youth. She was the colour of the blondest acacia wood finely polished. Her face was hidden by the mask of the goddess, made of gold; the wig that reached her shoulders was heavy and stiff with henna, Sekhmet's colour, ripe with knots of gold.

Her arms and shoulders, wrists and fingers, had gold all over them. She was clasped in it, enfolded by it.

The priestesses sang their clashing song.

They told how Sekhmet went to her husband, to his palace, which was the Temple of Ptah.

And the people standing by the road, and on the roofs of houses, echoed the song. Some threw flowers, convolvulus the bloom of love, lotus, the lily made for the dead.

Sparrows flew up from a purple street into the fire of the air.

They passed the slanting doors of the small temple of the Glory of the Solar Disc, and the winged sun above blinded the girl as she looked at it, and in turn her own face of gold blinded the people on the street.

She bowed to the temple.

Then the procession wound around the coloured houses with their steps and pillars and inscribed lintels hung with flowers and reeds, between the steep walls, past the first Great Wall, and out into the broad space before the place of Ptah, Father of Men-Nefer, Haven of the Good.

Two colossal pylons, maybe a hundred feet high, sloped up towards the blaze of Heaven. The gate between was wide open, only the line of priests standing there in their robes of white linen crossed by the skins of dead animals.

They greeted the visitor, Sekhmet, with gestures like the swooping of the birds above the River, then stood aside to let her in.

Simply by coming here, as was the custom, Sekhmet the female had married the male, Ptah. As she went in under his lintel, and the litter of the girl priestess after her, marriage was made.

Beyond the pylons, the enormous court, three hundred, four hundred feet across. It was already in shadow, but a shadow that was gold. Two tanks of water flamed, and fish leapt in them like blinking yellow eyes.

Across the court rose the portico, with the two vast statues, one Ousir, crowned by his reed, of a light green stone, the flail in one hand, and a sickle in the other. The second statue was of the artisan-maker, Ptah himself. He wore the mummy-wrappings of the tomb on his body; but for his head and feet. His emerging head was a man's head, beautiful and remote, graced with the sidelock of a child. He held a wand, tipped by the symbol of life.

The songs of the priestesses ended.

Deep silence came that was not silence at all. Far away the River moved, and in the streets were sounds, cicadas from the gardens, a child calling, somewhere the grunt of an apparatus for drawing water. Insects buzzed in haloes of light. The sky darkened to clear red.

The girl was assisted from her litter and stood before the goddess. She raised her hands, the girl, and then, turning, saluted Ptah the Maker of Life and Ousir the Lord of the Dead.

Then, Sekhmet was carried into the temple, and the girl, small in Sekhmet's fire of shadows, walked after.

In the long halls, whose pillars were square and painted black and ochre and green, offerings were made, on the altars of bread, wine and oil, and one, quickly, on the altar of blood.

The day died, and the night came, and all the torches were lit and the hanging bowls on chains of bronze.

Deep in the temple other holy noises moved, and breathed, as in the precincts of Sekhmet they did not. But here the doors led down into a labyrinth, and so to the gate of the land of Death. In his other form, Ptah waited there, the hawk-headed dwarf, Sokar.

The girl who was Sekhmet walked on behind the goddess.

They entered a vast stone room, and here, on a sort of altar, the girl lay down, and they parted the linen from her lower belly and legs and unclasped her girdle.

The Bull came, led by two priests who did not look at her, for to see the loins of Sekhmet was a danger.

But the Bull looked, knowing he must.

He was fair in his shade, though not so pale as the girl. On his broad forehead was the white triangle of Zehuti. He lowered his head, and sniffed at her genitals.

The girl did not flinch. This was needful.

And he was very gentle, smelling of perfume and bovine good health, and of the onions they gave him because he was a god, although the priests must never eat them.

The fine hairs of his nose prickled against her satin skin, and inadvertently, she laughed.

The Bull raised his head.

He was the incarnation of Amun, and looked now into her face, mildly.

Then she thought, *The next to touch me will be a man.* And then: *No. Ptah will touch me.*

The gentle Bull was led away, and they re-established her clothing and lifted her, and she and Sekhmet continued to the marriage chamber.

Her name was Ankhetari. She had been chosen many years before, as sometimes happened, from a village by the River. Here, at the rising of the water, the floors of the huts on their mound had grown wet. She had heard always the music of the River and the groaning of wooden things which took up the River and brought it in among the fields.

Then came the still interiors of the temple. She remembered her journey to the city in the golden boat, the priestess Nefertun with her blue nails. The high bank of Men-Nefer. And after that there had been the Temple of Sekhmet, the goddess with the red sun disc upon her head. The Lioness, bringer of plague and fire. Sekhmet, who could destroy like time, the wife of Ptah the Maker.

In the beginning, Ankhet had known her mother had committed adultery, but this was a terrible secret, for such a crime merited disfigurement. Even Ankhet's 'father' had protected the mother from it.

In the temple, where they trained her to serve the aspect

of God who was the lioness, Ankhetari knew that they also understood she was not wholly theirs. That they strove therefore to bind her to their ways. To *train* her like a vine.

But since she did not know herself what she might be, it did not much matter to her.

Yet he, it seemed, her husband for this night, selected to represent for the city, and for her, the god Ptah – he too had been chosen, plucked out of the River in a basket. He was six or seven years her junior.

The Temple of the Sun's Glory had wanted him, for he was a beautiful baby, a *clever* baby. But Khuen-Aten, the king's daughter, had not had him. Ptah took him, and now he was to be Ptah.

The outer room was of dark stone, and the lamps hung down through it in drifts of shady light. The shadows glowed as they had in the sunset. There was the scent of incense, khufre, oils of flowers.

The women left her by the altar, where the thin smoke rose and quivered at her breath, before the golden box that held concealed the image of Ptah.

It might strike her dead, were she to break the seal, and stare in.

Sekhmet they had left to one side. *She* might break the seal, and only she.

In a moment he would enter the room.

Ankhetari waited.

She was twenty-two years old, mature for a woman of Atert-Meht, the Upper Land. Yet she looked only fifteen, young, and perfect. Under the mask of Sekhmet, Ankhetari was more beautiful, yet with the beauty still of a mask. Her black hair would reach, unbound, to the backs of her knees. Her eyes also were black, but in the way of the River by night.

The doors opened, and Ptah came into the room.

As she looked younger than she was, so he, who was, they had told her, only sixteen, looked like a man, older than she.

He was straight and tall. Unlike the god, his head was not shaven or bound up, he wore – as she did – a massive wig, black locks that reached his shoulders, somehow not throwing his lean body out of proportion.

He was clothed in linen, his waist belted by gold, with the symbols of Ptah, hands and implements, the emblem of Life and For Ever.

She had never seen a face like his.

But then, cloistered with women, she had seen few men close, and these were guards or priests – yet this one was more a priest than any of them.

One ran before him, and set on the altar a vase, and Ptah's priest who was Ptah went to it, and broke it with his fist, so little jewels of oil and coloured glass lay on the stone.

He looked at her, and the other man went away.

The doors shut again, and outside, the great bar fell.

'I am Reptah,' he said. He was arrogant, cold and powerful as the pillars at his back, upholding the roof of the room.

'I am Ankhetari.'

Now they had made confession to each other, from their hearts. Their earthly names.

She said, 'But I welcome you as Ptah.'

And he answered, 'And you are welcome, lady. As Sekhmet who is Flame.'

His eyes, as was usual, were black. Like hers – and not like. If her eyes were the night River, his were the day River in shade. Some hint of lightness there, some ghost like the bird soul hovering, ready to fly out.

She had not been afraid, because it was her duty. And yet she was a virgin, and she knew, unlike the dulcet Bull of Amun, this man must pierce her, enter her, perhaps wake her womb to child.

Did she desire him? He was handsome and fine. But so young, even if he did not look it. Cruel with indifference.

They went, without any further dialogue, past the altar, into the second room behind the first.

Here things had been set for them, that they might bathe in the night, as a priest must, and again at dawn, that they might relieve themselves behind a painted screen. Food was set by, simple and plain, and wine, and two cups, a shallow bowl for a woman, the tall goblet of a man.

The bed was a bed for sex, inclined only slightly at the head, but with two headrests for sleep, like crescent moons.

She thought, it would be a night of Eset's searching for her husband, Ousir, a bright star above the crescent lunar boat.

But they would not see it, since there were no windows.

Ankhetari lay down meekly on the bed, and spread her legs a little, her hands loose at her sides.

Then, he laughed.

'Not as you did for the Bull,' he said. And then, more soberly, 'Take off your mask, at least, lady. I might want to taste your upper lips.'

Ankhetari, who knew nothing of sexual etiquette, who had had, in her time with Sekhmet, no sexual fantasy, all her sensual emotion drawn in to the goddess, obeyed him. She drew off the golden mask and put it carefully on the floor, where a wonderful woven rug was, of crimson and green.

'And the wig . . .' he said. 'Do they shave your head?'

'No.'

'Then let's both of us take off those. The night isn't cool yet.'

Compliantly, Ankhetari raised the red wig, and her own hair tumbled out, escaping silk, all over her breasts and shoulders and arms.

He watched her. Then he too lifted off the coffin of wig.

His own hair was also black as the wig, but it shone. It fell down his back, as hers did, to the knees. His hair was very strong, and again she thought of the River.

Then he filled the two cups with the red wine, and brought them. He sat on the bed and handed her the shallow cup.

'Are you afraid?'

'No.'

'Yes, you are. You're lying to me.'

'I'm not afraid, Reptah, First Born of Ptah.'

He raised his black brows. 'You honour me. But I am. Afraid. I don't like,' he said, coldly, 'to share.'

Ankhetari said, 'But you share the thought with me.'

'So I do. Maybe I can do the rest, then.'

'We must.'

'Oh no. I can deflower you with anything. My hand, or some suitable object in the room.'

'But,' she replied, 'won't it be – pleasure? They said—'

'For me, supposedly. But for you, girl, an act of great pain. Like giving birth, but going the other way.'

'Do we blaspheme?' she asked in wonder.

'It isn't blasphemy. Your seal must be broken and I must put something of myself inside you. My finger would do. And I must spill my seed for Ptah, but I've done that before.'

'What is it like?'

'Strange,' he said. 'A gift to the dark. Have you never touched yourself – where the Bull touched you?'

'Often, of course. When I bathe.'

'And did you never sense anything?'

Ankhetari lowered her eyes. 'Yes. Then I took my hand away.'

They drank a little.

A wick muttered in an oil lamp, and a vapour went up. They looked at it, and then looked back at each other.

'Let me see you naked,' he said.

Ankhetari put down her chalice, and slipped from the couch. She undid her girdle and let it fall, with the skirt of byssus, to the rug.

She was very slender, but curved like a vase. They had

298

shaven off all hair from her body, even from the mound of sex. Secretive and enclosed, the cup of her loins, like a lotus on a stem of shadow.

He observed her, and she must allow this, although now, for the first time, she felt a sort of anger. She wanted to say, *Why must you look at me?* His gaze was not friendly, not respectful. It seemed he hated her.

Then he got up, undid the fastening of his garments and let them drop.

His body was lean and muscled like a lion's, like a carving, wide at shoulder, narrow and straight at hip. They had taken all his body hair also and, without cover, the snake lay at his groin, large but motionless, of a tense dull colour. It was not erect, as they had explained to her it should be. He was quiescent. She had not stirred him.

Disdainfully he said, 'My body doesn't pay yours homage, lady. Forgive my body. I've been beaten for allowing it pleasure, and now it expects pain as a reward.'

Ankhetari said, cold as he was, 'Find some object, then, and take my virginity. If it isn't a blasphemy. Then you can go to sleep.'

And from her eyes, to her astonishment, two large tears sprang, leapt on to her cheeks, streamered down. She had not wept for years, not since the early days in Sekhmet's courts, when she had missed the crude family in the wet hut, and her adulterous mother.

But Reptah seemed perturbed by the two matched tears. He said, 'I didn't mean to distress you. No. If we must, then we'll lie together. Stretch out again, Ankhetari.'

'You don't distress me. I'm only nervous now. Yes. Let's do it and have done with it. It doesn't matter if you hurt me. I won't cry out.'

She lay down, and he, as if making an abrupt decision, lay beside her.

And the sides of their bodies touched.

Until that moment, there had been no actual fleshly contact between them.

Skin scraped softly skin, and through both of them seemed to pulse a ripple, a current, so both sat upright. They stared at each other.

'What is it?' she said.

'Knowledge,' he said. 'Once I touched the feet of the statue in the shrine. That was like this. And yet – it wasn't – like this.'

Ankhetari reached out slowly with her right hand, and put it on his right shoulder. He shuddered, and she felt go through her, the length of her arm, into her breasts and belly, a warm spasm like light or heat, yet something else.

He caught her hand before she could withdraw it, he held her hand in his and said, no longer cold but hard as metal taken from a fire, 'We have the same blood. Strangers in this land. They put me out in a basket in the River because I was nothing of theirs. And you—'

'My father,' she whispered, 'but who he was—'

'There were legends of Set hunting again in the marshes,' he said, 'and he fornicated with the women among the reeds. He came snuffling to the huts like a red pig with eyes as blue as lapis lazuli.'

'Are we cursed, then?'

'The god knows. But we're one. Brother and sister. Kindred. Not the children of the Upper Land.'

Something made her glance, and she saw that now he was upright, huge, like a statue, and too big for her, but in that moment, she wanted his invasion, wanted to be crushed and rent and taken, by him.

He kissed her and his tongue moved in her mouth and she could only lie against him, lost in the marvel of it, this first possession.

When he eased her gently on to her back, he lay over her, his feet clasping hers, his hands either side her head. He kissed her deeper and more deeply, and she felt the weight of him, and could not move, as if he anchored her to the earth.

Then he began on her body, seeking apparently to find out all of it. He mouthed her breasts, turning her nipples into sweets of joy. He kissed the scented pits of her arms, the softness inside the joints of her arms, he moulded her waist with his hands and tongue, and changed her navel to flame. At the gate of her sex he hesitated, but then his tongue found out this also, and an exquisite melting delight caused her after all, despite what she had said, to cry aloud.

He told her that she tasted of mint and honey.

He tongued her feet and the places behind her knees, he put even her hair between his teeth.

As he entered her, her entire structure seemed to give way, to break, and to reform.

She loved the pain, as if it were not pain at all, and somewhere she heard the sistrum bells, the notes of harps, in her ears of her veins.

And then he carried her, like the River, towards death.

She said to him that she was dying.

He told her this was not so, even though it was like that.

And then she did die, and out of her her soul burst, a blue bird with a human face, and she flew up into the ceiling, which was painted by golden stars. From there she saw the crisis of his own pleasure. Beheld him sink upon her. And then she opened her eyes, and she was beneath him, and she lived.

She knew at once terrible sadness, for she had not wanted to exist beyond that moment. To be obliterated with him – that was the culmination of all things. There could be no reason to live, and no life, beyond their union.

But after a little while he drew her up, and they bathed in the sacred water, sprinkled by petals, in which had dippered the beaks of ibises.

And after that, he made love to her a second and a third time.

Each occasion was like or better than the first. Each death more perfect. Each rebirth more sad and slow and dark.

Finally she wept.

He held her, and they did not speak.

They lay down, with the crescents under their necks, and saw the heavenly ceiling, until they slept.

Near dawn, the far outer door was loudly struck, waking them.

The lamps had burned out, but through a hundred tiny apertures, faint pearly light was seeping.

Soon Ra would ride up from the River of the dead and cleave the horizon. On the face and flanks of the great Sphinx in the desert, the goldenness of the sun would spread like oil. In the temple between the paws of the Sphinx, they would offer to the sun wine and flowers and blood. And from the obelisks of the city the sunbeams would ray out in blistering mathematical lines. The horns would sound over the high gates. Morning, in Egypt.

But for Ankhetari, a day of darkness. They would part. They would never glimpse each other again.

She felt a small soreness to one side of her neck. In his transports, he had bitten her, drawn blood like the blood of the sacrifice. Something of hers was always now in his body. And in her womb, perhaps, his seed. Although she doubted it. She felt empty there. And in her heart.

They bathed and dressed themselves. Still they did not speak, not until they came to the outer chamber with the altar.

'I don't want to go away from you,' he said. 'Maybe we can meet.'

'How? It would be death.'

'We're married. Husband and wife.'

'Only for one night.'

'You don't believe so,' he said. 'You're mine. In this life, in the life beyond life, in the golden fields of for ever, where Lord Ousir walks with the sickle.'

'I may never reach eternity,' she said. 'I may be devoured for my sins.'

He smiled. 'Never. What sins? My sister.'

They made the offering at the fire, the only fire which had kept alight, and round them the yellow jasper of the daylight began to come, through the miniature pores of those rooms.

'We'll be together again,' he said. 'There will be a way. You're mine, until death and beyond death. Until Ra dies on the River under the world.'

She lowered her eyes and the fire smoked. Had the gods heard?

When the door was opened, they went out, and in the corridor she saw a scribe painting writing upon the wall, a beetle above the sun. He used a can of red spray paint, and over its acidulous smell came the aroma of Heinz tomato soup from the thermos at his side.

Chapter Thirty-Four

WAKING WAS MORE CURIOUS THAN the dream. Anna was in her Egyptian 'flat', under the mountain. And this morning, at sunrise, it was Cain who had kissed her. He had done no more than that.

The dream concerned things Anna had never, until now, thought of. Sexual things that seemed a long way off.

Besides, the man in the dream, the priest called Reptah, was not Cain. Did not resemble him in any way.

Yet it had been so explicit and so evident. Everything. Even to the stars on the ceiling of the room, to the drop of blood that beaded her finger from Reptah's bite. To the pain and deliciousness of his penetration into her body.

Reptah also had seemed familiar. As if she had seen him often. But she never had.

It was very late in the day now, probably, for she had slept for hours after returning into the pyramid, the mountain.

She had felt calm and almost pleased, at first. Before she slept. Awake, she felt dismay. She was confused. And sitting on the side of her sloping bed, which was not designed specifically for sex, Anna cried. She was all child, very young, and lost. She wanted Althene. There would be no Althene. 'Mum' did not come, was not invited, as Harpokrates, Cain's pet, would surely understand by now.

304

Cain had said Althene was his own son – his *daughter*.
But even that would not count.

Anna had asked Cain for a music centre, and he had
said this might be arranged. A clock – and he had
laughed. Sekhmet, Lady of Time. She was to be Cain's.
Not Reptah's. Whoever Reptah had been – or was.

The woman called Ast came presently, and the repetitive
ritual of bathing and anointing took place. Anna was
dressed in the white Greek dress with a zip, and made
up in a modern way.

Anna did not ask any questions, and Ast only informed
her that later someone would come. Not who, or why,
or when.

She fastened a necklace of hammered golden shells about
Anna's neck. The necklace was genuinely, appallingly
old.

It was not to be a feast. It was a cosy little dinner party,
more Greek or Roman than Egyptian, perhaps. In a white
marble room that led from Nuit's Hall, there were low
couches with cushions by the low tables. The women –
two of them – sat upright, and the men reclined. There
were four men.

Lamps hung down. There were tall flowers in vases.

Somewhere music played, but it was ordinarily classical;
it was Bach. Some concealed music centre supplied it.

The first woman was Lilith. She wore one of her long
black dresses. No ornament beyond a garland of dark red
blooms, and a single dark red ring. The other woman
wore draped clothes, like Anna, several pieces of jewellery
that might have been real or superb copies of ancient
embellishments. She had also a garland of fresh yellow
flowers.

The four men had on contemporary dress, expensive,
very casual, shirts without ties, no dinner jackets. As if
one could be formal here only one way.

The fifth man, Cain, had on dark blue, the tunic garment

that was habitual to him. No jewellery, no rings. He did not recline, but sat, like the women.

There were bowls of nuts and sweets and fruits on the tables already, and flagons, Roman-looking jugs.

The men, and woman, who were not Lilith and Cain, were already, as before, utterly drunk and noisy.

There was something new about them. Something too alert, feverish and brilliant. They were afraid, of course.

Cain beckoned Anna to his side. She sat on the couch with him. He looked serene and friendly, at odds with all the rest of it. Lilith seemed only blank. Her tigers were not there. The boy, Harpokrates, also garlanded, came suddenly visible, sitting on a small child's chair, of gold, in Cain's shadow. Harpokrates was drinking wine from a small gold child's goblet.

'Describe the wine,' Cain said to him. The loud room hushed and listened respectfully.

'Roseate,' said the child.

The five guests made boisterous sounds. Lilith took no notice. Anna saw on her the mark of extreme old age, not senility, but pure self-removal. She might have been floating on a cloud. Only her albino tigers connected her to the ground, and they were absent.

How strange then that she had awaited Anna by the undersea window, had talked to Anna at any length. Why had that happened. Had Cain sent Lilith to do it? Or had it been some flash of awareness, that occurred like a planetary juxtaposition, once in a year or a hundred years only. Lilith had been a huntress for those moments, a slow and serpentine archer, sending off narrow arrows into the smoking air. But now, the quiver, empty. She was a doll which had come to life for half an hour, to show it could. No more. No *less*.

A girl dressed for Egypt came and placed on Anna's hair a white garland, like that of the boy.

'And now, you describe the wine,' Cain said, more intimately, to Anna.

She sipped it, she said, 'Burgundy.'

'Wrong,' he said, 'but not inept. Your father-mother will have taught you things.'

'Yes,' Anna said.

Cain said, 'And did she make love to you?'

'No.'

Cain said, 'What an opportunity missed.' His eyes had heat in them. He was intent, it seemed, on making her aware that he himself desired her. This was bizarre, after her long coherent dream, in which another man had been her lover, had taken her virginity and carried her through the River of Death and up again, into the morning.

Anna watched Cain. She seemed now to have the strength or only the temerity. She had known at once, obviously, his intention in bringing her to him. He had kissed her. But now was he too late after all? As if he guessed as much, he had asked her if anyone had been before him.

'Is this a Roman dinner?' Anna said. 'They won't serve dormice?'

'No. Dormice aren't to be had. A French meal. They,' he indicated the drunk noisy guests, 'like it. A treat for them.'

Lilith sighed.

Anna heard her, and glanced again.

Lilith sat quite still, her beautiful cat's head poised on her ringed paw. Slowly she raised a green goblet and drank from it the leaden roseate wine that tasted like Burgundy.

Anna said, softly, to him, 'Does she hate me?'

'Like the wicked step-mother in the fairy story? She hates no one. Her feelings are atrophied and must be manipulated. Perhaps we can do that. Or another. But not now. Not yet.'

Cain's Egyptian slaves came in with dishes that might have come from anywhere modern and expensive. The food was French, as he had said, or somewhat French: a white fish baked and stuffed with Brie and garlic, vegetables in pastry, with butter, chilled soup, strawberries that were sweet only by means of sugar.

The Bach played without pause. The tape or CD never ended, nor did it seem to repeat anything, yet it probably did. That then was like everything else, repetition that seemed always subtly altered, developed, but which maybe was quite static, *stuck*.

There had been something else, like this. Some other place.

Anna thought of the Scarabae house above the common. No, not there. Another house, earlier . . . A spangled dress, a great cat, a grave – a knife seemed to turn, painless and bright, in her brain.

She said, to him, 'Who are all these people?'

'You asked me before.'

'You didn't answer.'

'They're mine.'

'Are they old? Have they lived for hundreds, thousands of years?'

'Who knows?' he said, smiling. 'You sound like a little girl. Your little-girl's voice, I would call that. But you're not, are you, my Anna-Ankhet?' He gave her a strawberry, particularly bloodily red. The colour of Sekhmet—

'You,' she said. 'And you, look young. But *you're* not. You're Scarabae.'

'How tactful, my child. I don't look young to your young eyes. But then, I'm one of the very first,' he said. His voice was almost skittish. 'What is my name? Don't you recall? I killed my brother on the edge of a field, under the jealous eye of God. And God thrust me forth to endow the earth with my murderous children, and branded me, so they would beware of me, those children of others who already existed.'

'Yes,' she said.

'Ah, you believe it.'

'It's true,' she said. 'In some way, it is.'

'Eat the strawberry I gave you.'

'It doesn't taste of anything.'

'Strawberries are always tasteless. They only have a smell which is confused with taste.' He looked at her. 'The food comes to us from far off. It loses its savour. And we have no clocks. Here it's always day, or night. Anna will want to go away.'

'You won't let me.'

'No, I won't let you.'

She felt then a curious exhilaration. She said, randomly, 'Someone may come here, to find me.'

'Yes. How do you know?'

'Althene—' Anna said.

'Not Althene. Althene could never find the way.'

Anna bit into the strawberry. It tasted, now, red, but like red satin, material not fruit.

'What a prize you are to me, Anna. You must never leave.'

The meal was ending, with decanters of brandy, which had the aroma of smoke and pears. Even the little boy, who had stayed silent, was served a thimble of this.

The guests, as formerly, had grown more vociferous, smothering the Bach.

'Why are they so frightened,' Anna said.

'Can't you imagine?'

'Of you.'

'Of me, but for a definite reason. No, don't try to deduce. Observe.' He smiled out over the white room.

Then he stood, and massive soundlessness resulted. Even the Bach had ceased.

The woman in the Augustan jewels and yellow garland put her hand to her face, leaned sideways, and suddenly vomited, sharply, loudly, on the marble floor.

Cain, indeed no one, took any notice.

Cain said, 'The food, the music and flowers. And now, our lottery.'

In at the door from the red Hall outside, walked a woman

in a black robe. She was picturesque, almost funny, for she wore a crude bony mask like a skull. No one laughed.

Between her hands, which were smooth and quite youthful, she carried a copper bowl.

The stink of the jewelled woman's vomit had grown strong, as if it too had a special purpose.

The woman in black went to her, and offered the bowl. Quickly the sick woman thrust in her hand and drew out a small clay thing. She threw this down between her feet, and it broke. That was all. But the woman put her fist into her mouth and began to sob.

Death passed on with her bowl.

She came to the four men who had reclined, and who now sat bolt upright. They reached into the bowl and took, each of them, a thing of clay.

And each cast the clay down, where it broke.

Inside two of the objects, something black, like a calcified pea, rolled out.

Anna wanted to jump up and clap. The scene was absurd, theatrical and stupid. If the woman in the yellow garland had not been sick, Anna would have thought it all a game.

But the two men who had thrown the black peas stood up.

They looked identically drained and grey, though one was still foolishly smiling.

Cain moved across the room.

He embraced the two men, fondly, tenderly.

Then the death woman went out of the room into the Hall of Nuit, and the two men followed her.

In the red glowing gloom outside, there was movement as if of many people, and a scuffling, and the note of a blow.

That was all.

Cain returned to Anna. He ignored the rest of them, but for the boy. He put his hand on the boy's shoulder. Cain said, 'Anna, now I shall test you. Are you ready?' She only stared at him. To the boy he said, 'And you? Will you let me down, will you fail me?'

'No, Uncle Kay,' said Harpokrates. His eyes gleamed from the wine and the drop of brandy, and his garland was tilted, a small roué.

Cain glanced over at the woman who had vomited. She had stopped sobbing. 'Why were you so afraid? Don't you want to make me happy?'

'Forgive me,' said the woman. And then a stream of foreign chatter came from her (like the sickness), high and hissing.

Cain turned his back on her, and she grew dumb.

The Hall was very red, as if seen through a filter, as if lenses had been fixed across Anna's vision.

Red, the marriage colour.

Sekhmet's colour.

The woman's colour of sex, and birth, and life. Of fire. Of blood.

In this red sea, they moved.

Lilith and Cain, and after them Anna and the boy, Harpokrates.

There was no one else. Everyone had vanished. Save for the groups of gods about the Hall, Isis who was Eset, and her husband Ousir-Osiris, Set and his wife Nebthet. The Greek sphinx crouched in her cave of shadow – her whiteness blushed by red.

Harpokrates had taken Anna's hand. Not, she thought, for consolation, but in a kind of determination to lead her on.

She felt a weight of terror. It was inescapable. She would not, futilely, have attempted to run away.

Sekhmet stood up, her face like a gas-mask of gold, the flattened bottle of the muzzle, the neat rounded ears, and roundly slanting eyes.

To the colossal crimson pillar before her, the two men had been fastened, one each side, the men from the feast who had worn French and Italian clothes, hand-stitched shoes, and drunk too much and laughed hysterically.

They were naked now, blushed over their own yellowish white, like the evil sphynx.

Each man was in the shape of an X, the legs spread, as the arms were. They were chained by chains of bronze – so it seemed.

The head of one lolled. That must be the one who had – how had he thought he could? – attempted to resist. This, whatever this was and would be, was too absolute to evade.

The other man was awake.

His eyes were shut and he whispered something over and over, his face pressed into the cornelian limb of the column. Drool ran from his mouth. Was he praying?

They had stopped.

The child dropped Anna's hand.

The redness, the darkness, were so strange, that everything appeared two dimensional or partly as if it was not there. The torches burned from the miasma in spurling flights of yellow that seemed to make no true impression—

Cain.

Cain stood apart, and now a new type of power had come to him, that made him taller and more bulky. His shadow rose behind him, thrust out like a roar of blackness, yet beside him it looked worn, worn away, as if he had outlived it.

He put his hands out, parallel with the burning gems of the floor, and drew them in and took hold of his blue tunic. He tore it open with one vast tug, and in two pieces the garment sheered off from him.

He was, like the men tied to the pillar, naked now. His body was darker than theirs, terracotta in the blood-light. His black hair spilled down him like a rain of molten ink, and at his centre, from the black nest of his loins, a weapon towered, so sure it seemed almost false, almost some monstrous joke in some antique carnival of history where doubtless he had sported.

Anna was jolted, jarred. In her dream . . . she had seen a man revealed. Not like this. That had been a rod of power, but not this power. This was like a sword—

Cain strutted. Yes, he strutted forward, behind the prow of the great warlike erection.

The light went with him and smote on him and bled. A deeper, denser redness washed over everything.

Anna saw through blood.

She saw Cain reach the conscious man chained by bronze to the pillar, and make some manœuvre upon him, which drove the weapon of flesh into the body of the man.

The man shrieked.

Then Cain rode him.

Anna saw this, through blood and fire and smoke. Angles of arms and legs, the two serpents of torso on torso, adhering, slamming away, and back. A rhythm – she knew it from her dream. That was bliss. This was horror. Agony.

The man screamed over and over.

The shadow leapt and fumed across the Hall, in strips upon the pillars, going up into the arch of Nuit herself, as if to break into her also, to burglarize her womb—

And then, from the dance of snakes, Cain's face flashed snake-like forward. There were two white bars like lightning.

The man who had screamed, screamed yet once again, and from the side of his neck jutted out a huge bursting of redness that was black, that jetted away, that sprinkled down.

Cain had—

Cain had bitten out his throat.

Cain drank from the tap of blood, from the hose of it, stemming its violence.

And then he disengaged his body.

He stepped lightly and couthly away.

He was still big, engorged. But, for the moment, finished. His strength was no less.

Down his body, from his lips to his groin, over his legs on to the floor of jewels, the blood of his victim shimmered and ran like scarlet paint. But riper, more wet. The wettest liquid in all the world.

And he spoke to them, across the little distance, in his sane, beautiful and civilized voice.

'Come, Harpokrates. Come, Anna. Come and taste this blood.'

Harpokrates, his face clean and eager, started instantly forward.

And in that microcosm of time, Anna saw Cain see something other than his lust, and his taken children. Saw him see something behind her in the cavern of the shadow.

Perhaps only because it meant she need no longer look at him, Anna turned.

And sure enough, far off over the Hall, someone had come in.

There were others there, farther than he, an escort who had evidently had to allow him, but who dared not themselves venture so near.

He wore dark clothing, and over that ran a whiteness, just as the redness had poured down over Cain.

A tall man with white hair, dressed for the upper earth of ice. Bringing ice with him.

Anna, through all the blur and density of the Hall, made out his face. Eyes like glaciers, mouth like a line in snow.

She knew him.

Knew.

And in one split second, she remembered.

All of it.

Not Egypt, not anything momentous or wise between.

Only that one last time. The time when she had known him, maybe, the very best. When he found her and had her, and had been hers, and let her go. Betrayed her. Worse, not wanted her.

Her hand clutched at her left breast. Something hurt her there, as if she had been kicked.

She staggered, righted herself. Her brain boiled with things more awful even than she had just witnessed.

But it was not the white-haired man at the Hall's end who spoke to her.

It was Cain.

'Oh,' he said. '*Ruth*. Ruth, come here to me. Come and taste the blood, Ruth.'

And Ruth turned about and went to him, to Cain.

'It won't be as you remember,' he said. 'This will be sweet. Better than strawberries. Better than wine.'

And she walked to the corpse on the pillar and put her lips against its shattered neck, the mess of glands and veins and meat, and sucked the blood.

It was sweet. It was better.

Chapter Thirty-Five

MALACH ADVANCED THROUGH THE HALL of the Mountain King, the Hall of the Snow Queen. The servants of Cain had not dared stop him, or keep him from this central area. Cain was Cain, but they recognized Malach, too. Not so much who he was; *what* he was. Another king, a knight-priest-king, off the board of snow and darkness.

He wore the black thermal clothes he had put on for the waste. All but the hood and head coverings. Stripped of those, his hair flamed round him, extravagant, a banner.

Only he moved. The rest of them were a tableau.

Cain in his clothing of clay-red nakedness. Anna, who had been, and was, Ruth, still as a narrow white pillar at the side of the corpse. Only her lips were red, as they had once been painted to be. Something had ordained that her lips had kept a perfect shape, outlined in blood like lipstick. And then a single thread of scarlet slipped down her chin, and on to the breast of her white dress. The left breast. As if someone had thinly stabbed her.

Behind these two, Cain, the girl, the other man, unconscious but not dead. Then the child standing in his white and gold, and the fourth, black, pillar, of Lilith.

Malach negotiated all the distance.

He halted within ten feet of Cain, and of Ruth-who-was-Anna.

His face was composed of hollows, plains, like the world above. A snowscape. His paleness made his eyes far darker, almost black. He looked now, but for the pale hair and skin, very like the man in Anna's dream. Reptah, the priest of the god.

But she did not know him for that.

She knew him only as Malach, now. Ruth's Malach.

'Well,' he said. And then something short and rough, in Latin. Cain laughed, a braying noise.

Nothing else.

But it was Lilith who moved now, gliding, as if she went on wheels, to the dead thing. In a golden chalice she caught the last spasms of the blood.

Going around Anna-Ruth, around Cain, she came to Malach, and offered him the cup.

He looked at her, then dipped in two fingers.

They emerged bright red.

And these he touched to his lips.

Lilith, expressionless, turned from him. She took the cup to the goddess Sekhmet, and set it in the dark stone-woman's hand, which was humanly curved to receive it, under the muzzle of the lioness.

Malach looked at the young girl in red and white.

He said, flatly, 'Hunger.'

'*Full,*' she said. She smiled, and wiped the blood off her face with her hand.

'Anna,' Malach said, steady, still flat. He too licked the blood off his lips. They were pale again.

'Not Anna,' said the girl. 'And not to you.'

Cain laughed once more – now the briefest, most urbane sound. A host at a flawless dinner party where something had gone, just a whisper, amiss.

'You don't belong to him, Anna,' Malach said. 'Understand this. You're free to choose. That's why I came to find you.'

'So I could choose *you*?' she said. She grinned. She raised her head, and the cascade of white hair swung off her, and around her again like thick shining smoke.

She might have been his daughter, his sister. It appeared she had remade herself in his image. But that was before she remembered what he had done to her, for she had forgotten but not forgiven, and now she remembered, too.

He had taught her to kill choosingly – always, with him, *choice*. Spare this one. Take this one. *Some things belong to some people by right. A gift. A caress. Or even death.* But he was always the arbiter. He the instructor, the ultimate judge.

And finally she had made her inevitable mistake, even after his tuition. She had killed a man that Malach had not reckoned deserved his death. And so Malach left her. *Don't say my name*, he said to her. And screaming his name, they had carried her away to prison. But later she escaped, and in the wet wood, the knife went through her heart—

His had been the first of the knives. Her heart had already died. She had loved him. He had told her she was his soul. Yet he left her. *He left her.* And now, here again, *too late*.

'Anna,' he said.

In his face, behind the stone and snow, she glimpsed his strength, and his need.

'Don't,' she said to him, 'say my name.'

'Ah,' he said. 'You bear a grudge. Petty, Anna. After all this.'

'Then I'll be petty. I'll be so petty and so mean and so *changed*. You won't know me. Then you can go away.'

Cain said, gently, 'Is that all you want, Ruth?' And conversationally Cain added, to Malach, 'Your dog-team, of course, will be well treated. But, perhaps, not such niceness for you.'

'No,' said Ruth.

Ruth recalled Malach's beauty, his naked beauty, how she had watched him sleeping, aching with yearning. She had wanted to die for him. She met death over and again in his arms, death that burned—

And he was mixed now with the other image. The body of Reptah lying on hers in the chamber of the temple thousands of years before.

Something like orgasm moved through her now. And at the core of her belly an apple of glass broke. She felt the first blood-offering of Anna's young, young body sink through her loins, and the red rose of it bloomed on her dress. So that she was wounded twice now.

She had wanted to die for him.

She had died.

Anna who was Ruth crossed quickly over the small space, and reaching Malach, she looked at his eyes. She had grown during her time in the white mountain. Although he was taller than Cain, she could reach.

She spat into his face.

The spit, like silver, struck him.

He did nothing. Did not even wipe the spit away.

And she, she saw that Malach loved her, as Ruth had never truly known, despite the words he had spoken, despite his going away.

She was now Ruth and Anna. She was Anna, but Anna *knew*.

'No,' Anna said, 'it isn't all I want. Cain, take him somewhere for me. Tie him up and hurt him. For *me*. I want him to suffer now. I want him to suffer very much.'

Chapter Thirty-Six

✿ VIOLET CROCUSES HAD COME UP on the common, and in the gravel before the house.

Behind the house there was nothing unwise enough to emerge so early.

Dark-haired Sam, the gardener, had been cutting back the wild grass with a strimmer, leaving clots of grass intact around the old apple tree and the fountain with the fish. Nearby Terentia sat on a bench that had been bought, with the toy lion in her lap. She wore a long thick black jumper and over that a long black wool jacket, and a trailing, beaded black silk scarf.

Sam and Terentia did not speak, but they were involved, Miranda thought, in that silent communication so often found among the young, or very old.

Miranda had assumed it was good that Terentia should sit and watch Sam. Sam had not minded. He had seemed to switch his interest to Terentia as soon as he saw her, which was on the second occasion that he called at the house. He had been very respectful to Eric, and to Michael.

A strange boy. Like the eponymous hero of some short story entitled 'The Lodger', or 'The Dark Young Man'.

Sasha was not in the garden, but in front of the TV in her room, knitting another long black wool coat.

Eric was also in his room. He had leaned away from his re-writings of history and begun instead, with the aid of a jeweller's glass screwed into his left eye, to carve a tiny wooden figure. It was of a woman, and it had the head of a fox. Wooden memory?

They kept to their rooms now, like insects keeping to cells. Only Miranda did not do this.

She got easily, in her black jeans, on to the back of Connor's bike, and Viv yipped excitedly in the saddle-bag.

He had come back before he said he would, before the spring, unless the token crocuses made it all right.

'It means darkness,' said Miranda, absently.

'What's that?'

'Sam, in hieroglyphics.'

'Old Egyptian? You sound like Red . . .'

'Darkness strimmed the grass,' said Miranda. She laughed.

'Ready?' asked Connor.

'Oh, *yes*.'

He wondered, incoherently, if they would ever have sex, and if then he would also politely inquire if she was ready to begin.

The bike started with a thunderous roar and he heard Miranda exclaim. Not fright, possibly approbation.

Then they soared off down the drive, away from the dark glow of the looming house.

Miranda held on to Connor, her hands clasped on his leather belt. She wore the spare helmet. She and Viv gazed out through their goggles, and the world whirled by.

Miranda did not foolishly try to speak.

There was the silence of the bike's guttural roaring.

At turns, Miranda leaned, fearless and proper, as he had told her. Through the maze of buildings they went, under the red heights of buses, through currents of diesel and pollution, and now and then the rain slanted, light as mist, wavering, gone.

By twelve o'clock they had reached the outposts of the suburbs, and they pulled up in a pub yard. The owner knew Connor, and came out to admire his bike and his bint.

Miranda looked a wonder in her black long-booted

legs and slender body swathed by dauntless black velvet already veined from the road. Her hair foamed forth from the helmet. Her teeth were so white – like a child's. Had the originals dropped out and new ones grown, or had she just had everything capped. They did not look false.

They, Connor, Miranda and Viv, ate steaks and jacket potatoes, with two bottles of creamy red Gallo wine, Miranda's choice. Miranda paid overtly and stylishly, as if she enjoyed it. Connor was proud of her. She and Viv had had most of the booze.

In twenty minutes, the land changed, the far-off hills keeping up with them, while the middle ground ran in the other direction. Factories, schools, marooned office blocks. Then open country broken only by barns and crooked houses, old churches, the occasional oast house with a skirt of village.

They scored through places that seemed to be called Whippum and Flittham and Burrow and Warry. There were new quaint pubs with four-feet-high doors and beams and bright modern signs showing merry harvesters and bulls and porcupines.

In a rainy lane a daylight fox stared at them from a hedgerow, like a dog-rose, and Viv squeaked in affront.

They reached the shore by ten past three.

It was the place he had wanted, not popular, bleak and flat, with the fields sheering off, black and drained green, and great flattened cedars trenching up, and the stony beach empty but for two or three symbolic-looking huts, a man and his Labrador, and beyond everything, the sloping water, grey as turned cream, with a yellowish lace at its edges, and far out a hollow colourless half-non-existent sky.

The bike was stopped, on the muddy road above.

They sat, and looked at the end of the world.

'Oh, Connor. It's lovely. So devastated.'

'Yes,' he said, satisfied.

They walked along the beach, and Viv ran barking at the sea and the sea played with her, carelessly.

'Used to come here as a kid,' said Connor. It was a lie.

'Yes,' she said, 'we lived by the sea a long while.'

They did not talk very much, and the wind swarmed in, bringing breakers to their feet.

When Viv was exhausted, she too came to Connor, to be carried.

After the man and the Labrador, no one else hove in sight. They walked, and turned back, and got on the bike, and followed the road along above the shore.

Finally there was a long, low, flat hotel, looking wind-blown and deserted, but it was curiously occupied and open, and in the bar a woman, bleak as the sea, switched on an electric fire for them and served them tea and biscuits.

'You can't have a drink until six,' she announced. This was all she said.

Then they did talk. Connor, biker stories of the road, funny, sad, terrible stories, all true, scarcely embroidered, and she, strangely and perhaps disappointingly, London stories. The hotel where the piano played Cole Porter, and old men and young boys went mysteriously up to hidden rooms, the Indian gentleman who had wanted to give her an apartment, how she had been lost in Harrods one whole afternoon, never finding the way out until closing time.

'You don't,' he said, 'speak about the past.'

'Oh, the past. There's so much of it.'

'Is there?'

'Don't you,' elusively she said, 'find it so?'

He thought, considered, and felt compelled to agree. Since he was a child, centuries seemed indeed to have gone by, and besides he had been so many different people. And he did not want to speak of his beginning, the dire father and hard-handed mother, the sister he had loved who ran off with a married man and must never be spoken of, and who he had never managed to find.

'You told me once about a wedding,' he said, as they

drank the hot pale tea and dipped in the shortbread biscuits
for themselves and Viv.

'Did I?'

'An old wedding. You rode there on a horse.'

'Well, I'm old, Connor, you know. We did things like that
then. But now I've ridden on your wonderful bike.'

'We are honoured.'

She laughed. Pretty, her laughter.

There was a safe place for the honoured bike, and so
presently they went out and walked again along the stones
at the ocean's rim.

The light of the day was going away inland, grey sunset
without sun. But as the dark began, she turned to him and
Connor said, politely, 'May I kiss you, on the lips?'

'What do you think?' said Miranda.

'I think that you'll let me.'

'Then I shall.'

So he kissed her, decorously, his mouth closed.

Hers was sweet with a fresh rosy lipstick. He liked its
lollipop taste. Viv, jealous, ran off again and yapped at the
sea. Which came in with a great wave and showered her.

'Oh, poor Viv!' cried Miranda, but Viv only leapt back,
sneezed, and barked more furiously. 'When I was a little
girl,' said Miranda, 'once the sea did that to me. And I
wasn't brave. I cried. But then I pretended that my face
was only wet from the sea water.'

He thought, where had that been? What mediaeval or
Renaissance shore. He did not ask. He kissed her again,
and now he tried possession, and she allowed him to.
Inside her mouth was all the soft sunset warmth the day
had not provided, succulent, promising.

When he called, Viv ran up. Miranda took off her red silk
scarf and dried Viv, while Connor held them all together.

Back at the hotel, some lights had come on. The bar
looked like the *Mary Celeste*, the tea things uncleared, the
bottles dimly shining.

'Will you take a drink?' the bleak-sea woman asked,

rising up from below the counter, where perhaps she had lain folded.

'It isn't six yet,' said Miranda.

'Oh, well. Have the first one on the house.'

The electric fire burned bright. The woman made no demur at pouring half a pint into a bowl for Viv. She said, 'There's a room, if you want it. But I expect you're staying at the King's.'

'Never heard of it,' said Connor. 'We were going back.'

Miranda said, 'It would be nice to stay. Yes, I'd like that.'

Connor hesitated, and the woman said, 'You can have the best double for a single. Out of season.'

Connor looked at Miranda. Miranda said, 'That will be lovely.'

Resigned, Viv buried her snout in her drink.

In the night Connor woke, and watched Miranda sleeping peacefully and silently beside him.

Her naked shoulder gleamed in a ray of moonlight through the window, which had net only halfway up. They had left the outer curtains undrawn.

It was a quarter moon, a young-girl moon.

Miranda's body was mature, the moon at its ripened half, maybe. White and lush. The muscles firm. No inch or ounce of spare flesh, all taut and smooth as a white sweet plum.

They had lain in the sideways position. He did not think she had come, and yet, could not quite be sure. Her pleasure and contentment were very great, and completely genuine. Probably – for it was surely real, Miranda's age – she had not made love with a man for a while. Years, decades. She had said something . . . relearning her lines.

She had enjoyed him, any way. She had kissed his closed eyes.

And he, he had liked it very much. Too much. She had excited him in an odd new way. The way of the goddess on the hill. The way of perverse things, definitely. Too bad. A good lay. A glorious fucking lay.

Viv slept on the pillow, forgivingly.
Viv was his love, after all.
But what, what, was Miranda?

When the moon had gone and the sun had not yet decided
if it would rise, air like pearl, like sea water, he woke to find
Miranda's mouth curved round him, and, Oh Christ, the
swell of all the seas was in him then.

Almost too late she let him go that way, and got up on
him, slim and velvet pale, and he had to cram into his mind
the worst images, to hold off for her. Even Cardiff rose to aid
him, Cardiff burning dead on the beacon. And the granny
with her cake. But Cardiff would have forgiven him, like
Viv, who had opened one eye then closed it courteously.

This time she did come, for her back arched like a bow
and out of her mouth issued a long harsh hiss.

By then he could not let go, he could only sink
strengthless down. But it had been worth it, and fair.
Once for him, once for her.

'It's morning,' she said, presently.

The sun had made its decision.

'I'll have to take you back.'

'I'd have loved the night ride,' she said, 'but then, I had
the night ride, didn't I?'

He did not know if he should say he would want her
again, so he did not say it.

They lay relaxed, awake, and the yellow light lay on the
silver sea.

Viv climbed on to the windowsill to look.

When Miranda got up and went to the bathroom, Connor
saw a tiny darkness moving on her limbs, and for a
moment was concerned. Then it occurred to him she
had only started to menstruate; their activity must have
brought it on.

He heard her singing in the bathroom. He did not recognize the tune but it did not sound old. Of course not.

326

Chapter Thirty-Seven

CANDLELIGHT BURNED THROUGH ALL THE rooms, which ran about a rectangular courtyard. The court was from no particular period. It was only dark, like night, the high ceiling black and painted with gold stars. The candles burned also in the court, in tall wooden holders, as if on a still evening.

On one wall of the court was a fresco, faintly Pompeian, some sort of race in red and ochre, very faded.

Nacreous carp swam in the tank of water, hiding under large leaves. There was no other vegetation, not a single plant; no other life, but his.

Cain walked into and out of the rooms. On some days he would do this over and over. The rooms, of which there were ten, opened also into each other, except for the bathroom, which was modern, white and functional, and very small, having a shower not a tub, like something squeezed into a flat in Soho in London, as an essential afterthought.

Another of the rooms was a bedroom. It had a bed. The bed was of a somewhat Victorian or even Regency design. It was draped by dark blue that had pastelled with dust.

There was dust in all the rooms but for the bathroom, which the slave-servants of Cain cleaned every day. The dust did not come from the cold environ of the world outside. It was composed of shed particles of material,

327

of wood and fibre and cloth. And of Cain himself. For his skin, though evidently more than human, was human enough it sloughed, and his black hair also.

They had saved his hair once. His own pillows were once stuffed with it, and with the fallen or cut hair of women he had, now and then, fancied. But that was so long ago, the pillows themselves fell to pieces. Or had it even happened?

On some days, Cain did not go about the rooms. He sat still, hour by hour, in one of the chambers, on a seat or chair that was of European or antique Greek or Italian design.

There was very little furniture. Of all of it, only a vast black piano took up any space. The piano too was sheeted in dust. Its keys had swollen, turned yellow, and locked fast. Inside its harp-like entrails a spider had lived. Perhaps the spider had been imported, or had arrived in some case of books or fruit from another place where spiders were.

Other than furniture, there were objects.

They were possibly valuable by reason of age, but for no other reason. Stones and sticks, shards, stoppers, bottles, iron bolts, keys. In one area some cages of brass hung from the ceiling. On the floor of one lay the skull of something. The others were unoccupied.

In one room there were portraits or replicas. None were apparently of Cain, whose unique face was nowhere represented, save occasionally in a round bronze mirror that rested opposite the blue bed. There were, in the portrait room, three images of the woman, Lilith. One was a head in old brown marble, maybe Grecian, very lifelike, resembling her almost exactly. She had been crowned with marble flowers. Elsewhere she was shown in an oval of soft gold, a painting from the 1600s, a French school, wan and a-typical, still to be recognized under her visor of gauze.

The third image was a sepia photograph. Lilith did not look the same in this at all. She looked matronly under the plate of the great black hat, and in her stiff and studied pose, there was the hint of an aliveness she no longer had.

On a table stood a foot-high glass pyramid full of deep red liquid, with one silver bubble in it. The candlelight shone through the redness, which, perhaps, was blood. Or not.

When the candles burnt out, Cain himself would sometimes replace them. Otherwise the slave people did so when they came.

In the room that stood at the west end of the rectangle there were modern things. A flat-topped desk of black metal supported an Apple computer. Some software lay randomly beside it, as if it had been used at least once. There was a machine for playing music, but this conceivably had never been used, for it was thick with cobwebs, like the piano, almost. There was no evidence of disks or tapes.

Various gadgets were scattered about, with panels of buttons. These had been picked up, fingered, replaced quite recently.

Cain came into this room now, but only for a moment. He regarded it. Expressionless.

He did not look old, although maybe to a child or an animal he would have done. The boy, probably, thoughtlessly considered him to be well over sixty. Only Ankhet, still a child, seemed to see him timelessly. Ankhet-Ruth. Did Cain ponder her? Or Malach? Anything? Nothing?

Old men . . . might grow set, small-minded, spiteful. Physical youth might be full of itself, knowing everything. And Cain, was both. Too young. Too old.

Or was it all a carefully never-spoken lie. A fit and clever, intellectual, stupendously rich man of forty years. A madman, supposing himself to be so ancient that even his wife must be modelled and painted and photographed in a cunningly faked way. Surrounding himself with antiquarian treasures and, more cunning still, antiquarian mediocrities. As if he had picked them up along his path of thousands of years—

Cain turned and looked out at the pool of the elderly, white glistening carp.

His eyes were like tunnels into night.

He crossed from the room, and stood above the pool. On a silver dish were some scraps of something. And now he held it, down into the water, and the carp came and fed from his ringless hands.

Had some clever operation reinvented his eyes?

How had it been done? To put the black night of space behind the blue of earthly sky.

In the fifth room the stone was lying, on a granite ledge. The stone engraved with those words Lilith had mentioned to the white girl in the Hall of Nuit.

Tenebrae sum.

I am the darkness. Darkness, I—

The carp did not fear Cain, had no cause.

They nibbled his hands, and he let them, as he had let flies and beetles go over his flesh, lizards and serpents, crocodiles, unharmed.

Youth was fresh, and knew everything, and old age was locked and knew it too, two different and opposing intolerances, without mitigation.

More than human – yes, perhaps. But the mind, the psychology – *only* human.

Cain got up from the carp pool, where every regimented day he fed the carp, like clockwork.

Cain, who was Darkness, went across the court to the wall painted with a race, and the concealed automatic door slid open before him.

The woman was standing in the upper, actual world, at a spot where the river froze again, beyond the mountain. A vast greenish glacier spread away to the south, like a shadow under the ice.

Lilith was clothed over in grey and black fur. Like him,

330

she did not cover her face against the snarling cold, although it was today many degrees below zero.

A short distance from her were her attendants, dressed in thermal garments, but their faces similarly unshielded.

The group stood watching, as the two albino tigers hunted over the ice.

The tigers were about half a mile off, where some animals, taken at the coast, had been brought and let go. The cats had selected their kill, and, trapped in childhood by their association with Lilith, worked together in bringing down the prey.

They felled it, after the shortest dash, hardly enough to exercise them.

The two snow white beasts flung themselves down and began to rip the hot carcass apart, while the other prey animals waddled aimlessly away.

Steam rose like smoke from the kill, as if the ice were burning.

Soon enough they would run back to her, their feathery mouths dribbled red, their tongues red. They would bring her a morsel of death, and she would take it from them, to please their instinct. She, the old tigress, who had assumed the rôle of their dead mother.

Her brain . . . it was not senile, yet, like that. Glimpses of memory moving always within her, like the flicker and thrash of the two white barred tails on green-slotted whiteness, thought rising like the frail steam of the blood.

And she was on a sea that rocked her, quite gently, bore her on. But the ship had lost its sail (and that saying, a ship without a sail, a woman without breasts). Now, only a raft of black and white bones, Lilith.

Then, miles away, farther than the sight of her feeding sons, the tigers, rose the island of another thought. A child. Not the two *he* had named, Harpokrates, Ankhet – for there were others to come, *other children*. And one child, this child who was black skinned. He would appear so solid and real on the surface of the snow.

Faran.

Yes, the name, not minted by her lord, had been spoken to her. Faran, who was seven, or eight years old. Black knight to black queen. An island in her sea.

For he was something to her. She knew distinctly, inexplicably that he was – and oh the glimpse, the flicker of the thought. Hold it to her. Hold it before her.

Was it for this reason she had spoken to the girl called Ankhet, called Anna, called Ruth? Because that one was a foretaste of him. Of Faran. *Her* child. Lilith's child.

With him she would be, truly, a mother with a son.

And presently a lover. A wife.

And then at last, quickened by the newness of his new-made body, filled with seed, the vessel of a child that would be her own—

The darker tiger rose and shook itself.

Thought vanished from Lilith.

She saw only the two cats bounding towards her, the ice spinning from the runners of their paws.

She took from their red mouths the tiny slivers of flesh, and, turning, Cain, her lord, Phrah, Magus, husband, was at her side. And the slaves had drawn away.

He spoke to her now in one of the oldest tongues of the earth. Its very music almost robbed it of all meaning, yet she understood.

—*Soon, Lilitu. Are you anxious? Does your heart drum in your breast?*

—*Perhaps, my lord.*

—*But it must. Never disappoint me.*

—*Whatever you wish, my lord.*

And then Cain said to her, in French contemporary as his clothing – for he looked like a twentieth-century explorer of the ice-waste, all but the maskless face – 'Were you thinking of him? The boy I've taken for you. The black boy like smooth polished ebony. Fleecy haired. With cat's eyes. Yes?'

'Who?' she said.

'Or is it Malach you think about,' said Cain in an obscure dialect of Holland. 'Do you care about Malach?'

Lilith said nothing. The paler tiger licked her ungloved hand, streaking it with blood.

Cain said, in English, 'Maybe I'll have them both, after all. Your black boy. Her white priest. Leave only Cain for you women to fight over.'

Lilith's eyes quickened. They flared like points of mercury in her white face.

'You said the boy would come to me.'

'You care then?' he said in French. '*Hélas. J'ai perdu, mon amour.*'

But the life in her eyes had sunk. She glanced at him. She spoke in a tongue almost as old as the first one he had employed, calling him *Phrah* – Pharaoh – quirkishly, some eldritch remembered coquetry.

'You have Ankhet,' she said. 'You have *got* Ankhet.'

But her eyes were soft, dim, like the distance, where now a wind was lifting on the snow.

Ankhet Persephone Anna Ruth had dressed for Ruth, as Ruth would have wanted.

She had told the women, Shesat, Mesit, Ast, what they must do, and they obeyed instantly, faultlessly. She was very polite to them, in Ruth's way. *Thank you*, she said. Like Ruth, too, she was a little prim, but then she put that aside. The Egyptians had gone bare breasted often.

The wig hung to her shoulders. It was of thick black hair, many strands of which were plaited and ended in golden lunettes pierced by cornelians. Her earrings were also of gold, with three angelica crystalizations of green jasper.

The dress was transparent milky linen, tight on her legs so she could hardly walk, leaving one breast free – the right, and thus the left breast, which bore the blue wisp of scar, was hidden. Crossed braces of gold held up the skirt, and where they joined was a red scarab. Her pubic hair was covered by a mesh of gold which shone through the fabric.

Her eyelids were painted gold and outlined in dark green. She allowed them to add mascara. Her lips were the red of the scarab, dark as blood which oxidized.

She had taken off her turmaline ring. Rachaela had given it to Anna.

She was delighted by her looks. More than herself it was not herself at all, but someone else that she really was.

Down in the dark, the darkness Cain had made under the white pyramid, Malach was.

As Ankhet Ruth had been dressed, he had been, appropriately, stripped. Naked.

It would not surprise her. Cain had told her of it. It was what was done. And Ruth – had seen Malach naked. Even Anna had done so, in the dream.

His body, in the unlight light of a torch stuck high up in a wall of stone, was a universal sigil of the bodies of all prisoners. Although hard, proportionate, and beautiful in other circumstances, now it was debased, made vulnerable, horrible. In tint almost grey, streaked by fire.

The scene was again a set from some film, most likely a *bad* film. And Malach was a character, the way he had always seemed to behave, a person invented in romance, song and story. Doomed, glamorous, motivated – pointless. A revenger of wrongs, a rescuer, a white knight.

His head hung, and the long, long hair fell round him. They had not hacked it off. Ruth who was Ankhet Persephone had said she did not want that. She would do it, if she wished. No one else.

Imperious little spoilt and angry child. Child killed for love. Child dead of love's death.

Pointless too. Another character.

If they had lived so extensively, those centuries, and where they had not continued in one body, had returned, reborn, half remembering, how had they come to this pass? This utter stupid littleness?

They could have been gods, almost. They thought like people. Loved and hated and wanted to hurt and save the way only people excusably can, *people* who are tortured and maimed and have only one life.

And this was what he was saying, quietly, but it was in another language and she did not understand.

But then Ruth would never understand.

He had begun to teach her.

And then, he stopped.

'How are you, Malach?'

She asked him this, standing on the steps that led down to him, just like the wicked lady in the off-colour epic film.

'Very well,' he said. 'And you?'

'Shall we play the word game? I'll say a word and you say what comes into your head. *Mistake.*'

Malach smiled. He hung in the steel fetters Cain had epically arranged – Malach was strong – and smiled mildly.

'Go on,' she said. 'I want you to talk. I might forgive you if you talk.'

'And you might not.'

'Don't you want to ask, forgive you for what?'

'I know for what.'

'Good. He'll do anything to you I want. He'll have them hit you, whip you.'

'Don't you mean scourge?' he inquired softly, giving the softest inference that he had not quite accepted his status in her film, or, had accepted it humorously.

'Scourge then,' she said. Ruth's sense of humour had never developed. Perhaps Anna's had not. 'Castrate you, even.'

'No, I don't think he'll do that.'

'Because Scarabae revere generation? He doesn't care. You're my toy. He gave you to me.'

'No, Anna. *I* gave me to you.'

'Weren't you silly.'

'What else could I do. I thought he had you here against your will.'

'He'd never let me go.'

'He would. If I was here, and you wanted it.'

She seemed to be thinking of this. Then she said, 'But he wants me.'

'I want you.'

'No. It's too late. *Blood*, Malach. What do you think of when I say that?'

'That he likes to drink it. Or pretends that he does.'

'So do I.'

'Anna—'

'Now you sound different. But don't call me that. *They* called me that. I'm Ankhet, now.'

'Althene named you. You want to renounce Althene too?'

'Althene didn't come after me.'

'She would have tried. Something – No. Only I could find you. Was *meant* to find you.'

'Yes, that's true. So you could be *mine*. I was your prisoner once. You punished me.'

'Yes.'

'Now you're my property.'

'His,' he said. 'That's the mistake you mentioned.'

She came down the steps and walked into the space below Malach, where he hung forward from the chains. His arms were pulled up above his head. It must be painful, awkward to breathe, yet he seemed relaxed. There were no marks on him.

'I'm left-handed,' she said. She flexed the left hand. 'That's because of you. It's called sinister.'

'I know.'

'I'm sinister.'

'If I call you Ruth,' he said, 'will you listen?'

'Not if I don't want to.'

'Want to,' he said. 'Just for a moment.'

She looked into his eyes.

336

Her own, rimmed to the shape of two perfect fish by the malachite paste, glittered. Her gold gleamed. She said, 'Do you remember me like this?'

'No. I remember only *you*. And you've forgotten *you*. But I promise you this, whatever Cain does, or refuses to do, to me, what he wants with you is the old, old useless nothingness. What your mother's afraid of. A brood queen. His own woman can't do it. She's a husk. You've seen her. But you are the beginning. He wants to remake himself on you. That's what interests him. New creations of himself from your matrix. *Adamus*. Adamus was nothing to this one.'

'I hear you,' she said. 'What do I care? I can have babies. I can have babies easily over and over. And stay *me*. Why not? Make him happy. He wants me. There's more blue in his eyes than in yours.'

'Or you can go free with me. Think of it, Anna. Free with me, and of me, if you want.'

'How, he's subdued you? You've *succumbed*.'

'Appearances are deceptive.'

'You can't win,' she said.

'Yes, if you want it.'

'I want you,' she said, 'crushed, destroyed, ruined. I want you dead. I hate you,' she said quietly, 'I hate you so much I can't even feel it. I don't feel anything. I want to see you screaming in agony so I can feel again.'

'You could never feel,' he said. 'Don't wait for that.'

'*Yes*. I loved you. I did. I *did*.'

'Then come with me now. This is a place that isn't even real. It's a fantasy. Rubbish. The world goes on, it always has.'

'Let it go on without me,' she said.

Then she turned. She was like a slender glittering, gleaming icon, a beetle of gold, the way Ruth had always been, and Anna also, in her pale glowing way. Ankhet beckoned. To the man who had stood above in the shadow beyond the torch.

'Look,' she said.

The man wore a sort of leather kilt and iron on his big arms. He carried a *scourge*, its tails tipped by metal.

'Are you ready?' Ruth said to Malach.

He did not answer.

Ruth beckoned again and the man came down the steps, and stood before Malach's naked, held body, and raised the flail.

'Do it.' She put her head on one side.

And the arm of the man went back and back, and rushed forward like a fist of rain and hail that flamed.

Silence.

The blood that was unzipped from Malach's skin struck her in the face. She licked it off her lips, and stepped away a little distance, to avoid the deluge of the next blow.

Chapter Thirty-Eight

LOUIS THE PRIEST PICKED HIS nose.
He did it quickly, to get the business out of the way before the others, his congregation, came up.

It was not what he should do.

Not fitting. But then.

Then, nothing would be right, not really. After all, he no longer belonged to his church, the Children of Time, or Cot for short. Cot and God. And even his name had gone for a burton that last time, under the tooth of the guillotine, Paris 1793.

Once he had thought he remembered all that clearly. The tumbril and the shouting crowd, even the plank they had flung him on, and the nasty way the guillotine killed you—Thankfully the images had faded, dulled. Now, though he stuck to the teaching of reincarnation steadfastly, his own beliefs were blurred.

He had been fourteen when Cot got him. He had wandered into London off the train, eyes round, idiotic, ten pounds, stolen from his mother, in his pocket. He had wanted to get away from them, his parents, the back-to-back terrace house up north, the school, and the prospect of the factory after.

London could have done anything to him, given him away to heroin and prostitution, some quick death in an alley worthy of Paris 1793. But somehow London led

339

him, starving after three days without food, into the hall of Cot.

The Cot left their sect open to everyone. They believed in bodily cleanliness and free sex, between opposite or matched genders – after all, if you were attracted, it was probably because you had slept with this person before in a previous existence. And since reincarnation crossed the gender barriers, you could be a woman now when you had been male before, or vice versa, and that other woman you wanted had maybe previously been your legal wife.

This was all quite convenient.

The Cot ate well too. They begged in bands on the streets in neat green robes, and sometimes did odd jobs, having a common fund for all, which was administered by a committee.

The regression sessions had tickled Louis at first – his name had not been Louis then. Until he fell in love with a girl of seventeen, who reckoned she had died last time in France during the First World War.

The girl refused to make love with Louis because, she said, he was not ready yet. By this he understood that he was not yet initiated into the ranks of the Cot's true believers.

So then he began to try the regressions, allowing the priests of the order to attempt to put him into a trance. Whether hypnotized or not, Louis received no impressions of anything outstanding. Mostly the trances seemed to bring up memories of childhood, as when his mother had caught him masturbating, or he had had to help wash his Uncle Joseph's gangrenous foot.

Then Louis asked one of the priests of Cot if they would find out for him a recent life, so that he could try to feel about it.

One of the priests immediately sat down with Louis and scribbled out a long plethora of sentences in an exercise book from Woolworth's, with his eyes shut.

The other attending priest read this to Louis with some

difficulty. It explained that Louis was Louis, when he had perished, and why – he had been a pamphleteer who fell foul of the Paris Convention – and suggested that Louis should now research the subject himself.

Louis was oddly fired. It was a few days after his fifteenth birthday, and though he had no money of his own, the seventeen-year-old girl who would not sleep with him had bought him two bottles of Brown as a present.

Drunk, in his clean green, Louis went into a public library, and read all day about the French Revolution.

By the time he came out, he was bursting with conviction and urine – there had been no toilets in the library – and dizzy with it all, he had stood on Westminster Bridge, place of intimations, and felt that strangest of all schizophrenias, the awareness of living two lives at once.

He never got the girl into the sack, but there, she was hooked on someone else, who had been her mother two hundred years before. Louis ceased to mind.

He went through the world of 1970s London with a new bright joy, an almost tender amusement, content with everything, eager to know all, because everything was for ever, and it always changed, you always came back, death did not matter, and people, however badly they treated you and others, would one day be all good, all clever, and all one.

They were happy and exciting years for Louis.

He wanted and got to be a priest of the Cot, and all the disintegration and turmoil of the metropolis filled him only with bitter-sweet sad acceptance. He helped all he could. He was kind, forebearing, wise, seeing farther than anyone, the man who tried to knife him, the tramp who died in his arms (uncomforted by Louis' gentle words), the furious police and rankled young souls who thronged the cities of the world.

Louis' was not a young soul. His was a vintage spark of latest maturity, almost old. In ten more lives, maybe, he could make it out. But then again, how fascinating it would be to see even this devastated world unfold. For he would behold the future, everybody would. And in the end, the goodly clever meek ones would inherit the earth. It would be flawless.

The concept used to make him cry with happiness.

And then, somewhere in his early thirties, Louis lost his faith.

God knew – if God was really there after all – why this happened.

It just simply did.

One day it was as if he had seen through a glass darkly, seen as a child saw, and now he saw as a man. He saw the terror and horror of it all, and he knew, in one blinding Damascus moment, that there was, in fact, no point to anything. You did not live for ever. You suffered and you died, and that was it.

He tried to work through the crisis of his faith, but no one could help him, and in the end, he went away, out into the fallen city.

He still called himself Louis, after the one he had once thought he had been. He still boasted of how he had been a priest, and attended the dying, births and weddings of Cot members. He still insisted on reincarnation, although he no longer knew.

How could you *know*?

How could you? Until you were dead.

And then it was too fucking late.

Louis looked, and along the shoreline of the grey sunken river his congregation came.

It was Camillo who had wanted it, here, under the bridge.

And what the hell was Camillo? Old and young and crazy as a coot.

Louis, an innocent who had known too much and too little, brushed down the stained green robe he kept normally in his bag. His nose was clear now and so his head felt clear. He would do his best.

Lix had chopped her hair again, and shampooed the stubble. She wore her other pair of jeans, and on her coat Janice had pinned a soiled red poppy left over from Poppy Day.

Camillo had been offended.

'Too clean. You've washed again.'

Janice said, 'Yer goin' ter marry her.'

Kirstie giggled.

'It's not a real marriage,' said Lix.

'Yes,' said Camillo, 'it is.'

Lix did not care. She had washed because she always did. It was not that it mattered, only that she hated her own smell. The stink of the others she did not mind. Besides, Camillo did not smell at all, only the muck on his coat. He was like someone very old, odourless with age. Dry.

She went along with this since it had been foisted on her. It meant nothing.

The mad priest, the one who believed in reincarnation, was under the bridge, where Camillo had said he must be.

People did what Camillo said.

Even Two Hats, who had died when the bomb exploded. And Vinegar Tom, who was bombed half deaf now, hearing music in his head. He and Pug wore new trousers, already obscene, which Camillo had somehow found for the men denuded in the explosion.

Pug, with them now, had come for the drink.

Camillo had also found the money, simply produced it, for a box, a *good* box – red wine and brandy and white Martini. It had been mixed in a broken vase found among the dustbins, and smelled indolently of ancient chrysanthemums.

Lix thought suddenly of Ron, drinking from that. Poor Ron. She never thought of him now. One G and T before dinner, three glasses of a nice claret or a French white during the meal. The occasional whisky as a nightcap. Oh, yes, and whisky and hot milk for 'flu. Greg had drunk more. But Greg was young—

Wait. Why was she thinking of them? She had not thought of them for a great time. They were gone.

She could say, *Sorry, Camillo. I'm married.*

But that was not true either.

No, she was at liberty. No ring on her finger. Where had that gone? Oh, yes. Someone tore it off. She had been asleep. Pretended she still was. Thought they would take the finger, too, and then the ring came loose . . .

Had she cried afterwards?

She had never cried.

'There he is. He's nutty,' said Janice, indicating Louis under the bridge.

'All the better,' said Camillo. 'The mad are sacred.'

The afternoon was white, and noisy. About a quarter to four, probably.

Up on the bridge the traffic stormed along, and people passed like a speeded-up film.

Under the bridge, the thick shadow. Stasis.

Two feet of mud, and in the mud the effigies, like fossils, of shopping trolleys, dead fish, the jaw bone of a large dog, some hound of the Baskervilles, strayed here to die. They kicked through bleach bottles now, and bottles of fabric conditioner, as if, also, weird women came to the river bank to wash their laundry.

'Too clean, you bitch.'

'All right,' Lix said.

She sat down, then lay on the mud, and rolled.

She came up clotted, her face marked as if with war paint. 'Better?'

'Much. Much better. Lovely for me. Didn't know you would.'

Janice tut-tutted.

Camillo looked sixteen, the sixteen of the streets, a hundred.

344

He took Lix's elbow and slid with her under the bridge.

The others followed. Janice and Kirstie and the dog, Pug, bombed-deaf, grinning, smoking Vinegar Tom, listening to a Marseillaise in his head.

Louis conducted the service as he remembered it.

He addressed them all solemnly.

They acted well. Janice even looked quite reverential, and the dog did not bark. Sometimes Kirstie yawned, but she was possibly sick, always lethargic. A few years ago he would not have minded sharing the box of drink with such as Kirstie, but now he felt a lurking doubt. Then again, if there was nothing, why worry?

Louis spoke to them of what they shared, and they shared the box.

Then he addressed Lix.

He said was she free to be with Camillo, and would she? Lix said she was, she would. He did not ask her to love, honour and obey, but only to love. To love for always in whatever guise, and to observe the freedom of the other, and to cherish. The words were the same for Camillo. He was surprised, Louis, when both of them said *Yes*, and in a way, it brought home to him his own inadequacy. For if they had believed he had any authority to perpetrate this service, surely neither would have agreed.

The box went round again.

Louis uttered a prayer.

'Life is a hard teacher, and we learn through living, under the cane of experience. We smart and sting and are often sorry. But in the end, a golden light shines through our darkness. Though the way seems *made* of darkness, yet there is always a path. We have only to trust ourselves, and to trust the Infinite, which will always guide us.'

Janice's eyes were full of tears.

Louis felt a deep objective sorrow for her belief, stronger than his.

He concluded with a blessing.

They shared the box again.

Louis said, 'You can kiss your bride.'

Camillo turned and took Lix between his hands.

Camillo seemed like a boy, like Louis when he was fourteen and had stumbled into the Cot hall with his sick stomach growling and tuppence ha'penny in his pocket. And yet, Camillo was savage, and sure. Like a pigeon, for they were the best at survival. Camillo the pigeon kissed Lix with his cruel beaked lips.

She allowed it.

Janice said, 'There!'

And then a curious thing happened.

A wind must have scuffed along the bridge above. It stirred through the lightweight rubble of the day, raised it, and bore it over the parapet, and down, down, through the cold white air.

The scent of the rush-hour came with it, of cigarettes and the vacuum of the tube, the exhaust of cars and buses, fume of deodorized bodies cornered by emotions they must not feel.

Bile-green betting tickets torn up, love-letters on scented paper sealed with a Revlon kiss, technicolour beauty of butterfly papers from unwrapped Quality Street thieved and eaten swift above the river. Bus tickets, discarded bills not useful for tax evasion, a shredded card from a lover unwanted. Two coloured Kleenex, one containing a sneeze, the other full of tears.

These floated down, blew in under the bridge.

The wedding confetti.

'Ooh, look,' said Janice.

'It's like—' said Kirstie.

Pug stared and said, 'Yeah.'

And in the spiky hair of Lix, a golden chocolate wing, held, dropped away. Like a ring torn loose. Like a chip of the veiled sun.

'Now, honeymoon,' said Camillo. 'Who wants to come.'

'You don't take no one on your honeymoon,' advised
Janice.

Her dog barked disapprovingly.

Camillo said, 'This is different.'

He led them away, and even Louis followed, along the
dark white beach beside the river of phantom washing.

They climbed the slimy steps.

There against the grey marzipan kerb of the street,
where the world rushed, two great black vehicles.

'Blimey,' said Janice.

'S'Rolls,' said Pug.

'Be my guests,' said Camillo. 'Lix and I in one. Do you
see the white ribbons, Lix? And the rest of you in the
other.'

Janice stood sullen, clutching her bags and her dog.
Kirstie stood beside her, vacant as a house. Pug said,
'Yeah.' And Vinegar Tom, over his music, 'I'll do that.'

Camillo walked to the forward car and rapped on the
smoked glass of its windows.

A chauffeur got out. And another from the second car.

Around them the upper world of the bridge roared by.

Lix got into the first car, and then Camillo, and the door
was liquidly shut.

She did not turn to see who climbed into the second car.
She did note Janice and Kirstie and the dog, and Louis,
marooned on the pavement.

Then the car started.

The last car—

But it had not felt like this one.

'Here's some champagne,' said Camillo.

And she heard, from over the moon, the popping of
a cork.

Somewhere – it might have been near Euston – Camillo
ordered a halt.

He and Vinegar Tom and Pug went out to pull a man
in filthy black up off the pavement.

'Fokken, fokken, fokken,' said the man, his lower lip worn Rizla-thin by saying it.

But he made no other protest as they loaded him in the second Rolls Royce.

There he was sick after about ten minutes, stenching the calm interior.

But Pug and Vinegar Tom only plied him with the box, and themselves; no one complained.

Lix did not ask who he had been or where they went.

Camillo told her.

'There wouldn't be enough trouble without him, at my niece's.'

Chapter Thirty-Nine

❖ SOMEONE HAD STOLEN THE VAN. And so they were very sorry, they could not do the delivery this week. Maybe not next week either. They apologized profusely – after all, she was a very good customer. Thirty bottles of white wine every seven days, sometimes a rosé or a few red as well, and now and then a litre of Gordon's, about one a month. Aside from that, the mineral water, and sometimes orange juice. It was a pity, about the van.

Rachaela said it would be all right.

She would go down the hill and fetch some wine. Reg and Elizabeth she had sent away just before Christmas – she did not need all that cleaning and food and fuss, not for one. So there was no car. But there were cab firms. She would use one of those.

The man from the cab firm, seeing the man from the off-licence come out with the four boxes of wine, the water and juice and gin, said grimly: 'Having a party?'

'That's right.'

She thought, *A party just for me*. She tried to be lenient, the man probably only saw a bottle of wine at Christmas or birthdays, or when he took 'the wife' to the local Chinese. And driving, when could he ever drink, now? But he still annoyed her. His implicit jealousy. The old thing, enemies everywhere. She had seemed able to avoid them for so long.

349

But now, now she had to face the grimy world again, the insults and threats, the little peering eyes.

As they turned up the perpendicular hill to the house the cab-man said, 'Hardly worth a car. You should've got the bus. You could walk up this hill.'

Rachaela clenched her teeth. It seemed worse, after the interval. How much the Scarabae, Althene, had got between her and these people. A pane of bullet-proof glass.

Just then something else caught the driver's jealous, peering little eye.

'Look at that.'

Rachaela looked.

Two jet-black Rolls Royces skimmed past them, and floated up the hill.

'Bloody funeral, is it?'

Rachaela did not respond. She watched silently as the great sharks of cars pressed on between her own garden walls and away up the drive of the house.

Scarabae.

What else?

It must be.

Althene? No—

And then she felt vaguely a twist of fear, or interest, in the pit of her belly.

'I won't drive in,' said the driver. 'Those big cars'll make it difficult to turn round.' He glanced at the boxes in the boot. 'Can't carry nothing. My back.'

Rachaela waited until he opened the boot, then hauled the boxes out on to the space just inside the gate; the driver watched impassively. He overcharged her and she tipped him, wondering why – but then that too was a defence. He knew where she lived.

As he drove off, she stood by the boxes, and looked up at the two Rolls parked before the bare poplars.

No one had as yet got out.

Rachaela picked up the first box of wine and walked up the drive with it.

When she reached the white, two-storeyed house, she glanced back at the black cars. Not a hint of movement. Smoked-glass windows – nothing to be seen.

Rachaela keyed the door panel and the house opened itself. She carried the box through and deposited it in the hall.

As she was straightening, the foremost car put out a wing of door.

A man got out. No, not Althene, not even as she had become. He was slender, about thirty-seven, in a long, belted overcoat. Which she realized abruptly was stiff with mud and other dirt. She did not know him, only that he was Scarabae. He had their look. And his jaggedly hacked hair was white. Somebody to do with Malach?

Then he turned to summon someone else from the car. Something in his movement – the profile. He was older. He was fifty. It was Camillo.

The other passenger was a small thin girl-woman in jeans and an anorak. She carried a knapsack. Her hair too was a sort of spiked crew-cut. She was patterned by something black, clothes and face. Perhaps paint.

'Here we are,' the man who was Camillo said. 'Want some help with those boxes?'

A chauffeur, effortlessly and frighteningly smart, had got out of the car belatedly to see to the door.

'Fetch the boxes from the gate,' Camillo said to him.

And the elegant chauffeur went without a word.

Then Camillo stalked to the other car and rapped on it. And here another chauffeur, like clockwork, got out and opened the second door.

Two incredibly foul and fouled old men fell forth, bent almost double, coughing and laughing. They supported between them a sort of filthy black bolster with a slightly human head encrusted by grey hair and muck, which sank to its knees, saying, 'Fokken, fokken,' and spewed there, under the bird-bath.

'Friends,' said Camillo. 'Come to visit you for the weekend.'

'It isn't the weekend,' Rachaela said.

As she stood, watching Camillo, seeing the first chauffeur coming back with two boxes of wine, and the other one going down past him, presumably to help, one of the old men staggered by her. He stank, an incredible smell of sheer desolation that *lived*.

He was in through the door. He careered against the first box of wine. Paused to inspect it – she heard the bottles crack against each other.

The black-coated vomiter had finished.

'Fokken,' he said, glaring into her eyes like a rabid dog that knows.

Camillo said, 'Thought you'd like company. Not good to be alone.'

'I prefer to be alone.'

'Have to put up with it then, won't you.' He half turned again, 'This is my wife. *Mon amour. Ma femme.*'

Rachaela looked at the woman in jeans. She had very blue eyes. That was all there was to her face, eyes.

The second chauffeur was coming with the last of the wine, the water and the gin.

The other two dirty men rambled by and through into the house.

She had made no attempt to stop them; to attempt it would have meant contact. They were any way unstoppable. Why else had he brought them? Camillo the avenger. Always out to work some scheme of ill or accident on her for some reason—

Inside the house something, perhaps a bottle, broke.

'This is my niece, Rachaela,' Camillo said. 'Lix, say hallo.'

'Hallo,' said the blue-eyed woman, in an educated dead little voice.

How had he found her? Scarabae could always find Scarabae.

For a moment she thought of telephoning the house above the common, but the impulse faded. Camillo had spared them. And for her, well. So what? The rest of life had seeped through, and Camillo with his ghastly antics was only another facet of that. Strange he should have become so.

The old men milled into the kitchen first. They opened the fridge, and so presumably they knew what fridges were for – they seemed to be primeval, or at least from the era of Thomas Hardy, Dickens . . .

There was not much in the fridge, actually. A small raw steak, some ham in a packet, Camembert – they did not like its odour – tomatoes, and three cartons of yoghurt. However, there was also a last bottle of wine.

One of the old men did not care for that. He said that the wine was 'too noo'. And next Rachaela heard him go upstairs, just this one old man. She followed him, because she had now opened a bottle of wine herself, cool only from the cold day, and she was curious.

The old man went into the first bathroom, which had been Anna's. He began to rummage among the cabinets.

'Got any cleanser, missus?'

'There,' she said.

'Uh.'

The old man took out a half-full bottle of apricot cleanser, and another one of astringent. Anna had sometimes bought these things, and seldom used them, merely washing her white and flawless face, which was never too dry or too greasy.

The ghost of Anna came into the bathroom.

But the old man did not see.

He undid the cleanser and sampled it, smacking his lips. Pleased, then, he raised the bottle to Rachaela.

''S good. Any more?'

'I'll have a look.'

She went out, filling her glass as she went, bottle in one

hand, glass in the other, and opened the large cupboard in the other bathroom, which she had shared with Althene.

Oh, yes, he would like this.

He came in after her.

'Take your pick.'

'Cheers,' said the old man. He hovered behind her and his abysmal, knife-cuttable stink mingled with Coty and Lancôme, Boots No 7, and the ubiquitous marshmallow aroma of cold cream.

'Anything you want?' he asked her.

'No, it's all right. I only use it on my face.'

'Don't need to,' he said gallantly, 'lovely girl like you.'

He put his free hand, the one empty of apricot cleanser and astringent, into the cabinet, and things fell out, bursting in the wash-hand basin.

'Sorry, missus.'

Rachaela left him there. She could use the other bathroom or the downstairs loo if she had to pee. Or be sick. What if the other one were sick again? No doubt he would be.

Downstairs, *he* sat with a bottle of Colombard, on the Chinese rug. The rug had rucked up, already dispoiled. The last tramp was on the sofa, lying there, with his boots on the cushions. He too drank wine, dreamily.

Camillo sat on a chair, and the woman he had called Lix was on the floor, also, cross-legged. She did not drink. Nor did Camillo.

'That's Pug,' said Camillo. 'And the one upstairs – has he broken a lot of things? – is Vinegar Tom. This one we don't know. What's your name, daddy?'

'Fokken, fokken,' said the one who had been sick. 'Fokken mind your fokken fokken.'

'Adorable fellow,' said Camillo, with unsullied affection.

The nameless man surged on the rug, but did not quite come up. He relapsed, and drank from his particular bottle.

Rachaela went out again.

She stood in the hall and listened. She could hear the

other man – Vinegar Tom – lumbering about in slow-motion.

Suddenly the cat, Juliet, sprinted down the stairs. Her white face looked like a startled mask as she stopped and stared at Rachaela.

Rachaela's heart fell two or three other stairs behind her breast. The cats. She had forgotten them.

'Yes,' Rachaela said. She went to Juliet and picked her up. Juliet protested in a shrill coloratura. 'Don't struggle.' Rachaela bore Juliet to the cupboard opposite the stairs. As she undid the door and shoved Juliet, squeaking top E's with outrage, inside, the terrible stained-glass window flared its dying light on them, the red and green and gold of Persephone and her mother, Persephone who had been stolen away. 'Just for half an hour,' lied Rachaela.

She shut the door on Juliet and turned the key in the lock. This cupboard had always had the ability to be locked. God knew why. Useful, now. She kept the key in her hand, with her glass.

Probably Juliet would shit deliberately on the floor, and who could blame her?

Rachaela went upstairs again. She knew where the black cat, Jelka, was, or had been—

Jacob was normally outside. He would have too much sense to come in, hopefully.

Halfway up the stairs again, her hand with the key spilled her drink. She put the glass down and kept hold only of the bottle.

Vinegar Tom had gone into her bedroom, the room she had had with Althene. He was sitting on the bed, with a stub of fag in his mouth, sniffing at a pillow which maybe had scent on it, and which in a minute might catch alight.

Anna's door stood ajar.

Rachaela went in.

Jelka was curled asleep, oblivious, inside the coil of Ursula the fox-fur, with her head on the stomach of the white rabbit.

Something horrible assailed Rachaela.

She raised her bottle and tilted it into her mouth, but the mellow wine did not help her.

Christ, what was it. Reality. It was truth.

She put the bottle on the floor and crept up on Jelka with the stealth of dread. After all, she did not know any of the old men would harm a cat. Certainly Camillo would not. Or had that altered too?

Rachaela took up the fox, the rabbit, and Jelka, in a tray of softness. She held them to her bosom.

Jelka woke with a tiny purr and looked up, somnambulist, into her eyes.

'It's all right, darling. Come and sit with your mother.'

Jelka stayed quite calm, allowing Rachaela to carry her away downstairs.

It was difficult, unlocking the cupboard again, making sure Juliet did not get out. Rachaela could not have managed toting the bottle. She was glad she had got rid of it.

When she had insinuated the furry heap of cat, fox and rabbit into the cupboard, up against a forestalled, amazed and wowling Juliet, locked them in again, and clutched the key, Rachaela sat down on the stairs.

There were hardly any noises coming from anywhere. The man upstairs must be lying on her bed, sucking the pillow – she could not smell burning. The two downstairs were drinking. And Camillo and his wife – wife? – were still.

She could pretend she was alone.

But, she was not.

If she had been alone, she would have proceeded as always, drinking slowly and thoroughly her medicine of serenity. And the TV would have been on. And quiet night would have been gathering on the empty house.

It was odd. She had thought of Camillo when parts of London were blacked out by a bomb. Now here he was.

What did he truly want?

Rachaela did not care. She was aching, in dense, low waves, a sea of still pain coming in on her.

She had held it back so long.

The pain of everything. Sex and birth and loss. Mostly loss. Yes, that was right.

She thought of Althene, changed back into a man. So fragile as a man. And like steel, leaving her. First Adamus, then Ruth. Then Anna. Then Althene. Alone. But she liked to be alone. No, she was only used to it.

She wondered if she would cry. That would be a bad idea, for Camillo would sense it, come out and mock her, or worse.

Any way, she was not going to cry. Her pain, this new hurt, was far too arid for tears.

She looked, aslant as it were, for the bottle. Where had she left it? Never mind. There were other bottles in the kitchen where the courteous po-faced chauffeurs had left them.

Had the chauffeurs driven off? She had not heard the soft murmur of vehicles going.

She got up, walked to the front door, opened it, and looked out.

The Rolls Royce cars were yet on her drive, beyond the bird-bath with its garland of sick, which decoration gleamed salmon pink in the last of the daylight.

Rachaela shut the door.

She crossed back to the kitchen, and went in, switching on the overhead light.

As she was opening a new bottle, Camillo entered.

'There you are,' he said, 'I thought you'd run away.'

'Why should I? It's my house.'

'Is it? I thought it was Althene's house. Beautiful, glamorous Althene. Have you heard from her? Anything? What's she say?'

'I haven't heard anything.'

'Her male name is Johanon,' said Camillo. 'Did you know? The mother gave her that. You've been told about

Sofie. Crazy Sofie. Potty. God knows what she's up to. Just think. Tsk. To be mad.'

'Althene is searching for Anna,' Rachaela said.

'Anna got lost, like Ruth,' said Camillo. 'Yes, I know about it. Know everything. Althene went to Sofie first. Probably stayed with Sofie. Trapped by Sofie.'

Rachaela poured the new wine into three kitchen glasses of pale green crystal.

'I expect your wife will want some.'

'She might. Don't know her well.'

Camillo took a glass. They went together, out, and back into the main room.

Light was dying now in the zodiacs of the upper windows, in four places rich royal blue as the eyes of Camillo's wife.

Blue eyes. The eyes of Althene's father had been very blue. She had said. Cajanus. The one perhaps she had gone looking for. The one who might have taken Anna. If he existed. If Anna had existed.

Rachaela shut her eyes. She could not recall, now, what Althene had told her, what she had imagined, guessed, deduced for herself. None of it, any way, made sense. And so, she supposed, it was all ludicrously factual, had happened and did happen. And where did she fit inside it all?

'Thank you,' said the educated woman who was Camillo's wife or property.

Rachaela had handed her the glass, not looking.

Pug on the sofa had fallen asleep, his personal bottle drained.

On the rug, the man who said fokken hugged a brand-new bottle morosely.

'Do you remember my horsey?' said Camillo to Rachaela.

'Yes.'

'I left it somewhere safe. Poor thing, it misses me. No one else would. Nasty Camillo. Go away.'

Rachaela drank the wine. It was like leaden water. Useless.

Camillo said, 'You can tell she's depressed. Someone stole her daughter. And then Rachaela's lover went to find the stolen child and mad Sofie has got *her*. Heigh ho, this life is so jolly.'

Lix glanced at Rachaela.

Abruptly Lix said, 'Can I have a bath?'

'Yes, if you want. There are two bathrooms upstairs. Camillo's old tramp's in a bedroom. He's drunk the bath foam probably. There are towels in the cupboard on the landing.'

'Perfect hostess,' said Camillo.

Rachaela said, 'Will these people hurt the cats?'

Camillo shrugged.

But on the rug the fokken man looked up with a narrow gleam in his eye.

Rachaela said, 'They're out, the cats. Sometimes they're gone for days.'

Lix stood. She was very small, slim, compact. On her face the black was only some sort of mud. She looked clean under it, smelled clean. She went out.

Rachaela did not want to stay with Camillo. She rose too and followed Lix.

On the stair Lix turned. 'I'll wipe the bath round afterwards. I'm not diseased. So far as I know.'

'But you might not know,' said Rachaela.

'Yes, that's true.'

'It doesn't matter,' Rachaela said. 'This family is believed to be immune to most things. I only ever had 'flu twice in my life. Never badly. And one filling in one tooth when I was a child. We have babies like . . . shelling peas, practically.' She wondered why she had said this to Lix.

Lix said, 'You're very kind.'

'No, I'm completely callous. Just a coward.'

'I'm sorry. About your house.'

'Well, never mind.'

Lix lay in the bath, up to her small breasts in warm water.

Her body had a properly subaqueous look, like a painting by Waterhouse.

She had not been in a bath, an actual bath, for – well, it did not count.

They had had two bathrooms in that other house. Ron's house. One was Greg's, always a mess. The cleaning woman used to complain, but never much. Greg was so young and handsome. So full of that cliché, life. And any way, in the new house, there had been *three* bathrooms.

Ron was a sweet man, a bit dull, going very bald, getting a little tummy. But it made no difference. Lix might go to bed and fantasize, as Ron made love to her, that it was Sean Connery, but really she understood it was Ron, and she did not mind. No, she was secretly glad. For though Sean Connery was so wonderful, so apparently marvellous, she did not know him. And everything she knew of Ron – suited her.

They had married when she was sixteen and he twenty. They had known, from the first. Was it love? Or was it knowledge. It kept them, any way, very close. And Greg, the product of their love at its youthful fieriest, was a testament to the souls of them both.

She had been happy. Not riotously, not in vast sweeping passionate outcry. It had been so very ordinary. Just to wake up and to be. To fall asleep with. To rest in.

And why not for ever. Or, at least, until they were old.

There was no monetary fear either. How lucky they were. Their son at college, a designer with a future before him. And they, safe in Ron's safe business world. So safe they could afford the larger, prettier house with three bathrooms and six bedrooms they had gone to look at that evening.

They had had dinner in a country pub, and Ron was so sensible. He had only one glass of white wine. She and Greg had not had to abstain and they had drunk two bottles between them, and some Cointreau afterwards. Celebration. Greg was planning on a flat in town, and to come down to them at weekends. He had taken the micky out of it, liking it – a weekend in the country. He had said he would hunt foxes, shoot them – with his camera of course, no other way.

Foxes.

They drove back very late, and coming into London how empty and futile the city had looked, frozen in the orange static of its awful lights. Drunks and beggars. A wreck. So glad they would be leaving.

They were somewhere near Hyde Park, driving briskly but not too fast, and it was about one a.m. by then, somehow, and Greg said to Ron, 'Go on, Dad, just listen to it.' And Ron said, 'All right. All right.' Laughing. And Lix, who lay half asleep in the back of the soft, warm burring car, listened too. It was Greg's tape. *Killing Joke: Love like Blood.* Ron did listen. Then he said, 'Yes, it's not bad. No, it's good.' And she had thought, *Does he really like it or is he being wise?* But she quite liked it herself, and Ron had an open mind, a catholic taste.

And just then the fox ran across the road. The country fox, over the wide street of inner London.

The surface was probably wet. They had giggled, chasing through the light rain earlier.

Ron swung the wheel. He would rather die than hurt an animal.

Then the world turned round like a top. And then the world turned right over.

She did not know what happened, had never properly diagnosed. But presumably their seatbelts, the seatbelts of her husband and son in the front seats of the car, had held them fast, but not quite fast enough. And she, unsecured, her door giving way, had flown out as if on wings, thrown clear, to land hard, stunned, on a peculiar nothingness that was the pavement.

When she opened her eyes, all of ten or twenty seconds later, the car was burning, with Ron and Greg unconscious inside, securely held by their belts, and the horn, which any way had gone into Ron's chest, sounding dully, and, strangest of all, the music still playing. *Love like Blood*. Until the tape melted.

In the end, and that must have been fifty seconds after, Lix got up and tried to go round the car to see if they too had been thrown out, but she knew they had not. And they had not.

To be honest, she could see the shapes of them, inside, all lit by fire. Which in the frozen light was not realistic. Too flat. The shadows all wrong.

Somewhere a dog barked, miles away.

The city seemed otherwise totally deserted.

Lix walked slowly away. She was covered in smuts and sealing scabs.

She walked for an hour, until she found herself at the embankment, and there, because she felt ill, she sat down. And there she slept, or died. And in the first sere glow of morning, a young policeman shook her harshly and told her to move on.

And there she was, awake, reborn. There she was for the rest of her life.

Lix turned a little in her bath that did not count. Someone was at the door, maybe Vinegar Tom, but she had locked it.

That beautiful black-haired woman Camillo said was his niece.

Was it a fact she too had lost her lover and her child?

Rachaela leaned in the doorway of the main room, watching Camillo, and the fokken man who was drinking from his third bottle, and now and then glaring round the room at perhaps invisible entities, cursing them.

Faintly too she could hear the cats in the cupboard, irritatedly scratching and worriedly meowing. It would not do.

Then she heard the meowing again, much closer. She looked down. Jacob had appeared. He must have been secreted somewhere in the house.

Now he sauntered directly past her – she did not put down the new glass of wine in time to grab him. She should have dropped it.

Camillo half turned, but it was the fokken man who heaved up on to his knees.

'Fokken vermin,' he said, 'fokken, fokken.'

And he made a lunge, his black, broken nails intent for Jacob's white hide.

Jacob sprang aside, and the man reared up, was on his feet. He aimed a wide swinging kick.

Rachaela's heart hit her throat. She started forward and the glass after all fell. But Jacob was away again, up on the big table with the bowl of bananas.

The cat ran nimbly, and leapt free as the fokken man thudded into the table.

'Stop it!' Rachaela cried. Ineffectual, of course.

The tramp crashed his arm upon the banana bowl, picked it up, threw it straight at one of the windows. The bowl but not the window shattered. He turned with a roar. '*Fokken! Fokken!*' he shrieked. His eyes were red. Rachaela wished she had kept the glass – she might have cut him in the face. Torn between a wish to attack her and the other wish to damage the cat, he reeled from one side to the other.

Then Camillo came scuttling. A true scuttle, like some sort of crab. Camillo was smiling.

He whipped his white head forward, with the weight of his thin iron body behind it, and Rachaela heard the incredible crack of skull lammed on skull.

Camillo pranced back. The tramp went over with a deep lost glottal groan and lay under the table legs, making a snoring noise.

'He'll choke,' said Rachaela.

'Let's hope so. Here, cat, cat,' said Camillo. And reached on to a chair back, where Jacob had flown, and pulled him lightly off, pawfuls of ripped material coming out in Jacob's frightened, furious hooked claws.

Rachaela took the cat. He was not pleased, and lashed her with his tail, bruising smacks.

'All right,' Rachaela said.

She carried Jacob from the room, directly to the front door. Grasping him cruelly, she undid the door and marched out to the nearer of the two Rolls. The chauffeur, who stood beside it in the cold dusk, promptly opened the car for her. She cast Jacob, howling, inside. 'Close it, please. There are two more to come.'

She had difficulty only with Juliet, who scratched her and screamed, but when they were all, Jacob, Juliet and Jelka, in the back of the car, loose, amid the tumble of fox-fur and rabbit, the door was shut, and she said to the chauffeur, 'You'll drive me back to London. To the house on the common. Do you know where I mean?' The man said, 'Yes, madame.' 'I won't be long.'

It did not surprise her particularly when Camillo began to assist her as she gathered up Althene's lighter treasures, the skulls, and all Anna's toys from the room upstairs. Even Lix came in, her grubby clothes back in place over the bathed body, and began to point out things Rachaela might need to stuff into the weekend bag.

Had it all been a plan simply to get rid of her? The other tramp in the bedroom slept through everything. His fag was out. The bedroom was full of stink.

She did not really know what she took, what she did. She took Althene's lingerie, in crushed handfuls, stuffing it in the bag. There were a few things in the cellar, but perhaps they would never find their way into that.

Lix carried the bags of skulls and clothes downstairs.

Pug had wandered blandly into the hall in search of more wine. ''E's out,' he said, jerking his thumb back at the fokken man on the floor.

'Beachy Head,' said Camillo. 'In the car boot. Yes.'

They all helped Rachaela, Pug too, to get the bags into the first Rolls without allowing the cats to escape.

*   *   *

When the Rolls had been driven away, Camillo poured three *small* gin and tonics, for Pug, Lix and himself.

'Beachy Head,' he said again, raising his glass to the snoring fokken man.

Chapter Forty

ALCHEMICAL: A SEA-JOURNEY BY NIGHT.
She had been startled at the size of the ship, like a
white wedding-cake on the darkness, festooned
with lights.

It looked sound and indestructible, and inside it was
luxurious, full of cafés and shops, lifts and carpeted stairs,
which last, once it had parted from the shore, pushed
against her with only the slightest intimation of external
side-to-side movement.

The ocean was calm. The night vast. From an outer deck,
she viewed it all, feeling she should, for she had never
travelled in this way before. She had not wanted to fly.

A narrow moon hung low. The stars were bright. And
the black sea.

She must not call the ship a boat, or it. It was *she*.
Feminine. It was the fish that had swallowed her up,
and she would try to sleep inside the fish. In the morning she would come forth, out of the belly of the fish,
reborn.

She did not avail herself of the restaurants, but went
straight to the first-class cabin. As she lay on the sea green
bed, someone knocked.

There was no room service to the cabin. But, of course . . .
They had brought her a chicken salad and warm fresh

bread, a baked potato, dark amber juice, and two bottles of white Grenache. There was coffee too in a silver pot.

Gone for ever, those first Scarabae days, when she had had to ask in vain for coffee.

She ate and drank on the gently rocking bed. The rhythm was pleasant. It would help her to sleep, like the wine, of which she drank only three glasses.

After she had showered and cleaned her teeth, she got naked into the smooth white sheets, and lay in the dark, under a fleeting yet perpetual glimmer cast upon the ceiling.

I am Rachaela. My name.

But I am more than that.

It passed before her eyes, her whole life, as perhaps was proper, since in a way she had given herself over to drowning. The stunted beginning. The contact with the Scarabae. The first house above the ocean. Adamus. And then the travail. Ruth. Ruth's own fearsome life that came and went like that burning wind of the eastern desert, the khamsin—

And so Althene. And so Anna. Who passed like snow.

Lying there, it was Anna Rachaela tried to picture. Not Althene, her lover-husband-wife, that she was travelling now to find in turn. Althene was known to her. It was Anna she sought.

The whiteness of her, the flax of hair with its silver flush of roots growing from the moon-quartz of her skin. Her dark lashes. The little mark on her breast.

But Anna was gone. It was as if Anna had now died, just as Ruth died, in the woods, or at the moment when Malach abandoned her.

Anna was no more.

That made it easier, really. It was Althene who she wanted.

The decision had been simple. She had not even made it, it had merely come to be. When she packed her bag and the skulls – and for some curious comfort, the toys – then, she had known. As Rachaela sat in the back of the Rolls Royce, with Juliet growling on her lap, Jacob burrowing in her side, and Jelka, abruptly alert, her paws up on the window frame, staring out like a hyperactive child, then Rachaela had felt clear as glass. She could see through herself to what she was and what she wanted.

Had that ever happened before?

They reached the Scarabae house in darkness, but coloured windows were burning, like a welcome.

Cheta let her in, and then almost instantly there they all were, Miranda looking about twenty in the lamplight, and Sasha looking elderly, and Eric somewhere between. (Tray-Terentia was not present.) Michael served them an ample cold supper – Scarabae greed – and she told them what Camillo had told her, as if she had never heard of it before, that Althene's mother was mad, and since she had not heard from Althene at all, she, Rachaela, meant to go after her.

None of them contradicted.

Eric said it would be arranged.

And, by the following morning, it had been.

Lying in that unmoving earth-bound bed, in the room that had been hers once before, she did consider that she might be wrong, and Camillo only, solely, malicious. Althene might have passed on from the woman called Sofie, who was her mother. Althene might be anywhere at all.

Eric, perhaps with this in mind, had told her she would not be 'alone' in Amsterdam. Other Scarabae, apparently, would assist her. Not Malach. Malach was absent. But someone. Some people.

In the morning, the dove window of the room lightened and Cheta came with greedy breakfast, and later Miranda, who sat on the bed, playing with Jelka and her two black and white siblings. Miranda explained that the sea crossing had been arranged for that night.

'You're looking very well,' Rachaela said to Miranda.

Miranda smiled, as a woman would behind a fan. 'Yes, I am.'

She had been ancient, once. Like Sasha, now. Grey, webby, with long discoloured teeth. Rachaela said, 'Do they fall out?' She meant the teeth. It was an ugly, tactless, earnest question.

Miranda understood. 'Yes. Rather horrid. They break, you see. But then the new one comes. Like a child. But I don't leave the old ones for the tooth fairy. They're not pretty enough.'

The three cats played wildly. Only Juliet and Jacob were sulkily ensconced downstairs, where a fire burned, and several dishes of fish had been temptingly set out.

'Thank you for telling me. I wondered. What about the rest of it?'

'The rest of it?'

'I mean, you grow younger. Does – everything happen as it did?'

Again, the invisible lace fan and the smile. 'Oh, yes. Naturally.'

'Is it natural?' Rachaela waited, then said, 'Will it all happen to me, Miranda? Does it – frighten you?'

Miranda laughed, and Jelka and the other two sprang on to the bed again, chirruping for total attention.

'What did you call them?'

'They don't have names. They are the Cats.'

They don't have names. They are the family.

They are the Scarabae. Genus *not* title.

The car that took her to the ship was just a limousine.

Only Eric and Miranda said goodbye, Sasha was knitting, apparently, in her room. She was a little tired today. Was Sasha due to die, that other thing the Scarabae did? It tugged at Rachaela's emotions; she remembered Sasha and Anna embracing that day at the house, when Sasha had fainted, and then produced the shawl. The shawl had come home with Anna's toys, had had to, it was wrapped about two small brown bears to keep them warm.

She meant to hold them, the family, but somehow it did not happen. Well. She would be coming back.

Rachaela turned on her side.

To lie above the sea was to lie in the womb.

She had felt this gentle motion before, in the blood-heart-cave of her own mother. That was the essence of the lullaby. For that was a night-sea journey too.

Chapter Forty-One

THEY HAD SAILED ON 1ST April, an unlucky day. There had been no choice. The cargo was probably wood and wines and cloth. But then, they had not been sure of that. Bribed, the ship went out. The passage would be a long one, but the land journey had also been onerous. It was as if they had been travelling for years.

Not liking the light, they had kept inside the ship by day. The women shared one of the cabins, the men, the other. It was makeshift. They had expected nothing else.

The sailors especially did not care for the idea of so many women on board. Even a single female could make the sea angry. The sea became angry on the fifteenth day. The sky was green and the water white.

She began, the ship, to roll, to heave.

That was the day Camillo got away from them. The day too that Stephan's child started to move in the womb of Sasha.

Vain hope, that it would not be until they reached shore, that rough English shore they had been promised. The violence of the sea. Inevitable. And it was more than a month too early.

They had tied her to the bunk, they had had to, to keep her secure.

As the spasms of the sea came, lifting everything, Sasha

371

kept quiet. At her own spasms, the turmoil of the churning child, she did not cry out.

She looked young, in the way Anna and Miriam and Livia did, about twenty-five or twenty-eight. Sasha's long black hair lay coiled along the pillow in a plait. Grusha had seen to this, and now set wet cloths on the panting woman's forehead. Of them all, only Anna, and Sasha, were calm. The others were nervous, distraught.

The labour of the sea, Sasha's labour—

Night came. Then a day indistinguishable from night. And another night.

The sailors were muttering curses, and since Camillo had got out among them, they were worse. A man had been washed overboard by then, and Camillo clung to the great mast, its sails long since taken in. Camillo laughed, and now and then he screamed above the gale, foolishly, dreadfully: '*A tenger! A tenger!*' (The sea! the sea!)

They had tried to persuade him back. But he would not come. The polite epithet of *Uncle* did not solace him, although he had insisted on it before, in the stone house where they had kept him firmly under lock and key.

That house was far behind them now. Miles of tundra, mountains, wheat, roads burnt by dust, and later thick with mud when the rain came. Miles of water finally, smashed green glass.

Above, the sky rocked and pieces of it seemed to fall on the ship. There was no still place in the world for them. It was all like this, like the ocean, in frenzy, trying to thrust them off.

And the sailors spoke of murdering them. Last night the sailors had drawn lots, some of them, when drunk, to find three men to come down and club the unwanted passengers to death, and over the side with them, into the refuse pit of the water. Who would know?

'*They* would know,' the captain had said. 'Would I have taken them if I hadn't had to take them? Let them alone.' He spoke in a dialect of the Ukraine, but then repeated his words in a kind of Gaelic, for many of the crew were Irish. 'If one of you touches one of them, I'll do for him. I'll gut him. Understand me.'

Dawn broke, the third day of Sasha's labour.

The storm had darkened the sun, and four of them, George and Kare, Dorian and Stephan, went up on deck.

They spoke to the captain. More gold passed over hands. They had paid him to broach another cask of wine. Drunk, the sailors were mostly ultimately more amenable, and all of them less handy.

The man who had been swept overboard was whispered about. There had been marks on his neck.

Stephan laughed out loud when he heard this reported. He was vigorous and strong, seeming about thirty-five, with a mane of black hair. Handsome people, even the muttering sailors did not deny it, and their women, beautiful, but that only made the sea more angry.

In their dreams, the crew were seduced and poisoned. Five days into the voyage, seven men had fallen sick, complaining of feeling the weight of bodies lying on them in sleep.

'Do you think we would touch this scum?' said Stephan to the captain, straight out, in the language of Russia.

The captain shrugged. 'I don't ask questions. But they're near to mutiny. They're frightened of that girl of yours – your wife, is it? Giving birth! That's enough to tempt all the gods of the waters.'

The fourth night came. Sasha was no longer conscious.

Grusha bent over her, and Anna, rubbing carefully at the swollen belly, trying to ease the child on its way.

Frances and Stephan and Jack stood outside with Michael and Carlo, at the door of the women's cabin. They had four pistols, and Carlo carried the great axe he had brought away with him.

Usually, birth was swift.

The sea poured down into black valleys and slung them up again to pinnacles of white foam.

Sasha screamed.

She opened herself wide, the dilated orifices of mouth and loins.

The child came forth quickly at last, slipping in a wave of blood, water and slime.

The women were astonished. They stood, they too in terror.

For Sasha had sea-birthed a mermaid.

It was streaked in crimson, but through this gleamed a marble whiteness, as if the creature had been made of ice not flesh.

Nor was it a baby. It was mature. Almost two months too early, it had the appearance of a small infant of two years, wholly proportionate, and from the fair white face, framed in soaking blood, the long white hair had formed a wet rope that, going round its throat, had choked it.

There was no umbilical cord. Its wise dead eyes, rimmed by red, were the grey of ancient silver dredged up from the sea. It looked, it looked at them, as if, even dead, it saw.

And the slender legs were just visible, held in the silken jelly of the tail.

It was Anna who rushed forward and pulled the noose of hair away from its throat, who snatched it up, held it head down, slapped it, shook it, to try to make it live.

But the neck was crushed. It had been dead some while.

Only, the activity loosened the placenta which had tangled its lower limbs, and as that slid away, they saw it was only a child after all.

About the ship the sea quaked one more time, and shuddered, and fell back.

It was as though a sacrifice had been fed to it. A dead thing, that it had craved.

In the lulling cabin, the women washed Sasha clean, and cleaned the white baby that was too old.

They assisted Sasha, allowing her to sit up.

'Give her to me.'

'Sasha, Shasha, she's dead.'

374

'She was born dead, Sasha. The journey killed her. Rest, Sasha.'

'No, let me hold her.'

So they gave to her the beautiful snowy cadaver, and Sasha held it, wrapped in the shawl that Alice had made, a shawl like a moth's wings. And Sasha rocked the dead child gently, teaching the wicked sea how it might be.

'Oh, Sasha, Sasha. She's dead.'

'I know. Just for a little while.'

Then she asked that Stephan should come in, and he did so. He stood and looked at Sasha, and the white albino lovely child, whose starry eyes had refused to close.

Outside, up on the deck, the curses of the sailors came more clearly as the storm abated.

But Camillo was still shrieking, '*A tenger! A tenger!*'

Finally Stephan bent and kissed the dead thing, between its watching eyes.

'I know she would have been so good to us,' Sasha said. 'I know she had been with us before.'

Stephan took the corpse quietly from her arms, and she allowed it.

Then he carried it away, up into the dark incoming silence of the settling ship.

When he returned, he carried only the shawl. He offered it to Alice, but she, taking it, gave it again to Sasha.

And Sasha slept, smiling, with the shawl, that had held her dead child, soft under her cheek.

Camillo screamed, 'The sea! The sea!'

Stephan said, 'She sleeps now in the sea.'

'Why,' said Unice, 'must everything be taken from us? The first child – for so long—'

But Anna looked at Stephan. Anna, who would come to bear Stephan's living son, some years in the future, in the English land to which they went. Anna said, 'We must be strong. We must endure.'

Stephan said, 'And we do, my Anna. Don't we?'

Chapter Forty-Two

During the morning, they were taken to the big room.

There, a man talked to them, in English and French.

He was a newcomer, tall and rather fat, with spectacles that glinted distractingly. It was like one of the lessons they had already been given there, informal, quite interesting.

First of all he said general things about their backgrounds, nothing personal, although each of them bristled uneasily as he began. They had not told each other very much of their parents or guardians, or their homes, apart from Berenice, who had mentioned her unpleasant father to Faran.

The Greek boy, Christos, corrected the teacher – or whatever he was – at one point. Something about a statue. Faran was not very concerned.

Then the man in spectacles spoke about where they were going. This had happened before. None of them was alerted, until he said, 'This afternoon you'll set out on the last part of your journey.'

They all reacted, whispered and murmured, if only to themselves. The Swede, Jan, who was six, said boldly, 'Do you mean we are finally going there?'

'Yes,' said the man, nicely. 'At last. It's been a long wait, I know. You've been good. Patient.'

The Greek boy said, 'We had no choice.'

The French Canadian, Pierre, said, '*Tais-toi. Continuez, monsieur, s'il vous plaît.*'

'Yes, I will go on,' said Spectacles. He glanced at Faran as if expecting him, now, to raise some objection. Faran nodded, to encourage. 'You've been told it's going to be very cold. You'll be given special clothing for the last part of the trip. You must do exactly as you're instructed. That's for your own protection. Inez will speak to you later, give you full details. I know you'll all be sensible.'

The Welsh girl hissed something, in Welsh.

The tall fat man took no notice. He knew she understood English.

'Now,' said the man. He made an expansive gesture. He lifted his head, the way some people did during religious moments – even Faran had seen this, on television. 'Now, I have to say something that I know you may not grasp. I want you to be very quiet, and consider the concept, with an open mind.'

Faran decided Spectacles was treating them, not as children, but as young scholars, fifteen or sixteen, maybe, something like that. Faran waited, to see what the 'concept' would be.

'I know that Señor Stampa has given you some talks on the subject of reincarnation. I think that you understand the principle of it. When he asked you, I believe you all agreed that it was possible, such a thing. To be born again after death.'

Faran grimaced. The fat man was somehow embarrassing. Obviously they had agreed. You did agree with teachers who bored you. It was the quickest way to shut them up. And of all the people who had come into their lives here, Señor Stampa, with his guttural lisp and crumpled white suit, had delighted them the least. He had black teeth, and smoked continually. That was what they had come to associate with his quasi-spiritual subject – smoke. It was like, the Canadian had said, compulsory prayers.

'Now the family to which you are being taken,' said the fat man, 'is very important. A great family. Comparable only to the grand houses of Renaissance Europe, or pre-war Italy and France. And the gentleman who is to be in charge of you, he is one of the heads of this house.'

Faran glanced at Berenice. She was sitting very still with the toy cat in her lap, watching the speaker attentively. She always did this. As if nervously she felt she must try to help everyone.

The fat man said, 'Cain is the name of this gentleman. And you were selected by Cain. Now I shall explain why. You may not grasp it, but you must attempt to. Mr Cain believes that you are, all of you, reincarnations of members of the great family to which he belongs. That only accident has put you outside his house. Now you are to be brought back.'

There was no reaction this time.

Faran thought that all of them knew, knew at least that this was supposed to be what had happened. For himself – well, he had recognized the lioness-woman in the photograph. But that might have occurred in some other fashion. He felt irked at Spectacles, his mundane way of citing something so preposterous that was perhaps true. But then, adults had so frequently offended.

The fat man seemed somewhat thrown out of stride by the childrens' lack of response. What had he anticipated?

He stared at Berenice, who blushed and said; '*Merci, monsieur.*'

That was all.

Another bus conveyed them to the airfield. The first plane ride took some hours. They did not dislike it, since it made a change, being in the air, to being in some place, month after month, on the ground.

The green hills sank away.

On the plane they had hamburgers in sesame seed buns, fries and tomatoes, and then fruit salad and ice-cream.

They drank lemonade or kola or Pepsi. Then they watched some films, first *Superman*, which the Swedish boy and the Welsh girl had already seen, but did not seem to mind seeing over again. Then cartoons, mostly *Bugs Bunny* and *Tom and Jerry*, old cartoons in fact, but they laughed. Even Faran laughed. Even Berenice, sometimes.

Berenice though was rather troubled, and she looked very pale.

Faran decided he should sit with her. He changed his seat.

'Are you scared? Come on, tell me.'

'Yes, but it isn't that.' Her English had improved a vast amount through her talks to Faran, and she had acquired a lot of London slang, which he now used with impunity, having no Cimmie to stop him. 'It's that other thing. About being born again.'

'Oh, that.' Faran watched Tom Cat hit in the mouth by an iron bar. All the cat's teeth fell out and Berenice squirmed. 'It's all right. Look, next scene they've grown back.'

Berenice said, 'Papa said there wasn't God. There wasn't anything. Only this life.' She looked at her toy cat. She said to it, 'There was a sister – a *nun* came to the apartment once. She knew my mummy. When Papa came home, he threw her out. He threw her nearly downstairs, and she screamed. It was mega bad.'

'Your father was a thing from outer space,' said Faran. He liked this expression and thought he had coined it. It summed up Berenice's father very well.

'He just left me, on the boat. And then the lady came. But he left me.'

'Forget him,' said Faran. 'This Cain is bound to be better.'

Berenice said, 'But I'll do something wrong. I'm stupid. Then he won't like me.'

'You're not stupid. *I* like you.' Faran wondered if it had been well advised, to say that, but it was too late now. And she looked happy. She said to the cat, '*Tu est fou!*' and made the cat waggle its head.

Jerry sploshed into some butter.

The sky was very bright with sun, nearly sharp, when they came off the second bus, on to the second airfield.

Faran did not know the time, but he thought somehow the sun should not still be shining. The skin of the sky looked too thin, and perhaps could not keep the light inside for darkness.

It was here, in a long low building, that they were dressed in new, different, warm clothes, bulky and lined with wool, in bright cheerful greens and oranges. It was already cold, and a wind blew over the plain, twisting the dry grasses. There were bony hills in the distance.

They were given hot chocolate.

They stood looking out at the small red plane.

'What is it?' the Greek boy asked.

One of their companions told him it was a DC 6 four-engined fixed-wheel aircraft.

The companions were not going on the plane with them, only the pilot. The pilot would tell them what they must do, and they must obey him. The journey would be some hours. They would need to refuel only once.

'There's the pilot,' said Jan, pointing.

A man of average height and build, dark-faced, muffled against the wind.

He walked along beside the barbed-wire fence, and cast a glance at something whitish, some little statue or other standing there, perhaps to the Virgin Mary, like the votive images on the track they had gone by, coming down.

Miguel Chodil walked.

As he did so, the tiny medallion of the Madonna, which he had hung about his neck, moved against his chest.

They had told him only yesterday it would be this plane, and this cargo – not fruit or meat or books, but live children, six of them. He had not cared for it. Children were like monkeys. Unwatched, what might they not do, like the explorers' dogs that time, fighting in the midst of the cockpit – but it was no use to protest. He had agreed long ago.

He could see them inside a wide window of the building, watching. Five pale faces and one black. They looked quiet enough. Probably anxious.

Chodil reached the plane. He put one hand on its cold side. It felt lifeless to him. He knew this type of aircraft, had flown it, did not relate to it. It was not feminine.

He had not asked himself anything about the live cargo, beyond whether or not they would be submissive.

Chodil got up into the plane.

He sat, thinking of the woman he had had in the city. It was always a different woman. And afterwards, he had taken the medallion from the box where he kept relics of his mother's life, and hung it on himself.

Out on the runway, two of the guards, with Kalashnikovs, idling.

Then the children emerged from the building in a well-coordinated stream, guided by two adults. The children did not run or shout. Yes, they were docile. The black one was very handsome, like a carving in ebony. And that little fair girl with a toy. Something about her.

He turned his mind from them.

They must do as he said, but that had been impressed upon them, of course. And they would have been given something to make them sleepy. He had been assured of that.

Chodil touched the controls. For a moment he had, as never before, a sense of the alienness of this plane, and of the place whereto he went, and of himself, even, extraordinarily, a being with a head and torso, legs and arms, hands and feet, and an image of the Virgin Mother hanging inside his clothes on his naked breast—

But this passed.

*   *   *

'I've been asleep ages,' Berenice said. 'But look, it's still light. Look – look – what are those?'

Faran craned across her to the small window.

They were out over the pack-ice now, the sea like dark blue ink, ice sheets like white floating papers.

'It's snow,' Faran said.

'Will there be penguins?'

'Perhaps.'

'And polar bears?'

'No, I don't think so. Not here.'

'Oh.' She was disappointed.

Some of the others were waking up, the Swedish boy and the Canadian. The Greek snored, as he had not done in natural sleep.

Faran knew they had been drugged. He did not tell Berenice. Like Cimmie's tablets which she had sometimes swallowed after a row with Wellington.

A picture came into Faran's mind, a shelf of coast, mountains behind like black-and-white whales. Had they shown him a picture? Perhaps Mr Thorpe had done so. He could not recall.

'Do you think we'll be there soon?' Berenice asked, in a little voice.

'Yes. Don't be scared.'

'No.'

Faran wondered how he would cope with Berenice once his perception had centred on the woman, Lilith. He would have to be kind.

'My cat's excited,' Berenice said, placatingly.

'Good.'

The cat did look more alive, assuming personality as Berenice poured attention into it. This happened with people too. Faran hoped Cain would value Berenice. But he must, he did already, or why else had she been chosen?

Something tugged at Faran's soporific thought. They were all only children. Even the Welsh girl and the Greek. All – what was it? – First Born.

Why had he remembered that? The First Born in Egypt, and the angel passing over. What had the angel done?

'I keep thinking of Mama,' said Berenice. 'My mother. I never did before. I wonder if she's happy.'

'Perhaps you'll be able to see her one day,' he said. His ideas of biblical things had scattered.

'Yes, that would be great. Yes, I'd like to. When I'm grown up.'

'Do you want to be grown up?'

'Yes. I'll be more comfortable then.'

'Or will it be the same?'

'No, it couldn't be,' she said, making a decision, for all of them.

The plane rocked and purred. The pilot had not spoken. He was like a robot.

A roller of sleep came up on Faran again and he pushed it off, not wanting it.

'Isn't the sea dark?' he said.

'Yes,' said Berenice, and then something must have caught her eye, for she moved eagerly, and again she said, '*Look*, Faran!'

And Faran looked.

But in that second the sky went white.

Seen from below, the plane was, and then was not. It changed. It became a soft image, furry almost, and very bright, a puffball of rosy flame. And out of that, dark objects poked and popped, and sheered, soundless away, in the seconds before the explosion came.

The noise, unlike the vision, was hard and coarse, yet also somehow far away. Irrelevant. An afterthought.

Pieces of the plane, of seats and metal sinews, and fuselage, and dead burned bodies, fell quietly down, or sometimes with a little grating and rattling, and went in under the plates of ice, sizzling in the inky sea.

A smoke trail marred the sky, then faded.

Nothing at all remained.

Chapter Forty-Three

CAIN MOVED THROUGH THE TORCHLIT darkness of his mountain, his pyramid, and came to the courtyard with the four statues in it. Of Anubis and Bast, Hercules and Astarte: Soul, joy, strength, lust. And the tank of lotuses in alabaster lamplight.

There he paused.

He wore black, and the hood of his black silk hair, so living and viable it was like some animal that enclosed his face, some symbiote, just as his eyes were, set in that face, symbiotic eyes. Yet, now, his eyes were smouldered over, and calm.

He looked once towards the apartment he had allocated the boy. Then he moved on, and opened the outer door to the woman's rooms.

In his hand he carried the gadget of black plastic, with the single red button. That was all.

He passed the guardian statue.

At the inner door, he knocked.

She spoke, the woman. 'Is it you?'

'Cain,' he said.

He uttered his own name with inexpressible appetite, the way men speak the names of those they want and will have. He did not speak her name that way, though he had given her her name and now she used it.

It was she who opened the door.

He went inside, into the ornate, golden, painted room.

'I wondered when you'd come. Why were you so long?'

'You should never question me,' he said. 'I only answer when I wish to, and in that case I'd tell you any way.'

'All right,' she said. She was not discommoded. Now she was Ankhet, as he had meant her to be, neither quite Ruth nor, definitely, Anna. A new person. His?

'Ankhet,' he said, 'you're alone with me now.'

'Yes.'

'I don't mean that you and I are together here. I mean that there will be no others.'

'Others?'

'I've destroyed them. It's only you who matter to me. And you've renounced your lover.'

'Malach,' she said. 'Yes. The man whipped him with the thongs. Then I came away.'

'And I,' he said, 'came away to you. There's the boy, naturally. He means something to me, was something to me, once. He'd come to recollect that. Great loyalty, and in his adult life, more. But if you want, Ankhet, I'll have them kill him. Painlessly and quickly. Then, only you and I.'

'And Lilith?' she said. Her face was the mask face that Ruth's had been, porcelain perfection of nothingness. Blank. Divine. Empty. Yet now, the very emptiness was a sort of fullness and satiety.

'Lilith. Lilith and I are parted.'

'And you'd kill the little boy, Harpokrates.'

'Andrew,' he said carelessly.

'No,' she said. 'I don't mind. It's all right. Keep him.'

'And now,' Cain said.

'Now you want to make love to me,' she said. It seemed to her she remembered many times of love-making. Malach's, other men. Or were they all Malach, Malach in altered bodies, other lives? She herself must have died and come back often. She could visualize it now, like a winding passage with doors. She said, 'Do what you want.'

'That isn't inviting,' he said. 'Invite me.'

'Then I do. I'll sleep with you. I'll have your babies.'

'Oh,' he said. He smiled. 'Ankhet. Try to recall.'

'What? You and I, before?'

'No. That would be new, perhaps. You and I.'

He came forward, and put his hands softly on her arms. She gazed up at him, unafraid. She said, 'Will you hurt me?'

'Never. I'd never harm you.'

She frowned. 'But it should hurt, love, shouldn't it?'

He lowered his head and gazed into her eyes with his, so blue and quiet and shining. He looked near laughter again, like the boy he had been on the boat above, as they sailed the quick-silver cold river, that was the replica of the Nile.

Yet it was he, this one, who she had seen tear out the throat of a man, sodomizing him, murdering him, at once, and the scene running with blood—

She put her arms up round his neck.

He made a small sound, approval, pleasure.

Then he leaned into her body and drew her against him, and kissed her in the way she now recollected, his tongue swelling into her mouth, a kind of willing asphyxia.

Behind her shut lids, the other stirred, as if he were already in her body. *Malach.*

Ankhet flexed her will. It was far greater than she had suspected. She cast Malach out.

Cain was leading her over to the bed, pushing away its draperies, making her lie with her head at its foot.

He undressed her slowly and simply, but not himself. She did not remonstrate. She concentrated on his touch, which was electric, rousing her, for she knew her body should be ready.

He had said he would not hurt her, but obviously, he must. Anna was a virgin, tight. Now the vast weapon, which so far she had seen used only as a means to a death, would be thrust into her also, thrust in to her very core. He *would* hurt her, but not, it was true, harm.

She saw him through a fine veil of tears.

She did not know why she wept, or if she did.

He licked her tears away, his tongue rough like a cat's.

Then he suckled at her breasts.

Her blood began to flow to the rhythm of his heart, for she felt his heart beat hard against her stomach. And after that he put his face into her loins, feeding on her sweetly, so she was melted like burning honey.

But she kept her eyes wide on him. She did not mean, even for a second, to forget that he was Cain.

Finally he pierced her, and she knew the pain once more, but it was different, less, and greater. As then, she forced herself along the measure of the blade. She took hold of his waist. She stared at him, seeing him and only him. Now they were joined, perhaps the only moment in the world when two things can be said to be one.

'Will you drink my blood?'

'Yes, Ankhet Persephone.'

'Then am I yours?'

'From the beginning, you were. But we'll seal it.'

'Are your gods real?' she said.

'I have no gods.'

He moved in her like thunder. Then she closed her eyes at last. It was not the same. She did not need to see.

When he pierced also into her neck, she did not protest. She felt her blood run hot along her throat as his seed ran through her inner spaces. A spasm shook her distantly, the orgasm of who she had been, once, or who she would come to be. It was not ecstatic, not even enjoyable. It was not yet hers.

Cain lay on Ankhet. His body was heavy, warm and hard, but flexible, like the form of some large beast.

She spread under him, immobile, and felt him draw out of her. And away.

He looked grave, almost stoical, as if he had foregone sex rather than having taken it.

'Get up,' he said, 'look into the mirror.'

She did as he said. She would always have to do as he said. She must not disobey. This was nearly a relief.

In the ordinary, unsuitable glass, Ankhet beheld the reflection of herself, the young white naked girl, and of Cain standing behind her, clothed, sombre. He slipped his left arm about her body, and his hand cupped and gently crushed her left breast over the heart. With the right hand he smoothed her neck, where he had bitten her and drunk her blood.

'Why?' she said. It was not her question – they were vampires, that was why. Ruth had known. Yet, she asked it. To test him?

'The law of God,' he said, surprising her, for she had no memory to fit this.

'You told me you didn't believe in any gods.'

He smiled. He said, 'Habit. Perhaps there was a god long ago.' Then he put down his face, like a father with a child, beside hers.

She watched them, both faces, his, and hers. Her wig was gone. She was like his white shadow. A *living* shadow. He was relaxed, playful, now. Her own face was tense and alert.

He said, 'Now are you mine? Tell me so.'

'I'm yours.'

'For ever,' he said.

'Yes.'

'Then I can let him go,' Cain said.

She did not say, *Malach*. She said, 'But if I wanted you to kill him?'

'I've killed enough for the moment,' he said. He said, 'I shall have to carry them with me, for three days.'

She said, 'The children.'

'Yes. It was that,' he pointed. She saw the black plastic thing with the button lying on a table. Next to it was a sort of mediaeval pouch that had been at his belt. He said, 'They are there. Go and look.'

So she went to the purse, and undid the clasp, and inside there were six conventional blurry snapshots. Of six children. They had been captured unawares in various spots: a dusty street, a pillared way, outside an ancient building, a railway station, the entrance to Harrods, one on a bicycle in a green field. The boy outside Harrods was black, and his hand was held by a smartly dressed black woman with large white earrings.

'My sacrifice,' he said, 'to you. To the goddess Ankhet.'

She returned the photographs into the purse. She too, once, had killed children. But not remotely. She had done it face to face, with sharp implements.

'Thank you,' she said. Ruth's voice. Prim and cool.

Then it was as if he laughed, but without sound, like a cat meowing silently.

'I can't bring them back,' he said, as if she had inquired. He sounded – satisfied. 'They're dead.'

'Can Malach die?' she said.

'Oh, yes. Each of us can do that. But I shall let Malach live. I'll let him live with the memory of you, and how you told him to go away from you.'

She said, 'I'm afraid of boredom.'

'I know.'

'This place,' she said.

'I'll show you the ice world,' he said. 'I'll be with you. And when you tire of the things that are here, we can go elsewhere. I haven't troubled with it, but it's there. It may have some interest again for me. The world. Boredom, Ankhet. We'll amuse each other.'

She thought of them out on the earth, and Malach somewhere else, left behind, growing small with distance. Vanishing. A pain clenched behind her breast, where her heart was, and then the pain grew delicious, under his hand, the hand of her lover, who wanted her for ever, and would take her into the world. If anything, he had been too gentle with her.

'Make love to me again,' she said, 'I want to see—'

'She gives me orders,' he said, but he only smiled. He said, 'Then make me want you again.'

Sure in memory, she turned, her white spine to the mirror, and put her narrow hands, empty of rings, on to his amber flesh.

Lilith watched the child, Harpokrates, playing with the two white tigers. She had watched him for an hour.

Before and beyond them, the enormous Hall stretched away, the crimson pillars and the iron roof of Nuit's lamps. At Lilith's back, in the blue window, nothing moved. It was as if the window were finally dead. A dead blue eye.

He had told her, when he brought the boy.

As the boy took hold, fearlessly, of the two great cats, Cain had said to her, in a language of a dead sea, that now there would be no more children.

And on the horizon of Lilith's mind, there in the mist, a black icon winked away. Was gone. Cain too left her.

Then she sat still, and the little boy played and the cats played with him.

Now, when she rose, only the paler tiger turned its head on its gold collar, like a clockwork thing.

She said the word to it which meant it might stay, and then it looked off from her, and raised one vast paw, claws all sheathed, to cuff lightly the boy so he rolled down giggling against its side.

This child must be the one who had known cats before. He did not fear them. And the tigers played beautifully, majestic and careful, as with a young cub.

The darker did not even glance after her, as she left them.

In the thoughts of black Faran, Lilith had been fixed.

But his thoughts were ended. His brain was ashes.

It was as if she had been put out.

She did not know him, who he was, had been, would be, only the intuitive premonition of their life, jointly.

But now he did not think of her, she had ceased.

Lilith, too, moved through the mountain, and came into a place beyond the corridors and courts and rooms.

There was a door which, like the bomb on the plane, responded to the touch of a finger on a button.

Beyond this door was a fearful cold.

The woman in her black dress, the golden diadem of a serpent on her head, went out into this, and the door shut behind her.

Ice had formed, like walls and barriers, screens and windows. And behind, within, the ice, were shapes.

It was a burial chamber, a necropolis.

Unnecessary to pass over a river or a lake to reach it, perhaps unneedful the rites of old embalmings that seemed to have been carried out.

The mummy-cases stood upright in their shields of ice, black and emerald and gold. And between stood the slender statues of Anubis and Thot-Zehuti, the conductors of souls, images of the Balance, of the serpent of Hell, Aataru, the drinker of blood, of monsters which tore, and winged guides, and painted on the walls behind membranes of white crystal, the golden fields of endless day, the land of Ra beyond the River.

A great barge rose, green-dyed, like all the cases, for resurrection, the hue of the Osiris. Ice shards tapered from it.

On hedges of crystal hovered the personification of life and sexual energy, the human-headed bird, the Ba, overseeing what must be done.

Lilith, while she moved forward, drifting between the objects of death, murmured the names of those who lay there. A limitless list, no one must be left out: *You that pass me by, speak my name that I be remembered—*

In alcoves were dolls for servants to serve the dead, vases of date and pomegranate wine, or what passed for them, turned to maroon sand.

It was an Egyptian vision, slightly flawed . . . Here a

Greek amphora, there a bowl with a view of Bacchus, a woman's glove in the style of 1700 – items left deliberately, offerings, and frozen garlands of flowers turned black inside the claws of the ice.

There were butterflies too, in stasis, coloured like blood and gilt and sapphire. Butterflies that perhaps had lived, resting now with folded wings thin as breath on outstretched hands of stone, the snout of Anubis the Jackal, the curls of an Assyrian lion.

Lilith passed across the lines of sarcophagi, the boats of death, under the shade of cold gods.

This area was like some other element of her mind, some dream made real, for a few moments.

Then she had gone beyond it.

A tunnel of darkness littered by bits of pottery, fake or actual gems, whispers of things that had smashed. And after that the open grotto of ice, hollowed through some glacier beneath Cain's mountain.

Grey-blue, the walls ran up, shimmering with stone-still wetness. Strands like hair, or swords, stalactites of ice pointing down, framing the outer whiteness of the day-locked snow.

Lilith kicked off – a light gesture, girlish – her sandals.

Barefoot, bare and empty-handed, her face and head uncovered, and only the dress of black linen on her body, and the gold snake on her hair. So she walked, alone, from the grotto.

Her silhouette became, on the light, all darkness.

Black as Faran, she walked out across the slope of whitest snow.

She walked into the ice-scape, not fast, nor slowly, not looking back. Growing smaller with distance. Vanishing.

Malach's face, under the torch, now lit, now lost. Impossible to read there anything . . .

White hair streaming over him, into dim darkness.

White bandaging too, across his upper body. After the

whip-man, another came to clean and bind the cuts. Red
that was black in the half-light stained out on the white.

If he was waiting no one would know, and perhaps
Malach did not know. But logic might have forewarned
him.

Cain would come down to him. Cain would have to.

And Cain did enter the prison vault, or whatever it was,
that dungeon from a film circa 1958.

Cain in black, appropriately, for Malach's whiteness.

Cain said, as others had, 'Here I am.'

And Malach? Malach did not speak.

'She doesn't want you, then,' Cain said, 'after all that.
Not at all. A pity, that you bothered. Such a long journey.'
His voice, so musical, halting between every three or four
words, conceivably savouring what was said, or only
rehearsing it, since it was a fact. 'What shall I do with you?'

Malach still silent.

Cain said, 'Why not talk to me? We have talked, in
the past.'

'That was then,' Malach said.

'And when?' asked Cain, nearly coyly.

'Now and then. Here and there.'

The language Cain had elected to use was Dutch,
Malach's adopted tongue. But he employed it casually, with other words, of French, Latin, even German
inserted. Malach had responded exactly. Now Cain said,
'*U vergist zich.*'

'No error,' said Malach. 'Or wasn't it you?'

'You and I,' Cain said, '*Skheru* – the damned. But I
change. I alter. Malach remains the same.'

'Constant,' Malach said.

He had not raised his head, and did not now, as Cain
went closer to him. Cain spoke in an older tongue.

'Do you recall Set and Hor, how the two gods toyed in
Set's garden, and Hor sprayed his semen on the salad, and
Set ate the salad unknowing. And later the semen cried
Here I am inside Set.'

Malach, again, did not speak.

Cain said, 'You are my slave, here. You have put yourself under my hand. You know what I must do to you.'

Malach's face flashed up into the light. It was the visor of a starved wolf. His eyes were like the ice.

'Your ideas of revenge are both crass and melodramatic.'

'And I shall hurt you,' Cain said, 'my love.'

As Cain moved now, Malach moved in the fetters of steel. He could not get very far. Someone, besides bandaging his torso after the lashes of the whip, had secured his ankles. In the chains, Malach fell, and Cain was on him like a tiger, feeling after him in the most certain and absolute manner, his hands hot as an oven.

'*She* would have done this to you if she could,' he said. His marvellous voice now was thick with lust, but it was the lust of power not sex. It had been the most ancient method, this, to subdue an enemy. The most demeaning, the most damnable. To make of him *kat tahut*, the cunt of a whore.

Cain found the entry to Malach's lower body, and drew up the skirt of his robe, holding Malach twisted with his other arm.

Malach had stopped struggling. He said, in the purest, oldest Egyptian, 'May Set fuck you.'

Cain found the muscles of Malach's body had shut against him, hard as rock. Cain forced with his hand, to thrust his blazing penis, charged with the semen of Horus, into Malach's body. Cain forced, and could not. Malach had won.

Cain let Malach go and stepped away.

Cain was imperious, chill now, almost feminine in his disdain at defeat.

It was Malach who hung, shaking and sweating, his mouth shaped into a noiseless screaming oblong, the torch lighting up his eyes to madness. Malach, intact, who had lost.

'Well, then, I'll do without the felicity,' Cain said.

Then Malach made a sound. It was low and hoarse, the note a dog gives when it is hurt, and feels the hurt for the first.

Cain shrugged.

'They'll offer you food. They'll take you up and return you your sled and your team, and the clothing, and what else you need. Then you can go back.'

Malach's face gradually cleared. Voided itself.

He stood still. Ludicrously shackled.

'Do you have any message for her?' Cain asked in Dutch. 'She'll listen, if I tell her to.'

Malach lowered his head.

The white hair dropped forward over his face.

'I could take you now,' Cain said. 'But now there isn't any reason to. Is there?'

'No,' Malach said.

'Then we've finished with each other.'

'Yes.'

'Go back,' Cain said, 'to your charming life. Find some other less interesting woman to fawn on you and keep you warm.'

In the silence someone said, 'Warm.'

That was all.

Chapter Forty-Four

AT THE PORT SHE HAD been met by a large black car.

The driver spoke English. He assured her that nearly everyone did.

They went, as Rachaela requested, directly to the city by straight roads lapped with water-colour green. Lorries passed them, with *floris* written on the sides. The air was tinged by rain.

Amsterdam, swarming with bicycles and trams, verged on full morning. They drove through and up into the cobbled quiet beside the canals. The city seemed to her familiar. All cities would, perhaps. It occurred to her she had seen them before, long ago. When she was someone else.

Her mind was made up. She could feel it in her skull, programmed, like a computer.

The buildings were like doll's houses, and Sofie's was a deep lavender pink. It looked friendly, kind. Not a Scarabae house.

Rachaela walked up the steps and rang the bell.

Then she waited.

No one came.

There had been a message at the port. It had told her Sofie was at home. It was not, however, from Sofie. Perhaps Sofie had gone out for groceries – no, there was a servant, Grete, who did that. For some social occasion then, something the family did not know about.

Rachaela glanced up the pink-confectionary length of the house. Nothing. Not a movement. It was as if the architecture held its breath. *She was there.*

Rachaela rang the bell again. With her other hand, she struck the door.

Suddenly the door flew open.

The woman was small, smaller than Rachaela. She reminded Rachaela of a small quaint bird. A striped dress of grey and dull red, a necklace like three matchboxes made of silver. Round aquamarine eyes. Sofie.

The woman said, shrilly, *'Wat is er aan de hand?'*

'I'm sorry, I don't speak Dutch,' Rachaela answered.

The woman backed away from her. She looked, did she, younger than Rachaela, and only about five feet tall, so that she seemed to decrease excessively, as if seen through the wrong end of a bottle.

'What?' she said in English. 'Who are you?'

'My name's Rachaela. I'm the partner of Althene.' Rachaela paused. She added, firmly, 'Your son.'

The door was still open wide.

Rachaela walked forward into the black-carpeted hall. There was a peculiar statue thing, and Sofie was cowering against it. She squeaked – *tweeted* – 'Don't dare come in. How dare you come in? What do you want?'

'I want to see Althene.'

'There's no – there's no one here.'

'I think you call her Johanon. Johanon, then.'

'No. He left. He left weeks ago.'

Rachaela did not believe Sofie. Sofie was insane. And Sofie, palpably, was also very scared.

'I'm sorry,' Rachaela said, 'I'll have to see for myself. Please excuse me. Excuse my not believing you.'

'You bitch,' said Sofie, calmly now.

'Oh, would you say so? But you hardly know me.'

'Bitch! Bitch! You slut! Get out! Get out!'

Calm all miraculously gone.

Rachaela said, 'I'm not leaving. Not until I'm certain Althene isn't here. Where shall I start?'

Then Sofie flighted at her on outspread grey and red wings.

Rachaela did not plan what she did, but the programme in her brain must have done. Rachaela struck Sofie violently, with the back of her ringed right hand, and Sofie did fly then, straight over, to fall under the statue with a moan.

Sofie lay there crumpled. She cried, huge round tears, gushing out of her round eyes. 'Scarabae,' she said, 'Scarabae.'

Rachaela said, 'I *am* Scarabae.'

Then she crossed to the door adjacent to the hallway, and opened it.

It was a sort of dusty study, done in glaring puce, with a kidney-shaped desk. Beyond was another room, in murky orange. Both were vacant.

When Rachaela came out, Sofie still lay on the carpet. On her face was a thick rouged stripe that seemed to have migrated from her dress.

Rachaela thought, *Who am I now, Adamus or Malach?* And this faintly amused her.

'Are you going to take me there, or am I going to go all through your house?'

'The attic,' said Sofie.

'The attic?' Rachaela thought of mad Mrs Rochester, and she did laugh, out loud. Sofie buried her face in two thin hands.

Rachaela ran up the humped, bumpy, twisting black stairs. An engine drove her, and blood fuelled her, pumping through her heart like a drum.

She passed Sofie's ugly rooms, with hideous paintings like road accidents on the walls. The house was icy, but Rachaela scarcely felt it, scalded with purpose.

The last stair was bizarre, and she went more cautiously. At the door her own speed made her hesitate.

She had not thought before. What had the mad mother *done* to this errant child?

'*Christ.*'

The door was not locked. It gave.

An unspeakable lavatory stench pushed out.

Rachaela caught her breath.

Then, swimming at her on this tide of filth, she saw an image. Something lay on a bed, just there, where the ceiling sloped to windows which admitted a boned morning light. Something—

She went forward. She stopped.

There was a diseased man lying on the bed.

He had long dirty hair, in which something had been squashed, some essence – God knew what – red, pink, unthinkable – and his face was a mass of hair and sores, open cuts that had tried to heal, pus, and, incredibly, cosmetics. Blusher and powder. Fragrances, gone fetid, mingled with the effluvia.

It was cosmetics in the hair, too. They had been spilled . . . She could see.

The body was a sodden mass.

Every excrescence of physical need had gone on, and been permitted to go on. And all that into and over a nightdress of coral pink silk, trimmed with very expensive, rosy lace.

The heart of the pink house. Pink horror.

Rachaela stood there, and the coffee she had drunk at the café by the port, rushed back into her throat. She swallowed it a second time.

Who was this?

Was it alive?

'Rachaela,' the monster said. Somehow. Out of a mouth encrusted by mucus and sores and bright scarlet lip-gloss and thick coarse beard. 'Or am I – still dreaming you.'

'You're not dreaming.'

It was Althene.

None of this mattered. The stink, the horror. Althene

was there. Alive. Under the coverlet of the heavy leaves of darkness. *Althene*.

'I'll need to get some help,' Rachaela said, 'there's a man downstairs—'

The rustling jangle in the doorway made Rachaela turn. A weird sight.

Silent-footed, Sofie had re-manifested, like the internal image of *Psycho*, her thin arm upraised, but on a silly, tiny little knife, and there was indeed a man behind her, but not the driver. He wore a beret and his long brown wooden face was strung in attention. He was twisting the knife away.

It fell.

Sofie screeched. Like an owl.

The man thrust her, and she was gone. Magic.

The man said in English, 'Yes, you will need assistance, madame.'

'She looked like a fourteen-year-old schoolgirl that some-one has exposed himself to.'

Rachaela said, 'Yes. I'm sorry.'

'Don't be – sorry. *I'm* sorry. All – this.'

Wrapped in blankets, Althene lay against her in the back of the car. The shower had been possible, but little else. At some point, by the expensive hotel the family had arranged, they would have to get out. But it would be dealt with. They would get through it. And then more assistance would arrive. It always arrived, for the family.

'I think,' Althene said, 'she's got me addicted – to something. I don't – even know what. She'd leave me alone – months, is it? I tried to keep score, how long. But I didn't. Useless. What a fool. She lost interest, you see.'

'Yes, thank God.'

'I won't die, Rachaela. Whatever she did to me. I'm very strong.'

'I know. I know you won't die. I won't let you.'

'I didn't – I didn't find—'

'We can think about that later.'

'She was so frightened,' Althene said, 'what they'd do to her. Sofie. How she hates me.'

Rachaela felt the car turning in against a white and yellow building, a daffodil above a canal. 'We're going to have to walk. About five yards. He – Roman – will help. Can you—'

'Oh, yes.' Althene lay back, her full weight, which was too light.

The car stopped.

The man with the face like a clever fiddle got out. Two people were coming purposefully from the hotel as well.

Rachaela did not want to let go, but she must. Just until they were inside.

Chapter Forty-Five

THE SUMMER HAD TURNED THE city to a box of heat. The trees were green, but the waters had, in spots, a sour-vegetable smell. Red flowers flamed in windows. Car fumes condensed the skies.

Within the hotel, the old rooms had kept some coolness.

In the salon the sunlight sparkled on the polished chandelier and pristine ashtrays, made bright patches on sofas of white silk with a lemon stripe, the armchairs of a deep regal green. The floor was burnished wood. The beautiful woman, coming in, had crossed it with care in her high-heeled sandals.

She looked frail, the woman, as if she had been ill. Her fair skin, immaculately made up in soft tawny shades, was a little stretched and dry. Her eyes, though fabulous, were not entirely clear.

Althene wore a dress of creamy blue, clinging lightly to her body. Her thinness was only fashionable. Under her right shoulder was pinned a leaf of dull articulated gold. On her left hand was a large ring, a type of cow-snake, the golden horned head resting on the circle of its tail.

She sat now, waiting.

Beside her on the table was the gilded tray of Earl Grey tea, the little formal French cakes that she knew neither of them would touch.

She leaned to the tray, and poured a cup of the tea. Impartially, she watched her hand shaking. It had been worse, two months before. And before that – much, much worse.

When the door to the salon opened, she did not at once look up.

He came over the room, and touched her shoulder very quietly. He had never treated her as other than a woman.

She did look at him then.

He had altered. She had known he must.

Malach seemed now a man of fifty, fifty-five, gaunt rather than thin. A wolf's face, hungry and unappeased. And from the planes of it, which would still delight any artist, and perhaps rather more, the long white mane had been curbed, drawn back and strictly tied.

His clothes were dark, nondescript, light for summer, nothing more.

He had wanted, it seemed, to go unnoted.

She offered him, therefore, a commonplace.

'It's hot.'

'Yes. Where is she?'

'Rachaela has gone to the street by the green iron bridge, as we call it, to buy jewellery. She's developed a passion for odd rings. Look at this, my cow – Hathor at her most winning.'

'It must be heavy.'

'Yes. For three months I couldn't wear it. I used to put it under my pillow, for luck.'

'And now you can.'

'Now I can.'

'You look,' he said, 'as beautiful as ever.'

She said, 'Thank you for your lie. You look old.'

He smiled. 'Don't be unkind to me, *lieveling*. I've had enough of that.'

Althene poured tea for him. He watched her. She had stopped her hand from shaking.

'You think,' he said, 'I should expect nothing else. I have been harsh. Now, it comes back to me.'

'That's never worried you in the past.'

'The past. That other country.' They had spoken in English. She had begun it, used to Rachaela. Now he said, in Dutch, 'I have to tell you only that I found her. Anna. Where you and I understood that she would be.'

Althene sat back. She frowned. She said, 'That place truly exists, then.'

'It does. Of course it does. What else, for someone like him.'

'And – *he* has her.'

'And she has him.'

'You must explain what you mean,' she said.

'No. I won't do that. He's made her his lover, wife, daughter. And she wants all he wants.'

'Did you speak to her?' Althene asked softly.

'Oh, yes.'

'And she preferred – she wished—'

'She wished to remain with him.'

'He's a sorcerer,' she said. 'He could put a spell on her.'

'You forget,' he said, 'what she is.'

'My child.'

'No,' he said. 'She used you. You and Rachaela. No one's child, except his.' Malach picked up the china cup and looked at the tea inside it, and set it down. 'Have another child.'

'It's so simple. It takes two.'

'Find another woman—' he stopped. He said, 'To keep you warm.'

'Rachaela is who I want.'

'Then make do with Rachaela.'

Althene said, 'I won't ask—'

'No, don't ask.'

'But I do need to know – one thing. Is he – is he the way he was?'

'How was he?'

'His power,' she said, 'his difference. Is he older – younger – changed—'

'He changes the way land-masses move,' Malach said. 'Imperceptible but finite. He looked very young. He feeds on everyone and everything. Nothing sickens him. No rules. No obstacles. And he must have wanted her always. We believed he'd forgotten. But none of us does that.'

Althene said, 'Was there no moment when you could—'

'When I could have killed him. Yes. Several. But he sucked the heart out of me.' Malach leaned back. Inside its age, his face was very young, torn open, and the eyes like deserts of pale light. 'He drained me. But, *vampires*. What else?'

'You'll heal,' she said. 'We do.'

'Do we? Then that must be because we want to.'

Somewhere, down in the serenity of the hotel, there was a little sound of something.

Althene said, 'Rachaela may come back. Will you—'

'No. I don't want to look at Rachaela. Tell her what you like.'

'The truth,' Althene said. 'It will take some hours, I think.'

'Only such a little time?'

He stood up. Althene stood. They regarded each other over the blades of sunlight and the undrunk tea.

'You helped me once very much,' she said. 'I wish that I could return the favour.'

'But you can't. One life is enough for any of us to manage. And our lives, of course, are so long.'

When he had left her she took up one of the little cakes and crumbled it gently. She did not know why. Something delicate and sweet, something wasted.

Jutka, the old woman who served the castle of crows, had told him about the fox, the vixen. He did not often meet Jutka. But he had found her in the bedchamber, the woman's room, sweeping the floor in a slow attending way. She made no apology. She stood before the curtained bed and looked at the painted cradle.

She told him a white vixen had been coming into her garden.

He said it must be a dog. There were no foxes, here.

She did not argue. Jutka never argued.

'I leave out a cooked chicken for her,' said Jutka.

Perhaps the vixen had escaped from some private collection of animals. Or possibly Jutka had dreamed it all.

The dogs had been pleased at first, galloping about the castle after him, Firs and Kraai the silliest, bounding on to and off furniture, their claws skittering on the flagstones.

His mood infected them gradually. He was sorry to see it. They ran through the maze of the overgrown garden, which represented eternity, barking, trying to intrigue him. They bit at the fires of tulips, remnants of the mania of the 1600s, then scowled because he did not shout. Their tails drooped.

Enki and Oscar bore with him best, refusing quite to give in, nuzzling his hands.

He could not foresee a day when it would be otherwise.

The story of the white fox angered him.

It was Ruth, evidently, the symbol of Ruth and Anna joined. Some projection of his own unconscious, or some ghost of her living ka far off in Cain's white tomb.

He drank through the afternoon, beer, Jenever, brandy, in the bar with copper pots and horned skulls.

No one remarked him, but for the elderly man he always bought a few drinks.

Later, the hyacinth colour of dusk came down, the neons woke and the street-lamps and the loops of bulbs above the canals.

He waited even then, watching the drunks pass through the bar, sober as the death's head at the feast, with the second bottle of brandy standing hollow.

It was two in the morning when he went to her, along the cranny of street. The man by the door knew him, but the tired sooty girl did not, and tried to call him back.

Above the squinny of stair, he knocked. Then listened for her rasping. The city was very, uncharacteristically, still. At length, a dribble of a voice, not hers, bade him come in.

She was seated at her table, amid the litter and clutter and stink of her room. The Jewess. No, his blood had not done her good, though she had been so intent to get it. She had grown fatter, into a vast wallow of flesh, and her hair was thinner and more brittle, burnt straw now. Only her dark eyes grinned at him, her purple mouth turned down.

The other was a woman ancient and thin as a stick, with matchstick hands, in which she held, muzzle towards his chest, a .357 Magnum. Without a tremble. She cackled, too, liking what she did. From her lips protruded a smoking Lucky Strike, its blue thread rising like a tendril of her soul.

'No need. Put it away,' said the Jewess. 'This is the wicked one. He is my friend, the shit-beast.'

The second crone lowered the gun without effort. She plucked her cigarette and let out a gust of blue. 'This one is the one they call the Prince.'

'Prince,' said the Jewess, 'Prince of Smokes.'

'Tell her to go,' Malach said.

'Private, is it, Pretty? Not so pretty now. I won't have your blood this time. Not worth it.'

'No you won't have my blood. I've brought you an armful of guilders.'

The thin crone shuffled up. She left the Magnum lying on the table among the packs of cards, the greasy candles stuck into dented tin mugs. Moths clustered on a plate of crumbs, feeding, their wings fluttering, ignoring the candlelight.

Near the table's centre a dead rose, its head perfectly preserved and the colour of tobacco, stood in a cracked grey glass.

'See,' she said, 'I keep mementoes of you.'

'How unwise,' he said.

He sat at the table facing her, as the other one stick-cackled out of the door.

The Jewess raised her head. In the white suet of her face, all folds and creases, the eyes moved independently of the rest of her. Her fat dark lips.

'What do you want?' she said.

'Tell me about her,' he said.

'Let her go,' said the Jewess.

'Never.'

'Through me, the only fashion he can come at her. Why didn't you take her while you could? She would have fallen like a fruit into your mouth.'

'Why,' he said. 'I don't know. Perhaps I only want the pain of loss. I'm used to it.'

She glared into his dry cold eyes. 'Don't weep at my table,' she said. 'You'll bring bad luck.'

'You are bad luck, lady.'

'Not so bad as yours.'

Then she heaved herself together, pulling shamelessly inward with her hands, her breasts and thighs. She stared down into some space under the world.

'Already,' said the Jewess, 'she is his. Already. And what do I see? There in her belly. His child.'

Malach watched the witch.

He blinked once, that was all.

The Jewess coughed. Her breath was intolerably foul, but he did not flinch away. 'Give me the money.'

He put a brown packet on to the table, slitting it at one end as he did so. The coloured notes poured out, looking like some parody of her cards.

'Then,' she said, 'I can tell you one last thing.'

He waited.

The Jewess said, 'She is white as snow, but the child in her womb is black. Black as coal.'

She lifted her head and added, to the silent entity of the room:

'A *new* darkness.'

7/96

YOU CAN RENEW
BY PHONE!
623-3300

GAYLORD M